If

This

World

Were

Mine

Also by E. Lynn Harris

INVISIBLE LIFE

JUST AS I AM

AND THIS TOO SHALL PASS

If This World Were Mine

a novel by **E. Lynn Harris**

ANCHOR BOOKS
DOUBLEDAY
New York London Toronto Sydney Auckland

AN ANCHOR BOOK
PUBLISHED BY DOUBLEDAY
a division of Bantam Doubleday Dell Publishing Group, Inc.
1540 Broadway, New York, New York 10036

ANCHOR BOOKS, DOUBLEDAY, and the portrayal of an anchor
are trademarks of Doubleday, a division of Bantam Doubleday Dell
Publishing Group, Inc.

The poem "The Summer Scorches" from *Metamorphosis—A Life Journey*,
written by Pat J. Schulz (Enheart Publishing). Used by permission.

The poems "Blue" and "Fall Rhapsody" © Sonya Jackson.
Used by permission.

Book design by Brian Mulligan

If This World Were Mine was originally published in hardcover by Doubleday in 1997.

The Library of Congress has cataloged the hardcover edition of this book as follows:

Harris, E. Lynn.
If this world were mine : a novel / by E. Lynn Harris. — 1st ed.
p. cm.
I. Title.
PS3558.A64438I38   1997
813'.54—dc21   97-18795
CIP

ISBN 0-385-48656-1

Printed in the United States of America
First Anchor Books edition: July 1998

10 9 8 7 6 5 4

For Judge **Vanessa D. Gilmore** *(Hampton Institute, 1977) for the honor . . . the pleasure . . . and the joy of friendship for over two decades.* **And Everick** *for giving me the love I prayed for . . . a friendship I treasure . . . and making me feel like I'm dreaming even when I'm awake.*

The Author Thanks . . .

I am thankful for living each day protected by God's amazing grace. I know it's a blessing and privilege to be able to write the stories that dance inside my head and have people read them. I realize the stories are gifts, and not a tool to alter lives, but hopefully change hearts.

There is much and many to whom I must give thanks. I am thankful for my family, all of them, but most especially my mother, Etta Harris, and my aunt, Jessie Phillips, for being constant with their unconditional love and support.

I am thankful for my friends, most whom I've named in previous novels. I'm happy I can say ditto on all my friends previously mentioned. I've made some new friends—remarkable people who began as supporters and became cherished friends: Debra Martin Chase, Yolanda Starks, Tavis Smiley, Sybil Wilkes, Gordon Chambers, Derrick Thompson, and Linda Villarosa. I also want to thank a couple of friends, Dyanna Williams and Chester Jones, for their valuable information regarding some of my characters, and Sonya Jackson and Pat Schulz for the wonderful poetry used in the novel. Riley should only wish to write as well.

I am thankful for my Doubleday family, most especially Martha Levin for her publishing brilliance and friendship. My publicists Sherri Steinfeld and Patricia Blythe for taking great care of me when I'm on the road. And Mario Pulice for great covers and a smile I know I can always depend on.

There are several people whose support I couldn't live without and who deserve mention in everything I publish. Regina Brown Daniels, Lencola Sullivan, Tim Douglas, and Carlton Brown. My agent and friend, John Hawkins, for guiding my career from beauty shops to the bestseller list. I extend my gratitude to Moses Cardona for his support and for selling my novels abroad, and my film agent, Irv Schwartz, for his belief in my work. My deep appreciation to Laura Gilmore, whose attention and care of my personal and business life allow me to write without worry. Special shout-outs and kudos to the men who help with Basil, who asked to remain nameless, and a big shout and high-five to the students at Hampton University, University of Arkansas-Fayetteville, Tennessee State University, and Florida A. & M. University. Thanks for showing me so much love. Special thanks to Austin Foxxe for his editing contributions.

I would like to thank all the booksellers, escorts, writers, and radio personnel who have supported me throughout my career. You know who you are.

I could not close without special mention of two people who make my life and writing a joy. Blanche Richardson and Charles Flowers are both brilliant editors and two of the finest people I know. I'm proud to call them friends.

I close this chapter in my writing career by thanking all the marvelous people who buy my books and support me so warmly during my tours. I thank you for the prayers, letters, and gifts of love. They mean the world to me. That's it for now. Raymond, Nicole, Jared, Delaney, Trent, and Peaches are waiting. I promise.

Being a friend means mastering the art of timing. There is a time for silence. A time to let go and allow people to hurl themselves into their own history. And a time to pick up the pieces when it's all over.

—Gloria Naylor, *The Women of Brewster Place*

If
This
World
Were
Mine

Before

Now

Dear Friend of Hampton University:

It was so great seeing you at the recent reunion. I'm so happy you're considering joining the journal-writing group. As I mentioned at the brunch, all you need to do for membership is write a small journal entry for the first meeting.

Please share with us your dreams, your goal in five years, and your favorite season and why. Also any other information you want to share about your life since we left Hampton Institute, now Hampton University. It seems like those of us who married aren't the only ones whose name has changed (smile). Please keep it to five hundred words or less. I look forward to seeing you at the first meeting. Now get to writing!

Blue and White Kisses,
Riley Denise Woodson

The Life of . . . Riley

Sometimes I come up with the most brilliant ideas! I think this journal-writing group is going to be a big hit. The people I've invited to join are absolutely wonderful. First, there is Leland, whom I met in the Hampton Marching Pirate band; he was the drum major, I was a majorette. Yolanda and I met at a Delta Sigma Theta rush session, when we were numbers 78 and 80. I don't remember who was number 79, because she didn't make line. Finally, my VC (Virginia Cleveland) Hall suitemates, Kelli and Dana. And Dwight and Selwyn because he married Kelli and Selwyn married me.

My life has become everything I dreamed it would be after I met Selwyn Curtis Woodson in front of The Grill on my first day at Hampton. I was having a hard time reading the schedule of classes, and he guided me through registration. It was love at first kiss. Even my mother, Clarice, *a diva before her time*, has fallen in love with Selwyn. So what if it took fifteen years, three promotions, and a six-figure salary to melt her opposition. She only demands, I mean wants, the best for her children.

I remember when I first told her about Selwyn and she asked me who was his family. When I said he's from a foster family, Clarice asked, "The Fosters from Richmond?" Mother was shocked when I explained that Selwyn, a self-described *Grady baby* (born in Atlanta's Grady Hospital), was raised in several foster homes and didn't know who his parents were. The way Selwyn overcame adversity is one of the things I love about him. My mother's trauma at Selwyn's roots, or lack of, was nothing compared to the lashing I got when I announced during my junior year that I was pregnant with twins. Of course, she fell in love with my little boy (Reginald) and girl (Ryan) hours after they were born. So much that she felt the need to raise them for the first eight years of their life. My children are adorable, but Mother didn't give a hoot about adorable, she was trying to make sure I had a B.S. to go with my *M.R.S.*

So that's enough about my family and me. My desire is for life to stay as wonderful as it is now. A loving husband, two perfect preteens, and a life my mother dreamed for herself.

My personal dreams? First I want to quit my job as vice president of marketing, at Wanda Mae Cosmetics simply because I've outgrown peddling blushes and lip gloss to welfare mothers. In five years I want to be a singer and poet who will make even Gwendolyn Brooks and Whitney Houston green with envy. I want my children at Hampton, studying something impressive and challenging. And I want my husband to be even more in love with me than he is today. If that's possible. I hope by then my mother and father have given up their post as members of Black Chicago society and moved to Florida or *somewhere*.

My favorite season? Fall. It's when I met Selwyn, when my children were born. I love the way leaves change colors. Change is good. I want to say more about my wonderful life, but I think I'm over my limit.

Riley

Mad As I Wanna Be

I love my wife. I think I love my wife. I want to love my wife. I can't say that we're *in love* anymore, but that's why we're joining this group. Kelli thinks I'm angry at the world, and she just may be right. The problem is that she thinks my anger is spilling over into our marriage. So, instead of paying somebody to listen to our problems, I've agreed to join this journal-writing group with her.

I met Kelli Chambers Long during our freshman year at Hampton. We were at a Sigma-Zeta mixer. Kelli pledged Zeta Phi Beta and wanted me to pledge Phi Beta Sigma. But I decided to remain independent. I'm Black, not Greek. The only colors I wanted to wear were the red, black, and green colors of liberation. The only thing I've ever joined was church, and that was when I was ten years old. I quit that when the minister tried to hit on my mother. Sunday dinner, my foot! He was already married. But Kelli loves being part of a group. She's in everything from the Links to the Doubleday Book Club.

It's not that I'm angry per se. There's just a lot of shit I don't care for. I don't like white folks and I don't like Black folks who try and be like white folks. I don't know which I dislike the most. I'm sick and tired of the subtle racism inflicted by whites and I'm real sick of Uncle Tom Blacks who accept it without protest. I never dreamed when I was at Hampton that I would run into so many people who were ashamed of being working-class Black folks. They actually believe everything they see about themselves on television or in the white press, where Black folks are "murdered" or "killed" and white folks are "slain." Black folks are crackheads, white folks have drug problems. The only paper I read is the *Chicago Defender*. Same goes for movies. I won't go to any movies unless they've hired at least one Black actor or actress in a meaningful role. This really pisses Kelli off, because she loves that Meryl Streep chick.

I have to work around a lot of white men on my job, but the only men I address as "sir" are Black men. As far as I'm concerned, they're the only ones who deserve my respect.

My dreams? I don't dream. That's all I need to say about that. I have nightmares occasionally—usually about incidents in my childhood, but I don't want to go there. Ever.

My favorite season is summer. It's the one time of the year that I know I will feel warm in an otherwise cold and lonely world.

My goal in five years is to not have to deal with white folks on any level. I want either to have my own business or work for a Black-owned company. I also want to make the brothers who ain't here—including my own brother—proud. I want them to look down and see that all Black men aren't in prison, on drugs, part-time heterosexuals, or in the ground over some silly shit. On a material tip, I'd like to buy my mother a house so she can move out of the two-bedroom apartment she's been living in for the last twenty-two years.

And maybe by the time five years rolls around, me and Kelli will be like that old LTD song, "Back in Love Again."

Dwight

Sisterfriend

I guess you could call me a springtime kind of girl. Spring is such a lush season, when the sky, beautiful in colors of pink, blue, and gray, seems endless in every direction. Spring isn't harsh like winter, or suffocating like summer. Spring is hopeful. And right now I'm feeling hopeful. I finally feel I'm ready to make some progress toward my dream life. The last time I was this optimistic was the spring I graduated from Hampton Institute. When I was at Hampton, life was deliciously uncomplicated, like my childhood. Then, my yesterdays and tomorrows always had a great deal in common. Full of promise. I felt I could do anything and I'm feeling that way again.

I just completed my business plan for my banker to secure an SBA loan to start my own company, and she tells me things look good. I'm so confident, I've already put down a deposit on a downtown office location. I've ordered my business cards and can envision the day when I'll need a larger work space. My professional goals are in place, and soon I can turn my attention toward having a special someone in my life.

Over the years, I have established a formula for men and love. I like to call it *Yolanda's Plan for a Man*. First, I let men know they're not the be-all and end-all. Then I tell them how much I love men and how that love is shown when I'm treated the way I treat them. Plain and simple. Don't start no *s-h*, it won't be no *i-t!* I tell them, treat me the way you *want* to be treated. When men don't return my calls, I don't return calls. When men can't give me honesty, can't find the truth, I book. I can't deal with liars.

In my twenties I stayed in a relationship six years before I realized he wasn't the one. In my thirties a man gets six months to show his stuff or it's "see ya." If I'm still looking in my forties, I'll give a man six weeks before I say "next." I won't have time for love games. I'll be too old, and I'll have a business empire to run.

So while I'm building my queendom and waiting on Mr. Right, I think this group will be fine. I'm looking forward to renewing old friendships and getting to know you guys even better. To see how much we've changed. Besides, my daddy told me when I started dating that "only fools and the very brave dare love with all their hearts." And Daddy didn't raise no fools. Though secretly in my heart of hearts I think we all want someone that makes our skin dance.

Friendship is the one thing that's always been constant in my life. When I was growing up, my best friend was my sister, Sybil. She still is, but Sybil has found her perfect mate and she lives in another city. She didn't mind when I went to Hampton and she stayed home for college. I used to tell her about all the wonderful people I met at Hampton, and I know she'll be happy we're all hooking up again.

Okay, I've told you my favorite season, my goals and dreams, and a little about the woman I am. Now, Miss Riley, I hope this is the last time we have to do this, because I like to show what kind of friend I can be rather than tell.

Yolanda

Doctor, Doctor

I had a dream once. His name was Donald. I don't know what you dream about when your dreams are gone. Do you start new ones? I think that's tough when everything you've ever dreamed of comes true and then suddenly disappears like a thin cloud after the sun shows up.

I had to think hard about joining this group. Not because I don't think it's a good idea, but because things are different now. Two years later the dream of Donald has faded, and I'm different. I'm no longer the man who was consumed by dreams, music, and his plans to be a doctor. I was a man who once envied most of your lives. I watched you join fraternities and sororities, dance and flirt with one another and then fall in love, while I immersed myself in music and my studies. I can't tell you how many nights I went back to James Hall alone, and wished I were you. I don't anymore.

After leaving Hampton Institute, I went to medical school at Howard. I had planned to be a family practitioner in a community clinic, but while I was at Howard, a little boy entered my life. I don't know his name, but I will never forget his face. He was nine years old and he had a venereal disease, but he couldn't tell us how he got it, because his mother's boyfriend was looking at him with an evil eye. I remember those sad eyes that wouldn't meet mine, but every now and then would move toward the man who had brought him in to the clinic. I thought, *this young man is going to have a difficult life if he survives this.* Who will he talk to? This little boy convinced me I could be an asset to my community if I went into psychiatry. I wanted to be the someone that little boy could talk to about what was burning inside. So my goal is to have a practice that will help those little boys and girls who cannot speak when the unspeakable greets them. I know I sound like Miss America, but I want to help people deal with life. To make up for the little boy I didn't know how to help.

After Howard, I did my residence at Columbia University and Harlem Hospital. It was in New York where I met my dream. There were so many times with Donald when I felt he was some type of angel whose responsibility was to make my dreams come true.

One winter night, after a movie and dinner, we sat in Donald's apartment, listening to the music of the seventies. You know, the Isley Brothers, the O'Jays, Marvin Gaye, and Aretha Franklin. A tear rolled from my eye as ribbons of a winter moonlight moved into the darkened room. Without knowing where my tear came from or why, Donald looked at me and said, "Dance with me." So on the terrace of a Harlem brownstone we slow-danced to the music of all the songs I loved in my teens, like "If This World Were Mine," "Stairway to Heaven," "Giving Him Something He Can Feel," and "Hello, It's Me." I had never slow-danced with anyone, but with Donald I was suddenly a Black Fred Astaire. Snow was falling, and it landed on our bodies like tiny sparks. It felt magical. I learned to appreciate the beauty and power of snow. Honest. Silent. Pure.

My favorite season is winter. And so I keep that winter night, dancing with Donald, deep inside me and look forward to the day when I can once again enjoy its splendor.

Leland

This
Is
Now

Player Hater

Something's not right. I'm moving mirrors again.

I'm feeling mellow, a moody sadness like being in a dimly lit room listening to some Miles Davis. Last time I felt this down, I removed all the mirrors except the one attached to the wall in the bathroom. Removing the mirrors was a better option than putting out my own eyes. Made me feel a little crazy, like I just couldn't stand the sight of myself. My own reflection in other people's eyes was better than how I felt about myself then. In their eyes I look *good*, I look strong. They can't see what I see, or what I've seen.

I was happy once. When? I don't exactly remember. But what does "happy" mean anyway? Does it mean that you're always grinning at everybody like a fool? That your body feels like it's dancing even when it's not? I think the last time I was happy was in my senior year at college. Me and my football team, the Miami Hurricanes, were the national champs, and I was one of the star players. Made all-American that year. I was engaged to a beautiful woman, Chase Lewis, a dead ringer for Halle Berry. I was in love for the first time and it was like the sun had dropped down from the sky and kissed me.

I just don't feel right. It's not like I-wanna-kill-myself sad. I wouldn't punk out like that. Maybe it's just that my life is getting ready to change. Big-time.

I have lived the life many men dream about. Picked in the first round in the NFL draft. Setting receiving records nobody has come close to touching. I was making big bank, had a shoe contract, made a few commercials, and was on everybody's wish list when it came to making an appearance at an opening or party.

I figured I had at least two more good years to play, but my football career has ended prematurely because of an ACL injury to my right knee. I'm okay though. You know I still got my walk. A player gotta have his walk. But the team doctor and my own personal physician have warned me that if I sustain another injury to my knee, I might not be so lucky, might wind up spending the rest of my life limping around on crutches. I ain't with that. I don't love football enough to risk never walking again. Besides, the last time I played football or any sport for the pure joy of it, I was ten years old, playing Pop Warner football with the guys from my neighborhood. To be honest, I was getting sick of sports, especially football. Maybe I'll start shooting pool again like I did when I was a youngster. I could get into a game like pool, where it's just me against the game. I have no desire to even watch any pro or college games this fall. I am holding tickets to all the prime track and field events at the Olympics. I should go since the tickets were a gift. Yeah, that's what I'll do, go to Atlanta and then quit sports cold turkey. Get a head start on my new career. Whatever that may be.

A literary agent suggested that I write a book about myself. What would I call it? Something like *The Man in the Mirror Has Two or Three Faces.* But would a publisher be interested in my story? What story would they want to hear? What would I write? I was born in Jacksonville, Florida, right around Thanksgiving, on November 22. I never knew my mother, who died right after I was born. I'm an only child and I don't think I'm spoiled, but I might be. I lived in Magnolia Gardens and graduated from William M. Raines High

School. I was raised by my dad; my aunt Lois, his younger sister; and my dad's younger brother, Mac. I could write how much I love my dad, though our relationship is more like a player-coach thing than a typical father-son thing. But I'm cool with that, 'cause Dad treats me like a star player. Always has. I have much love for my dad!

I could write that most people think I'm biracial because of my honey-brown skin and gray eyes. I'm not. I can't give them that tragic, confused, what-color-am-I story. I'm Black. Believe that. Most people consider me arrogant. I'm not; I'm confident. I'm sick and tired of hearing Black people talk about their lack of self-esteem. They need to get over it and get on with it. But I guess when I'm feeling the way I do now, I sorta understand.

If I wrote a book, would they want to hear how many women I've made scream my name at the top of their lungs? How many of these women think I'm a real dog? I may be. But that's just my way of keeping those chicken-heads in check. I mean, what do they expect when they give up the draws too quick? That ain't the kinda woman I want to marry. Done that. Now, *that* would be a story: how I got rid of that skeezer. But the truth might get my ass in serious trouble. Can you say blackmail?

Would they believe me if I said I don't have any really close male friends? How the media image of the so-called male bonding ends the moment you walk out of the locker room? Most men I know are dogs, and they're weak. Always frontin' with that fake macho thang. Most men, including myself, don't really want to be close friends with other men, but we still want to be all up in each other's faces. Making sure somebody ain't getting more than the next brother. If a mofo ain't got his shit together, then he can't hang tough with me. Mofo, that's short for motherfucker, a term I don't like to use. But since it does apply to a lot of people, I just shorten it to "mofo" for my own purposes. To me, a mofo is somebody who doesn't have a clue on his or her dumb ass. You can usually spot them the moment they open their mouths.

What they probably want to hear is a lot of inside football shit. I don't know why people are interested in a bunch of grown-ass men still playing games, living in a dream world, getting physically abused on a regular basis for big money. I've played most of my career for a losing team, the New Jersey Warriors. But to show you how my life is f'd up, check this out: Right before I got hurt, my agent heard from my dream team, the Dallas Cowboys, inquiring about my skills. They haven't called since the injury. And to make matters worse, the first year I'm not with the Warriors, those mofos are finally getting their shit together and might even make the play-offs. Ain't that some shit. My dad wasn't kidding when he told me at a very young age that life wasn't fair. No shit, Sherlock.

My agent got a call from ESPN. They expressed an interest in me trying out as an announcer for college games, or maybe Canadian football. 'Course, they got to be willing to pay a pretty mofo like me. We'll just have to wait and see what kinda money they're talking. If they don't come correct, then it's Hollywood, here I come.

Maybe I should just wait on writing a book, maybe see if I make the Pro Football Hall of Fame, or I could head to Hollywood and become a big movie star or even some kind of porn star. Yeah, that could work. My name, John, is the only thing common about me. My body is still da bomb. I'm 6'3", 220 pounds. I got chest. I got legs. I got ass. I got dick. I could put that Calvin Klein underwear model in the unemployment line. Calvin would do well to give a brother like me a shot at being a sex symbol. Yeah, yeah, I, could get with that. Naw, naw, I'm tripping. My body already gets me in enough trouble, and if any more mofos saw my shit up there on the screen, well, let's face it, I'd never get any rest. My agent has been receiving some calls for my services in Hollywood, including a cameo appearance in an action feature film. I could do the Jim Brown–Fred Williamson action-hero thang for a minute. But if I'm gonna be up on the big screen for real, it's got to be all about the face. Give Denzel some comp.

You know, writing a book might not be such a bad idea. I heard Dennis Rodman got paid big-time for his book. But money ain't everything, and thanks to a smart business manager and my own common sense, money won't ever be a problem. Anyhow, I wouldn't tell as much as Rodman did. Man, I couldn't believe what that mofo wrote! And the public just ate that shit up. Put *all* his business in the street. Rodman, now, that's a crazy mofo.

All I know right now is that I got to get my life out of this melancholy jazz set and back to some old school pumpin' soul jam like the Isley Brothers' fight-the-power kinda groove, where I'm dancing with myself in a full-length mirror. Know what I'm saying?

Chapter 1

I've just stepped out of the shower and I'm standing in front of the full-length mirror on the bathroom door of my junior suite at the Omni Berkshire in New York City, near Fifty-second and Madison. I *like* what I see. Thanks to a steady regimen of diet and exercise, plus enough vitamins and beauty aids to keep a small drugstore chain in business.

Everything is just as it should be—firm and tight on my tall frame with just enough hips to keep the boys looking. My red linen suit with pearl buttons should do the trick. Red looks good against my chocolate-colored skin. I'm meeting another potential client for lunch, but to be honest, my red suit isn't just to impress a client. I don't want to be caught short like I was last night.

My name is Yolanda Diane Williams, and I'm from Chicago. Well, that's not totally true. I live and work in Chicago, but I grew up in Des Moines. Now, how many Black people do you know from Iowa? Like I always say, it's a good place to be *from*. I get defensive when people ask me where I'm from. I'm afraid I sound like a white girl, so I lay some ebonics on them: "Whatsup wit cha dippin into my buziness?"

I'm presently single, and, unlike most of my female friends, I haven't been looking for a man. Besides, I get more than my share of date requests, and I've got a great ex-husband, Chauncey, for conversation when I'm feeling a little blue or when my batteries are low. The only reason we aren't still married is because Chauncey wanted a life of traveling all over the world, playing his saxophone. Which, when I was younger, seemed exciting. Me, I need something a little more stable, like a regular mailbox to receive my letters and bills. I want a home, not a different hotel room every night.

After working for over ten years in the advertising field at Burrell Communications, Inc., I started my own business about five years ago, called Media Magic, A Consulting Concern, Inc. The years I spent at Burrell were among the best in my life. I learned a lot there from people like the founder, Tom Burrell. But I wanted a job where I could call *me* the boss! I figured out a way to get paid doing something I absolutely love: preparing entertainers and aspiring artists to deal with success. I advise them on how to deal with the press and their adoring fans. I handle special events like musical showcases when they come to the Midwest to promote their latest project. And I do crisis management when some of these music stars get their celebrity butts in a sling. And I'm good at what I do. I have several major record and video companies under contract. I come to New York twice a month to meet with regular and prospective clients. New York is my second favorite city—after Chicago, where I feel safe and have several good, make that *great*, friends.

Around the time I started my business, me and five friends from college renewed our friendship at a Hampton alumni reunion. We had such a good time, we decided to start getting together socially and writing journals like we had in an English class at Hampton. Keeping the journal and meeting with friends at least once a month couldn't have come at a better time for me. I had just lost both my parents within a year. My daddy to a heart attack and Mama, nine months later, to a broken heart. So now it's just me and my baby sister, Sybil, who lives in Iowa City. I was nervous about stepping out on my own, and more than money, I needed friends I could count on and who believed in me.

Right now the group includes me, and my best friend in the whole world, Leland, make that Dr. Leland Thompson, single and gay. Then there's Riley (poetic justice) Woodson, who could best be described as a BAP (Black American princess) from the day she was born. I call her my high-maintenance soror. She's married, but I'm not convinced she's still in love. Her husband, Selwyn, used to be cool, but now he's strictly business. And there is Dwight Leon Scott, a computer engineer, divorced and mad at the world. He was married to one of our former members, Kelli, who left the group when Dwight wouldn't. I think Dwight stayed just to spite Kelli. We lost one of the original members, Dana, to marriage and Atlanta, Georgia.

Our monthly meetings are big fun. We eat, drink a little wine, listen to music, and read from our journals. We talk about our lives and our dreams, then share affirmations that might help us in times of need. Most of my journal entries that I share with the group (I also keep a private journal) have been about my career, good dirt on some of the celebrities I've worked with, and my dreams for the future. Dreams that, quite frankly, have not included a Mr. Right. Like I said, I have a great ex-husband and a wonderful male friend who listens to every and any thing I have to say. And I had a wonderful relationship with my deceased father.

I've already exceeded my goal for this trip by landing not one, but three new clients. Pretty soon I'm going to have to hire someone to help me and Monica, my assistant, with the extra workload. I've got a whole file of résumés from recent college grads looking to get in the media music business.

Today is Thursday, and I've been in New York for four days. Usually by day five I'm ready to return to my adopted hometown. Day four and suddenly I'm not in such a hurry to leave the Big Apple. In fact, I'm standing here humming Toni Braxton's "I Love Me Some Him," and thinking about this truly over man I met last night at the Motown Cafe. I'm still trying to figure out exactly what happened. Now, it's not like I'm a believe-anything-you-tell-me type of woman. I mean, I'm in the twilight—make that pitch black— of my thirties. In other words, I'll be forty in February. I've been to the Male State Fair a few times, rode a few rides, then got off. In fact, I'd forgotten what the tunnel of love looked like, when Mr. Fine walked into my life.

I was feeling tired and probably looked like it after three days of meetings and presentations. I'd spent about an hour on the phone with Sybil. It was her thirty-fifth birthday and I was telling her what she had to look forward to. But Sybil already has her stuff together. My little sis is working on her Ph.D. in social work while raising two children and a husband. Sister got it going on strong.

I could've ordered room service, but I'd been in the suite most of the day and figured fresh night air would do me some good. It must have been fate, because I wasn't planning on eating at the Motown Cafe. It's not the kind of place I would choose to eat alone, something I hardly ever do, since I usually find a way to combine my meals with meetings. I wound up there because I couldn't get a reservation at my current favorite restaurant, Cafe Beulah in the Flatiron District.

So there I was, sitting in a booth and enjoying some tasty catfish fingers with a little macaroni and cheese on the side. I was gazing up at this huge ceiling, at a platter of the Supremes' single, "Stop! In the Name of Love," and listening to the Motown Moments sing all the hits I love. I have to admit I wasn't looking all that cute; like I said, I was real tired. It had been a week since I'd seen my hair technician. Although I'm wearing a short, curly Afro, I still need my salon time. I had on a simple V-neck top and a wide black silk skirt. I was licking catfish juice off my fingers, when I felt a strong presence approaching my booth. Up walked one of the most gorgeous men I've ever seen! He leaned into my booth and said something (Don't ask me what 'cause I don't know) and then I said something (Again, don't ask me 'cause I don't know that either) and then he kissed me like I've never been kissed before. Yes, he did, he did! I *do* remember the kiss being sensual, and him whispering in my ear in a smooth and dreamy voice, "It's so great seeing you again. Please, don't make me wait so long ever again." I mumbled, "I won't." His lips were warm and gentle—and the kiss felt whisper-soft.

I swear I've never seen this man in my life, but I went along to get along. I don't do drugs. Maybe a glass of wine or champagne every now and then. But I would have *remembered* this man. He had this great smile, startling winter-gray eyes, and a body that was bumping. He was tall. I like tall. He was fine. I love fine. And like I said, the man could kiss! I don't even remember his name, I'm not sure he even told me what it was. But I did manage to give him my card. I hope it was my card and not one of my clients'.

As I watched him walk out of the restaurant alone, I realized I still had a catfish finger in one hand. The Motown Moments were still singing, and the scent of his cologne hung like a promise in the air. I walked back to my hotel humming "I Hear a Symphony" and floating through the summer air. I've been in a daze ever since. But I've got to come back, get on the first thing flying back to Chicago tomorrow. On Sunday I've got a meeting I just can't miss. My friends aren't going to believe this.

Chapter 2

It's Friday and I'm wondering why God ever created sex. It just so happens that on this last day of the week, each one of my eight patients is dealing with how sex has messed up their lives. Maybe I'm pissed off because despite all their problems, at least they're getting some. More than I can say for myself. It's usually on Fridays that I seriously consider switching from psychiatry to being a general practitioner in some small, uncomplicated, slow-paced southern town near my hometown of New Orleans.

Sometimes on Fridays I long to be back at Hampton, sitting under Emancipation Oak or in the library, trying to solve a complicated chemistry problem. I wish I were back at Booker T. Washington Junior High, when sex was something I only pretended to know about.

On this particular humid mid-July Friday I had made it through the first five clients then managed to finish a tuna and American cheese on rye while jotting down a few notes on the morning patients. I was praying for the strength to give my final three clients my undivided attention.

I had a good thirty minutes before my afternoon patients, so I decided to write an entry to read to the group on Sunday. When my office was quiet, like it was now, I was grateful that Riley had suggested that I join a group of her friends keeping journals: My journals had become much-needed therapy for me.

 It's been a good week. I feel like some of my patients are making progress. I'm trying not to get too excited, but a couple of my patients who are HIV-positive (and who months ago were at death's door) have started taking some of these new drugs and now they look great! Could we be close to beating this AIDS thing? I'm excited, yet frightened to even think about something so miraculous and wonderful.

I know you guys have been worrying about my social life. I don't know if you're really worried or you're all homoerotic voyeurs. I don't think you'll ever understand that dating for a Black gay man is different than with you guys. Anyway, I had a date this week and in my world you never know what you're gonna get.

This was a rugged-looking guy I met near my office. He was part of a work crew widening the streets close to Grant Park. He caught my eye one day when I was having lunch in the park and I guess I caught his, because he came over and started a conversation. I didn't know at first if he was gay, but I was hoping. Then he told me I should be eating something more substantial and then he offered to cook dinner. His invitation surprised me. I never figured he might be gay, but only wished. He had a wonderful smile and was very masculine. You guys know I like macho.

When I got to his apartment I thought I was walking into my great-great-auntie's apartment. It smelled like an old person's house! I mean, it was decorated with all this old-timey furniture with shawls and plastic covering everything. It looked like the showroom of **The Price Is Right.** *In the seventies. When I asked him if he lived with his mother, he smiled and said no, he had decorated the place himself. That's when I noticed his voice was softer than it had been at the park, and he was wearing a long, flowing blousy kind of shirt with huge exotic flowers all over it. Thank God I had instructed my answering service to page me thirty minutes after my* *arrival. I know the operator must have thought I was crazy when I kept saying "Oh, no. No. I'll be right there." When I explained to him I had a medical emergency, he said, "I hope you feel better soon." I started to tell him I was a doctor, but decided it might take too long. He insisted on fixing me a plate, and the food did smell good, so I agreed to take some food home. When I left, he was standing at the door in that outrageous outfit, his head posed ever so Doris Day–like. "You got a rain check you can cash anytime, man friend." Man friend, what exactly is that? Sounds like something my uncle would call his trade. All I could think of was I had been faked out again.*

Before I knew it, I had made it through two more clients, including my married, closeted ex-judge and "Joyless Joey," my Friday ABM (angry black man) who still hadn't confessed the sexual secret that was causing him so much pain. As usual, he had spent his fifty minutes blaming everyone, especially white folks and faggots, for his lack of social skills. Several times I had been tempted to tell him, "Excuse me, but you're sitting here depending on a 'faggot' to help you with all your problems." I thought he and my journal member Dwight might make good buddies. Not because I think Dwight is *that* homophobic—just mad at everybody.

While waiting for my last patient, I picked up a pink message slip from the receptionist's desk. My best friend, Yolanda, had called, saying that she would pick me up at six P.M. sharp on the Michigan Avenue side of my office. There was a special instruction for me to be on time because she had "big news." I guess she had finished her business in New York early enough to get a midday flight back to O'Hare.

Yolanda, or Yogi as I sometimes called her, and I had a standing Friday-night date when she was in town. We left Saturdays open for dates that for me never seemed to happen. Before she left for New York, we made tentative plans to check out Vanessa Williams in the movie *Eraser*, and then grab a bite at my uncle Doc's South Side eatery. I was still wondering what her big news was, when I heard the outer office door open. My three o'clock appointment called out, "Whatsup, Dr. Thompson?"

I turned toward the door and gave my best I'm-a-doctor-who-cares smile.

"Michael, come on in," I said. I had been seeing Michael Hunter for a little over a year. We hadn't made much progress with his sexual addiction. He was a handsome man, slender, yet well muscled with white, slightly crooked teeth under a trim auburn mustache. For the past two years he had made a living as a high-priced escort for both men and women, even though he considered himself gay. I was thankful we didn't have to deal with the bisexual thing. He had, on occasion, modeled for legitimate clients like Marshall Field. Michael had convinced himself that the reason he was working as an escort was that the Chicago modeling opportunities hadn't panned out. He denied the fact that he enjoyed the sex with as many as a dozen clients a week.

I followed Michael into my office and placed Yolanda's message on my desk, picked up my yellow legal pad, and sat in my well-worn chair. Michael plopped in the black leather wing chair facing me. It looked as though the chair had swallowed him whole. I spent a few minutes trying to remember if he normally sat in the chair or the sofa. Some of my patients always sat on the sofa, while my more uptight patients, like the judge, favored the chair. I didn't consider Michael uptight.

"I've got some exciting news, Dr. Thompson," Michael said. "I'm moving back to New York."

"I thought you enjoyed living in Chicago," I said. He had been living in Chicago for less than two years.

"Yeah, I do, but I think things are changing with the New York modeling scene," he said.

"What do you mean?" I asked.

"The Tyson look, you know, all that dark skin, is finally wearing thin and agencies are going to be looking for light-skinned men. You just *know* light skin is coming back." He smiled as if he had heard some special news bulletin interrupting his favorite soap. I didn't know whether to get up and shake this fool or to laugh. My people never fail to amaze me.

·   ·   ·

I was worried. It was nearly eight o'clock and I hadn't heard from Yolanda. I had waited outside on Michigan Avenue for over an hour before returning to my office. I tried her cellular. I called her office phone and home number. I checked my home answering machine to see if she had left a message for me there. Nothing. I checked to see if her flight had arrived on time. It had. I called the Omni in New York, where Yolanda always stayed. She had checked out. I was eager to see my girl and to hear her "big news" as well. I smiled when I thought about *my* big news. I had to warn my Hershey bar–colored friend that light skin was making a comeback.

I decided to take a taxi over to Uncle Doc's. Yolanda would know to find me there.

I paid for my taxi, and as I approached Miss Thing's Wings, I could see a long line leading up to the door. The door itself defied logic. It was a ramshackle wooden door with a wire mesh screen inserted into its upper half. Like rings on a tree, different colors told the history of the door, which had been painted again and again over the years. Currently, it was a reddish-brown with bits of hospital green peeking through. The door hung on spring hinges, so it was easy to push open and could shut by itself. With the constant flow of customers in and out of the place, the banging of that door was as familiar to me as Uncle Doc's voice shouting out orders to Miss Mavis in the kitchen.

While many small businesses in the area had come and gone, Miss Thing's Wings was entering its twentieth year, despite competition from the chicken franchise down the block. My uncle had refused several good offers to move and expand, because as he put it, "I don't want nobody in my skillets or my business." It was located just past the 1200 block of South Michigan, where it had always been. Its address should have been thirteen something, but Uncle Doc thought that would be unlucky and had somehow managed to convince city officials to give him a 1200-numbered address. Uncle Doc had changed the name from Doug's Chicken Shack during the early '80s, when every gay man in the country started using the term "Miss Thing" to describe each other and close girlfriends. Some of my uncle's closest friends would call him after leaving the club with the same question Friday after Friday: "Miss Thing, you got any of them wings fryin'?" And the ever-popular "Miss Thing know she can put a fryin' on some wings."

A full block before you entered the one-story building you could smell the barbecue smoking in the huge barrel smoke pit out back. The tiny dining room was the size of a project bedroom, with a kitchen the size of a walk-in closet. The place was packed—as always. Each of the six tables was covered with a plastic pink and green checked tablecloth (a tribute to my mother's sorority, Alpha Kappa Alpha; Uncle Doc had declared himself an honorary member of the AKAs). They were wedged between the used-to-be-white, greased-stained walls. Each plastic upholstered chair was spoken for. A red Formica counter with three stools stood at the back of the room in front of the kitchen, and beside the fully occupied counter was the cash register and takeout window. In the corner, the jukebox still offered three selections for a quarter and was belting out some serious B. B. King over the roar of voices. Two pay phones were attached to the wall near the front door. Most of the wall space was covered with mismatched framed pictures of Uncle Doc's favorites like Lena Horne, Billie Holiday, and Nat King Cole, as well as Chicago dignitaries like the late Mayor Harold Washington, John H. Johnson, Michael Jordan, Oprah Winfrey, Jesse Jackson, Senator Carol Mosely Braun, and the latest edition—Dennis Rodman. The frequent visiting celebrities like Vanessa Williams, Babyface, Laurence Fishburne and even Elton John were also showcased shaking hands with Uncle Doc.

The remaining reachable wall space was dotted with every possible handwritten sign indicating the acceptable behavior in Miss Thing's Wings: NO FEETS ON THE WALL, NO SHOES, NO SERVICE, and my favorite, IF IT AIN'T RIGHT, IT'S WRONG!

One summer I had come to Chicago from college to work with Uncle Doc. I was full of myself, cocky and feeling college-boy smarter than anyone else. Clearly, it was up to me to save my uncle from himself. Or so I thought. I decided I would take down all the misspelled signs and correct them while Uncle Doc was out. Sort of my surprise thank-you for all the financial help he was giving me. I was tacking up the last sign, EXTRA POTATO SALAD, 50 CENTS, when the door banged. It was Uncle Doc. I stood there grinning, waiting for my well-deserved thanks, but Uncle Doc just walked right past me up to the counter. He called out to Miss Mavis, "Love, has *any*body ever had any trouble reading the signs in my place?"

"Naw, not to my knowledge, Doc," she answered thoughtfully. "Well," Uncle Doc said, turning to look me right in the eye, "has *any*body ever questioned the 's' on 'feets'? Or maybe the 'e' on 'p-o-t-a-t-o-e'?"

"Naw, Doc, don't you think maybe it's because we's just too stupid?" Mavis asked.

" 'Cause we ain't been to no big fancy c-o-l-l-e-g-e?" Uncle Doc chimed in.

I changed the signs back. Uncle Doc never said a word directly to me, but he did give me a large circle pop and a smile, as if to say, "Now, there," one of his favorite lines.

The takeout line snaked into the establishment along the walls and ended at the cash register, where orders were placed from the chalkboard price list that hung from the ceiling over the register. The menu included a "Girlfriend Basket" (five wings, fries, and slaw with a thin slice of white bread on top), a "Snap 'N Pop Plate" (short ribs and potato salad), and my own personal favorite, the "Trade Basket" (a combination of wings, hot links, short ribs, and fries, drenched in hot barbecue sauce with two slices of white bread).

The orders were served in too-small green plastic baskets. If it was a "bird flying," meaning to go, the baskets were covered with plain brown paper bags that the sauce would seep through before the customers banged the door on their way out.

There was no denying the food. It was simply among the best in Chicago. The lines told the story. The steady stream of celebrities or their assistants, rich white folks slumming, gangstas, Chicago Bulls, Bears, and Blackhawks, and regular folks all proved that Miss Thing's Wings was putting out something almost everybody wanted. The clientele was as much a part of the ambience as the smell of smoking hot links. Tonight a Buppie couple in formal wear—she in sequins, he in a tux—sat greasy-fingered at one of the tables, poring over plates of short ribs and slaw. Now I knew who owned the limo double-parked outside. Or maybe it had delivered the two white businessmen whispering conspiratorially over steaming Trade Baskets. I smiled to myself, thinking they probably had no idea where Uncle Doc had gotten the name from. Maybe they thought it was a part of the NAFTA agreement.

Two of Chicago's finest were finishing off their Hot 'N Spicy wings and potato salad with long swallows of Uncle Doc's famous red fruit punch. He had another version of the punch he wasn't allowed by law to serve, something about a liquor license. No one paid the cops or the white businessmen any mind, and the cops seemed oblivious to the noisy flurry of activity all around them. The table in the back corner was occupied by a middle-aged, diamond-studded blonde and a brother who appeared at least twenty-five years her junior. They had moved their chairs close together, and their blue plastic tumblers were raised in a toast. Their other hands were not visible above the table as they gazed feverishly into each other's eyes.

Four open-shirted, gold-chained, Jheri-curled young men were hunched over their food like they were afraid somebody was gonna take it away. Their many-ringed fingers were dripping with sauce, and the table was littered with greasy used paper napkins.

My stomach was growling for some of Uncle Doc's throw-down food. I couldn't wait on Yolanda.

"Hey, hey! Here comes my baby!" Aunt Thelma's booming voice greeted me from clear across the room like a warm bear hug. She was ringing up orders and calling them out to Miss Mavis in the kitchen. Thelma Washington, a hefty brown sweet-faced woman, was no more my aunt than Patti LaBelle was my mother, but she was family. Aunt Thelma had worked for my uncle for over fifteen years. When Uncle Doc wasn't there, Thelma ruled Miss Thing's Wings with an iron fist. Sometimes gloved in velvet, more often not. She was not only headwaitress-in-charge, but often the entertainment for the evening. Aunt Thelma wouldn't hesitate to *read* first-timers who behaved like they had no home training, much to the delight of the old-timers, who'd laugh openly, remembering their own trial by fire. I still remember the day she snatched my baseball cap off my head just as me and some friends were getting ready to dive into plates of short ribs and potato salad. Took me forever to live that one down.

"How's my favorite chile? You shrunk any heads this week?" Thelma asked. We both laughed and hugged the best we could across the counter. I always got the shrink joke from Aunt Thelma when I came in wearing my uniform: khaki slacks, oxford shirt, tie with a vest, and regulation penny loafers. "I'm doing okay. And I'm doing the best I can on the other tip. What's going on with you?" I answered back.

"Chicken and customers. Customers and chicken," she replied.

"Where's my uncle?" I wanted to see my wiry, fun-loving uncle, my father's brother with the big smile. Uncle Doc's aging features came at you in waves, a button nose, large teeth, and lips almost too big for his oval-shaped face. He dyed his hair constantly, so it was always too black for peanut-butter-brown skin.

"Now, Doc, Jr. You know he's running the stand over at the Taste," Thelma said. Sometimes she called me Doc, Jr., because I had given Uncle Doc my medical degree when I graduated from

Howard Medical School. He had paid my tuition all the way through school. He was so touched and proud that he had a duplicate made so that he could have one at home and one in his restaurant, right next to the triple chicken fryers.

"I forgot the Taste of Chicago is going on. Couldn't tell by this packed house," I said. This was Uncle Doc's fifth year of participating in the huge and popular Chicago food festival. Only the best restaurateurs were invited, and this year was supposed to be extra special because First Eater President Bill Clinton was making a visit. Uncle Doc had been busy for months trying to figure out a way to make sure the President tasted at least one of his wings.

"I'm sure there's a line over there too. You want your usual?"

"Yes, ma'am. But don't rush yourself, wait on your paying customers. Yolanda hasn't called here, has she?"

"Now, you know you askin' the wrong one. I don't answer that contraption 'less I have to," Thelma said.

"I wonder what happened?" Before I could answer myself, I felt two delicate hands cover my eyes. I knew those hands, and her exquisite vanilla perfume confirmed it.

"Guess who's my favorite boyfriend?" Yolanda said as I turned around and gave her a quick kiss on the lips and then a big hug. She looked great in a cranberry-colored silk dress with thin straps.

"Where have you been? I've been worried about you," I said.

"I'm sorry. I had to take a later flight. You forgive me?"

"Of course, but why didn't you call me?"

"Didn't have my phone. I must be losing my mind 'cause I put that girl in my luggage. And then this jerk I was sitting next to on the plane tied up the phone the entire trip. You would have thought that phone was attached to his ear when he came on the plane," Yolanda joked.

"It's good to see you, but a diva like you wouldn't have a phone problem if you were riding up in first class," I said.

"I know that's right, but I don't have enough clients to have first-class money," Yolanda said.

"One day . . . one day very soon. What's the big news?"

"Hold up, Leland. Let me catch my breath and place my order. I'm starving," she said as she lifted her leather shoulder bag from around her neck.

"I've already ordered. What would you like to eat?"

"You oughta know. One Sweet Thing, please," Yolanda shouted toward Thelma. A "Sweet Thing" was two fried chicken legs on a syrup-covered waffle. I noticed one of the security guards escorting the sequins and tux outside, so Yolanda and I grabbed their empty table.

"Yogi, what's the big news?"

"My news will have to wait. I'm waiting on some real food!"

Chapter 3

One look at her lavish surroundings, and it appeared that Riley had it all. Her friends and family were certain she was living a charmed life. She lived in a spacious twelve-room residence in a tony gold-coast condo, with Lake Michigan facing her office window and downtown Chicago sprawled beneath her bedroom balcony. She had her choice of not one, but two luxury cars to drive, every credit card known to man, a maid, wonderful teenage twins . . . and Selwyn, the perfect businessman and husband. Riley had bulging bank accounts, trust funds for the twins, a safe full of expensive jewelry and papers documenting the wealth she and Selwyn had accumulated, and her own manically organized walk-in closet full of designer clothes and shoes.

But in reality Riley Denise Woodson was living the life her parents had dreamed of and planned for their firstborn daughter. She was also living her life according to Selwyn's latest ten-year plan. Her reality had little in common with her dreams, which were filled with drama and desire. Since she quit her job as vice president of

sales for a minority-owned cosmetics company, she viewed herself
merely wife and mother—a kept woman with kids. Born and raised
in Chicago's Pill Hill area, Riley had lived in the Windy City all her
life with the brief exception of five years at Hampton Institute and
three more years she spent in Cambridge while Selwyn studied for
his J.D. and M.B.A. degrees at Harvard.

Although Riley was the perfect wife and the perfect mother, the
mask of perfection was slipping. She was neither a famous singer nor
a world-renowned poet, but these were her aspirations. Riley Denise
Woodson was living a lie.

It was early Sunday morning. Sire, her maid, was singing an up-
beat song in her native Spanish and busying herself around the
apartment in preparation for the journal group's meeting. The ca-
tering people were setting up the buffet, arranging flowers, and doing some last-minute cooking in the kitchen. Five hours to show
time, and Riley felt none of her usual excitement when she was
planning a party.

Riley closed the massive mahogany doors behind her. The library
was quiet and she found comfort in the silence. Her footsteps were
muted by the Oriental rug as she walked to her antique cherry-wood
desk and placed her crystal juice glass on the silver coaster. She
slumped heavily into the leather wing chair and retrieved a small key
from its hiding place under the lamp on top of the desk. She un-
locked the top left-hand desk drawer and pulled out two leather-
bound journals. The group kept one journal to share and another
personal diary that remained confidential. She opened the group
journal and stared at her own neat handwriting, then turned to the
first available blank page.

July 14, 1996 was all she wrote before closing the journal and
reaching for her private diary. She stared blankly at the bookcase-
lined walls filled with gold-trimmed books that neither she nor Selwyn had read. She picked up her black ball-point and began to
write:

I've been looking forward to this meeting for months, but, as usual, Selwyn has put a damper on my special day. He says he's stuck in San Francisco with a client—again. It's not like I really expected him to be here for me. It's not like family comes first with him. Besides, he thinks the group is childish and a waste of time. I could be doing something for him with my time. I'm sure that's what he really thinks. It's just that I thought his being here would lay to rest the rumors that our storybook marriage is in trouble. It's not. It's way past trouble.

I want romance back in my life. I dream of a passion like we once shared. What if I wrote in my journal that I haven't had sex with my husband in close to two years. The last time we made love, Selwyn didn't even look at me afterward. He pressed his head deep into the pillows and moaned, to let me know he had finished. I guess to call what happened as making love would be inappropriate. I can just see their mouths drop open. They would never believe that Selwyn and I were the same two people who couldn't keep their hands off each other in college. But the skinny boy I fell in love with my first year of college has become a grown man I don't even know anymore. Maybe they wouldn't be shocked at all? Maybe I should write a poem, no, a song, about how love once beautiful can gradually become boring and brutal.

I don't think I'll write about rejection letter No. 10 I just received. I'll just tell them I'm still waiting to hear something about the last batch of poetry I sent out. I'm not so certain they believe I can really write poetry. Right before Selwyn left for his trip, I tried to read him one of my poems, like I did in college, but he gave me a quick and firm "Not now, Riley, I'm busy." But I know one day I'll be as popular as my she-roes, Maya, Gwendolyn, and Nikki. Maybe this time someone will ask me to read one of my poems at the end of the evening. Maybe if I plant myself at the baby grand, they will ask me to sing.

I could write about my children. I haven't talked about Ryan and Reggie for a while. Ryan is so bright. She's going to Hampton on an academic scholarship and Reggie on an athletic scholarship. I make sure I tell the group that even though our children are going there on scholarship, we still *send a generous check to Hampton every year. I'll be the first one in the group to have my children attend our alma mater. Third-generation Hamptonians. Reggie is especially going to love that beautiful campus with its historic buildings and Hampton Creek. Selwyn and I used to have poetry-sharing picnics near the creek. My kids have never given Selwyn and me an ounce of trouble. No gangs. No drugs. They're polite, obedient, and independent. I'm not really sure they even need me around. I wonder what would happen if I didn't come back when I take them to Hampton. I wonder how long it would take Selwyn to notice I was gone.*

*My weight. Now, there's a subject I could write about ad nauseam. I have a new plan to get rid of the same fifteen pounds I lost last year (plus the five of friends they brought back with them) before I go to Virginia. I'm beginning to feel like I will always be just one biscuit away from permanent Jenny Craig membership. But I hate talking about my weight with Yolanda looking me dead in the face. **She** still looks like she just made the majorette line at Hampton. She wasn't a majorette, **I** was. No, if I'm going to really lose the weight in time, I'd better keep it to myself.*

Somehow I will make it through the day without Selwyn being present. If only I could do that every day. Be alone but not feel lonely. I see my loneliness as solitude, not punishment. I guess a live body next to me some nights is better than no nights at all. Besides, who else would want me?

Riley laid her pen down momentarily and felt the tears well up in her eyes. She sipped some iced tea and hoped it would quell the sob rising from her chest. She had an urge to call her mother but didn't feel like praying for approval, let alone understanding. Her mother would tell her she needed to be in church, making social connections, instead of planning some party for friends who had not managed to move up to Riley's social class.

These depressive periods in her life were when she felt she wrote her best poetry, but today she picked up her pen and wrote in her group journal about her perfect children, her perfect husband, her perfect life. When she was finished, she locked her diary in her desk, hid the key, and took her journal and glass into the kitchen, where a white-aproned, white-faced caterer's assistant was putting the final touches on the hors d'oeuvres and uncorking the wine so that it would have time to breathe. Maybe that's what Riley needed—time to breathe, but appearances were everything, her image more important than her tattered feelings. Riley had a party to dress for, and even if she didn't feel it, she would at least *look* great.

As Riley was walking to her dressing area, her private phone rang.

"Hello," Riley said.

"Riley, this is your mother." Riley was thinking this was one voice she could always remember.

"Hello, Mother. How are you?" Riley braced herself for a typical no-win conversation with Clarice Elizabeth Wade. Her mother tended to dominate and manipulate every situation and every relationship she was in. Riley always felt like a three-year-old when she had to talk with her mother. Though she occasionally rose to the level of a rebellious teenager, she doubted she would ever be on an equal adult level with Clarice.

Clarice had dangled her love and approval before Riley like a carrot on a stick, and Riley felt she had never been quick enough or smart enough to catch the carrot whole, only small pieces every now and then. Her mother had a subtle way of letting Riley know that she was neither as good a mother nor as good a wife as Clarice. When Riley complained about Selwyn's long and frequent absences, Clarice simply told her that it was a wife's place to be patient and keep the home fires burning until her husband returned. Clarice also told her that complaining was probably what kept Selwyn away.

Clarice knew what to do with her idle time. She controlled people. She was an officer in both the National Council of Negro Women and Links. A lifetime member of Zeta Phi Beta Sorority, Inc. She had a closet full of size-seven pastel suits and tasteful evening wear. Her hair, which she had dyed a honey blond long before any of her friends did, was always beauty-parlor fresh. Her lips and nails were always perfect, painted in pale peach and deep pink shades to accent her oatmeal-colored complexion.

Riley had long ago given up on ever winning her mother's approval, and certainly her mother's respect was out of the question. But Riley had her moments of sweet revenge. At Hampton, where Clarice attended, Riley pledged Delta instead of Zeta. In her early thirties, when Clarice said the Links were interested in Riley, she rushed to the arms of the Junior League. For Riley it was One Hundred Black Women, not the National Council of Negro Women. While Clarice always wore Mary Kay, Riley went to work for a minority competitor, Wanda Mae Cosmetics. Clarice was not impressed when Riley was named executive vice president in charge of marketing after only five years. When Clarice became close friends with the *real* Wanda Mae, Riley knew it was time to leave her powerful position. Riley convinced herself she no longer agreed with the direction the company was taking with marketing. Wanda Mae sounded like Clarice when she chastised Riley for hiring a white woman as her executive assistant, instead of the Black woman Wanda Mae preferred.

Clarice got on Riley's last nerve each and every time they spoke, but she had yet to summon the courage to tell her mother to butt out of her life.

"Listen, Riley. The reason I'm calling is to tell you to be sure and wear something to your little party that will accentuate your pretty face. You know, you've gained quite a bit of weight, and if you emphasize your one good feature, well, maybe no one will notice. Wear a dark shade, something loose-fitting. And don't slouch! You tend to slouch when you're overweight."

"Yes, Mother, I'll try and remember that," Riley said.

"Have you tried that new shade Wanda Mae sent you? That stuff you've been wearing is going to break your face out as sure as I'm standing here talking to you," Clarice said.

"I've been using a product by Iman, and it's working just fine," Riley said.

"What does some former model know about makeup? Wanda Mae just hired a new chemist who's come up with some great products. I've been using them and you should see my face. And Wanda Mae asked if you were working and if . . ."

Riley interrupted Clarice.

"Mother, for the last time, I quit Wanda Mae because I didn't like the way she does business. I know she's your new best friend, but I'm fine with things just the way they are. Thanks for calling. Give Daddy my love. But I've got to go. I think I hear someone at the door."

"Where is that maid of yours?"

"Good-bye, Mother."

"Good-bye, Riley. Have a nice time."

Riley muttered to herself, *yeah, right.*

•   •   •

Dwight Leon Scott sat at the desk in his cluttered Hyde Park studio and decided it was time to write something for the group. Just like in college, he had waited until the last minute, which usually meant Sunday morning. He had never been fond of journal writing in college, but since he had joined the group, he noticed how writing things down helped extinguish his anger. Dwight's ex-wife, Kelli, had been right about something, he thought when he realized how soothed the writing left him. Before Dwight told Kelli he wanted a divorce, he wrote in his journal how unhappy he was with marriage. Dwight felt the differences in their upbringing were more than he could handle. Kelli didn't understand why Dwight was more inter-ested in buying a house for his mother, rather than building the new house she dreamed of in Lake Forest.

He had already had a long telephone conversation with one of his basketball buddies, and he had turned down an insistent offer to go shoot some hoops while his buddy's wife was at church. A place he should have been. His mother had just asked him when was the last time he had been inside a church. She didn't understand his joke when he told her he attended Bedside Baptist regularly. Dwight looked around his apartment for his cellular phone. It was time to make his Sunday-morning call to his mother, Sarah, who lived in Oakland, California, where Dwight was born and raised until he left for Hampton Institute in 1974 to study computer science.

Dwight's studio was a large space divided by partitions of wood that had been painted a brown-orange color. The kitchen-dining area was separated by a small bar, where Dwight would pull his meals from the microwave and eat alone most mornings and evenings.

There was only one picture on the dull gray walls—a high-flying Michael Jordan—and no photographs on the two low-standing bookshelves. Thin, dusty miniblinds hung from unwashed windows. Dwight spotted his phone on the windowsill, picked it up, and dialed his favorite girl's number.

"Miss Sarah, this here is ya boy, Dwight Leon Scott," he said in a teasing southern drawl. Sarah was originally from a small town in Texas.

"Hey there, baby. I was just thinkin' 'bout you. Wondering what time it was there in Chicago and if it was okay to call you. I know how you like to sleep on your day off. It wouldn't hurt you to get up and go to church though," Sarah said.

"I told you I'm a member in good standing at Bedside Baptist," Dwight joked.

"I hope the good Lord knows about Bedside," his mother joked.

"I think I've seen him there," Dwight said.

Dwight and his mother spent about thirty minutes reviewing each other's week and Sarah gave him the 411 on everybody in the family in California, Texas, and the few living in Oklahoma. When Dwight noticed what time it was, he told his mother he loved her and he was still working on buying her a real house.

"Don't you worry 'bout me. I'm fine right where I'm at. You just take care of yourself and that helps me out. And I love you too, Mr. Dwight *big shot* Scott."

When Dwight clicked off the phone, he decided to write in his personal journal. The journal he kept on his personal computer. He took a swig of his orange juice, clicked on his PC, and began to type.

I know the group is sick and tired of hearing me rant and rave about white folks. Too bad. I get sick and tired of hearing Riley go on about Selwyn and their great middle-class adventure. I know she was separated at birth from my ex-wife, Kelli. Sometimes I feel kinda sorry for Riley with her lame poetry and can't-sing-a-lick ass. Yolanda's pretty cool with her fine self. But she won't give this brother the time of day. I mean, she gets all up in Leland's gay-ass face. Talk about separated at birth. The doc is okay, he's cool, but no way can he do for her what a real man can do. I really do not get the gay man/straight woman thang. What's the big attraction? Maybe I'm just not assimilated enough to hang with the in crowd. I shoulda left when I dumped Kelli. She's the one that got me in this mess. Fuck 'em! Today I don't give a shit.

Dwight turned off his PC, stood up and stretched long and hard. He took a deep breath and picked up his pen and journal to write one more angry Black man story he knew would annoy the entire group of sell-out Negroes:

*There I was, sitting in first class, minding my own business, when this overdressed, plump white woman sat down next to me. Of course, she didn't speak, but gave me one of those **what-are-you-doing-in-first-class** looks. She got situated and pulled out a fancy laptop computer. I figured she was some kind of computer guru with her thick glasses and frumpy wanna-be-a-man business suit. Now, even though I don't like engaging in personal conversation with white folks, I will on occasion break my rule if I think I'll learn something that will help me in the white man's business world. I started to ask her about her PC, when she asked a stewardess, I mean flight attendant, to watch her computer while she went to the rest room.*

I've gotten used to that kinda snide racist shit from other passengers and from the airline personnel. They always ask me if they can help me find my seat when I slow down in the first-class section and try and store my luggage. They always want to see my boarding pass, which I never show them. I just give them my seat number in a low, deep voice, and they leave me the fuck alone. But I like first class, it's one of the few luxuries I allow myself. I've met some kick-ass, good-looking sisters in first class, even though most of them were stuck up like my ex and other people I know. But every now and again I've met a sister who is good-looking, smart, and hasn't forgotten her people. Of course, when they're all that, they're usually married too. I ain't with that married-woman shit.

Anyway, while lard-ass was in the john, the flight attendant came over and asked whether I preferred the steak or the chicken breast. Now, even though I like me some chicken, I didn't want to feed in to that stereotype that all Black folks love chicken. I've been known to get down with some smoking Harold's painted with hot sauce, but that's in the company of my own people. Besides, when was the last or first time they had some kick-ass fried chicken on an airplane? So I ordered the steak.

When my seat mate returned, the flight attendant returned her computer and asked her if the chicken breast would be okay, since I had ordered the last of the steak. Well, you would have thought she had told the bitch that we were on a twelve-hour flight to China and they had forgotten to put food on the plane.

"What do you mean, that's all you have? I want the steak!" When the attendant repeated herself, the laptop lady got all loud the way only white folks can. "I paid full price to sit in first class," she yelled. Then she looked me dead in my face and said, "I should at least get the first choice at the dinner selections before all these people using upgrades." I had to sit on my hands to keep from hitting the bitch upside her fat face, but I don't hit women. My mama taught me right. I don't even like calling them bitches, but sometimes what's a man gonna do? I gave her my most understanding, sympathetic, I'm-so-sorry-God-made-you-ugly, apologetic nod. She thought I was getting ready to say that she could have my steak, but instead I smiled up at the attendant and said, "I'll have a merlot with my meal."

Chapter 4

Dwight and I arrived at Leland's at precisely the same moment. Actually I think Dwight had waited around the corner until he saw me walking down Ohio Street, so we'd just happen to get to Leland's apartment building at the same time. I don't think he feels comfortable being in Leland's apartment alone. I don't think he's really homophobic, but Leland's lifestyle, conservative though it is, threatens Dwight's manhood. He doesn't have a clue that he's not even close to Leland's type. But I'd never tell him so. We chitchatted in the elevator for thirty-two floors. Nothing serious, just playful small talk. Twice I caught Dwight sneaking a peek at my body, then quickly averting his eyes when he was busted. I didn't really mind: In fact, I was flattered. Those early morning workouts have gotten the old girl on a roll, sorta like in my early twenties.

"What are you smiling about so hard?" Dwight asked.

"You, Dwight Scott. I see you trying to check me out on the sly. Is that any way to look at your sister? I thought we were like family," I kidded.

"I was just checking out your new 'do, my sister. It looks good on you. Got that seventies thing going. You don't mind if a brother admires your natural, do you?"

"Don't mind at all, thank you very much." But we both knew his eyes had fallen far south of my hairdo.

When we reached Leland's apartment, he opened the door on the first ring.

"We've got exactly twenty-three minutes and forty-seven seconds to get to Riley's," he announced as Dwight and I stepped inside. Every time I entered Leland's apartment, I was struck by its orderliness. A place for everything and everything in its place, like my mother tried unsuccessfully to drum into my thick young skull. The apartment reflected Leland's fastidious personality to a T.

Leland grabbed his jacket and his keys and escorted us back out his front door. As he turned to lock the door, he added, "You know Miz Riley don't play no CP time!" We laughed in agreement and headed for the elevator and the midafternoon Chicago humidity. The sky was beginning to cloud and threatened a sudden downpour. Whenever the group was to meet at Riley's place, the three of us would hook up at Leland's and walk or cab it together. No one wanted to be the first to arrive alone at Chez Woodson, for fear of a poetry reading or concert. We linked arms, Dwight on my right and Leland on my left. Turning from Ohio onto McClurg Court toward Riley's condo, I got several envious looks from sisters and some brothers we passed on the streets. I didn't blame them; both Leland and Dwight were good-looking men.

Leland still had the same casual good looks he had some sixteen years earlier in college. He carried himself with an appealing air of confidence that most women and men found inviting. He had close-cropped, wavy dark brown hair and a well-trimmed mustache over full lips. His light brown skin was the color of butter pecan ice cream.

He was, as always, dressed impeccably, wearing not-too-tight white jeans, silk T-shirt, and navy linen jacket that draped casually over well-formed hips. His nails were freshly manicured, and I caught the faintest scent of cologne. Leland had piercing brown eyes and darker brown thick eyebrows that gave the impression he was deeply interested in each and every word that fell from your lips. It's the doctor in him, people feel safe, like they can tell him anything.

I guess the best word to describe Dwight is "intense." He is strikingly handsome, though I don't think he realizes it. His face and body appear to have been sculpted from a block of bittersweet chocolate. His brown bedroom eyes hide beneath long, thick lashes that I would personally die for. There is a sadness and tenderness in his clean-shaven face, especially when he doesn't know anyone is looking, that make him seem so vulnerable. There is the slightest hunch in his strong shoulders, a litheness to his movements that makes him always appear on the defense. The three of us were as different as our shoes, stepping along in unison, Leland in his reptile loafers with no socks, me in my basic black pumps, and Dwight in his sweat socks and gym shoes. But at that moment we were as close as cereal and milk, thankful for one another's company and friendship.

A little before three o'clock we stepped off the small elevator directly into the Woodsons' gray marble foyer. The color reminded me of John's eyes. That was mystery man's name, John. He had called me twice and left messages with Monica, who couldn't stop describing his silky, deep voice. All I could think of were those lips and those gray eyes. I didn't want to appear too eager, so I hadn't responded yet. On Friday night, Leland had agreed with my strategy of taking it slow.

Riley greeted each of us warmly with her angelic smile and a delicate hug. She looked great—as usual—in a peach silk pantsuit. And, as usual, I felt underdressed in a black mid-length skirt and black knit top. I always felt the need to wear a formal ball gown just to stand in the Woodson foyer. Dwight, on the other hand, didn't share my sentiments and wore a red and black Chicago Bulls warmup suit. We followed Riley into her den, where white wine was chilling in a silver bucket on the glass coffee table. The heavy scent of fresh flowers filled the room, and I started to ask Riley if Selwyn had given her the bouquet of gladiolas by the terrace.

"It's just going to be the four of us, gang. Selwyn is stuck in San Francisco. Ryan is still in New York and Reggie is at basketball camp at Ohio State." Riley answered my unspoken question.

"What's Ryan doing in New York?" Leland asked. I suddenly remembered that Riley had asked me to check in with her daughter while I was in New York. But after my Motown experience, I had completely forgotten to call her.

"Didn't Yolanda tell you? She's doing a summer internship with the New York City Ballet," Riley said proudly. I knew and fully expected Dwight to ask why not the Dance Theater of Harlem, but he surprised us all and just smiled politely. I guess he didn't want to get off on the wrong foot with our hostess, at least not yet.

"That's just wonderful," Leland said. "I know you must be so proud."

"Yes, I am. Very proud. I tell Selwyn all the time that we done good."

Riley's maid quietly entered, carrying a tray of prawns and cock-tail sauce arranged on a bed of watercress. The last time we met here, Riley had a white maid. This one looked Colombian. This is the fourth or fifth maid I've seen since the group started. I wanted to ask her why she can't keep good help, or find a Black maid, but I didn't. This was Riley's show, and I didn't want to put her on the defense. I was certain Dwight would do that soon enough.

The four of us were sitting, eating, sipping wine and catching up on each other's lives from the previous month, when Dwight broke loose.

"You know, I'm really pissed off at what they did to those broth-ers." We all exchanged a *what-else-is-new* look.

"What brothers are you talking about, Dwight?" Riley asked.

"You know, the brothers they just let out of jail after serving eighteen years for a murder they didn't commit."

"Yeah, I've been following that in the newspapers. It's been on all the newscasts," Leland said.

I didn't quite know what they were talking about, so I assumed it was something that happened while I was in New York.

"Dwight, you're watching the news? When did you go back to the mass media?" I asked.

"I don't watch just anybody. I look when the brothers and sisters are on. You know, like Hosea Sanders in the morning before I go to work, and those beautiful sisters, Cheryl Burton and Allison Payne. That's it," Dwight said. "And I dig that sister with the braids on CNN."

"I think her name is Farai Chideya," Leland said.

"Oh, so you don't mind when the brothers and sisters bring you the bad news," I teased.

"Naw, I still get mad at some of the stuff I hear. Like with these brothers," Dwight added.

"But they're out of jail now, Dwight. Aren't you happy about that?" Riley asked. "Thank God for those wonderful Northwestern students who got them out."

"Yeah, I'm glad the brothers are out, but all you see on the news are those 'wonderful' white students that got them out. Nothing 'bout the brothers. The media probably wouldn't have even covered the story if white folks weren't involved. Mark my word, if they make a movie about this, it will be told from the white folks' point of view," Dwight said. He was on a roll. A very familiar roll.

"Dwight, come on," Riley pleaded. "Why can't you just be happy that the system is working?"

"The system *ain't* working! Four Black men just spent eighteen years in prison for a crime they didn't commit," Dwight said firmly.

Then Riley said something I wished she hadn't.

"But didn't some other Black men actually kill that woman?" Dwight looked exasperated. He was just fixing his mouth to give Riley the what-for, when Riley put her own foot in her mouth.

"You know, Dwight, we all care. I mean, you're not the only person sitting here who was born Black!"

"Yeah, but I'm the only one who still is," he said as he grabbed the last shrimp from the tray and rolled his eyes toward Riley.

She pretended not to notice, a familiar pattern. Instead, she asked, "Who wants to read from their journal first?"

"I've got something that might change the tone," I said. Leland and Dwight both gave me looks that could kill. I'd forgotten our agreement on the walk over. We'd make sure Riley read first. Whenever she was the last to read from her journal, she felt compelled to wind up the evening with one of her poems.

"But I can wait, it's your party, Riley. You go first," I said. Leland and Dwight nodded their enthusiastic approval, and Riley gave us this month's version of the same old fantasy. Her kids were great, her marriage was fabulous. She was hopeful that her poems would soon be published. And, of course, her singing career was sure to jump off any minute now. The woman is in complete denial. I mean, her kids barely speak to her. I think they're pissed off that their mother and father didn't become mom and dad until after Selwyn finished Business and law school. Her parents really raised them. We haven't seen Selwyn in months, and as for her writing and singing—I don't *think* so! I love Riley. I really do, but I wish she'd pull her head out of the sand. None of us, including Dwight, had the nerve or the heart to tell her we knew better. We didn't want to hurt her. Riley smiled and closed her journal and turned to me and said, "Your time, Yolanda."

"I'm trying not to get excited, but I met this really wonderful guy while I was in New York. I know I said I was going to put my love life on hold, but this is one I might not want to pass up. He's so fine. Light-skinned with sort of winter-gray eyes." I paused and sipped my wine, but before I could resume, Dwight jumped in.

"Time-out! I got something I want to put in the *If This World Were Mine* journal."

The group had started a journal we had named *If This World Were Mine*. The notebook contained wishes and suggestions on what we would like to see happen in the world. Sometimes they were affirmations and sometimes personal wishes or pet peeves. I knew from the tone of Dwight's voice that he wasn't getting ready to add a positive platitude.

"What do you want to add, Dwight?" I asked a little impatiently.

"I want us to stop describing one another with terms like 'light-skinned' and 'dark-complected.'"

"I'm sorry, Dwight, I didn't mean to offend you. I was just describing the brother I met," I said defensively.

"I know. But you know what that does? It continues to separate us when we use terms like that," he said.

"I guess you have a point, Dwight," Leland said. "But isn't that one of the wonderful things about Black people? That we come in so many beautiful colors? I don't think Yogi meant anything by it."

"And I'm not jumping on her. We set up the journal so we could wish for things. I know it's not going to change. I know people will keep doing it. Let's just not do it here in the group," Dwight said.

I could tell from the look on his face that he was real serious, and he did have a point. Dwight and I were almost the same dark brown color. I loved my color, and I assume Dwight loved his too.

"I agree," Leland said.

"I don't see what the big deal is. Nobody means any harm," Riley said. "I mean, white folks do it. The only difference is they use things like eye color and hair color. I bet you don't hear them talking about how that separates their race," Riley said.

"Well, I think you're going to lose this one," Dwight said. "I think it's three to one."

"Whatever," Riley said, and rolled her eyes. "Go ahead, put it in the journal."

I picked up the journal from under the coffee table and wrote, "*If this world were mine, Black people wouldn't use skin color as a way to describe each other. What a wonderful world it would be!"* Under that I wrote Dwight's name and the date.

"If this ever happens in the real world . . . then it's going to make one of my patients very sad," Leland said with a sly smile on his face.

"What are you talking about?" Riley asked.

"Just this last week one of my clients said his modeling career was taking a major turn because light skin was coming back." Leland laughed. Riley and I grinned. Dwight didn't flinch. I guess he didn't think it was funny at all.

"See what I mean. It separates us," Dwight said sternly.

"Let's take a break," Riley said. We all agreed and headed for the lavish supper laid out in the formal dining room. Riley may not be the poet or the singer she thinks she is, but Lord, Lord, the woman knows how to entertain. The extravagant buffet was all that. We each heaped our gold-edged plates with shrimp, oysters, and smoked salmon. Leland and I praised Riley to the high heavens. It made her so happy to be appreciated. Dwight, of course, shared with us the latest statistics on world hunger.

That's when Riley ushered us all into the living room, which made the rest of us a little nervous. Anytime she got close to that white baby grand piano, we knew there was a good chance she would feel the need to share one of her latest songs. It wasn't that Riley had a bad voice, it's that she just didn't have the vocal chops to match her formal expressions and dramatic movements. She didn't know if she wanted to be Eartha Kitt or Jennifer Holiday. I'm sure she would have blended in with a large mass choir. Maybe.

While we finished eating, I finished reading my journal entry. Dwight was noticeably unresponsive, but Riley asked for all the details. Dwight shared his latest victory over the white man, and even he had to laugh at Leland's dashiki-wearing construction worker.

Later we were drinking coffee and admiring Riley's latest acquisition, a Paul Goodnight painting, when Riley decided to recite a poem about friendship. It was a sweet and simple poem. I sighed with relief. Could Riley's poetry actually be getting better? It was a rare occasion when we were treated to both a poem *and* a song. All three of us told Riley what a moving poem it was and demanded personal copies. The woman must be psychic, because she had laminated copies already prepared. This woman really needs to find something to do with all this time she has on her hands, I thought.

"Since this was the fifth anniversary for the group, I had something else special made that I'd like to start using at our meeting. I think it will help us to be closer, and to talk about things that we might not include in our journals," Riley said as she held out a silver-colored shopping bag.

"What are you talking about?" Leland asked.

"Yeah, whatsup, Riley?" Dwight asked.

"See, I had these cards made. They're really quite wonderful," Riley said proudly.

"Cards? Like playing cards?" I asked.

"Kinda." Riley reached in the bag and retrieved a single card. "You see, each of the cards has a question on the back. Some are serious, thought-provoking questions, and some are really simple. Each of us will pull out one card and answer the question on the back. The rest of the group can then ask the cardholder something about their answer. But we must, as friends, promise to tell the truth even if it's hurtful."

"Are we sure we want to do this?" Dwight asked.

"I don't see any harm in it. Let's give it a try," Leland said.

"I'm game," I said.

"Great," Riley said, and passed around the cards for us to see. Riley was truly amazing. On the back of each was a picture. Some were photographs of us individually and some were group shots from previous meetings and other events we had attended together. There was a picture of Leland in his band uniform at a homecoming game, and one of Riley and me when we were pledging Delta Sigma

Theta. Riley even had pictures of us when we were at Hampton and some from our ten-year reunion.

"Riley, these are wonderful. Where did you get these made?" I asked.

"At a printing shop in Evanston. Do you like them?"

"They're great," I said. Dwight and Leland laughed and gave each other a high-five.

"What are you laughing at?" Riley asked.

"Look at Yogi with these Afro puffs." Dwight laughed. "She looks like Thelma on *Good Times*."

"Let me see," I said as I grabbed the cards from his hands. There I was, some twenty years ago, with Afro puffs and big loop earrings. I guess I was in my Angela Davis phase.

"I look a mess," I said.

"No, you don't," Riley offered. "That was the style back then. And, as I recall, nobody kept up with the styles more than you, Yolanda."

"This is too cool," Leland said. "Where did you get all these pictures from?"

"From mine and Selwyn's collection. Here, look at Dwight in his glasses," Riley said.

"Man, I look like Mr. Dufus," he said.

"I think you look smart," I said.

"I was. I mean, I am," Dwight countered. "But I was sure glad when I could afford contacts."

"How do we play the game?" Leland asked.

"It's really not a game. Just a way to, you know, think about things. We'll take turns pulling a card out of the bag and then giving it to the host or hostess, which today would be me. I will read the question and then the person answers. And then we each get to ask a question. If something really important or funny comes up, maybe we can write it in the journal. Now, who wants to be brave and go first?"

"I will," Dwight volunteered.

"Wonderful," Riley said as she gathered the cards and placed them back in the bag. We had been so busy looking at the pictures that no one had looked at the questions. With Dwight going first, I didn't know what we were in for. The wrong question and this game could be over before it even began. Dwight twirled his hand around in the bag for a few seconds, then pulled out a card and handed it to Riley.

"Are you ready for the question, Mr. Scott?" Riley asked like she was the emcee at a beauty contest.

"I'm ready," Dwight said.

"What is your favorite album of all time?" Riley read from the card.

"Oh, that's easy, Marvin Gaye's *What's Going On*. Both the man and the album were brilliant."

I breathed a sigh of relief that this wasn't going to be that bad.

"Who has a question for Dwight?" Riley asked.

"Do we have to ask a question about his answer or can we ask a question related to the general area of the question?" Leland asked.

"We can kinda make the rules up as we go along," Riley said as she made a silly face and bunched up her shoulders. "What do you guys think?"

"Since this is the first time, why don't we try both ways," I suggested.

"That's cool," Dwight replied.

"Okay, then I have a question," Leland said.

"Shoot," Dwight said.

"How does Marvin's violent death at the hands of his father reflect on the Black family?"

"Ooh, that's deep," I said.

Dwight frowned at Leland and said, "I don't think it says anything about the Black family as a whole. All it says to me is that Marvin's father was a crazy son of a bitch. End of story," Dwight said.

"Sho' you right," Leland said.

I raised my hand. "I've got a question. Are there any artists today that you think come close to Marvin's genius?"

"Naw, naw, there will never be another Marvin, but this new guy Maxwell is smooth and so is this guy Kenny Lattimore. But even they can't match Marvin's skills."

"Are there any white artists as great as Marvin Gaye?" Riley asked. I could suddenly hear that old saying ringing in my ear: Katie bar the door. All hell was getting ready to break loose.

"What kinda dumb-assed question is that? Hell, the fuck no!" Dwight shouted. Riley looked wounded. To break the sudden chill, Leland pulled a card from the bag and handed it to Riley. "Here, ask me a question, sweetheart." He cut his eyes at Dwight. Riley looked relieved as she took the card from Leland and smiled.

"Who is the person you had your greatest sexual experience with?"

"That's easy. Besides Donald, since I'm making a rule that life partners don't count, I would say from my senior year at Hampton. Eric Hughes, that fine, coffee-colored, oh, I'm sorry, my bad. The great-looking and fine-body boy from Charleston, South Carolina, who ran track. He was the shit." Leland smiled. I was giving him a low-five because I had already heard that story, but Riley's mouth fell open and Dwight had a look of disgust on his face.

"Not Eric Hughes," Riley said in an exasperated tone.

"Yes, Eric Hughes," Leland said.

"Oh, that can't be," Riley said.

"Why not?" Leland countered.

"I thought he was straight. I mean, you guys remember when Selwyn and I agreed to see other people while he did that year of study in London?" Riley asked.

"Yeah, yeah, what about it?" I asked.

"I dated Eric for a little while," Riley said shyly.

"Then you know what I'm talking about," Leland said confidently.

"But I thought he was straight," Riley said.

"And he might be. But for a couple of nights. First question," Leland said.

Riley's mouth was hanging open, and Dwight was making eye contact with the nearest wall, so I asked a question.

"Leland, what do you remember most about Eric?"

"That we didn't have to use a condom. Man, those were the good old days. Next question."

"I think I'll pass," Dwight said soberly.

"Can he do that?" I asked. Riley didn't answer.

"Whatever clever," Leland said. "Riley, do you have a question?"

"Eric Hughes," she muttered as she shook her head. We didn't know if she was still in shock or if her head motion meant she didn't have a question. I wanted to tease her about always advertising that Selwyn was the only man she had been with. Instead, I reached in and grabbed a card and handed it to her. Riley came out of her trance and asked, "What's your greatest fear about the future?"

"I guess that's kinda easy. I'm scared that my biological clock is going to sound the alarm before I have children. And even if I have a child, say within the next couple of years, will I be too old to enjoy him . . . or her," I said.

"Do you have any prospects?" Riley asked.

"I've got several men who'd like to make deposits, but I want to at least be *in like* with the father. And I haven't ruled out adoption."

"What about this new guy? The one you met in New York?" Leland asked.

"Who knows, I'd like to think he's a candidate. He's so fine."

"And let's not forget he fits the most important criterion," Dwight offered.

"What's that?" I asked. I felt like I was falling into a mine shaft.

"Mr. New York is light-skinned, or is the term light-complected?" he said with a nasty grin.

"Why are you even going there? What did you say not an hour ago?" I demanded.

"Yeah, Dwight, that was cold," Leland said.

"I know, I'm sorry. My bad. But I do have a serious question."

"What's that?"

"Do you look at men in terms of their color, I mean, like how they look when you think of a father of your child? Tell the truth now."

"Absolutely not," I said confidently. But did I mean it? I wasn't going to give Dwight the satisfaction of watching me hesitate for one second.

The game and evening ended with Riley getting a question about her dreams. Of course she said something predictable about wanting to have a successful writing and music career, but she ended her answer with a far-off look in her eyes and muttered something about having more love in her life. None of us questioned her about that.

Chapter 5

"**This is** John Basil Henderson. Do I have any messages?"

"Let me check, sir," the female voice said. A few seconds later she came back and said, "Yes, sir. You have one. A Keith Meadows called. The message is please call him if you still want the tickets to the game for your father."

"That's all?" I asked.

"Yes, sir."

I muttered "damn" to myself as I hung up the phone and clicked on my music system. Keith is not the message I was looking for. I needed to chill.

One of the things that really bothers me about women is they can't make up their minds about what they want. They are the most indecisive creatures on God's green earth. I hear women all the time say how they can't find a good brother, when most times they wouldn't recognize a correct brother if he walked right up and kissed them on the lips. This woman I met a few days ago at the Motown Cafe really seemed spellbound by me. Especially after my old kiss and then it's-so-great-to-see-you routine. I noticed her eating alone in the restaurant and I thought, maybe a good-looking woman can bring me out of this funk. It couldn't hurt.

She gave me her card and I've called her twice. It's Tuesday, and I still haven't heard from her! I can't remember the last time I called a woman more than twice without a return call. Yolanda, that's her name, told me she was up in New York all the time, so I'm trying to reach her to see when she comes back this way. I need to see if she's somebody that's worth my time. Somebody who will come in handy when I'm feeling like a hot fudge sundae.

Sister is a beautiful smooth color with nice, full kissable lips, and from what I can tell when I held her, she's probably got an awesome body. Nice and lean.

When I was playing ball and showing up on the sports shows almost every week, all I had to do was put it out there that I was interested in someone, and the call would happen, like bam. My recent career change better not mean I'm going to have to chase some of these ladies like a regular brother. You know, I can't even comprehend that shit.

I remember once, I saw this actress on a television soap. She was sexy and I thought she would be great under the sheets. I called my agent, told him the show she played on, and the name of her character. Eight hours later he called back with digits. I didn't even have to know her real name. I called her once and six months later Dyanna had my town house as her East Coast address. I usually didn't even have to go through that much trouble. Sometimes I'd just get in contact with a lady because one of the guys on the team would be talking about her while looking in a magazine or a movie on the team charter plane. Had to let them know who was the man. I'd go out with a lady a couple times and when I got the draws I'd dash. Usually when I do my hit-and-run routine it's, you know, just physical. To capture my attention for more than a moment, a woman has to satisfy me on every level, which means emotional, mental, and, of course, sexual. I'm like most men in that visual is the first thing that grabs me, and then I see if she has the other things I need to keep me from straying. Like the class of a lady like Lena Horne and the sexual appetite of a female porn star.

Most of the times the women contact me, so I guess it's visual for them also. They usually go through my agent or the team offices, by sending me, you know, pictures of themselves in lacy underwear, their numbers, and a list of things they wanted to do with me. Sometimes I give the pictures, panties, and numbers to some of my physically in-the-face challenged teammates. We had a lot of mofos like that on the team. One of them ended up marrying some girl who had sent her nude pictures to me. Ain't that some shit? I tried to warn old boy, but I guess he got whipped and that was that.

I met my ex when she was dating one of my teammates. Every time I saw her she was giving me the look. I went for it. Next thing I know I'm married. But I should have known it wasn't going to work. At the time I thought I wanted to be married and start a family. First thing she tells me, she doesn't particularly like athletes. You see what I'm talking 'bout with women and knowing what they want? Said most jocks were dumb and interested only in sex. That was cool with me 'cause I know I'm not a dumb mofo. I hate to admit it, but I need a woman in my life! But our marriage was difficult because we went into it too fast, and she wasn't athletic and wasn't hip to the life of a professional athlete. Since sports was my life at the time, I found myself spending time explaining everything about what I did and why I had to do some things that seem unrelated to sports. You know like playing golf and shit with people who I really didn't give a shit about. She was into the celebrity thang and getting fucked up and then trying to jump my bones all the time. A star fucker. In the end it was she who was dumb and interested in sex all the time. You know, sometimes I thought she was trying to run a game on me.

I guess I'm not going to worry about Miss Yolanda. I'm not looking for a main woman in my life. I have three decent women I keep on hold. Usually a sister, a white chick, and maybe a Latina or Asian woman. Variety is the sex of life.

If Yolanda got good sense, she'll come around. I got a lot on my plate. I've got to visit my dad. Might not see him as much since we don't have football games as a regular meeting place. And I've got to find me a new place to live besides my Lower East Side sublet. That is, if I decide to hang around New York. Maybe I'll buy me a place on the Upper West Side or Lincoln Center area. I've got to decide if I'm going to pursue this book deal. Get ready for my audition with ESPN. But that reminds me of something else I liked about Yolanda. This chick at her office told me she works musicians and such, helping them with everything from interviews to their diction. I know how to walk the walk and talk the talk when I need to, but a little private session with a media professional couldn't hurt. I get this vibe that she's smart. I like that in a woman.

I know if I leave Yolanda alone, put it out there in the universe that I'd like a little sample of that chocolate pudding, then it will be. Or else I'll just switch back to a tasty vanilla sundae. Believe that.

●　　●　　●

I weighed the pros and cons of calling Mr. John Henderson. It was a stall tactic—I knew I was going to call, but I at least wanted to go through the motions of letting my mind, not my body, make the decision.

He was a great kisser, one of the main qualifications I look for in a man. I like them to kiss me softly and gently. I'm a firm believer in the *If-the-kiss-ain't-right-keep-the-legs-tight* school of love. But I've learned not to start a relationship based on sexual attraction.

Take, for instance, my ex, Chauncey. The sex was fierce, but in the long run we were both looking for different things outside the bedroom.

He sure could kiss though. Years after our divorce he would still drop in when he was in town for a tune-up.

I thought about Dwight's comments at the last group meeting. Was I color struck? Did I believe in marrying light so I'd produce a light-skinned child? I don't think so. I mean, my mother and father used to say all the time what a stunningly brown-skinned baby I was. But just to be on the safe side, I asked Leland. He told me to chill, and reminded me that the majority of the guys I dated—including the one I married—were, at the very least, cocoa-colored.

I'm not going to lie. I love the company of fine, sweet-talking men no matter what color they are. I like men. And intellect is definitely a turn-on. I also need honesty, and a sensitive man makes me weak. They don't need to cry, but at least have eyes that look like they might sprout tears at any moment.

It's Thursday and John's card has been propped up on my desk for days. I picked it up and dialed. It would be noon in New York, and frankly, I was hoping for an answering machine. First, it would take me out of the awkward position of being the one to call. Second, it would tell me something about John. Any man home in the middle of the day was most likely unemployed. Call me whatever, but a man with a job was an essential qualification in my book. It's like buying a car. Do you want the standard package or do you want some options, like cruise control?

The phone rang once. Twice. I was already composing a noncommittal message for his machine. Something vague yet promising.

"Speak to me," a deep, sexy male voice answered.

"Yes, I mean, hello. Is John Henderson in?" I winced at my total lack of cool.

"Speaking." His voice gave me the shivers.

"John, this is Yolanda. Yolanda Williams? From the Motown Cafe? We met last week?"

"Of course. Miss Sweet Lips," he said.

Boy, did he sound good. My smile must have been a mile wide. Good thing we were on the telephone. I was surprised at how quickly I relaxed with this man. He was so smooth, I could feel myself sliding right along with him, and he'd spoken only five words to me.

"I guess I could say the same thing to you," I replied, pressing the phone closer to my ear.

"Yeah, you know, I guess you could," he said confidently. "So, Yolanda, when are we going to get together?" He wasn't wasting any time.

"When are you planning to come to Chicago, John? You know it's beautiful here in the summertime."

"Yeah, sure, you're right. I've been to Chicago a few times," he said.

"Really? On business?"

"You could call it business," he said slyly.

"What type of business? Or am I dipping?" I was praying, please, Lord, don't let this man be a drug dealer or professional gangster.

"Don't you know what I do for a living?" he asked.

"No," I said. "Why, are you somebody famous?"

"Most people know me as Basil Henderson. Does that ring any bells?" I was thinking what kind of name was Basil and where did the John come in.

"I'm sorry, but no. No bells."

"Guess you're not much into sports, huh?"

"Well, I like to work out, and I've been watching the Olympics. I've been to a football and basketball game before. What are you, some sort of sports star."

"You could say that. I've been playing for the New Jersey War-riors for over nine years. You know, the NFL? The Chicago Bears? The Cougars? You've got two NFL teams right there in Chicago."

"I know the Chicago Bulls, but I don't really follow them until the championships. So, you're a famous football player, that's good. I thought when you answered the phone in the middle of a weekday, you *must be* unemployed." I couldn't believe I was being so honest with this man.

"As a matter of fact, I've just retired from football. I'm sorta in transition. I'm looking at sports broadcasting. That's why I might be interested in your professional services, you know, and whatever else you might have to offer."

I acted as though I didn't hear the last part. And how did he know what I did? He must have done some homework. "So, John, whatsup with this name thing? You told me your name was John. Where does Basil come from? Is that just part of your game, like acting like we knew each other?" I said.

"My full name is John Basil Henderson. Most people call me Basil, but you can call me what you like. And—we *do* know each other," he said playfully.

"Whatever. I think I like John. It sounds powerful, spiritual."

"Fine. Just so you call me something," he laughed. "Besides, since I'm starting a new phase in my life, I've started to introduce myself as John more often. So, Miss Lady, when am I going to see you again? Do I need to make an appointment? Let me show you New York."

"I've already seen New York. The good, the bad, and the ugly. But I will be in the city this weekend or early next week. Maybe we can get together for a drink."

"Sounds like a plan. Where will you be staying?"

"Hold on. First I've got a couple of questions for you—if you don't mind?" Who was interviewing who? I wondered.

"I'm listening. Shoot."

"Are you married?"

"No, I'm divorced," he said firmly.

"How long were you married, and how long have you been divorced?"

"I was married a couple of years, and I've been divorced for almost a year. Now, that's three questions. You said you had a couple, and where I come from, a couple means two."

"Just a few more, pretty please?"

"All right."

"Are you involved with anyone, living with someone, seeing anybody? And have you ever been in a relationship with a man?" I guess this was one football star who knew how to handle a reporter.

"No, no, definitely not and I don't roll like that. I've got a few questions for you too. But I'll wait till I see you face-to-face. Will you call when you get to New York and we can set something up?"

"I'll do that."

"Yolanda?"

"Yes, John?"

"Thanks for calling me back."

"Good-bye, John. Have a blessed day."

•   •   •

I knew she'd call. They always do. Believe that. In fact, I'd be willing to bet money that Yolanda Williams will be in my bed before midnight the first night she's back in New York.

My boys are always quizzing me on how I get women to drop the draws so quick. Besides the obvious that they don't look like me, most men just don't know how to get a woman. Some of my teammates complain about how their women won't suck dick. Especially Black women. All women will suck dick. It's all in the approach. You can't just say "suck my dick." You've got to invest in a little gentle foreplay. Start with a soft kiss. Kiss the neck, ease down to the breasts, the nipples. Then get them to follow suit. Sometimes you have to direct them ever so gently. Tell them your navel is sensitive and how much you'd like to feel their tongue inside it. Once a woman has her face that close to your manhood, the lips will naturally find the dick.

Of course, it's not always that easy. I remember this one gal I went out with for almost a month. No matter what I did, I couldn't get her lips nowhere near the dick. She loved me inside her, but she wouldn't even touch my stuff. One morning, I woke up and my stuff was harder than a roll of quarters. Make that two rolls of quarters. I straddled her and slowly lowered myself until it was laying on her face. When she woke up to the weight of my manhood so close to her lips, well, hey! It was over. I finally had to pull her off the johnson. She acted like that was her first time. I did have to tell her to watch her teeth. But I said it gently. I know one thing, it sure wasn't her last, and ole girl got pretty good at it.

Yolanda might be different. I get this funny feeling about her. Sounds like she figured out she didn't know me when I walked up and kissed her. But she called me anyway. Maybe she's trying to play me. She made it perfectly clear that she didn't know who I was or what I did. But that's okay because that's not who I am anymore. Still, I've got to be on my guard. If a player ain't careful, he can be played. Not that that ever happened to me.

I can tell from our conversation, I'm probably gonna have to do the theater/dinner thing before I make the first move. I'll charm her with my quick wit, my intellect, and dress in my good shit, from my silk tailor-made slacks to my form-fitting boxers that leave nuthin', and I mean nuthin', to the imagination. But if that's what it takes to dip my stick in this fine-ass female, then a player's gotta do what a player's gotta do.

If my basic night-on-the-town doesn't work, I'll go straight to Plan B—the super deluxe way to win a woman. This plan calls for all the above, plus a gift of some kind. Sometimes a first-class flight to a secret location is required. Of course, one hotel room only. Women are so impressed with Plan B, they start singing that old Marvin Gaye song, "Got to Give It Up." Believe that!

Chapter 6

My work week began with something that rarely happens in my life: a disagreement with my Uncle Doc. He called me early this morning to see if I had made plans for our annual family reunion in New Orleans. When I informed him I wasn't attending, he asked why.

"You know I'm still not talking to my mama," I said.

"Now, love," he said gently. "You got to get over yourself. The good Lord didn't give you but one mama and you have to allow her to be. A mama is the only one who would leave heaven to come and see about one of her children."

"She's the one that's not talking to me," I said.

"It don't matter. You need to make her talk to you."

I ended the conversation abruptly by telling Uncle Doc that I had more important things to do than worrying with some old woman who wasn't ever going to change and admit that she was wrong. He said, "She don't have to. She's a mama."

I love my mother, and for most of my life we've enjoyed a warm and loving relationship. And although I know she would have been happier if I were born heterosexual like my older brother, Dennis, she never seemed to have a major problem with my sexual orienta-tion. I mean, Uncle Doc paved the road of acceptance in our family by never lying about who he was. He remains one of the most popular family members at funerals and reunions.

The dilemma with my mother started about two years ago, when she called me on a day when I was really feeling depressed. It was the fifth anniversary of my partner Donald's death. When I told my mother why I was so down, she acted as though I hadn't said a word. When I said I didn't know if I would ever find another husband like Donald, she started telling me Donald wasn't my husband. And that by referring to him as my husband I was disrespecting her marriage to my father and all other couples, including my brother, Dennis, and his wife. Her voice kept getting louder and higher, as if she were trying not to explode. When I asked her what I should call him, she said, "Your friend, your bed buddy. I don't know, but he was *not* your husband." This was the last conversation I had with my mother. That was two years and two reunions ago.

I sometimes think back on that last dialogue with my mother and wonder if I'm being fair. *Husband* is not a term I used to describe my relationship with Donald. The years we were a team I referred to him as my partner or lover. I think maybe I used the term "hus-band" in this particular instance because my depression had caused me to feel lonely and weak, and I felt I needed the strength Donald provided me, the strength I had observed between my mother and father on countless occasions. My mother's reaction made me feel like my relationship wasn't a real one. She was not showing me the respect I had always given her. I had often told family members who questioned my sexuality that they were not required to accept my homosexuality, but they must respect me as I respected them. It was something I wouldn't give up, even for my mother.

•   •   •

When Riley turned on her computer Monday afternoon and logged on to America Online, the mechanical voice announced, "You've got mail."

For Riley this usually meant a message from her mother or father or some subscription service, but today her message made her smile.

Dear Dreamseekr: Read your poetry on the Poet Power Bulletin. You are obviously very talented and a woman with a sweet and tender heart. Does the man in your life know how lucky he is? If you're interested in sharing some poetry on a private basis, e-mail me back. Thanks for the wonderful poetry you shared and for making a lonely man smile. Keep writing, from a lucky admirer. Lonelyboy.

Riley let out a delighted "Yes!" She read the message again and hit the reply button on her computer screen and typed:

Dear Lonelyboy: Thank you for the wonderful message and words of encouragement. You've made my day, my week, my year! Sure, I would love to exchange some poems with a man who appreciates the joy good poetry can bring. E-mail me some of your work. I look forward to reading it. And you keep writing and reading. Yours in the words, Dreamseekr.

When she clicked the send box with her message, Riley felt a surge of adventure and her mind was full of questions. She daydreamed her own answers. Maybe this man could love her like he did her poetry. They could spend their days and nights writing poetry together and reading them over wine or coffee at a sidewalk cafe. Perhaps this stranger could bring some much-needed excitement in her life. Maybe he would listen to her the way Selwyn used to. She hadn't thought of getting a response when she posted her poem of lost love some weeks before. Riley located the poem in the loose-leaf notebook she used for her poetry and read the poem out loud, breaking the silence in her office.

"With love, I am reborn
 I sing with the birds
 Float on the clouds
 Feel as soft as a baby
 Nothing is as radiant as I
 When I am in love."

She paused and took a sip of her cold coffee and then continued.

"But, when you take it away
 I cannot sing
 Too heavy to float
 All feeling is gone
 When you take love away
 I cease to exist."

Riley placed the poem next to her computer and smiled to herself. She had discovered the poetry workshop section one day while surfing on the computer Selwyn bought her three Christmases before. He had hoped she would use it to start a business of her own. Riley mainly used the computer for word processing when she transferred her poetry, songs, and selected journal entries to the computer. She also used it for her household budgets and for keeping up with her schedule of charity commitments and events. It was her son, Reggie, who had introduced her to America Online, and she found it kept her company on the many nights when Selwyn was working late at the office, out of town, or just too tired to care.

•   •   •

Monday's tension had left Dwight after a strenuous two-hour workout. He was walking briskly and minding his own business, when he heard a high-pitched voice.

"Please don't hit me! I promise not to talk to him anymore," a frightened female voice screamed. Dwight looked toward an alley-way as he walked from the Bally's spa located near his apartment. He saw a tall and lean man pounding his fists on the shoulders and face of a young lady who was trying to use her gym bag to shield his fist while she screamed for help.

"Man, what the fuck are you doing?" Dwight shouted as he ran toward the couple.

"Mind your own fucking business," the man said as he stopped hitting the young lady and looked toward Dwight with a cruel grin.

"You want to hit somebody? Then bring your ass on over here," Dwight said as he lifted his fists in a defensive posture. He was standing a few feet from the man, who was still holding on to the frightened lady.

"You want some of this?" the man yelled as he released her and pounded his chest with a balled fist.

"Sir, please leave us alone. He doesn't mean any harm," she cried.

"Shut the fuck up, Chanel," the man said.

Dwight couldn't believe his ears. Did she say he didn't mean any harm? As he stared at the young lady whose face was badly swollen, he felt something crash against his left eye, like someone had hit him with a sock filled with marbles. "Mind your own business, mutherfucker," he heard the man say.

"Maurice . . . stop it. Stop it," the lady screamed. For a moment Dwight was stunned, but he quickly regained his composure and started pumping his attacker's face with his fists. The man seemed amazed, like he hadn't been hit before. He started to back away from Dwight's punches and tripped over himself. There he was, laid out on his back as Dwight plopped down on top of him. He grabbed the bully by the collar of his sweatshirt and pulled him close to himself with his fist pulled back. "You want some mo' of this?" Dwight said.

"Naw, man, naw, I quit," he said, sounding like a little boy who had suddenly grown tired of a childhood prank. By then a crowd was beginning to form at the entrance of the alleyway, and several on-lookers started clapping as Dwight got up and dusted himself off.

"Do you want me to call the police?" an elderly lady asked Dwight.

"I think you should ask her," Dwight said as he pointed toward the victim.

"Naw, I don't need no police," she said. Dwight looked at her and shook his head and turned north toward his apartment. He had walked past the record store where he bought his music and rented videos, when he heard a female voice call out, "Hey, Mister . . . you . . . in the black warmups."

Dwight turned, and the young lady walked up to him and placed a piece of paper in his hands. "Thank you. Why don't you call me so I can show you how much I 'preciate what you did for me," she said as her smile broadened, and she winked at him.

Dwight didn't respond, he simply slipped the piece of paper in his warmups and headed home. For a Monday, it had been longer than even he could stand.

•   •   •

Tuesday is a slow day for me, only three patients. It's one of the only days when I have time to deal with my own problems. After a carry-out dinner from Miss Thing's, I decided to write in my journal.

I'm having second thoughts about this family reunion. I guess I can thank Uncle Doc for that. I do miss my family, and I can almost taste my mother's gumbo. But I'm worried that Mama wouldn't welcome me with open arms. Too bad we both share a streak of being stubborn. Daddy always said I was just like her.

For the last two years, the group and Uncle Doc have been my family. Maybe this new guy is gonna take a lot of Yolanda's time and attention. I don't recall her being that excited about a man in a long time. Dwight and

I have never really been that close, and long talks with Riley would surely include a poem or a song about the way I'm feeling. I can hear it now, some type of tribute to the power of family.

I know it's strange, but when my patients talk to me about family problems, I always seem to have the answers. Rarely do I tell them what to do; most times I get the patient to realize how they ought to approach a situation. Most times it's a solution all parties can live with, so that no one has given up everything. Now I've got to take my own medicine to find a solution for my family drama.

If I don't go to the reunion, I can avoid the questions of why I'm not married. All my relatives ask me this even though they know I've been gay since kitty was a cat. But they will ask anyway. And this includes my male cousin (now married with children) who loved to bump and grind with me when we were all little boys. Tarki, the best-looking of my cousins, used to put towels and pillowcases on his head and play like he had long hair. Today he's bald with three girls, all with long hair, weaves no less, but long hair.

Maybe I'll go on the last day, fly in during the morning, plead medical emergency, and fly out that evening. I don't know why I'm letting this get to me. I guess it's kinda like when I pretend my life hasn't changed since the eighties, when life for me was really one big party. But the party is over now simply because there isn't anyone left to attend.

Yolanda, Riley, and Dwight talk about missing the seventies and Hampton, and I do too. But for me, the mid-eighties is the time I miss most. The life and the kids were at full tilt. On weekends when I didn't have to study I would hop a train to New York City and party the entire weekend. I would get a room at the Howard Johnson's on Eighth Avenue just to change clothes. I'd meet friends at the Nickel Bar on 72nd, between Broadway and Columbus, and party until the wee hours. Saturdays would mean Better Days and Ninety-six West. Sunday morning brunch in the Village. How I miss those times and those people. I can still hear Chaka, Melba, and, of course, Miss Ross ringing in my ear.

Just as I was about to relive one of my one-night stands in my journal, the phone rang.

"Hello," I said.

"Whatsup, my boyfriend?" Yolanda asked. She sounded quite happy.

"What's the word? Where are you? Didn't you have a date?" I asked.

"Which question do you want answered first?" Yolanda asked.

"Where are you?"

"In my hotel."

"Didn't you have a date with Mr. Wonderful?"

"Yes, and it was." Yolanda sighed.

"Tell me about it and where is he?"

"On his way home, I suppose. It was all that and a bag of chips. He picked me up in a car. A regular limo, nothing really flashy, but a car nonetheless. We went to B. Smith's for drinks, and then we went to see *Bring in da Noise, Bring in da Funk*, which, by the way, Leland, is just all that. Absolutely awesome, we have to come back here and see it together. We need to see *Smokey Joe's Cafe* too," Yolanda said.

"Yeah, yeah. Tell me about the man. Did he kiss you again?" I was thinking how I want to see the musical, but wondering if Yolanda's new toyboy would want to tag along and who would be the third wheel. Me or him?

"Yes, and it was all that. Damn, that boy knows he can kiss. But that's as far as I let him go. Homeboy, I know, had other plans, but I'm taking this smooth talker slow," Yolanda said. I couldn't remember her gushing over a man like this in a long, long time.

"What did you do after the play?"

"We went to dinner at some seafood restaurant near the Four Seasons Hotel. Plush deluxe, baby. You know, John is not only charming and fine, but he's very smart. I mean, he didn't mention sports once during the night. We talked about everything but that. I think he thinks he's a player, but there is something very sensitive and special about him," Yolanda said.

"Does he have any brothers?" I was thinking if he had a lot of brothers there was bound to be a gay one in the bunch. I wanted to gush a little bit myself.

"I don't know, we haven't gotten to his family yet. I mean, not all of them. I know his mother is dead, and he's real close to his father and his aunt."

"Speaking of family. I was just jotting down in my journal some stuff about my family reunion," I said.

"You still haven't decided what you're going to do?"

"Naw. Uncle Doc is giving me the blues about not going. Giving me the you-ain't-got-but-one-mama speech."

"You know he's right. You want me to go with you? I could go for some of your mama's gumbo. When is it?" Yolanda asked.

"It's in August. Now, you going with me . . . that's a plan. That way I won't have to talk to members of my family," I joked.

"Now, come on, Leland. Be nice."

"I am."

"I'm getting ready to crash. I've got a meeting over at Arista Records tomorrow with my good girlfriend, Lajoyce. My girl has some possible acts she wants me to work with. I can't forget the real reason I came to New York, I gotta work some! I just wanted you to know that your sisterfriend is alive and doing quite well, thank you very much, in New York City. And I love you . . . that's all," Yolanda said.

"I love you too . . . that's all. Am I going to have to wait until Friday for the rest of the details, or is this something you're going to share with the group?"

"Both. Good night, sweetie."

"Good night, Yogi. Sleep tight."

After I hung up the phone I went back to my journal, but before I resumed writing, I went to my kitchen and poured myself a glass of orange juice and located my Diana Ross *The Boss* CD. I needed Miss Ross and the music to take me back to New York and the eighties like only Diana could.

 I love me some Yolanda, so I'm really happy with recent developments with her love life. It sounds like she's found a winner in this John guy. But what will I do if my girl gets hooked? I don't think I'm ready for the dating scene again. When I think about Yogi dating someone serious, I realize how much I depend on her and how I've removed myself from the children. I know one of the main reasons is the fear of losing someone else. Either a friend or a new lover. But we can lose people all kinds of ways. Lose them even when they're physically still in our lives. I'm wondering if Yogi and I would be so tight if I hadn't lost so many friends to AIDS, crack, and crazy trade. Would she have liked me (heaven forbid, loved me) in the eighties? AIDS changed everything. Could I put up with Dwight's macho routine and Riley's want-to-be-white bull if I hadn't lost Donald?

While listening to Yolanda talk about John, a vivid memory came to life. I was trying hard to keep it out, because I wanted to focus my attention on Yolanda's joy. But there it was despite my protests. A vision of Donald the first time I saw him, at the Nickel Bar on a Wednesday afternoon. A tall, trim, broad-shouldered man who looked at me and smiled and asked, "What do we have here?" I thought of how we talked at the 72nd Street subway stop for three hours. How many trains passed us by before we finally parted. How our first official date lasted forty-eight hours. I miss that. I miss stopping at Sylvia's on the way to his apartment some evenings and picking up orders of smothered chicken and fried chicken, and then sitting on the floor of his apartment, feeding each other. Drinking some wine and maybe smoking a joint. And then making mad, crazy love. Oh, how I miss Donald.

Listening to Miss Ross has me thinking of putting my dancing shoes on, throwing caution to the wind, and giving that dating wheel a spin. But the thought of being dizzy again scares me.

• • •

I'm tripping right now! I just got home from my date with Yolanda, and I didn't get the draws, but I'm not upset! I mean, I had a *mad* time with this lady. She looked good and smelled even better. And when it comes to kissing, you know old girl can hold her own without showing her trump card. Her kisses are sweet, sensual, and very gentle. Exactly how I imagine she'll be inside.

When we were alone, we just talked and she seemed to enjoy talking with me and vice versa. We didn't talk about sports or sex. Instead, Yolanda had me thinking about what I was going to do the rest of my life. When I talked, I looked into her thoughtful brown eyes, and saw somebody who, even though she doesn't know me, seemed interested in what I had to say. She asked questions I had never been asked, like without a woman in my life as a child, how was I able to appreciate women? I guess she meant for things other than sex. I told her about my aunt Lois, and that seemed to satisfy her, but I had never thought about whether or not I appreciated women. I can be a big dog. It's like she was giving me the benefit. Most women naturally assume men are dogs, and you know most men don't let them down. Yolanda acts as though she expects only the best from men. She's so in control, so confident. She carries herself like *I'm worth nothing but the best and if you want to even get within sniffing distance of this good loving, then you've got to come correct.* I haven't even come close to feeling this way on a date since the first time I went out with Chase. I never felt that with my ex-wife.

Yeah, I made my standard attempt by inviting her back to my place, and when she said no, I offered to keep her company. I snapped out of my trying-to-be-a-gentleman stance long enough to do my player move, but then I got over myself and began telling this woman everything there was to know about me. Shit, dreams and stuff I hadn't even admitted to myself. I told her about this dream I had of buying a big ranch and having about five kids. I want a lot of children because I was an only child. I told Yolanda I wanted my father and maybe his lady friend to come and live with me and help me raise my family. I had forgotten all about that dream. When I was in the position to buy such a place, I hadn't met a woman I wanted to bear my children. Maybe that's changing.

Usually I wait for a woman to show her weakness and then I go for the kill, just like in sports, when you figure out your opponent's weakness and go for it. For me, success in the game of seduction is to get them naked. I love the different variations of the body. Make that most bodies. I have been known to get a lady naked, then tell the skeezer to get dressed and get to stepping if I don't like what I see.

But what's really tripping me out about tonight is the ride home. On the way back to my apartment I made a call from the limo to this freak of the week I know who lives on the Upper East Side, named Linda. I told her to meet me at my place and to leave her panties and bra at home. She responded, "I'm on my way."

But when I got home, all I could think about was Yolanda and our evening together. I managed to shower and slip into my robe. When Linda showed up at my place around two A.M., I thought I was ready for something real freaky. But I couldn't get Yolanda out of my mind even when Linda tried to kiss my lips. When I didn't respond, she went for the dick. But even my dick was in a place I feared my heart was headed with Yolanda.

I told Linda I would have to take a rain check and gave her a twenty-dollar bill to pay for a cab home. She gave me that *you-ain't-shit* look, but I didn't give a damn.

I think I'm in real trouble. I wanted to call Yolanda, but I didn't want to wake her up. She said something about having an important meeting in the morning. So I called her machine in Chicago a couple of times just to hear her voice. The third call I just put the phone close to my music, Marvin Gaye moaning "Distant Lover." On the fourth call I finally left a sappy message, mumbling something about what a sweet time I had. I can't remember ever doing that. And then I called FTD and ordered a dozen red roses, a dozen yellow roses, and a dozen white and had them scheduled for delivery the first thing the following day. I went to sleep thinking about Yolanda and me covered by those roses.

Chapter 7

Riley slowly finished her second cup of coffee and enjoyed the August heat of the morning sun coming through her office window. The sky was a hopeful blue. Riley started to go to her kitchen and pour herself another cup of coffee, but instead she turned on her computer, waited for a few seconds as the modem made the connection she needed and had looked forward to the last two weeks. When she heard the automated voice announcing she had mail, her face broke into a wide smile. She clicked a few keys with a sense of joy and wondered what message would greet her.

Her message felt like a loving touch after a long trip.

Dreamseekr: Just wanted to say good morning and to let you know that someone out here in cyberspace thinks you're wonderful and is hoping that this Friday will be a good day in your life. I'll have something special for you later. Lonelyboy.

Riley punched a button that would save the message in a folder she called True Dreams, then turned off her computer, located her journal, and began to write:

I love the computer age! Every morning and sometimes in the evening when I log on to my computer there is a very sweet message from my secret admirer. One day he even downloaded a picture of a vase full of beautiful roses, with a note below saying he hoped I could smell the roses and that they brightened up my day. He has been sending me poems, and I send some poetry and a few song lyrics back to him. For the first time in a long time I feel like someone appreciates my talents, besides my kids, who I think don't really get the poems, but at least they try and be supportive.

I don't have any idea how my secret admirer looks, or even if he's Black. I don't think I care. All I know is that whenever I hear the computer tell me I have mail, my heart skips faster than double-dutch jumping. At night I can't sleep for wondering how my secret admirer might look. This happens even when Selwyn is here. A few nights ago he startled me when he reached over to kiss me good-night. I was thinking about my mystery man, and when I felt his lips brush against mine, I looked at him like he was a total stranger and asked, "What are you doing?" He didn't respond. He just rolled back over to his side of the bed. The next morning he didn't even say good-bye when he left for the office. I didn't even know he had gone back to the West Coast until his executive assistant called to make sure the car service had shown up to take him to the airport. She explained they had recently switched services and hadn't heard from Selwyn. I told her they had shown up, even though I wasn't certain. But knowing Selwyn, he would have been back upstairs on the phone raising hell with somebody.

I was through with Selwyn. When he didn't make the trip back to Hampton with me to take Ryan and Reggie to school, I thought seriously about divorcing his butt as soon as I got back home. He came up with some lame excuse about a client making a million-dollar decision and he needed to be there to make sure his firm got the business. Most times I tell him I understand, but I just looked at him like he's not even there. The children didn't seem to mind, but it ruined the trip for me. All the plans I had made about visiting some of the places I thought were special to the two of us were destroyed. My mother and father offered to make the trip with us, but I told them I would be fine. I helped my kids check into the dorms, went out and spent a ton of our money on dorm goodies for Ryan and Reggie, then spent two days eating and watching movies in my Radisson Hotel suite. Instead of rekindling a romance, his absence made me realize how silly my plans were.

While sitting in my hotel room, watching a sad movie and eating some lifeless popcorn, the weight of the loneliness I feel every day in my own house hit me full force. Maybe it was the realization that I could no longer look forward to the sound of the door opening and one of my children coming in and greeting me with a hug and kiss and sometimes a kind word. I looked out on the city of Hampton, Virginia, a city where I had enjoyed so many happy times, and I just couldn't stop the tears. But I don't want to write and think about that sadness again. I want to enjoy this surge of joy my computer and this special man is bringing me.

On the evening I returned from Hampton, my admirer surprised me again. I was on my computer, composing some poetry in the workshop area, when this little message popped up my screen: *Your poetry and messages have given me something to look forward to.* There was a little box where I could respond to his message. At first the message scared me and I was wondering how he knew I was on my computer. I was feeling a bit paranoid. But he explained this feature called the *Buddy List* that notified him when his friends were on-line. When he told me I was the only person he ever sent messages on his *Buddy List*, I had to fight back tears. We spent the next hour writing messages to each other on the computer like we were grade-school kids exchanging notes. He must live in California, because he said something about the Bay Area's warm days and cool nights. I also get the impression he's some type of executive, because a couple of times it took him a little longer to respond to my question. He would then explain he was talking with his assistant. During this session I told him I was married and he told me he was also. I asked him if he was in love and he said he didn't know. That his wife didn't understand him and had let herself go. When he posed the same question to me, I said I was beginning to wonder if I had ever been in love. He said he had figured that out from some of my poetry.

I don't feel like I'm doing anything wrong. I view this as a way of *satisfying my emotional needs like I use other things to quench my sexual desires, like my little mechanical friend, Frank Faithful, I keep hidden in my lingerie drawer. And this man has inspired me. Two days after this chat with my mystery man, I went out to the fitness warehouse and insisted they deliver a treadmill the following morning. I've been on it every day, listening to music and motivational tapes. Sometimes I feel like I'm chasing Gail Devers. I'm starting to feel better about this ole body.*

●   ●   ●

Dwight poured himself his first cup of coffee and then hit the mute button on his small color television sitting on the counter. Dwight always hit the button when his favorite newscaster, Hosea Sanders, turned to his white co-anchor. Dwight wasn't interested in any news she might be reading. He started to pick up his phone and call his mother and share the morning with her, as he often did. But he looked at the clock and realized that it was already a few minutes past seven A.M. in Oakland. His mother had most likely left for the hospital where she had worked as an LPN since he was in the eighth grade. So he pulled out his journal and began to write something he might even share with the group:

I don't know why I called the sister, but I did. Maybe I thought I could be her Black knight and save her from an abusive boyfriend. I noticed her name, Chanel, and her digits on the tiny piece of paper sitting on top of my dresser. I didn't even remember how she looked, but she must have been checking me out, because while I was standing outside the Hyde Park movie theater, she rushed up and hugged me. I didn't even invite her on the date. She had asked me if I was married, and when I said no she said, "Good. Take me to the movies." Since women weren't beating down my door or ringing my phone, I said sure, why not. She wasn't that bad-looking, kind of a cute little girl who had already seen a lot of life. I could tell that in the ten minutes we waited to get tickets, popcorn, and sodas.

She talked too much, and obviously didn't think that much of herself. I think all the talking was to keep herself from thinking about her situation. She talked during the movies, causing me to miss a lot of the funny lines in **The Nutty Professor.** *I guess there were funny lines from all the laughter from the audience. She told me about all her boyfriends, her two kids, pausing to ask: "You don't have anything against a woman with children, do you?" I must have said no, because all I remember is her smiling and saying "good" as she continued to talk endlessly. The only question I got her to answer was about the guy who was beating her. She started by saying he was one of her babies' daddy and he had gotten upset with her for speaking to her other baby's daddy in the health club. I was going to ask her why she hadn't married, but she gave me that information during one of her monologues: She hadn't found the right man. I wanted to tell her she still hadn't, but I couldn't get a word in.*

After the movies I should have run like Michael Johnson, but I couldn't leave well enough alone. I had suggested we do dinner. We went to a Black-owned seafood restaurant that has some of the best shrimp creole I've ever had in Chicago. The first sign that dinner was also going to be adventure was when she asked the waiter if they had Red Bull in a can. At least she didn't ask for a forty-ounce! I suggested a glass of wine and she agreed. I ordered a fried shrimp platter, and Chanel ordered the crab legs. While I was digging into the fries and cole slaw, I heard this loud crunching sound coming from across the table. When I looked up, I couldn't believe my eyes. This woman had the entire crab leg in her mouth. I asked her how her food was, and she said, "Oh, it's good, but these things sho' are crunchy." The waiter was pouring water in our glasses and looking at her like she was a fool, and I think he was going to show her how to use her utensils to eat the food, but I beat him to the punch by grabbing the crab cracker and saying in a very polite way, they might taste a little better if you use this. At least she smiled and said thank-you.

I hope this date and my reaction doesn't mean that I'm becoming too much of a Buppie. I mean, I'm thinking that I am better than Chanel and that's the reason I'm certain I won't ever dial her number again. When I think about it, she was funny. I like my women a little rough around the edges, but this was a little too much for even me! I guess I'm looking for a happy-in-between kinda thing. Somebody who's not stuck up and full of themselves like my ex, Kelli, but not as around the way as Chanel. Someone who knows what a forty-ounce is but can also appreciate a nice warm bath and the taste of fine wine.

Chapter 8

Sometimes my mouth gets me into trouble. My mother always used to say, "Yolanda, you talk too much." Mama ain't never lied!

There I was, enjoying a nice, leisurely lunch at Riley's a couple of days ago, when she asked me a simple question: What was I working on? I mentioned the new record label I had signed the last time I was in New York. The company had a new male group, Goodfellaz, they thought were going to be big, and I had been contracted to pull together a showcase at Park West, one of the city's top small concert venues. That's when my mouth lost contact with my brain. I told Riley how much I was dreading having to listen to all the local Chicago talent in search of an opening act for the group.

Riley seized the moment. "You're looking for an opening act? Please, please, Yolanda. Let me do it."

The last of my mango sorbet refused to be swallowed. "Let you do what?" I croaked.

"Let me open for the group. Please, Yolanda, this is the big break I've been praying for. To perform at a place like Park West would be just too wonderful. I already have a set prepared. Please, Yolanda, please."

"Riley, I don't know. I think the record company wants a group," I said weakly. The truth was, the record company had left it completely up to me, but letting Riley open would ensure that my first contract with this client would also be my last. I know I should have told Riley right then and there that I didn't think she could handle it. But I didn't want to hurt her feelings or risk losing her friendship.

While Riley ran off to find the tape of her latest singing session, I recalled her last public performance—Sally Turner's funeral.

Sally Turner was one of our sorority sisters who had died suddenly from breast cancer. Now, I don't do sad, fall-in-the-casket Black folks' funerals, but the family had requested that Sally's funeral be a true celebration of her life, so I agreed to tag along with Riley. It was a beautiful and joyous service, and I found myself feeling happy that I'd known Sally rather than sad about her death. That's when the minister asked if anyone wanted to stand and share a personal anecdote or pay tribute to Sally. Several people got up and offered wonderful memories that brought out the Kleenex. Riley and I gently comforted each other as our sorors expressed our same feeling for Sally and her family.

One of the sisters, Olivia, who had appeared with the New York Metropolitan Opera, got up and sang a brief and beautiful aria. I felt the tiny hairs on my arm stand up as she hit her final note. She could blow! I mean, sister sang us slaphappy. That's when Riley patted me on the knee and whispered, "I think I'll sing a song."

Dear God, not a song. A poem maybe, but not a song. "Are you sure you want to do that?" I asked gently.

"Yes, I think I'll sing 'Walk Around Heaven All Day.' " I was thinking we might all need a chorus of "Standing in the Need of Prayer." I gripped her arm. "Riley, you don't want to sing after Olivia, do you?" But Riley, the diva-in-waiting, had no fear. Next thing I knew, Riley was standing up next to me, singing a *cappella*.

She sounded like a frog on crack. Everyone was looking around in disbelief. The woman on my left was rocking back and forth, crying and laughing at the same time. "That's okay, chile, let Him use you . . . let Him use you."

People turned to look at me like it was my fault. Like I should just pull Miss Riley back to her seat. I could hear whispers and muted laughter all around us. But Riley heard nothing but her own voice. She couldn't see the looks on the mourners' faces because she was singing with her eyes closed. Her hands were clasped in a prayerful pose, her long neck arched and her head thrown back. When she mercifully finished, she bowed toward Sally's shocked family as though she had just given a command performance for the queen. She even gave Olivia a *take-that-diva* look.

After the service, several sorors came over and whispered to me. "Is Riley all right?" "Is she on some kind of medication?" A few confided that it took everything they had not to burst out laughing. It was bad. Real bad. But the really sad thing was Riley didn't have a clue.

"Just have them listen to this," Riley said as she plopped a cassette down on the dining room table.

"Have who what?" I asked.

"Have whoever's in charge listen to this tape. I pulled it together with a new producer I paid a lot of money to work with. Please, Yolanda. This is the break I need." Riley sounded like a small child pleading for a special toy she wanted for Christmas. Did I look like Santa Claus to her?

"I'll see what I can do," I lied.

"Yolanda, I know if you just put in a good word for me, they'll say yes. You're the best friend in the world!" Riley gave me a big hug. I gave her a half-smile and slid the cassette into my purse. It's been there ever since.

I called Leland as soon as I got home.

"I think you should tell her," Leland said.

"Tell her she can't sing?"

"If that's how you feel."

"How *I* feel? We all know Riley can't carry a tune in a paper bag, let alone a bucket. I just don't want to hurt her feelings. Riley is already so emotional, and now with her kids gone and Selwyn being Selwyn, she's a little depressed. I guess I'm feeling sorry for her," I said.

"Sorry enough to risk your reputation with a new client? Do we owe our friends that? Aren't we getting too old for this? We sound like high school kids," Leland said.

"I do hear what you're saying, and deep down I don't think I would ever allow Riley to sing. It would embarrass her and I'd be out of work. I guess what I'm asking you for is a way out. I mean, I could tell her that the record company turned her down, but it's high time one of us told her the truth about her singing. I just don't want to be the one to hurt her feelings. And I don't think it's high-schoolish to concern yourself with another person's feelings. Especially someone you care a great deal about," I said.

"Well, do we owe each other the truth? Or should we always say what we think our friends want to hear?" Leland asked.

"We should tell true friends the truth," I said.

"Then why hasn't one of us told Riley she can't sing?"

"I don't know."

"Do you consider Riley a true friend?"

"You know I love Riley," I said.

"That's not what I asked. Do you consider Riley a true friend?"

"Is that my answer?"

"It might be, my friend. It might be."

Chapter 9

"**So, did my mama** ask about me?"

"Now, Boo, what kinda fool question is that? Of course your mama asked about you. She's your mama!" Uncle Doc said as he took a long drag on his cigarette. "Boo" was one of the many nicknames he called me, depending on the mood he was in. "Stinker," my pet name from childhood, still meant Uncle Doc wasn't pleased with something I did.

"I'm sorry now I didn't go. How was it?"

"Chile, it was a hoot! A whole lot of food, drankin', and cussin'."

"No fights?" I asked.

"Not really. Well, almost. Yo aunt Mayline and cuzin Ruby Jean almost came to blows after they both made the same pineapple upside down cake. Ruby Jean said Mayline had stole her recipe just like she tried to take her husband. Some of your strong young cuzins had to keep them apart. Both of them had been drinkin', you know." Uncle Doc laughed. "I had me a few drinks too, and was feelin' pretty good, so I kept yellin' 'turn 'em loose! Let them ole hussies fight!' It would have been better than that tired ole talent show we keep having. When it's my time to head the reunion, that talent show is the first thang to go. It's history. I'm so sick and tired of little nappy-headed children trying to rap about plenty of nuthin'."

Miss Thing's Wings was quiet. Almost one in the morning. It had been closed for an hour before I stopped by to get something to take home and to get Uncle Doc's report on the family reunion I had missed. I had no real excuse. The group had decided to take August off. Yolanda was spending a lot of time in New York, with work she said, and Riley had to take her twins to school. Dwight didn't say what he was going to do, but he was in total agreement on taking August off. Our next meeting was scheduled for the first Sunday after Labor Day.

I had decided to forgo the reunion and meet up with a man. I was sorry that I had changed my mind, because the man had faked me out. I didn't think Uncle Doc knew the real reason I had stayed in Chicago, even when everyone was trying to leave because of the Democratic Convention. But then he asked: "So, when are you going to learn that you don't put trade before yo' family? Haven't you learned anything from me?"

"What are you talking about?" I asked, trying to sound innocent.

"Don't try and pull that mess on me. I'm from the ol' school. The last time we talked about the reunion, you was telling me to get a suite at the hotel so you could crash with me. I know it musta been some man that kept you here. But to be honest, I'm glad your ol' rusty butt decided to stay. Gave me a chance to hang out with some of my girlfriends from the ol' days."

"You still have friends living in New Orleans?" I asked. What I really wanted to ask was how did he still have friends his age alive and kicking, when all my gay male friends were either dead or sick.

"Yeah, Boo. 'Bout three or four of my friends I used to run with when I was at Southern still livin' 'round New Orleans. I think the good Lord done forgot them girls still down here, they so ol'. But don't try and change the subject. Who was he?"

"Who was who?" Uncle Doc gave me one of those *chile, please!* looks.

But he was right. I had met this guy a couple of weeks before the reunion right there at Miss Thing's Wings. I had stopped by late one night after one of the Democratic Convention parties in early August. I think it was the JFK, Jr., party. Lots of celebrities but hardly any food that I could get to. I spent time gawking at people like Kevin Costner and Juanita Jordan, Michael's wife. Yolanda had invitations to all the major parties, and she invited me. I tried to get her to join me for some late-night wings, but she was expecting a call from John and wanted to get home. It didn't matter that she had already talked to him at least three times on her cellular.

I was sitting at this exact same table I was now sharing with Uncle Doc, when this handsome hunk of a man came over and asked if he could share my table.

To make a long story a short one, Medgar Allen Douglas ended up at my apartment instead of at the Marriott. We had actually been at the same party. It was a wonderful night. The boy had a dick that could change your life. He told me he was an attorney, single and looking. I saw him two more times before he left for home. We made plans for him to return to Chicago the same weekend as my family reunion.

But Medgar didn't show, didn't call, and when I called him, I heard *the number you have just dialed has been changed, at the customer's request, the new number is not in my records.* When I tried to page him, I discovered that his pager had been disconnected. I had stubbornly waited by the phone, praying that it would ring or that the doorman would buzz me from downstairs and tell me that Medgar was waiting for me in the lobby. But my phone never rang. The doorman never buzzed.

"Just some man," I said nonchalantly.

"Some man? That ain't what I heard," Uncle Doc said with a snide little laugh.

"So what did you hear?"

"Now, Boo, you know that don't nuthin' go on in this place that I don't hear about. Mavis and Thelma can't hold water, let alone some good gossip. I hear he was a fine, tall thing. Did you give him some of that sweet potato pie of yours?"

"You dipping, Uncle," I said, blushing.

"Well, I hope he was worth giving your family shade. I ain't met *no* man like that in all my years. Family always comes first," he said firmly.

"I know, Uncle Doc, but I didn't think it would matter. I've missed the last three reunions, and no one seems to care."

"Yeah, well, don't blame that on some silly argument you had two years ago with yo' mama. Who, by the way, was lookin' good. I tell you, that ol' Mattie could do an advertisement for good-Black-don't-crack lotion!"

"You know, you ain't got a bit of sense," I said.

"And that's the way I like it," Uncle Doc said.

"Mama looked good, huh? Still wearing her hair in that French roll style?"

"Yes! Miss Mother looked real good. And let's just say the French roll is lookin' a little more *French* these days. Got her a man too. She had on those beautiful pearls you bought her for Mother's Day. Guess we ain't the only ones in the family that got pullin' power," he said. I knew my mother couldn't out on those pearls without thinking about me. She had cried for days when I gave them to her.

"What? Mama got a boyfriend. Who is he?"

"I ain't sayin'. But she seems quite taken, and he ain't bad on the eyes neither. I think yo' aunt Mayline was trying to make a play. Making sure his plate was full and askin' him if he had any brothers still living. And, if not, did he have any sons!" Uncle Doc slapped his knee and laughed.

"Does he treat her nice?" I asked, trying to imagine my mother with another man besides Daddy. But Daddy has been dead almost ten years. It's hard to believe it had been that long. Seems like only yesterday when my daddy died suddenly from a heart attack. The family was devastated, especially Uncle Doc, who was so proud of his older brother.

"Now, you know yo' mama ain't going to have it any other way. You could learn a thing or two from her."

"What are you talking about?"

"You think I got to be this ol' being stupid, Boo? I can tell from that face of yours that whoever you put in front of your family either didn't show up or didn't look as good as he looked the night he swept you outta here."

"He didn't show up," I said sheepishly.

"I figured as much," Uncle Doc replied. "Don't tell me yo' uncle can't read you like the Bible."

"How's my brother, Dennis? Does he like Mama's new friend?" I wanted to get Uncle Doc off me and back to my family.

"He was fine. He likes Andrew. That fool kept teasing me, callin' me Uncle Pussy and rubbing his nose against mine like we some kinda Eskimos," Uncle Doc laughed.

"So he's still a fool?" My older brother was a prankster from day one. Whenever he did something horrible to me, I couldn't stay mad long, because he always had a joke that would make me laugh. When that didn't work, he would resort to tickling.

"Still a fool."

"Did you bring me back a T-shirt and some gumbo?" I asked. Our family always had great family reunion T-shirts. I still had some from ten years back. My favorite was Uncle Doc's WE ARE FAMILY over a portrait of the year-before reunion.

"Maybe and maybe not. You'll just have to wait and see how I feel the next time you drop by my place." Uncle Doc smiled.

●　　　●　　　●

The group didn't meet this month, and to tell the truth, Yolanda needs a break. I mean, with all the Democratic activities in Chicago during the usually mild month of August. Trying to stay one step in front of Mr. John Henderson can be more than one girl can stand. I needed some private time and some private thoughts for my own journal.

Last night I had one of the best dates of my life. Date— how silly does that sound at my age? But whatever I choose to call last night, wonderful and magical are the only two words to describe it.

John asked me to trust him for twenty-four hours. When I asked him what he meant, he told me he had a special evening for me, but he couldn't give me the details and all I needed was clothing for an overnight stay. When I asked where we were going, all he would say was it was a surprise. I told him, of course I trusted him—but I still called Leland and told him I was with John, so if I came up missing he'd know where to start looking! When he picked me up at my hotel, he came bearing gifts. Three very strange gifts. The first was a beautiful pair of silver crescent-shaped earrings, which he said was a clue concerning our outing. The second gift was a black silk mask which he told me I had to put on once we got inside the limo that was waiting downstairs. The final gift was a pair of earplugs. I like adventures, so I went along. About an hour later I knew that I was being led on a plane, destination unknown.

*Once we were airborne, John removed the mask and the earplugs. When I asked where we were headed, he said I'd know in a couple of hours and told me not to bother asking the flight attendants, because they wouldn't tell me. So I just sat back and enjoyed the latest issues of **Essence** and **Sister 2 Sister** magazines and orange juice the attendants offered. John had this pleased look on his face like he was really pulling one over on me. I looked over at the passengers sitting across the aisle from us, hoping for a newspaper or some type of sign that might let me know where I was headed. No such luck. After we had been up in the air a couple of hours, the flight attendant came over and whispered something to John, and he put the earplugs and mask back on me. It took me a few minutes to get my* bearing once we had deplaned, then I smelled the sweet scent of food. Creole food. I was in one of my favorite cities and the birthplace of Leland. I wanted to call him right away and say, "Guess where I am, baby-boy?"

A driver met us at the baggage claim area and whisked us into a waiting limo. Inside I found a dozen red roses, a bottle of champagne, and a note saying welcome to an evening of magic. And it was. We checked into a suite at the beautiful Windsor Court Hotel, right outside the French Quarter. After a few minutes of a little hugging and kissing, John and I headed for a workout at the New Orleans Athletic Club. We worked out for about an hour and then came back to the hotel, showered and changed clothes, then headed for dinner at the Commander's Palace, a renowned restaurant located in this great old house. Dinner was different from anything I had ever experienced. John had arranged for us to sit at the captain's table, which actually meant the kitchen. Our table setting of fine china was in the center of the busy kitchen on a butcher-block cutting station. There we were served samples of everything that left this wonderful kitchen. Every time the chef would put something on our plate, he would describe its origin and how it was prepared. We sampled everything from beef to lobster. A wine steward served us a different type of wine with each entree. It was simply exquisite.

After dinner John had a horse and carriage waiting in front of the restaurant. We strolled the Garden District and viewed the beautiful Victorian houses. It was humid and the bugs were out, but I didn't mind a bit. The driver gave us bits of New Orleans history and pointed out the hotel where Tennessee Williams finished his play *A Streetcar Named Desire.* We got out of the carriage and walked for about an hour around the French Quarter, which seemed packed with visitors.

When we got back to the hotel, he had both tea and champagne waiting. We took separate showers, then listened to the music of Sherrie Winston and Cassandra Wilson while we talked. John attempted a move by letting his hand slip to my left breast, but I was able to keep him at bay. But I was tempted, especially when he walked out in nothing but some form-fitting Versace boxers. His body brought to life a pair of underwear the way few men could. It looked like he was also trying to hide a couple of packages of

Now 'n' Laters in his fancy underwear. He saw me look, but fair's fair: I caught him looking at my chest when I came out wearing a peach satin nightgown. I was glad I didn't bring my little-girl cotton gown, what I wear every night at home, plain and simple. Whenever he would try to make his move, I would engage him in conversation or bring him over to the terrace and point out one of the many strange people walking around the French Quarter. I know I'm sexually attracted to him, but it will be on my terms, and only when I'm good and ready.

John likes talking to me and hearing himself talk. Sometimes when he talks it seems like he's saying things he never shared with anyone. It makes me feel special and I try and return that feeling back to him. I don't know why, but I'm not so surprised that someone so handsome still might be insecure about certain aspects of their lives. Before we knew it, daybreak was coming and he fell asleep in my lap, just like a little baby. I woke him and we got in the canopy bed. The closest we came to doing the do was when he wrapped his large legs around my body and drew me close to him. But that was as far as he went. He was tired and so was I.

The next morning we went for an early morning run and stopped at the Café du Monde, a cafe across from Jackson Square, where we enjoyed sugar-drenched beignets and flavored coffee while sharing parts of the local newspaper. I couldn't help smiling as the sunlight began to fill the cafe and everything just filled with warmth—me, John, the whole wide world.

Chapter 10

Dwight sat in his small cubicle in the Wrigley Building staring at his black computer screen with the orange screen saver, asking: *Has it changed your life yet?* He was mad. Dwight started to pick up his phone and call his mother, but realized she was still at work and might not understand his anger. He started to call Henry, one of his basketball-playing buddies, but thought he would have to explain everything he said, and he never knew who might be eavesdropping in his office. Dwight started to simply grab his gym bag and leave early to work out some of his steam, when he noticed his journal sticking out of it, inviting him to express his anger on its pages.

I don't care when white folks try and f over each other in business. They do it all the time. But when they try and pull that shit on a brother and try and get me involved—then that's when I have to say to hell with the bonus and stuff and speak my piece.

I got a situation going on like that in my office. I just came out of a meeting with a sales representative and his manager. I know in this office

*the salesmen and their managers run the shit. It's that way in most orga-
nizations that're trying to sell something to other companies. Employees
look to them like they're some kinda gods. The secretaries perk up when
they walk in and they get the best parking spaces and no one ever questions
their 500-dollar lunch and dinner tabs. But if the real truth be known,
most of them don't know jack. Just bullshitters who've faked their way to
the top and are getting paid big-time to f over people. It's the good ole boy
network in its purest form. That's one of the main reasons I won't consider
ever going into sales—I'm not a bullshitter. I have to say what's on my
mind. Salesmen will say whatever they think you want to hear.*

*This white salesman (we don't have but one brother in sales and he's a
Tom—never even talks to me unless he has some technical question) I
usually work with, Barry Slaughter, wanted me to sign off on this proposal
for over three million dollars worth of new equipment for this client. All
the sales proposals have to be signed off by a sales engineer, basically stating
that the equipment the company is proposing will work together and do
what the sales representative has promised. On a deal like this, the sales rep
will make a killing in commissions (in this case over 50K) and sometimes,
not always, the sales engineer—that's me, who's responsible for installing
the equipment and working with the customers will get some type of
jive bonus. The sales rep is the one who gets the Cubs, Bears, and Bulls
tickets, and who can actually claim a day on the golf course as a full day's
work.*

*The reason we had this meeting was because I refused to sign off on this
proposal and I think Barry needs it to make quota or else his ass might be
looking for a new job. The customer is one of my favorites, MedMac, an
African American medical information service company that started out
small, a family operation. But over the years they have grown tremen-
dously and recently went public and had sales of over $75 million a year. I
like the president and the MIS director, who's a young brother who worked
his way up from a programmer. This was one of the few accounts that I
really looked forward to visiting, so I was all for installing new equipment.
It made me feel proud to see what Black people could do when we put our
minds on something constructive. MedMac was one of the things I loved*

about Chicago—that being so many African American businesses were thriving here despite a white mayor and his cronies.

Well, Barry is trying to sell them a lot of equipment they don't need and won't need until five or maybe even ten years from now. At the bare minimum they need about $750,000 worth of equipment to add to their existing computer system. When I told Barry this, he looked at me with a smirk and said, "I know they don't need all this equipment, but what they don't know won't hurt them. I got a mortgage to pay." I start to tell him I didn't give a flying fuck about what he had to pay, he wasn't going to fuck over the brothers to pay for his house out in Arlington Heights or wherever the fuck he lived. I didn't go off on him, I just told him I wasn't going to sign off on the proposal.

Next thing I know they're beeping me while I'm in a meeting and telling me to get back to the office right away. When I get back, he and his boss are jumping up and down saying I got to sign this and help them convince the customer they need this equipment. When I tell them no, they said something like I'm not being a team player and this isn't going to look good on my next evaluation and raise. I tell them I don't care. They can write and say all they want about how I'm not a team player—but they can't ever say I don't know my shit when it comes to computers. I still study hard to make damn sure of that.

One of the reasons I left Digital Plus was for bullshit like this. I thought a smaller computer company wouldn't try and mess over their customers to make quota. Now, I ain't saying they did that at Digital Plus, but there were a lot of politics when it came to assignments, and if a salesman didn't want you on his accounts, then your ass was gone. The real reason I left Digital Plus was because of all the money I was able to collect when they were downsizing. I figured I could use that money toward building my mom a new house real soon. I remember how she thought I was crazy leaving a good company like Digital Plus, no matter how much money they were offering me to leave. I told her they were all the same and if they wanted to pay me money to not have to look at my Black ass—then it was, see ya, I'm outta here.

During the meeting Barry and his manager pointed out that I hadn't taken this stance before, that I knew they usually recommended more equipment for a customer for backup and I had signed off before. I countered with the fact that the equipment was more than enough for backup. The customer had spent over three million the year before on a new system. I started to tell them I didn't really care when they were messing over each other. Then they tried to imply that I was doing this because the customers were African American, but they didn't have the nerve, so they said something about maybe I was too close to this account. I got so mad at what they were trying to pull that I went further than I should and told them, not only was I not going to sign the proposal—but if they went over me and brought another engineer on the account, I would go to the customer directly. They knew I had a great relationship with MedMac, and this was one of the few customers old Barry couldn't sell shit to on the golf course. When these brothers did lunch, it wasn't at some fancy downtown restaurant, but maybe Glady's or Army and Lou's.

After I made the statement, they both looked at me like I had gone postal, threatening to bring in the branch manager and the vice president and recommend my immediate termination if I did such a thing. I told them do what you must—but that's the way I feel about it and you guys ain't going to f over the brothers, and I walked out. I'm just waiting for them to make their next move. I've made mine.

•　　•　　•

Riley was preparing to turn on her computer and send a poem to her secret admirer, when Selwyn walked in. His presence surprised her. Selwyn never came into the office when he knew Riley was there; usually he would take his laptop or his work into the library. But there he was with his clean-shaven nutmeg-hued face, looking a bit tired in his white shirt and tie. Then his first question shocked Riley even more.

"I'm thinking about going up to Hampton for a football game and check in on the kids. Are you interested in joining me?" Selwyn asked. Riley was noticing how gently he was smiling.

"Excuse me?" Riley said as she moved a white sheet of paper over the yellow legal pad where she composed her poetry. She didn't feel like having Selwyn patronize her by asking to hear her latest piece of poetry. In recent years, the only time Selwyn asked Riley about her poetry was when he needed her to do something for him, like dress up nicely and attend a party of one of his partners.

"I'm heading east. I've got to see a client in Washington, D.C., and I thought it would be nice if we rented a car or hired a driver and went to see the kids," he said.

Riley wanted to ask him why now, almost a month later, instead of the opening of school as they had planned. Was there some other motive? Were the partners at his firm the ones actually requesting her presence? They did that on occasion.

"I don't know if I'm going to be available. I'm waiting to hear about a singing engagement."

"A singing engagement?"

"Yes. I might be singing at Park West," she said proudly.

"With who?"

"Solo."

Selwyn looked at Riley like he wanted to walk over and put his hand over her forehead and see if she had a fever. He stayed leaning in the doorway and his curiosity got the best of him and he asked, "So when did this happen?"

"It's not official yet, but I'm pretty certain I'm going to get the gig. I'm just waiting to hear from the record company executive," Riley said. Selwyn placed his hand on his chin and walked closer to his wife. Maybe something in her eyes would let him know if she was serious.

"So you're going to sing? That's wonderful," he said, facing Riley and the black and chrome desk he had picked out when Riley told him she wanted her own office at home. As distant as Selwyn could be with his emotions, he always tried to provide Riley and their children with any material possession they requested. Selwyn scratched his itching back against the doorway in a right to left sliding motion and began to unloosen his gold and blue tie. He was staring at his wife. Selwyn removed his oxford red glasses and rubbed his eyes in a defeated gesture.

"Is there something wrong, Selwyn?" Riley asked.

"No, I guess I'm just a bit surprised," he said.

"Surprised at what?" Riley asked. She wondered if he was surprised that she was charting out a life of her own or that she was going to sing in a top spot like Park West.

"Just surprised that you're turning down a chance to see the kids. I know you must miss them and I thought you enjoyed visiting Hampton," he said.

"I do miss the kids. But they're not kids anymore, and besides, I talk to them every other day. When's the last time you've talked to them?"

"At least once a week. I talked with Reggie just yesterday and Ryan has my 800 number that she uses often," he said.

"Who knows, I don't have the exact date. Maybe I will be able to go. I have to make sure it doesn't interfere with my rehearsals," Riley said. She was thinking, maybe her dreams about a Hampton reunion with her husband might happen after all. But she also questioned if she desired such a return to the place they fell in love.

"Let me know," Selwyn said as he lowered his tall and lean body into a blood-red leather chair. "I'm going into the library and look over some work before I call it a night," he said.

"I'll do that. Maybe I'll call you and leave you a message on your 800 number," Riley said.

"Do you have that number?" Selwyn asked, trying to recall if he had given his wife one of the plastic cards with his personal 800 number.

"No, but our daughter does. Remember?"

"Oh, yeah, I remember," Selwyn said.

•   •   •

I could tell from my caller ID box that Yolanda wasn't phoning from Chicago, so when I picked up the receiver I said, "Miss Yogi . . . do you still have any clients in Chicago, and if so when do you see them?"

"Whatcha talking about, boyfriend? How do you know I'm not right down the street from you," she laughed.

"You forgot. I'm Black. I got caller ID," I joked.

"I know that's right. Busted! I'm back in New York, but I'm working."

"Working what? Or should I say working whom?"

"That too. How ya doing?"

"I'm doing fine. How is Mr. Wonderful?"

"Just great. Matter fact, I'm waiting on him right now. He going to pick me up when he leaves the gym," Yolanda said.

"Why didn't you go with him? Afraid you might show him up?"

"Naw, from what I've seen, he has nothing to worry about," Yolanda said.

"So you still holding on to your stuff? As Uncle Doc would say, you keeping that wax paper over your sweet potato pie?" I teased.

"Trust me, honey, I've got aluminum foil over my pie. How is Uncle Doc?"

"Fine. Crazy as ever. I was hanging out with him a few nights ago," I said.

"Tell him I said hello," Yolanda said. I told her I would, and then I noticed a brief silence, which usually meant she had something important she needed to ask me.

"So whatsup?" I asked.

"I have a little favor I need to ask you," Yolanda said shyly.

"Why am I not surprised? I'm listening."

"You know the next meeting, which is this coming Sunday, is supposed to be at my place. And, well, I've been so busy with my new clients in New York, and, well, would you switch with me and take September? I know it's short notice, but it would be a big help," Yolanda pleaded.

"Is that all?" I thought she was looking for man advice.

"Yes, that's all," Yolanda said.

"Sure, Yogi. I can do that. All I got to do is call Uncle Doc. Tell him to fry up some extra wings on Sunday and go pick up a loaf of light bread and we'll be set," I said.

"Thanks, baby-boy. Miss Riley will be too through with all those wings she says she don't like to eat," Yolanda said.

"Speaking of Poetic Justice, have you decided what you're going to do?"

"I have decided that she won't be singing at a showcase I'm producing. I just haven't figured out how I'm going to tell her. You want to do me one more small favor?"

"Sure," I said without thinking.

"Tell her," Yolanda joked.

"Not for all the wings in the world," I said.

"I guess that's my clue to know I'm pushing it and to say good night. Oh, before I get off, John is coming with me Friday night when we meet at Uncle Doc's. I want you guys to meet him, so will you give Riley and Dwight a call and see if they want to come?"

"Sure, but now you better quit while you're ahead."

"Good night."

"I can at least hope for that. A good night would be nice," I said as I hung up my phone.

•   •   •

I honestly thought I was above being jealous of anyone, until the moment Yolanda walked into Uncle Doc's with her new man. Not only was I jealous of John getting so much of Yolanda's attention, I was envious of Yolanda for catching one of the finest-looking Black men I've seen in a long time. As the *kids* say, Yolanda has met the baby's daddy. A daddy with handsome, athletic good looks and a body to match. He was wearing jeans so tight that it appeared the jeans were wearing him.

And they looked so happy, it was contagious. It seemed like the crowd at Miss Thing's Wings just opened up and made a space for them to get through. I saw a couple of brothers stop John to shake his hand or pat him on his back as they made their way toward me. *Damn*, I thought as I looked at John and Yolanda walking toward me, they look happy!

Yolanda came up and gave me my usual "Hey, baby-boy!" greeting and a big warm hug. Yolanda had a way of making everyone around her feel special, and my brief jealousy quickly dissolved. Her smile does that to me.

"Yogi! Whatsup? Whatsup?" I asked as she released me from her hug.

"Dr. Leland Thompson, I would like you to meet John Henderson. John, meet Leland," Yolanda said in a mock-formal tone. She did a half-step back, signaling us to shake hands.

"John," I said, "it's good to finally meet you, man."

"Good to meet you, Leland. Thanks for letting me crash your Friday-night time with Yolanda." Now I knew what Yolanda was talking about. John's voice seem to emanate not from his diaphragm, but from a much more southern locale. I flashed back on a scene Dwight had made at the group meeting when Yolanda talked about John's eyes. I would have said exactly the same thing—they were a startling gray color. Intense considering their lightness. They seem to draw you deeper into his soul than one would go on a first meeting.

"Yolanda," I said, "can you believe that Uncle Doc managed to reserve us a table, with chairs, on Friday night?" We all took a seat, and John moved his chair a little closer to Yolanda's. "Dwight and Riley said they'd try to stop by for a minute and Uncle Doc has been peeking his head out of the kitchen every half-second or so to see if you've arrived."

"Uncle Doc? Is this the uncle you mentioned, Yolanda?" John asked.

"Yes baby, that's him," Yolanda said.

"So is he really your uncle, Leland?"

"Oh, yeah. One hundred percent. My daddy's baby brother," I said.

"This is the best food in the city of Chicago," Yolanda said. "Just wait. This food alone will bring you back."

"Oh, I think I've found something better than food to bring me back," John said as he smiled at Yolanda. I think John and Yolanda were holding hands under the table when they spoke to me, 'cause I couldn't see their hands on the table. I felt kind of left out, but that was okay. Sisterfriend was happy, and John seemed to appreciate what he had.

"Let me see what Uncle Doc is doing. He really wants to meet you, John. I'll be right back." As soon as I stood up, two old dudes walked up to the table and asked John if he was Basil Henderson, the football player.

"I tole you it was him!" old dude number one said. "Man, see that what I be talking 'bout. I know my football shit!"

"Good to meet you, Mister Basil," old dude number two said. "Don't pay him no mind, Mister Basil. He thinks he knows everything and most times he don't know nuthin'!"

John rose and shook hands with both men. "It's good to meet you both," he said. He seemed very much at ease with his public.

"C'mon, man. Let's get out of the man's face. We got chicken waiting and Mister Basil here with this pretty woman," said old dude number two as they nodded their heads at Yolanda and went back to their stools at the counter.

"My, my, my," said Uncle Doc as he approached the table. "Ain't you something? Look just like two little love doves. Douglas Thompson's the name, son. But you can call me Uncle Doc. Mightily pleased to meet you." Uncle Doc shook John's hand across the table as he sat himself down.

"Miss Yolanda, you've been mighty scarce around here since this young man came on the scene," Uncle Doc said as he gave John the twice-over. "Now, I don't like to git in nobody's business, but this here little girl is real precious to me. You taking good care with her, right?"

"Yes, sir," John answered. "She's real precious to me too, sir." I had to give it to John. He was polite, courteous, confident, and sincere.

Just as Uncle Doc and I sat back down, I saw Dwight making his way through the people standing in line to place their orders.

"Dwight," I called over the noisy Friday-night crowd, "over here!" Dwight looked his usual intense self, though he seemed to warm a little when he saw Yolanda.

"Glad you made it, Dwight," I said. "Let me introduce you to John—also known as Basil—Henderson. John, meet Dwight Scott."

"Nice meeting you, Dwight," John said, standing to shake Dwight's hand. "I understand you're also in Yolanda's journal group?"

"Yeah, man, that's right. It's a long story how I got there. An ex-wife. Like I said, a long story. But it's a pleasure to meet you, man." Dwight's voice went from warm to cool. "How's it hanging, Uncle Doc? Yolanda." Dwight seemed even more uncomfortable around Yolanda than usual. He avoided her smiling face even when he said "You're looking beautiful, as usual, Yolanda."

An awkward silence fell across the table for a second until Uncle Doc lightened the mood with a long litany of all the football players who had been in his place. He asked what we'd like to eat—on the house—and called Aunt Thelma over to take our orders. I got my Trade Platter, but Dwight said he had "another commitment," and Yolanda said she had to get John to his hotel so he could get his "beauty sleep" before his ESPN debut the next day. Oh, so that's how he does it, I thought.

Dwight gave us a curt good-bye and left. Moments later Yolanda and John followed suit after Uncle Doc made them promise to return soon and gave them two Sweet Thangs to go.

"Man seem o-kay to me," Uncle Doc offered as the two of us watched John and Yolanda disappear into the crowd. "Yolanda sure does look happy. Makes this ole heart glad," he said.

"Me too," I said, ashamed of my earlier selfish feeling. "I think this one's a keeper, Uncle Doc. This might be the one."

Chapter 11

Sometimes a man's past comes and kicks him in the ass at the most inopportune time. For me, it happened on a crisp autumn Saturday in September. I was in Chicago, on my first assignment for ESPN, covering a Northwestern football game. It wasn't the play-by-play assignment I'd hoped for, but a sideline gig. My job was to get interviews with the coaches before, during, and after the game. I was also responsible for interviews with key players after the game. I was looking forward to the experience, but, I have to admit, I was a little nervous also.

Everything associated with the game had gone well, thanks to Yolanda's pregame prep. She showed me how to take the *you-knows* out of my conversation and suggested I ask players questions I wanted answers to. Her point was to think like Oprah or somebody instead of going with the canned questions the producers had written out for me. "Just imagine you're at home watching the game and think of the things you'd want to know," Yolanda advised me.

I was walking back to the limo with Yolanda's soft hands in mine. This was going to be a special weekend for us. I'd had the chance to meet some of her friends the previous night, and she had planned a special evening for the two of us in her city. I had my own plans. It was time to see if Miss Yolanda had been worth the wait. Just as I was looking in the window of the black sedan, making sure this was my driver, I heard someone call my name. "Mr. Henderson." When I turned around, a young man ran toward me and said, "Mr. Henderson, I was hoping I hadn't missed you. I'm a big fan of yours. Would you sign this football for me?" He was an imposing young man, brawny and tall with a warm smile and big whiskey-colored eyes. He looked like a football player.

"Sure, young man. Do you play ball?" I asked as I took his football and looked inside my jacket for a pen. Signing autographs for children and young high school and college players was one of the things I missed most about playing pro ball.

"Yes, sir. I play for Northwestern. I'm a wide receiver just like you were," he said.

"You certainly have the size for it. Congratulations on the win. Did you play today?"

"No, sir, I'm just a freshman. But already I'm number three on the depth chart. I'm just waiting for my chance," he said confidently.

"Well, by the way, what's the starter's name? I should know that."

"Bates. Bill Bates. He's a senior. Made all Big Ten," he said.

"Yeah, that's right, Bates. But you never know. I guess you know you've always got to be prepared," I advised.

"Yes, sir, I know you're right. How's your knee? I was really sorry when I heard about your injury."

"The knee is fine. Thanks for asking. What's your name? Who do you want me to sign this to?"

"My name is Kirby. Kirby Tyler. But I want you to sign the football to my father. He's a big fan also," he said.

"What's your father's name?"

"Raymond Tyler," he said proudly.

"Raymond Tyler?"

"Yes, sir. But you can just put Ray Sr."

My hand suddenly became moist with perspiration, and I stopped writing and looked up at him. I asked, "Where are you from, Kirby?"

"I'm from Birmingham, Alabama. Graduated from Ramsey High School."

"I know a Raymond Tyler from Birmingham, but I don't think he's old enough to be your father. This guy I know used to live in Atlanta and New York. He's an attorney, but he's not old enough to have a son your age," I said.

"You're probably talking about my big brother, Raymond Jr. You know my brother?"

"I think so," I said.

"Aw naw, that's mad real. He's here. He's waiting on me at the locker room door. Hold up, and I'll run over there and grab him," he said. Before I could stop him to suggest I see his brother later, he was gone.

"Isn't that something else, running into the little brother of someone you know?" Yolanda said. She had been standing there patiently and quietly. So quietly I had forgotten that she was right next to me. I wondered if my face had changed. Did she notice my reaction when I heard the name Raymond Tyler? Raymond Tyler. My past had showed up.

I kissed a man once. It shocked me. It shocked me even more when I did it again. It blew me away when I enjoyed it. Raymond Tyler was that man. While I was waiting on Kirby to return with his brother, I tried to remember what I had blocked out successfully for years. My attraction, naw, make that distraction, I had with men. I stood there, motionless, noticing only the gold and red leaves fall slowly from the trees.

Despite a cool wind blowing, my body felt warm.

"John, did you hear me?" Yolanda asked.

"What? Aw . . . baby, I'm sorry. What did you say?" I turned to face Yolanda, who looked concerned.

"I said, isn't that something, running into an old friend, and from what's walking in this direction, a fine old friend," she said as she noticed Kirby and Raymond a few feet away from the two of us. Thoughts of shame and pleasure that had taken me years to forget now flooded my mind. I felt like I was drowning in fear. Raymond was smiling, but I couldn't tell if it was a glad-to-see-you smile, or a mofo-I'm-gonna-bust-you smile.

He looked me dead in the eye when he reached to shake my hand. He seemed to look right through me to our shared past, like he was pulling the secret from me. Secrets I kept from everybody, even myself.

"Basil, what a surprise. It's so good seeing you," Raymond said.

"Indeed it is, Ray Tyler—what a surprise," I said, trying to smile, but I had the feeling it was coming off more like a chilly stare. I wanted to grab Yolanda and run for the limo, but instead, I stood there like a dumb mofo—my palms all sweaty.

"Whatsup? My kid brother tells me you're an announcer now. I thought you were still playing for New Jersey," he said.

"Naw, you know, that's all over. Had to find a new gig, you know, and this one came up. Do you live here in Chicago?"

"No, I'm just here to see if they gonna give my little bro some playing time. My partner and I live in Seattle," he said. Just as I was preparing to ask another question, I felt Yolanda nudge me, and when I looked at her, I realized I hadn't introduced her and Raymond. I slowly grabbed her hand and pulled her in front of me and said, "Let me introduce you to my lady. Yolanda Williams, meet an old friend, Raymond Tyler, Jr.," I said.

Yolanda smiled, extended her hand, and said, "Nice meeting you, Raymond. Did I hear you say you live in Seattle?"

"Nice meeting you also, Yolanda. Yeah, my partner and I built a house there. It's one of the most beautiful cities in the world." He beamed. As I looked at Raymond, I was wondering why he had referred to his *partner* twice in less than a minute. Was he trying to prove something, and did Yolanda know what he meant by "partner"? Did I even know what he meant? Raymond was one of those guys who I believed could go either way. If he ended up with a wife and kids, I wouldn't have been surprised. While I was busy thinking where this meeting was going, Yolanda and Raymond were engaged in pleasant conversation. I couldn't help but notice how handsome and confident Raymond looked in his charcoal-colored slacks and mustard-yellow V-neck sweater. He looked more muscular than I remembered.

"Doesn't that sound like a great idea, John?" Yolanda asked, interrupting my thoughts.

"What?"

"Raymond just invited the two of us to visit him . . . and what did you say your partner's name was, Raymond?" Yolanda asked as she looked toward Raymond.

"Trent. My partner's name is Trent, and I'm sure he'd love to meet the both of you. Let me give you my card, and maybe when the football season is over or when it gets too cold here in Chicago, you guys will pay us a visit," he said.

"Thank you. I'll give you one of my cards and one to your little brother, just in case he needs help getting adjusted to Chicago. You don't have family here, do you, Kirby?"

"No, ma'am," he said shyly as he looked toward Yolanda.

"First of all, baby, don't call me ma'am," Yolanda teased. "I'm old, but not that old."

"Yes, ma'am," Kirby said.

"What are you two doing this evening?" Yolanda asked. "Do you have plans for dinner?"

"Yeah, I'm sorry, but we do. I've got to help this knucklehead get settled and make sure he realizes he's up here to get an education, not just play football," Raymond said as he playfully knocked on his little brother's head.

"Maybe the next time," Yolanda said.

"Yeah, next time. Basil, it was great seeing you. I hope to hear from the both of you soon," Raymond said as he gave me his card and shook my sweaty hands once again.

"Yeah . . . you know it was good seeing you too, Ray. Nice meeting you, Kirby. Good luck with the rest of the season," I said.

"Thanks a lot! Thanks for the autograph, Mr. Henderson. Now I know what my pops is getting for Christmas," he said as he admired the football I had signed. As I watched Raymond and Kirby run toward the stadium playing catch with the football, Yolanda said, "Ain't that a blimp. A fine-looking man like that gone to the other side." I pretended not to hear.

Chapter 12

My cellular phone rang as I drove down the Dan Ryan freeway. "Hello," I said.

"What's going on, big sis? I tried reaching you at home all morning. Are you on your way to church?" Sybil asked.

"No, darling. On my way back from the airport. Dropping off that man of mine," I joked. "Is everything okay? Are the children and Martin okay?"

"Oh, everybody's just fine. I just wanted to hear my big sister's voice. I'm on my way to Sunday school," Sybil said.

"It's good hearing from you. I'm going to make it up there real soon, or better yet, we should plan a weekend where you can come here. I know this wonderful place that Riley turned me on to, where we can get facials and massages. A day spa."

"That sounds nice, but how much is it?" Sybil asked.

"Oh, don't worry about that. My treat. But I think it's around two hundred a day."

"Honey, for two hundred dollars, they are gonna have to come and clean my house for a month also," Sybil laughed.

"Girl, you are too crazy. I'm coming up on my exit. I'll call you later on tonight."

"Do that. I love you, sis," Sybil said.

"And I love you more! Give the kids and Martin a big hug and kisses from me."

"I will," Sybil said. I clicked off the phone and took the Ohio Street exit.

I arrived at Leland's a couple of hours before our scheduled meeting. John had an early morning flight back to New York, and after dropping him off at O'Hare, I decided to go and see if I could help out and find out what Leland really thought of Mr. Wonderful. The prior evening with John had been relaxing and romantic, even though there were a few times when John seemed preoccupied. When I asked him what was wrong, he said he was worried about how the executives at ESPN viewed his performance. I thought that was understandable.

I was looking forward to seeing Leland and catching up before the rest of the group arrived. When I got there, Leland and Uncle Doc were putting the final touches on the food and seemed involved in their preparations and conversations. I asked if I could help, and they both gave me a firm yet polite *no*. So I kept myself busy by wandering around Leland's condo to see if he had purchased anything new since my last visit.

I loved Leland's place. It had been decorated by the same woman who had created just the right balance of intimacy and personal comfort at his downtown office. Andrea (she gave only her first name) had met Leland at Uncle Doc's when Leland was opening up his practice and she was just beginning to build an impressive reputation as one of Chicago's finest interior designers. She had come into the restaurant trying to convince Uncle Doc to become one of her clients, but instead she had become one of Uncle Doc's regular customers. Leland told her to give up any hopes of changing Miss Thing's Wings' decor, because the only decorating done there would be by the original Miss Thing herself—Uncle Doc.

When Leland bought this upscale condo in Chicago's Streeterville area, he was lucky to get Andrea to work on both his office and condo at a reasonable price. I don't know if they did any bartering, you know, a few free sessions on his couch for a room, since Leland never really talked about who his patients were. I do know that she talked with Leland for hours over a three-week period, getting as close to him as he would allow. Assuming he let her in, Andrea discovered that my friend was a complex, sensitive man given to reflective thought. He had a quiet need for order and harmony in all things and cherished books, singers, and his solitude.

Leland had told Andrea he knew his way around the kitchen but had no real passion for cooking. Uncle Doc and I were the most frequent visitors to his home, and we usually spent hours talking in the kitchen. So she remodeled the sterile white kitchen with oak cabinets, terra-cotta countertops and floor, and a copper-plated refrigerator and oven. He installed hand-painted ceramic tiles with African symbols in the breakfast nook, where two tall chairs were tucked beneath a small oak table. Colorful woven baskets dotted the walls above the stainless-steel double sink and the six-burner stove and grill. An antique oak hutch displayed brightly colored china, cups, and a collection of lacquered gourds. Gourmet appliances and copper cookware were purchased more for Uncle Doc's use than Leland's.

Leland did little entertaining except for the occasional visiting colleague, the quarterly group meetings, and the rare romantic dinners he told me about. He wanted his home to be a comfortable reflection of what he had accomplished in life without being pretentious.

I loved the parquet floors laid throughout the condo and the creamy white walls. The furniture was a combination of European woodwork and African textiles that created a striking effect of sophistication, warmth, and comfort.

Each of us in the group had our own favorite spot in Leland's living room. I always nestled down into the corner in one of the deep-cushioned caramel-colored sofas that formed a semicircle in front of the brick fireplace. I'd snuggle up with one of the mud-cloth throw pillows where I could appreciate the carved Yoruba figures that lined the mantelpiece. Most times I'd kick off my shoes and rest my legs on the glass-topped Ashanti stool that served as a coffee table.

Dwight always anchored himself on one of the wood- and leather-backed chairs that flanked the sofas. From this vantage point, he could see past the tall palms potted in beaded baskets and the mahogany cabinet that held Leland's high-tech stereo system, and into the entryway. I think he sits there in his defensive position so he can see who's entering the room at all times.

Riley always sits center stage, claiming the entire middle sofa as her own. Leland usually sat on the antique Moroccan trunk beside the fireplace, facing the other members of the group.

Whenever Leland allows newcomers a tour of his home, the bedroom seems to draw the most praise. The headboard and frame of the massive bed were carved African mahogany. The thick down comforter and oversized pillows were fashioned from patterned African textiles of indigo and brown. A moody, unframed portrait of a male nude on the opposite wall was reflected in the large framed mirror over the bed. Black lacquered end tables posed at either side of the bed, a small French sculpture on one, a black glass reading lamp on the other. The door to the left of the bed opened into Leland's spacious walk-in closet, which in turn led into the master bath.

I could still hear the sounds of food frying and Leland's and Uncle Doc's voices, so I walked into Leland's small study. It was his sanctuary. A large L-shaped ebony desk and buffalo hide swivel chair dominated the space. A credenza stood against the wall behind the desk, covered with assorted framed photographs of friends and family, old photo albums, his Hampton degree, and his journals. A John Biggers painting of a father and son filled the wall space behind the credenza. His desk was cluttered with orderly stacks of file folders, magazines, trade publications, and mail. Well-worn psychiatry texts stood between carved elephant-head bookends I had given him, to the right of a computer and keypad. Most prominent on Leland's desk was a silver-framed photo of a smiling Donald with his arm around Leland's shoulders. A deep, red-based Oriental rug stretched from between the desk and bookcases to the worn leather couch against the shuttered windows. A brass floor lamp stood at attention next to the couch and end table that held the CD player. It was there that Leland like to sit and read or, I imagine, just sit and think. He once told me that sometimes he just sat in this room and stared at the picture of him and Donald, so happy, so long ago.

But despite the intimacy, comfort, and warmth of Leland's home, it was a study in contradiction. There was a vague sadness in the air, a sense of something missing, something lost.

While I was standing in the den thinking tenderly about Donald's last year of life, Leland walked in and hugged me from behind and whispered, "What you thinking about, doll? That new man?"

I turned and faced him and kissed him on the cheek and said, "No, baby-boy. I was thinking about you and Donald. I was missing him. How are you doing?"

"I'm all right now that everything's ready. Uncle Doc cooked up some food. You're going to have to take some of this stuff home, and I'm going to take some down to the homeless shelter," he said.

"That sounds like a plan. What time is it?"

Leland looked at his watch and said, "It's almost show time. Come on in the kitchen and let me see if Uncle Doc needs any help."

The two of us walked down the hallway into the kitchen, where Uncle Doc was removing his apron and surveying the buffet of chicken, ribs, and sides of baked beans, slaw, and potato salad. Positioned in the center of the table was a beautiful white coconut cake with strawberries dotting the edges. He heard the two of us walking close to him, and he turned and greeted me with a big smile and hug. "Hey, baby-girl. How ya doing?"

"I'm fine, Uncle Doc. Everything looks great."

"And look at you. You look fabulous," he said as he pulled for my hands and turned me in a circle like ring around the roses and gave me the Uncle Doc seal of approval.

"That new man better know what he's got hold of."

"I remind him every chance I get," I teased.

"You do that doll, and don't forget to see if he has an older brother or a daddy that can appreciate an old southern gal like myself," Uncle Doc joked.

"I can't believe you don't have people knocking down your door. I mean as sweet as you are and the way you cook," I said.

"Please don't encourage him," Leland said.

"The kids ain't lookin' for sweet these days, doll. They like them rough and tumble men. It ain't like it use to be," Uncle Doc said. "But enough about me. I'm getting out of here before your guests arrive. Now, remember, Leland, there is plenty of extra sauce and some more wings and ribs sitting in the oven. All you have to do is pull it out and dump them in the platter. But if you don't think you can do that, I can still have Thelma come over and help. The old gal should just now be gettin' home from church," he said as he looked at the gold watch on his thin wrist.

"I'll be fine, Uncle. I'll call you later on this evening so we can finish our conversation," Leland said.

"Yeah, you do that," Uncle Doc said as he headed toward the front door. Just as Leland was closing the door, the buzzer rang and the doorman announced that Riley and Dwight were in the lobby. Leland gave me a warm smile as he told the doorman to send them up. He then clapped his hands and said, "Let the games begin!"

The meeting started with Dwight suggesting that we either move the meeting to Sunday evening or Friday night since the football season had started. Every year we went through this with him, and although we usually conceded, it was three to one in favor of changing the meeting time. Since John had entered my life, I too was in favor of the change, despite John saying he was going to attend only games he was paid to cover.

Before we started to read from the journals, we talked about the recent Olympics, with Riley saying how sad she was that Dominique Dawes, the beautiful Black gymnast, had fallen during her individual events. Riley shared that she had been depressed for a couple of days after her events. Her statement led me to pose a question to the group.

"Why is it that we—meaning Black folks—take on the disappointment of people we don't even know. I know every time I hear about some tragic crime on television, I immediately begin praying . . . please, God, don't let them be Black," I said.

"I'm a card-carrying member of that club," Leland said. Riley and Dwight were silent.

"I remember when Debi Thomas was in the Winter Olympics some years ago. Honey, we had a major party the night she skated. I think it was about twenty-five of us all gathered around the television set, waiting for Miss Debi to beat that Katarina chick. But when Debi slipped on her ass in the first couple of minutes, the room was silent like somebody had died," I said.

"I remember that," Leland said. "I was at a Black gay bar in the Village in New York that night, and everybody was watching the television and it got dead quiet in there when she fell. A couple of the kids even had tears in their eyes."

"It's because we put so much hope in them. Like their success validates us as Black people," Dwight said. "And that ain't right. It's like we need to succeed in white folks' eyes to feel good about ourselves."

"I don't agree," Riley said. "I just want them to do well."

"I know one thing. I'm already sick of that little Miss broke-leg Kerri whatsherface," Leland laughed.

"I know that's right," I said as I gave him a high-five.

"See . . . we shouldn't feel bad for Dominique. She was the real star. If it hadn't been for her, the U.S. team never would have won the gold medal. She was the top scorer for the team on the night of the finals. But does the media point that out? Hell no! They had already won the medal before the little munchkin made her vault. But the great white hope hobbles away the star. Making all the bank," Dwight said.

"Dominique was the top scorer? Are you sure?" Riley asked.

"Yes, she was. But you wouldn't read it in the papers," Dwight said.

"See, I didn't even know that," Leland said. "I be damned. Learn something new every day."

We moved from the Olympics to our journals with Dwight reading something about his job. It sounded like he was headed for serious trouble, and I was wondering how he had managed to stay in corporate America so long with his strong feelings about white folks. Maybe it was because despite his personality problems, Dwight was a brilliant man. At Hampton, Dwight finished in the top five of our class, but very few people knew it until graduation because he didn't talk a lot about himself. The only way I knew was because Kelli was bragging on what a great catch Dwight was, and predicting how much money he would make.

Riley read something about how much fun she was having on the Internet in the chat areas and exchanging poetry with people she had met through her computer. She seemed happy and didn't mention her singing. We all tried to encourage her, but Dwight warned her about all the weirdos on the net, and made her promise not to give her name or phone number to anybody she met through her computer. It was really touching to see Dwight acting like a big brother toward Riley. He really seemed concerned. And Riley thanked him for his advice. She didn't say she was going to follow it, but her thanks sounded sincere.

Leland shared something about some famous political person cruising him at one of the parties I had taken him to during the Democratic Convention. He wouldn't give any names but said we all knew him and would be totally blown away. We all blushed as Leland read from his journal about what the mysterious politician had in mind for him. Riley kept quizzing him for clues, while

Dwight's only comment was he knew for sure it wasn't the now-jailed former Chicago congressman Mel Reynolds or one of his heroes, Louis Farrakhan. Leland quipped, "I'm Catholic, but I ain't a schoolgirl."

I read one of the entries I had written after helping John prepare for his first announcing gig. I told them how much fun it had been and how it had opened my eyes to another market I could attack when I was able to hire more personnel. Dwight joked he might be looking for a job and looked me dead in the face, then asked would I hire him. I smiled and said, "Of course, bro man, I'd hire you in a heartbeat."

After taking a break to eat some of Uncle Doc's delicious grub, I thought we would enter some affirmations in the group journal. But Riley had brought those cards and convinced everyone it was time to pull a card. We were having such a good time, and it seemed we were all feeling the same, because nobody protested. Not even Dwight, who offered to go first.

He pulled a card and handed it to Leland, since he was the host. "If you could ask God one question, what would it be?"

"That's easy. I'd ask if we Black people get any extra credit for putting up with white folks and all their shit while we down here on earth," he said confidently. I thought it was funny and started laughing, but Riley in a very serious tone asked Dwight if he believed in God.

"Of course I do. My mama had me in church every Sunday ever since I can remember. I think you'd have to be pretty stupid to believe man could be responsible for some of the wonderful things life has to offer. Like nature and good people you're fortunate enough to know and love." When he said this, he looked toward me and gave me a sweet, almost sensual smile. It made me slightly uncomfortable, but I smiled back.

"Aren't you asking for some type of affirmative action from God?" Leland asked.

I thought his question would change Dwight's pleasant mood, but it didn't. He just answered Leland's question without his normal defensive tone. "Not if you believe in a God that's fair. We know life here on earth hasn't been fair for a lot of people of color. So it has to be a more equitable way in heaven. To me that's not asking for special treatment," Dwight said.

"But what about white people who go through suffering themselves? Shouldn't they get some extra credit for their pain?" Riley asked.

"You've already had your question, Mrs. Woodson, but I'm feeling charitable today, so I'll answer you. God will have to decide if they deserve consideration or if they're paying the debt of some evil they committed before their bad luck."

"Let's go to the next person. Riley took my question," I said. I wasn't going to tempt fate by asking Dwight if he would worship with whites if he thought that would get him to heaven.

Riley pulled the next card and passed it to Leland. He smiled before he read the question. "Riley, your question is: What lesson has love taught you?" Riley looked at Leland and then around the room. She was silent for a moment, and then in a very eerie voice she said, "That forever isn't as long as it used to be." The three of us gazed at Riley for a few moments, and then I asked her if she believed you fall in love—real love—only one time.

"I think we're lucky if it happens that often," Riley answered.

"Do you think you need it to survive?" Dwight asked.

"I don't know about most people, but it's the one dream in my life that's never changed. To have someone love me as much as I love them," Riley said solemnly.

"Don't you think it best to have someone love you just a little bit more than you love them?" Leland asked.

"I don't think that's fair," Riley said. Now it was my turn. I pulled a card from the bag and handed it to Leland. "This must be the love-questions day," he said as he read the card. "Yolanda—what are the three most important things you look for in a potential spouse?"

"That's easy . . . the triple H," I said, laughing, because I knew they wouldn't understand my secret code.

"What's the triple H?" Leland asked.

"Honesty . . . humor . . . head—and not necessarily in that order," I said.

"You're some kinda crazy," Leland said.

"And you know it. First question."

"Since honesty is something you look for, please tell me why most women fall in love so easily with liars?" Dwight asked.

"Probably 'cause men are so good at lying," I snapped.

"Yolanda," Leland said.

"Yes, baby?"

"Do you think it better to give or receive?"

"I assume you're talking about trait number three. Both," I said. Riley had this disapproving look on her face. I started to tell her she should try it before she turned her nose up at it. Maybe that would bring Selwyn back to her side of the bed.

"Would you marry somebody who possessed only one of those traits?" Riley asked.

"Absolutely not."

Leland handed the bag to a surprised Dwight and pulled out a card and placed it in his hand and instructed him to read it.

"Aw, man . . . this is an easy one. I wish I had gotten this one. Name your favorite actress," Dwight said.

Leland put his index finger on his lip, hummed for a moment, then looked at us and said, "Can I pick two?" And then without waiting for us to respond, he said, "Of course I can, this is my house. Angela Bassett and Sheryl Lee Ralph."

"Why?" Riley asked.

" 'Cause they're both beautiful Black women who look Black and carry themselves like Black princesses. And because Donald and I saw Sheryl Lee in *Dreamgirls* over twenty-five times and each time we waited at the stage door and got her autograph and she took pictures with us. And she was always very nice," Leland said.

"Would you sleep with either one of them?" Dwight asked.

"Sure. I'd sleep with them both. I wouldn't have sex with them, but it would be a hoot to have a sleepover with them. I'd have them do scenes from their work. Like having Miss Angela dance like she did in *What's Love Got to Do With It* and then I'd have her destroy my closet with a cigarette hanging out of her mouth à la *Waiting to Exhale*. And Sheryl Lee and I would sing "When I First Saw You" and then I'd have her do a scene from *Mistress*. Did any of you guys see that movie? Miss Sheryl was fierce! If you haven't seen it, then rent it."

"I don't have any questions for you. You've answered them all," I said. I think we were all tired from Leland's nonstop oration.

After Dwight and Riley left, Leland and I were in the kitchen putting away food and cleaning up. We talked about how Riley seemed a little happier than usual. I was happy that she didn't mention the singing engagement, because she was not going to like my answer. I knew it would be a miracle if she never brought it up again. Leland joked about her new love on the computer and said he thought about going on the net to find one or running a personal. When he talked about his trouble in finding someone to date, I asked him if he ever thought he'd meet someone he would love as much as Donald.

"I don't know if that's what I'm looking for. I just want somebody I can turn to and hold, you know, after I hang up the phone from talking with you or Uncle Doc. My memories of Donald are so special that most times it's enough," he said.

"But how long are your memories going to be enough?" I asked.

"Until I meet someone who'll help me make new memories," he said.

Leland made some coffee and the two of us sat at the dining room table and talked about the upcoming week. I was walking back into the kitchen to get another cup, when Leland called my name: "Yolanda, will you do something with me? Something I think will help me start making those new memories."

"Sure baby-boy. What can I do?"

"Donald's fortieth birthday is the last week of October. I'd like the two of us to go to New York and celebrate. I want to visit some of the places he and I shared. We'll get a suite—maybe at the Four Seasons, and you and I will celebrate his birthday and his life. How does that sound?"

"Sounds like a plan to me. Do you want me to get my travel agent to make the plans?"

"No, I want to make all the plans myself. I'll keep you posted."

"You think this is what you need, baby?"

"It's a start. And I've got to start somewhere," Leland said as he took a long sip of his coffee and gazed out the window. That's when I noticed a long tear sliding down his face. I started to ask what was wrong, but I got the feeling he wanted to be alone, so I poured my second cup back into the coffeepot, walked over to Leland, and stood behind him and rubbed his shoulders for a few minutes. I kissed him on the top of his head and whispered, "You'll be fine, baby-boy. You'll be fine."

Chapter 13

I got one of those calls I had learned to dread from a patient. Taylor Wilson, a former family court judge from New Jersey, had called my service five times within an hour. I was with a patient, and when I called him about ninety minutes after his first call, I could hear the panic in his voice. He said, "Doc, I have to see you right away before I lose it." I tried to find out what the problem was, but he insisted that he needed to see me in person. I had the receptionist switch around a couple of patients, and about an hour later Taylor was knocking on my office door.

He was bothered. Taylor was huffing and puffing like he had run to my office. This patient, who was always dressed neatly, looked totally disheveled in wrinkled clothing.

"Calm down, Taylor. Tell me what happened?"

"I saw him. That motherfucker that ruined my life," he said, and then took a long drag of his cigarette. Normally I didn't allow patients to smoke in my office, but Taylor would have probably killed me rather than give up his smoke. He was pacing back and forth in the little area in front of my sofa.

"Why don't you sit down and tell me what happened," I asked gently.

"I can't believe this motherfucker is following me," he said.

I stood up from my chair and placed my pad on the floor. When I started toward Taylor, he suddenly plopped on the sofa. I took a deep sigh of relief.

"Okay, tell me about this guy."

"You know. The man who got me in the mess. The man who ended my career and my marriage. The reason I'm here right now," he said while twisting his gold wedding band.

"Are you talking about the football player that blackmailed you?"

"Who else would I be talking about?" he shouted.

"Come on now, calm down. You saw him here in Chicago? I thought you said he lived in New Jersey."

"That's what I thought."

"Did he say anything to you?"

"No, the motherfucker didn't even look my way. But I know it was him. I'll never forget that smug, arrogant sonofabitch as long as I live," he said as he reached in his shirt pocket and pulled out another cigarette.

"Where did you see him?" Part of my strategy to calm a patient down is to focus on the details, the reality of what happened versus all those wild emotions that come pounding in.

"Walking down Michigan Avenue, near the Water Tower. I was coming out of Borders bookstore when I saw him. He was looking in the window of Victoria's Secret with some lady. I wanted to run up to the lady and tell her to leave this crazy motherfucker alone. That he would ruin her life. But I punked out. I wanted to run up and just start kicking his ass. All the shit he did to me, it just all came back. All my dreams up in smoke," he said softly.

I started to say, speaking of smoke, you're going to give it up while you're in my office, but I didn't. For about ten minutes he went on ranting about how evil this man was. Taylor's horn-rimmed glasses were too low on his nose and he kept pushing them up.

Suddenly he stopped talking and stood up motionless for a second, his face vacant.

"Are you all right?" I asked after a couple of minutes of silence.

"I'm okay," he said as his voice trailed off like smoke from his cigarette.

"It's been a while since we've talked about him. Tell me what happened."

Taylor told me the story he had shared on our first meeting. How he, a promising Family Court judge in Jersey City, New Jersey, married with a child, had met a handsome pro football player at the gym. He told me how the player had befriended him, offered to be his workout partner and teach him some of the exercises that kept his body in top shape. They had become fast friends and Taylor was attracted to the player. Until this meeting he didn't consider himself gay or bisexual, since he was completely faithful to his wife. He told me in a later session that he had carried on a two-month affair with a fraternity brother his senior year of college but hadn't been with a man since he had met his wife during his first year of law school. But the handsome football player had seduced my patient, and the two became engaged in a torrid month-long affair. From the way Taylor described the sex, meeting the man had turned him out. He said all he could do was think of this man and the next time they could get together for sex. He neglected his wife and child and his work. He had even come to the conclusion that he would leave his wife for this man, when he discovered he was a pawn in a plan of revenge. It seems the player was getting a divorce from his wife of two years and didn't want her to get any of his holdings. He figured Taylor would probably get his case and had set out to meet him for a game of seduction. When he mentioned to Taylor that he had a case coming up in his court and he hoped he would look toward him favorably, Taylor told him there was no way he could hear the case. That he would have to remove himself from his friend's divorce case. That was when the old worm turned. The man threatened to expose Taylor and their affair, telling him he had taped phone conversations and even a video of the two of them getting busy. After days of deliberation, Taylor gave in and heard the case, granting his former bed partner a divorce without the penalty of alimony on the grounds that there were no children from the union. The player's betrayal had led to a nervous breakdown for Taylor, who left his wife and child to return to his boyhood home of Chicago for recovery. I was under the impression that we were headed in that direction. Now this.

"Do you really think he's following you?"

"What?"

"Do you think he knows where you live? I mean, how could he know what happened after you heard his case? Didn't you tell me that you didn't talk with him after that?"

"Yes, but he knows I'm from Chicago. In the early days of our meeting I told this man my entire history," Taylor said.

"Has he tried to contact you?"

"No."

"Then I think you don't have anything to worry about. Didn't you tell me he ended the affair even though you wanted to continue?"

"Yes, I must be a sick motherfucker to want to stay with that asshole after he played me like a fucking flute. But he changed my life."

"What do you mean?"

"I mean, when I met him and when he made love to me, it just opened a gate I thought was closed. It was like I was addicted to crack or something. I had to have him. My seemingly happy life with my wife suddenly seemed dull and lifeless. I would have done anything for him," he sighed. His face looked as though he were watching the two of them make love. He smiled and then suddenly his face darkened with a frown.

"It's normal to think back on that time in your life. But you can't let it destroy you again. I don't think he's looking for you. But if you really feel like you're in some kind of danger, you can take some measures to protect yourself. Do you think he's dangerous?"

"Hell, yeah."

"Really? Did he ever harm you physically?"

"Not really. Just the one time when I threatened not to go through with his plan. We were in the gym, and he grabbed me by the throat and pushed me against the locker, telling me he'd kick my ass and then send the tapes to my wife. I can still see those gray eyes. Those eyes I once thought were so beautiful suddenly looked like they belonged to a wild animal," Taylor said.

Gray eyes? I suddenly thought of Yolanda's new football-player friend with beautiful gray eyes. A thin film of sweat broke out over my body. This couldn't be.

"What was this guy's name?" I tried to ask calmly, though my voice wavered a bit. Taylor noticed the change in my tone and gave me a curious look and said, "Basil Henderson. Why do you ask?"

"No reason. I just don't remember you ever telling me his name," I said as I looked at my watch. I was no longer worried about my patient, but my best friend. This had to be the same man Yolanda was falling for or had already fallen in love with. The charming man I had told her to go for with a vengeance. Taylor interrupted my frightened thoughts.

"You probably don't remember his name because I always referred to him as motherfucker this and motherfucker that. I tried to forget his name, his face, that dick. I tried for the last couple of years to forget his smile and those eyes. And just when I'm getting close, this motherfucker shows up again. You know but I ain't scared of him. When I think about it, he's just a weak, simple-minded motherfucker."

"I think it's best not to let him affect you," I said. What simple-minded advice, I thought. This Basil obviously had some kind of sexual energy and power.

"Yeah, I hope the mutherfucker does come for me. This time I won't punk out. I'll kick his ass and then expose him. I wish I had gone up to the lady and warned her what a sick freak she was looking at with that look of love and lust. Women are so damn stupid."

I wanted to say men are too, but instead I said, "Time is up, Taylor. If you need me, just call my office and someone will page me immediately. I think you'll be all right. But I will increase the dosage on your medication. Just in case you have trouble sleeping again."

"Yeah, do that, Doc. More medication."

When Taylor left my office, my first reaction was to call Yolanda. To tell her the dream boy could be a nightmare. I picked up the phone and punched in the first three digits to her number, when I realized I couldn't tell her what I had just discovered. If I did, I would be breaking my professional oath. But Yolanda *had* to know.

I sat at my desk for a few minutes, trying to figure out a way to tell her about Basil without breaking my oath. I started to call Taylor and tell him I knew the woman Basil was with and would he allow me to share the information with my friend. I quickly decided against that, although it wasn't unethical. I had to consider my patient's mental state. If he thought I knew Basil, his paranoia would go through the roof. I thought of writing an anonymous note to Yolanda and dropping it in the mail. But I didn't know what to say, and I would still be breaking a doctor-patient confidence.

Maybe I was losing my ability to spot men who were hiding something with their sexuality. When I met Basil, he displayed a quiet and confident macho image. Now, I know there are thousands and thousands of gay and bisexual men who are tough and strong, but I just didn't pick up any vibe from Basil. Besides, I knew Yolanda always questioned the men she dated about being gay or bisexual. I had taught her how to ask the question and to recognize when she was getting the correct answer or an out-and-out lie.

What if she hadn't asked Basil this question, and if she did, what did he say?

Chapter 14

Let me make one thing clear. I am not gay. I'm not even what people call bisexual. I'm a pussy-loving, pussy-eating, one-hundred-percent man. Believe that. But I have on occasion strayed to the other side, for a purpose.

I've used men for being the dogs that we are. I try my damnedest to punish them for the shit they do to women and for trying to mess over me when I didn't know any better. I wouldn't be talking about this shit if I hadn't run into Raymond Tyler in Chicago. It really f'd up my entire weekend. I think I could have finally got the draws from Yolanda Saturday night, but I kept thinking about Raymond and that period in my life. Every time the phone rang, I flinched. After Yolanda fell asleep, I pulled his card out of my wallet and just stared at it. I started to tear it up and flush it down the toilet, but I decided to keep it. I was happy Yolanda didn't bring his name up. Sometimes women start tripping when they find out their man knows somebody gay. Yolanda seems cool with gay men, but I know she's not going to give up the draws to a man who goes both ways. When she asked me if I was gay or bi, I acted like I was convinced she was just teasing. I said, "I don't roll like that." It hasn't come up again.

I met Raymond in New York in the late eighties. He's a cool brother, and, I must admit, I enjoyed his company. I dug Raymond because he's not like a lot of faggot mofos I know. I catch them in the gym, trying to check out a brother's kibbles and bits. I've run into them in locker rooms in both college and the pros. We used to call them DWs in college, which stands for dick watcher. A lot of that shit goes on in the locker room. But can't nobody call me a DW. I keep my eyes on my own shit.

When I was in college, some of my team supporters would give a brother a few dollars to let them suck you off. We used to call them jock sniffers. I was game 'cause I didn't have much money. The way the NCAA rules work, I couldn't work while I was playing college ball. So what was I supposed to do? I had to have my clothes together 'cause women have always loved the way I dress. My dad tried to help out, but he wasn't making that much as a truck driver. My aunt Lois would send me a couple dollars every once in a while, but she had her own children to support. But these rich white boys had the ducats, and they didn't mind sharing them with a good-looking brother like myself.

Most of them were big shots in the community and married, so it wasn't like I had to worry about them talking, like some do. I've had to bust a few sissies for approaching me the wrong way in public. I don't know how my shit got out, 'cause I don't mess around with a whole lot of men. There were two Black punks in college, but that was because I needed one of them to type a term paper for me, and the other one had the best reefer in Miami. Thank God I don't smoke that shit anymore. When I've been with a dude, it wasn't any of that crazy shit you hear about. Just them servicing me. I mean, I didn't kiss them or anything. For me, kissing is serious, more so than sticking your dick in some warm place. I did kiss Raymond a couple of times, but like I said, he was different. Don't ask me why, he just was. You'd never catch me laying up in bed with some guy reading the sports page. I don't dig men that way.

Man, I guess when this starts—it starts. When I got back to New York, there were a trio of messages on my machine from this dude, Monty. I used to kick it with him about a year ago. He's in this hot R & B group, and his first message said he was just back from a European tour. I didn't even notice the mofo was gone.

I always figured Monty was cool, 'cause he had just as much to lose as I did. I met him at one of those Hollywood parties. I could tell he was a player like me. I mean, the women were all over him. And when the brother started singing—well, you could hear the panties dropping. I was a little surprised when he made his play for me, and it was kinda strange how he busted me.

The two of us started hanging out whenever he'd come to the East Coast to record. We'd shoot hoops, go to the malls over in Jersey, and run the ladies at some of the clubs. Once, we had a three-way with this stripper we met at Champs, one of the tittie bars. Another time we got these two strippers to make out while we jacked off, watching. One evening we were hanging out pretty late, and Monty spent the night at my place 'cause it was raining and shit. I had a custom-made bed big enough for four or five mofos, so he really wasn't putting me out. That's when he made his move. First our knees accidentally bumped: Then I felt his toes touch mine. Then old boy pretended like he was asleep, and his hands started going places they didn't have no business being. I knew what was up. But I didn't give in. I started to say something to Monty the next morning, but I let it slide.

A few weeks later I was over at his hotel and we were having a drink before we went out to run the women. We were drinking beer and I had to go to the bathroom a lot. On my third quick trip to the can I left the door open, and just as I was shaking my stuff, I looked up in the mirror and saw Monty coming in the bathroom. He shut the door behind him, and the next thing I know, old boy was on his knees sucking my stuff like he was a milking machine. I started to push him away, but my stuff was harder than Chinese algebra. I closed my eyes, and all I could hear was Monty's slurping sound and his head banging against the bathroom door.

When he finished, Monty didn't say a word. Just reached in his medicine cabinet, pulled out some mouthwash, and turned the bottle up like it was a carton of milk. He swished, spit, and walked back out of the bathroom. I stood there tripping, with my shit still hanging. He didn't say anything and neither did I. I was cool with that.

Later that night, after we got back to his place, I asked him how he knew I wouldn't go crazy on his ass. I wanted to make sure he hadn't heard any rumors. "I knew you'd be down," he said. Monty told me that when the two of us were out, he'd watch my eyes. Even when I was wearing sunglasses, he said, he could see my eyes following women and men. Ain't that some shit? Said our eyes were going the same places, so he knew I was game. I didn't say shit. Monty musta been checking me out all along. So we started kickin' it every now and then. It was cool. No pressure. We both still ran the women and we never talked about what happened at night. Like I said, he had as much to lose as I did. His picture was on the cover of *Right On, The Source*, and *Vibe*, on the walls of thousands of teenage girls and probably under the beds of a couple of teenage boys. Monty was kind of a sex symbol, so he had to keep his mouth shut.

But I'm not calling his ass back. If he calls me again, he'll get answering machine 24-7. I'm into women exclusively now. I got a good thing going with Yolanda and I ain't about to fuck it up. This is a woman who can change my life. So it's later for the dudes. And that includes Raymond Tyler, Jr. Believe that.

I'm gonna call Yolanda and find out when she's going to be back in New York. If it's not in the next couple of days, I'm going to get on a plane and carry my ass back to Chicago to close the deal. It's time for Ms. Yolanda Williams to hook up with a *real* man.

•   •   •

I wonder what it would feel like to make love to John. I thought we would have done the do on Saturday night, but it didn't happen. I could sit and fantasize about John Basil Henderson all day, but I'm worried about my baby-boy, Leland. He's been on my mind all day. I was sitting in a meeting with the Park West people and all I could think of was him. Even when I met my play little sister, Jazmine, after school, I was thinking of Leland. Jazmine asked if everything was all right and I told her I was fine, just worried about a good friend. It seems like he's still living in the past. How I wish someone like Donald would enter his life again. Too bad John's friend, Raymond, is attached. If he wasn't, I'd put Leland on the first thing jetting to Seattle. I know that's not realistic, but I want him to be happy. I want him to have someone in his life besides me and the group and Uncle Doc. Maybe I'll ask John just how serious Raymond is with this partner of his. Who knows, it may be just a casual relationship, and Raymond could be interested in knowing another gay man when he comes to visit his brother. What if his brother is gay? No, that wouldn't work, he's too young. Leland and I both have a rule of never dating anyone under the age of twenty-five.

I don't know what going to New York and visiting the places Leland and Donald used to frequent will do. Maybe he'll finally be able to say good-bye or maybe his trip will simply make those memories stronger. I'm going to go with him because I promised. But I think I'll talk to him and try and determine what he hopes to accomplish on this trip.

It's not like Leland talks about Donald constantly. But sometimes when he's quiet and has this far-off look in his eyes, I know he's thinking about him. I remember when Donald died. Leland and I weren't as close then as we are now. All I said was that I was sorry to hear his friend had died. I didn't say spouse or lover, but I knew they were closer than friends. My other gay friends who died were usually alone at the end. When my girl-friends have lost a husband or significant other, I've made a big deal out of it. I've sent over flowers, or fruit baskets, or even baked a cake. I didn't even send Leland a card. From what Leland told me, and from what I've gathered from Uncle Doc, Leland never left Donald's side. He even took a leave of absence from his residency program to spend every second with Donald during his first bout of pneumonia Now, that's love. Lifelong love. I can tell from the pictures of them together that they were in love, that secure look in their eyes. I guess memories like those are hard to forget.

·   ·   ·   ·

Riley splashed her face with lukewarm water and patted it dry with a cotton towel. Then she rubbed some aloe vera lotion into her hands and moisturized her face and neck. Riley had just finished a productive workout with her newly hired personal trainer, Jack. Riley hired him after interviewing two other candidates, including a beautiful, well-toned Black woman, Janice, who Riley thought was just a little too perky. She had also passed on Willie, a super-buffed Black guy who Riley thought was a bit arrogant. She settled on the muscular brown-eyed, blond Jack when he convinced her she could shed fifteen pounds in less than a month if she went along with his exercise and diet plan.

Jack had brought a scrapbook full of before-and-after pictures, as well as his certification as a personal trainer, something neither Janice nor Willie produced. If she was ever going to get down to a weight where she could wear one of her Barbara Bates evening gowns, Riley needed someone who meant business.

With the addition of her daily workouts, and her preparations for her opening at Park West, Riley had little time for her computer romance. She was still excited when she received messages, and early that morning she had completed the final draft of a poem she had written especially for Lonelyboy. Before sending the poem to him, she read her words aloud in front of the full-length bathroom mirror:

" 'Blue,' by Riley Denise Woodson," she said with a dramatic tone.

"I stood in the sunlight
Watching the sky change
From blue to gray to rain
Then back to blue
I was surrounded by blue
So I bathed in it
I let it seep deep into my pores
And I found peace there
I decided I'd never leave
Then out of nowhere
You appeared
And like a voyeur
You watched as I caressed my own skin
Massaging in more blue
Rubbing blue across my lips
Washing my hair
With Blue"

Riley paused like there was some serious music playing in the background and pursed her lips. She took the first sheet of yellow paper and moved it beneath the second sheet and continued:

"You were a vision
Dressed in white
Flaunting places I'd never seen
Or been before
And you opened up your arms to me
But you left one hand
On a rainbow
With the other hand
You extended
A pot of shiny new gold
And you said

'Don't rush, gold lasts forever'
So I withdrew my hand
Now I wait
For you to give me your gold
With both hands
Free"

Just as Riley was walking toward her office to send the poem, her private line in her bedroom rang. She picked up the phone and said, "Hello."

"Have you talked to Ryan?" her mother asked.

"Hello to you too, Mother. I talked to her a couple of days ago. Why?"

"Well, you should get on that phone right now and give her a call. How can you go a couple of weeks without talking to your children?" she asked in a voice full of judgment. Riley suddenly felt like she was in high school and her mother was scolding her for not calling when she was running late from school or twirling practice.

"I've been busy, Mother. What's going on with Ryan?" Riley asked, realizing it had been more than a couple of days since she had talked with either of her children. She had been busy and was trying to give them time to get adjusted to being away from home.

"Busy, my butt. I'm not telling you. That's your child. Call her and see. I'm through raising your children, Riley."

"Mama, what's the matter? Why are you giving me all this grief? Is my child all right?" Riley asked anxiously.

"Don't mama me. Call her and see," her mother said. Riley suddenly heard the dial tone.

She rushed to her office and located Ryan's dorm number. It was about two o'clock in Virginia and she knew Ryan had a biology lab in the afternoon, but she decided to call and leave a message with her roommate or on the answering machine. She was surprised when a deep voice answered the phone.

"I'm sorry. I must have the wrong number," she said.

"Who ya lookin' for?"

"Oh, I have the wrong number," Riley repeated.

"Are you lookin' for Ryan or Darcey?" he asked.

"I'm looking for Ryan Woodson."

"Hold on a minute," he said. Riley could hear the man say "I think it's yo moms."

"Hello," Ryan said.

"Ryan? Are you all right? Who was that answering your phone?" Riley asked.

"Hello to you too, Mother. Of course I'm all right. Whatsup?"

"Whatsup? Whatsup? Who is that answering your phone?"

"Oh, that's my boyfriend, Perry," Ryan said casually.

"Your boyfriend, Perry? Ryan, you haven't been up there two months. And why aren't you in class?"

"I didn't feel well, so I skipped. But don't worry, it's nothing. Perry's taking good care of me," Ryan said.

"Taking care of you? Then why is your grandmother calling me sounding all worried," Riley asked.

"I don't know. I talked to her a couple of times, but I told her everything was fine," Ryan said.

"Obviously, she doesn't think you're fine and I'm beginning to have my doubts also. Do I need to come up there?"

"Naw, Mama, please, everything is cool. Grandma's just tripping. I'm cool. I'll be back in class tomorrow. How's Daddy? Is he still coming up here this month? Are you coming with him?"

"He's all right and I think he's still coming. I don't know about myself. How's your brother?"

"He was fine the last time I saw him. Same old Reggie smile—basketball and books in hand," Ryan said.

"The last time you saw him? When was that?" Riley asked.

"A week ago. He was on his way to the library."

"A week ago? That's not like you, not seeing your brother every day. Ryan, are you sure you're all right?"

"I'm busy, Reggie's busy, and I guess you've been busy too. We're

only twins, not joined at the hip. Chill, Mama. Gotta go. Love ya,"
Ryan said. Again Riley heard the dial tone.

 *I wanted to pick up the phone and call Yolanda and say
girl, ask this guy again if he's gay or bisexual. Ask him if
he's been tested for HIV. But how can I do that without
breaking my patient's confidence? I'm still hoping that
Taylor is wrong. That there is some mistake. That we're talking about two
different people. I've been thinking a lot about my brief meeting with John.
He seemed like a nice guy. I didn't really have my gaydar on, because
Yolanda's usually pretty good about picking up signals. Most times when
guys are undercover, I can still tell by their actions. But John just seemed
confident, at ease, like he wasn't hiding a thing.*

*Maybe he's one of those guys from the early eighties, before AIDS, who
didn't think nothing about letting a guy go down on him or go a little
further if he could benefit from it. They never identified themselves as gay
or bisexual. And when AIDS came out, a lot of these men disappeared from
the scene. Back to the arms of their wives and girlfriends. Over the years
I've had more patients like him than I can count. But if Taylor's correct,
then John has been dipping recently, and from Taylor's description of their
affair . . . often. I do recall Taylor telling me he had tested negative for
HIV, but I don't remember if he's clear about practicing safe sex. I hope he
calls for another emergency appointment. I need to know more.*

Chapter 15

I was glad to be back in Chicago for longer than a couple of days. It was Thursday. It was a little after six, and I was headed home for an evening of takeout and television. It had been a busy day with me playing catch-up with some of my local clients and ending with an unpleasant meeting with my accountant, who informed me I was spending too much money on New York hotels. He suggested I look for a tiny studio if I was going to spend as much time there as I had the previous two months. I hadn't decided if I was ready to make such a commitment.

Thursday was my favorite night to climb in bed and watch *Living Single* and then switch over and watch *Seinfeld* and *ER*. But just as I was about to grab my bag and briefcase, my phone started ringing. Monica had already left for the evening, so I grabbed the phone after a couple of rings.

"Media Magic, Yolanda speaking."

"Yolanda, hey girl. This is Lajoyce."

"Lajoyce, how are you doing? I was going to call you first thing in the morning. What can I do for you," I asked.

"Just want to finalize the showcase we're doing. Have you booked an opening act?"

"No, not quite. I have a few people and a couple of groups in mind," I said.

"Great. As soon as you get some tapes on the acts you're considering, please overnight them to my office. I wanted to let you know that the guys would prefer a female opening act. It can be a solo artist or a group," she said.

"Any particular reasons why?" I asked.

"Think about it, darling. They're young, heterosexual men in a new city," Lajoyce laughed.

"You don't have to say another word," I said. "I'll have some tapes in your office early next week."

"I might have another project I want you to work on. When are you coming back to New York?"

"I can come anytime. What's the project?"

"It's top secret right now. But I think you'd be perfect!"

"Thank you for thinking of me. Whenever you're ready to talk about it, let me know. I can be in your office in a heartbeat," I said.

"Okay, Yolanda. Thanks a lot. I know you're going to do a super job," Lajoyce said.

"I'll do my best," I said. As soon as I hung up the phone, it rang again. It was Riley. It was as though she was sitting in the outer office listening to my conversation with Lajoyce.

"Yolanda, I haven't talked to you in a couple of days. I wanted to know what the people in New York thought of my tape. I've been practicing, working out, and I got some fierce gowns I've thinking about wearing. When do you think you can let me know something definite?" Riley asked. I started to say I can let you know now, but I was a chickenshit and said, "Riley, I'm still waiting to hear something. As soon as I do, you'll be the first one I call. But I want to warn you. I think they want a group."

"Why?"

"That I can't answer. Oops, I'm sorry, there's someone at my door and I'm here by myself. I'll talk with you later," I lied. Or at least I assumed I was telling a little tale, then I heard someone knock at my door. This late in the evening it was usually a courier picking up a package, but I remember Monica telling me she would take our overnight packages and drop them off on her way out. I went to the door and looked through the peephole and saw a white guy in a black suit, white shirt, and a hat.

"Can I help you?" I asked without opening the door. I looked at the lock to make sure it was turned south.

"Is there a Miss Yolanda Williams here?" he asked.

"Yes, who's asking?"

"Ma'am, my name is David, and I'm with the Desire Limo company. I have a pickup scheduled," he said.

"A pickup? I didn't order a limo," I said.

"I know, Miss Williams. There is a gentleman waiting on you downstairs in my car. A Mr. John Henderson," he said.

A smile broke out over my face a mile long. No wonder John wanted to know what time I was leaving the office. I opened the door and greeted the limo driver with a smile and a question, "He's downstairs?"

"Yes, Miss Williams, he is."

"Let me get my jacket," I said. I rushed back to my office to grab my jacket and bags and stuff, when the phone rang again. "What's going on," I shouted in exasperation. The phone wouldn't stop.

"Yolanda here," I answered.

"Yogi, what are you doing?"

"Leland! Hey, baby-boy. I'm on my way out. What's going on?"

"Do you have plans for dinner? I need to talk with you," he said quietly.

"I think I do. Are you all right?"

"Yeah, I'm okay. I just need to talk with you about something," he said.

"Can it wait until tomorrow? You know it's Friday. Our regular date night," I said.

"Oh, yeah. I guess so. You sound like you're in a hurry."

"Yes, I am. John is downstairs waiting on me," I said.

"I didn't know he was in town," Leland said.

"I didn't either until a few moments ago. He surprised me. Isn't that wonderful?"

"I guess," Leland said. He really sounded depressed, but he was usually so strong. Whatever was bothering him could wait until tomorrow, when I would try and cheer him up.

"Do you want me to ask him about his friend Raymond?" I asked.

"Raymond? What friend? What are you talking about?" Leland asked.

"Didn't I tell you about John's good-looking friend we ran into when he was here? The one that's gay," I said. "Remember I told you how fine he was."

"Naw, I don't remember. But don't worry about it. My plate is full," Leland said.

"I gotta run, Leland. Who knows? This night might be the night," I said cheerfully.

"Yolanda."

"Yes?"

"Be careful. Please be careful," he said sadly. I started to ask him what he meant, but I just said, "I'm always careful. You know that. I'll see you tomorrow."

When I got downstairs, David opened the door to the limo, and there he was, John Henderson, looking so handsome with a big smile on his face and pink roses in his hands. After the day I had endured, the smell of roses delighted me.

"Hey, sweet-lips. Looks like we're off on another adventure," he said.

"But, John, no out-of-town trips. I've got meetings tomorrow," I said.

"I promise to keep it local. Get in," he instructed.

I threw my bags to the floor of the limo and climbed in the plush backseat. Inside, John greeted me with a soft, simple kiss and then pulled me closer with a deeper kiss and definitely more tongue. He tasted and smelled great. His breath smelled of cinnamon and he was wearing cologne. John was dressed in a symphony of blue. Cobalt-blue silk pants and a matching shirt. I suddenly wondered what he was wearing under all his blue. Maybe tonight I would find out.

John had made reservations at one of Chicago's most popular restaurants, Lola's, a place I had heard of but had never been. When I asked him how he knew about Lola's, he said the concierge at his hotel had recommended it. As we drove over toward Wells Street, I enjoyed looking at John and a spectacular autumn sunset coming in through the clear sunroof. The sky was painted with coral and gold colors that were creeping into the heavens. I wasn't able to enjoy the view for long, because minutes later David was opening the back door.

I was impressed the moment I walked into Lola's. It was a forties-style supper club that had the feeling of a sexy theatrical production. I felt sexy although I was still wearing the buttermilk-white suit I had worn all day. There were murals on the walls, palm-leaf chandeliers, and golden ringtail monkeys accenting the bar, while a soaring ceiling crowned the main room. The crowd was mixed with both Black and white people, I noticed Allison Payne of WGN (Dwight's favorite) and Jon Kelly (my personal favorite), one of Chicago's handsome sportscasters talking at the bar with another lady I didn't recognize. I started to go over and introduce myself, but I didn't want to talk business. My John walked up to the hostess stand, whispered something to a beautiful brunette, and moments later we were seated at a velvet booth in the back of the crowded restaurant.

We hadn't been seated for longer than a minute when a waiter came up and welcomed us to Lola's and asked what we wanted to drink.

"I'll have a brandy and the lady will have the same," John said.

"No alcohol for me. I've got a busy day tomorrow. I'll just have cranberry and club soda with a twist of lime," I said.

"Are you sure? Maybe just a glass of wine?" the waiter asked.

"Yeah, come on, Yolanda. Just a glass of wine," John said.

"No, I think I'll stick with the cranberry juice. Maybe I'll have some wine a little later," I said. The waiter told us about the specials and John ordered oysters and salads and instructed the waiter to give us a few minutes before we ordered. He laid the menu facedown, and looked me in the eye and said, "So . . . you glad to see me?"

"Of course, I'm always glad to see you. But why didn't you tell me? Do you have another assignment in the area? Is that why you're here?"

"No. The only assignment I have is to make sure my lady has the evening of her life. I'm here to please you and you alone," he said.

"I see. But what is it going to cost me?" I teased.

"Nuthin' but your heart," John said as he took my hand, lifted it to his lips, and kissed it ever so gently. I was getting weak and was thankful I was sitting down.

"Have you heard any more from ESPN? Are they going to give you another assignment soon?" I asked.

"They've talked to my agent. But, come on, Yolanda, no business tonight. I just want to concentrate on you," he said, and he lifted my hand and kissed it, and then gave me the most irresistible smile.

After a wonderful meal of lobster and asparagus, all I wanted to do was crawl in my bed and sleep. But I could tell John had other things on his mind. I suggested that we go to my place, but he said his hotel, the Tremont, was only a few minutes away and that I had promised to have at least a glass of wine. So I agreed to go back to his hotel room with him for a glass of wine, mind you. We cuddled up in the back of the limo and toasted the evening with plastic cups of sparkling water the limo company provided. He put his big strong arms around my shoulders, and I laid my head on his firm chest. We rode the rest of the way in silence. There was no need for words. It was all so right, so perfect.

The limo slowed as it came to the front of the hotel's luxurious lobby. David got out and came around to open our door. John exited first, and I saw him hand the driver a single folded bill and then dismiss him for the evening. I was thinking I would take a taxi back to my office for my car, but I was also thinking I was exactly where I wanted to be, with the man I wanted to be with.

When we walked into the small but elegant suite, I noticed a platter of fresh fruit, a bottle of champagne, sparkling apple cider, and Evian. John read the white note card and smiled. "The management's glad I'm here," he said.

"Where's the rest room?" I asked. John pointed to an open door and I took my bag and went in and freshened my makeup. When I came out, John was on one knee in front of the fireplace. A fireplace I hadn't noticed.

"That's so romantic. Too bad it's not cold enough to use the fireplace," I said.

"Says who? Wait a few minutes. I've cranked up the air conditioner. Trust me, it will be cold enough in a matter of minutes," he said as he stood. The fire began to blaze, and the warm glow framed his stunning physique. He was one handsome man.

John dimmed the lights, took my hand in his, and walked us over to the pearl-gray sofa in front of the fireplace. He clasped his hands behind my back and gently embraced me. He was so tender.

"Yolanda," he whispered in my ear. "My beautiful Yolanda." He said my name like he was tasting each syllable. He licked my earlobe, then traced the outline of my ear with his tongue. He softly blew on my ear, then I felt his tongue on my neck. He kissed my neck ever so lightly and lowered his hands to my hips. I buried my face into the curve of his neck.

"Ooh, Yolanda," he said as he kissed my face and cupped my ass in his powerful hands. "Is everything you got this tight, baby?"

I pushed back from him slightly and began to unbutton his shirt. When his shirt slipped open and I felt the smoothness of his skin I was so ready, but I reminded myself to make sure the condom comes out before the penis goes up. He grabbed my hands in his.

"Naw, baby, tonight's your night. Let me do this for you." He asked me to guide his hands wherever I'd like. I placed them on my stomach and slid them slowly up to my chest. He massaged my breasts gently at first, then held them firmly. He bent down and sucked my nipples through my blouse, leaving wet circles on the pale blue silk. The skin around my nipples tingled and tightened.

He tilted my chin up toward him and kissed me so long and so good that I didn't realize he'd removed my blouse until it fell at my feet. I could feel his proud erection through his slacks.

"Take it all off, baby. I want to see you."

I kicked off my shoes, then reached under my skirt and removed my panty hose. John wrapped his arm around my waist and unzipped my skirt, then stepped back as it dropped silently to the floor. He walked over to me and unhooked my bra, and my breasts fell free in the warm air of the room.

"You're so beautiful, baby."

I stood there naked except for my French-cut bikini panties. The heat of the fire was at my back and the glow of John's smile before me. I felt so beautiful.

He placed one hand on my shoulder and turned me around. "Damn, damn, damn, baby. Look at you." He pressed himself to me, and I could feel him behind me unbuckling, then stepping out of his slacks so fast that he almost fell. I cupped my mouth to keep from laughing. John's shirt fell beside my blouse, and I could feel his muscular chest on my bare back. He reached around and rubbed the palms of his hands across my erect nipples. I threw my head back against him and slid his hands down between my legs.

John dropped to his knees and pulled my panties down with his teeth. He turned me toward him and nuzzled his face in the soft down of my pubic hair. When his tongue found the spot, I thought I was going to pass out.

He rose to his feet and led my trembling body to the sofa. He sat and pulled me toward him.

"Come here, Yolanda." I started to sit beside him. "Naw, baby, sit here. Sit your beautiful ass right here." He stroked himself with one hand. I could see the head of his penis protruding from the elastic waistband of the body-fitting briefs he wore. He stood and slipped his briefs off with his free hand, then pulled me to him. My heart was pounding at seeing him completely nude, his ass the perfect curve.

"I don't want to spoil the moment," I said, "but you do have a condom, don't you?"

"Back in a flash," he said as he raced naked into the adjoining bedroom. I decided to surprise him, so I followed him, and when he turned with the packaged condom in his mouth, I slowly removed it and kissed him softly—loving the citrus-like smell of him. We moved toward the bed, and I watched him place the condom on his still-erect penis. He then moved his body on top of mine in a motion so fluid, it seemed choreographed. It was like our whole bodies were kissing as I opened my legs and he pressed the weight of his body inside me so deeply, it felt as though he had located my center and then some.

"Does it feel good, Yolanda?" he panted as our bodies rose and fell in unison. "It feels good to you! Don't it, baby? Tell me how it feels, baby. You like having all this man inside of you? Tell me, baby."

We rode to ecstasy, twisting and turning, and arrived at the same time. I shouted out his name, "Oh, John, John . . . John," as one sexual wave followed another until I was totally spent. I collapsed breathless onto John's sweaty chest. And though I replayed it in my mind in slow motion—each kiss, each touch—I knew we had entered the room only minutes before. I had to smile at John's smoothness, and my entire body was flooded by his tenderness and compassion.

As the two of us nestled in the luxury of the king-sized bed covered with crisp ivory sheets, I whispered, "Thank you, John Basil Henderson."

"Don't thank me yet, Yolanda," he whispered back in his silky voice. "The best is still to come."

Chapter 16

Friday, I tried to reach Yolanda after each patient. No luck. She wasn't answering at home and Monica said she didn't expect her in the office until later. I was so preoccupied with trying to reach Yolanda that I'd forgotten that my next patient was Taylor. Today his clothing looked neatly pressed, and he seemed a lot calmer than when I'd seen him earlier in the week. The increased dosage of his medication was helping, he said. When he voiced a lingering concern about running into Basil again, I took it as an opening to get more information.

"What would you say to him if you did run into him?"

"I don't know," Taylor said.

"Are you sure? It sounds like you're still harboring a great deal of anger," I said.

"This motherfucker ruined my life," he said.

"Do you take any responsibility for allowing him to do this," I asked gently.

"What do you mean?"

"You did enter the relationship on your own free will, right?" I thought Taylor's paranoia and denial might be exaggerating Basil's cruelty in the situation, so I wanted him to see his role in the affair very clearly.

"I guess so. It's just that I didn't know what kind of person he was. If I had, I never would have given him a second look," Taylor said.

"What do you mean?"

"It's not just that he played with my emotions. He became mean about it. Even when I agreed to do what he wanted."

"Explain." Maybe Taylor would contradict himself. Again I was hoping Basil wasn't as evil as Taylor made him sound.

"Before his case even hit my docket, he would call my house, and when my wife answered, he would hang up. When he called and I answered, he would tell me that he wanted me to know he could reach me whenever he wanted."

"What did he mean by that?"

"He didn't have my phone number. I mean, I didn't *give* him my number. It's unlisted. When we got together, I either called or paged him. He knew I was married, so he understood. The first time I heard his voice on the other end of my home phone, I almost lost it," Taylor said.

"Did you ask him how he got your number?"

"Yes."

"What did he say?"

" 'I have my ways.' "

"Taylor, have you thought any more about resuming your marriage?"

"Yes, but my wife wants to make sure I'm cured," he said softly.

"Cured?" I knew what he meant, but I wanted him to put it in his own words. It still amazed me that so many intelligent folk thought somebody could be "cured" of their sexuality.

"Yes. She says she won't even consider taking me back unless I can promise her that I will never sleep with another man. That this phase of my life is over."

"How do you feel about that?"

"I love my wife," he said firmly.

"Okay, but what if you run into Basil again or someone like him?"

"There's nobody out there like Basil Henderson." He paused. "Nobody." When he spoke again, his voice was earnest and calm. "It's almost like he has some secret, eerie powers. You can see it in his eyes. If you met him, you'd know what I'm talking about."

"Did you practice safe sex?"

"For the most part. I didn't always with the oral stuff," Taylor said.

"Let's forget about Basil Henderson for a minute. What if you meet another man and find yourself attracted to him? What are you going to do then?"

"I won't allow anything to happen. I have control over that now. I'll stay away from certain places. If a man gives me the look, I'll turn away. I want to save my marriage and what's left of my career."

"Would you go back on the bench? You took a leave of absence, didn't you?"

"Yes, but I couldn't put the robe back on, knowing what I've done. I'm not worthy of the robe or the faith people put in me." I started to ask Taylor would he feel that way if he was "cured," but I didn't.

"Maybe you're being too hard on yourself. Though I don't think you've faced up to the real problem," I said.

"What do you mean?"

"Dealing with your bisexuality," I said. Looking over my notes on Taylor, I had noticed how much he had talked about what his family and peers would think. How important his marriage was for appearance's sake. Earlier he told me how much he loved his son, and how his wife had threatened to keep him away from his child unless he got some help.

"I kept it in check for all those years, I can do it again," Taylor said. "I can find other ways to satisfy that side of me," he added confidently.

"How so?"

"You know, I have a porn collection I used to keep in my office. I gave it to a friend for safekeeping. I can look without touching," he said. We didn't have enough time to pursue how empty that might prove in the long run. So I focused on what was working for him at this moment.

"So the medication is helping?"

"Yeah, I don't feel so helpless." I looked at my watch and realized Taylor's time was up. I still hadn't gotten any information that would help me with regard to Yolanda.

"Good, that's good. Taylor, I see here in your records you haven't taken another HIV test since you've been back in Chicago. Is that still true?"

"Yes, that's true."

"Don't you think maybe you should?"

"I can't deal with that right now. Besides, we always practiced safe sex and Basil told me he was HIV-negative."

"Can you trust this Basil guy on something so important?"

"I guess not. But isn't oral sex safe without a condom?"

"The verdict is still out on that. You don't have to make a decision right now. Just think about it," I said.

Taylor stood and stretched his long, thin arms. "I'm not making any promises, Doc, but I'll think about it."

I stood up and opened the door. "Do that," I said. Maybe there was hope for Taylor. When I walked him into the reception area, the receptionist said she had a message from Yolanda canceling our regular Friday-evening date.

"Was that all she said?" I asked her.

"Yes, Dr. Thompson."

"How did she sound?"

"Excuse me?" she asked with a puzzled look on her face.

"I'm sorry, did she sound okay to you?"

"She sounded very happy. Like a woman in love, if you ask me," she said cheerfully.

Let's pray you're wrong, I thought.

· · ·

In the lingering warmth of an early October evening, Dwight walked into a crowded bar near Navy Pier. He promised himself that he was too old and serious for the happy-hour scene, but there he was, standing amid a group of well-dressed, mostly Black professionals. His reasons for being there were different from when he used to come looking for a weekend, maybe a month if she was good, romance. He was a former card-carrying member of the new pussy club. But the older Dwight got, the more he wanted something more permanent, like he once had with Kelli.

Tonight it was strictly business and he came armed with business cards and a stack of newly revised résumés in his black leather portfolio. Dwight had a feeling he'd be looking for a job soon, and First Fridays were a good place to start. Popular for years with those looking for love and/or career opportunities, First Fridays were sponsored by the local chapter of the National Association of Black MBAs, and Dwight was a paying nonparticipating member. The couple of meetings he attended had bored Dwight to sleep.

All week long the sales management at Dwight's office had been hounding him to reconsider his position. One manager had even told him if the company didn't get this million-plus deal, they might have to lay off some employees. At the very least, they said year-end bonuses would be next to nothing. But Dwight had stood his ground, offering a two-page memo detailing why MedMac didn't need the proposed equipment. He had even offered to identify existing customers who might actually need the equipment. But no one wanted to hear what Dwight had to say. All they wanted was for him to sign the proposal and keep his mouth shut. Dwight told them he couldn't do that. They threatened to take him off the account. He sat silent and rigid in a chair, grimacing his disapproval. The sales manager, Kent Larson, became so unnerved by Dwight's steely gaze, he chain-smoked three cigarettes in the office's smoke-free environment. When Dwight finally broke the silence by saying he had some calls to make and asked if there was anything else, the manager puffed out a weak no.

While he was deciding if he should have a drink before he passed out his first résumé, he felt someone come up behind him and place hands over his eyes.

"Guess who?" a squeaky female voice asked.

The voice didn't sound familiar, but the hands were soft and sweet-smelling. "You got me. Who is it?" Dwight asked as he felt the hands move from his eyes. He turned around and saw a short woman with a comfortable bosom. As she positioned herself at the bar, Dwight couldn't help but notice her spectacularly round bottom. Her smile had a sensual fullness to it, like a bowl of peaches. Dwight vaguely remembered tapping her last year when he was in his *baby-gotta-have-back* phase. One of his last new pussy conquests.

"Ah, how ya doing, sweetheart," he said, and gave her a hug.

"I'm fine, Dwight. How you doing? It's been a long time no hear from," she said as she reached toward the bar for her half-empty glass of white wine.

"Baby, I've been fine. Everything is good in the neighborhood," he said.

"You don't even remember my name, do you?" He was caught.

"Sure, I remember you. It's Cynthia, right?"

"No," she said, her full lips pouting.

"It starts with a C, right?"

"No, it don't. It's Priscilla, and my friends call me Cilla," she said.

"Cilla, that's right. I knew there was a C in there somewhere. You still lookin' good," Dwight said as he gazed at Priscilla's full hips in her tight-fitting green dress.

"You don't look so bad yourself. Why haven't you called me?"

"I lost my electronic date book. That's why I'm so glad I ran into you. I was wondering if I would ever see you again. Didn't have your work number either. Now, who do you work for?"

"I work for the city," she said. This will definitely be a pleasure play, Dwight thought. He knew he didn't want to work for the city.

"Yeah, I remember. You're in public relations, right?"

"Community relations," Priscilla said. Dwight started to give her a smart *same-thing* response, but instead said, "That's right, community relations. Sounds real cool."

"It's a job. Most of these people in here are looking for jobs. I already got one," she said.

"Is that so," Dwight said as he tried to make eye contact with the bartender. He needed a drink before every inch of his body starting showing annoyance.

"Can I have a Beck's?" Dwight asked the bartender. He smelled the tortilla chips and guacamole placed along the bar for drink-buying customers.

"In a minute," he replied. When Dwight turned back toward Priscilla, a tall, slender woman had joined them. "This is my soror, Tasha," Priscilla said.

"Hello, Tasha, I'm Dwight Scott."

"Nice meeting you, Dwight," Tasha said as she flashed a beautiful smile.

"What sorority are you ladies members of?" Dwight asked.

"You don't remember nothing I told you," Priscilla said. "Sigma Gamma Rho at FAMU."

"The only sorority," Tasha said as she gave a high-five to Priscilla.

"Are you in a fraternity, Dwight?" Tasha asked.

"Naw, that ain't me. So you both from Florida?" Dwight asked.

"I'm from Miami and Tasha's from Jackson, Mississippi," Priscilla said.

"Southern girls," Dwight said. "There's a whole lot of southern people living in Chicago." He felt a tap on his shoulder. He turned around and was greeted with a cold Beck's from the bartender. "How much, fella?" Dwight asked.

"No charge. The gentleman down there paid for it." He pointed toward a crowd of men at the opposite end of the bar.

"What gentleman?" Dwight asked.

"I don't know his name. He's an older man," the bartender said, trying to find Dwight's benefactor. Dwight was looking too, when he heard Tasha call his name, "Hey, Dwight . . . Dwight." He turned around and said, "Yeah, whatsup?"

"Did anybody ever tell you that you look like R. Kelly?" Dwight frowned. Women were always asking if he was any relation to Chicago's popular R & B singer. Before he could say yes, Tasha said, "I don't know why you making that face. R. Kelly looks *good.*" Dwight decided not to respond: He needed to locate the man who had bought him the beer. The music in the club was blasting like summer thunder and Blackstreet's "No Diggity" was rocking the packed club. On the dance floor, couples were whirling and sweating in tight rhythm. Tasha waved her long, scarlet fingernails in the air and started singing, "Party over here . . . party over here." The dance floor was filling up quicker than a Bulls game. "You want to dance?" Dwight asked Priscilla. "Not off this song. Too many people on the floor. But I promise you a dance when the next good song comes on." Dwight smiled and then turned to Tasha and repeated his question. "I can't. I'm with somebody. And I ain't having him go off on me in this packed club."

Dwight muttered *whatever* under his breath and cursed himself for even asking. He started looking toward the end of the bar to see if he recognized anyone. He saw Dan Stickens from MedMac walking toward him and smiling with a Beck's in hand. He was a stocky, silver-haired man in his early fifties with a raspy voice. "Don't tell me you gonna act like you don't know a brother. Not when I'm getting ready to buy over a million dollars worth of equipment from your boys," Dan said.

"Dan, my man. What's going on? Are you the one who sent me the brew? Thanks."

"You're welcome, my man. I didn't know you were a *First Friday* kinda guy," Dan said.

"Naw, I haven't been to one of these things in years," Dwight said.

"What brings you out this evening?"

"Just trying to see if there's anything new out here. A brother needs to update his address book and his résumé every now and then."

"You're not quitting your job, are you? We depend on you over at that company," Dan said.

"Naw, it's the address book today," Dwight lied. He wondered what Dan would say if he told him about the problems at his office. Dwight decided it wouldn't be right to confide in Dan, even though he considered him more than a customer.

"From the looks of things, you're well on your way," Dan said, motioning his beer toward Tasha and Priscilla a few feet away, munching down on the chips and guacamole.

"Naw, that ain't me. I'm just passing time," Dwight said. "What's this about you spending some big money?"

"I thought you knew. I heard you're the one who made the recommendation that we upgrade our equipment. That white boy you work with set up a meeting at our office for early next week to go over the contract. I've already talked to our accounting department about preparing the draft if we like what we hear. We're going to be on the cutting edge when it comes to information processing," Dan said proudly.

Dwight took a swig of his beer. Should he tell Dan what was really going on? He was praying Dan wouldn't ask him what he really thought. "Then, I guess I'll have to see that mug of yours again next week." Dan smiled and offered up a toast to their mutual success. Dwight heard the clinking of their beer bottles so clearly over the loud music. Maybe the clinking was inside his head. He suddenly had a piercing headache and "No Diggity" wasn't helping.

●   ●   ●

Riley stopped reading Susan Taylor's *Lessons in Living* and tried to decide if she should mention her conversation with Ryan to Selwyn. She was sitting up in their king-sized bed with six pillows assembled behind her head and back. Her cotton nightgown hung loose around her body like the sheets after a night of sleep. Selwyn would always pull the covers to his side during the night until Riley retrieved them in the early morning.

Riley decided to lie down and close her eyes, but just when she did, the phone rang.

"Hello?"

"Riley, did you speak with your daughter?" her mother asked.

"Hello, Mother. Yes, I called her," Riley said. This was all she needed to ensure another sleepless night.

"So what did she say?"

"About what?"

"Now, Riley, I hoped you would have figured out what's going on. That child has started having sex. And you and Selwyn better get up there and talk with her, or bring her behind back home. I told you sending her up there with all those potential hoodlums wasn't a good idea. Ryan should have stayed home and gone to the University of Chicago like her grandpa and I suggested. I don't want her to end up in the same predicament as you."

Her words pierced Riley's heart, and tears began to form in her eyes. "Good night, Mother, I don't feel like discussing this tonight," and she hung up the phone. Her mother should have just come out and said it: "If Ryan's not careful, she's gonna end up pregnant just like you did your junior year in college." She wiped the tears from her face with her nightgown just as Selwyn entered the room. Dressed in green plaid pajamas, he was carrying a mug of hot chocolate and a copy of *Black Enterprise*.

Riley didn't want Selwyn to see her tears, so she looked away. But Selwyn did notice and asked, "Are you all right?"

"I'm fine, I've just got something in my eye."

"Did I hear the phone ring while I was in the shower?"

"Yes," Riley said softly.

"Who was it?"

"It was my mother."

"Is everything all right? They're doing okay?"

"Yes, they're fine, Selwyn. Mother's just trying to run my life," Riley said.

"What is it this time?"

Riley paused for a moment, then decided Selwyn had a right to know about her conversation with her mother and about their daughter. Even during the very dark periods of their marriage, their children were the one thing about which they could communicate. It was the common bridge they always tried to cross together.

"Mother's worried about Ryan. But I spoke with her today and she's okay. She just had a bit of a bug. And it sounds like she has a boyfriend."

"A boyfriend?"

"Yes, some guy named Perry," Riley said.

"What do you know about this Perry? Is it serious? Have you talked with Reggie about him," Selwyn asked with some concern in his voice.

"No, I haven't talked with Reggie, and I don't know much about this guy. Ryan must have said something to Mother about him though. She's worried Ryan's going to get herself into trouble."

"What type of trouble?"

"Sex, I think. But we've talked with both our children about sex. Ryan will be responsible," Riley said.

"Be responsible, my ass! I hope she's not up there sleeping with this guy. I'm heading up there the first of the week, and if your mother's right, then Ryan's coming home and I'm taking her tail to Northwestern or De Paul," Selwyn said firmly. "Where is her number? I think I'll call her right now."

"Selwyn, don't. I think we might be jumping the gun. Let's wait and talk with Reggie. Maybe I should go up there with you next week," Riley said.

"Suit yourself. But I'm not going to let some knucklehead ruin my daughter's life while I'm spending my hard-earned money to get her an education," Selwyn said as he set his mug on the nightstand and pulled back the covers on the left side of the bed. Riley closed her eyes and pretended to fall asleep. But when Selwyn turned the lights out thirty minutes later, Riley was still awake.

In the darkness that covered the room like a dream, Riley thought about her mother and husband being so concerned that Ryan would repeat her own mistake. She tried to convince herself that Ryan and Reggie were more educated about sex than she had been. With AIDS, students were now taught to practice safe sex. Riley had tried to maintain a big-sister attitude with Ryan, though a subject as loaded as sex smacked her back into mother mode. When Ryan was a junior in high school, she shared her curiosity about sex, and had told Riley that she was still a virgin, and intended to remain so until she met the right man. Riley told her daughter how she had made Selwyn wait for sex, almost two years, but left out the part where she got pregnant because of getting caught in the heat of passion. Despite what her mother thought, Riley never considered her children a mistake. A little early, maybe, but not a mistake. Could history be repeating itself for Riley's daughter? She wondered where Ryan had met Perry and if he was anything like her father. The right man. Clarice had drummed that phrase into Riley's head as a young girl. *Wait for the right man.* Riley fell asleep wondering if Perry was that man.

Chapter 17

Late Sunday evening Uncle Doc stopped by for a surprise visit after leaving his second church service that day. He said I didn't sound good when he spoke to me early that morning, and he wanted to make sure everything was all right. I poured the two of us glasses of cranberry juice and spiced Uncle Doc's with a capful of vodka. "Just right." He smiled as he took his first sip. We moved to my dining room table, and Uncle Doc pulled out a cigarette, kicked off his shoes, and said, "Whew, there's a time limit on these shoes, and it's up!" My uncle was the only person I allowed to smoke in my home. He situated himself in the dining room chair, looked at me, and said, "Now, Boo—tell me what's wrong."

"Nothing's wrong. Just some things I have to work out," I said.

"Who with?"

"Myself and a friend," I said.

"Do I know this friend?"

"Of course. It's Yolanda and her new man," I said softly.

"He ain't beatin' her or nuthin' like that, is he?"

"Naw, it's nothing like that."

"Then why the long face?"

I explained my dilemma to Uncle Doc without going into specific details about my patient. I knew anything I told him would remain between the two of us. He listened intently as he drank and smoked a couple more cigarettes. When I finished, he looked at me and said, "I know you want to help Yolanda. You're her friend. I understand that. But, Boo, you worked too hard to git where you're at now to risk it. You accepted an oath. Yolanda will understand that. Anyhow, trust me, she'll find out. Yolanda's too smart a girl not to."

"But what if she doesn't? She could be putting herself at risk."

"What are you talking about? You said this man doesn't beat her."

"I'm talking about AIDS. If this guy is sleeping around, he could be infected."

"No, Boo, you're a doctor and know that not all bisexuals or whatever you want to call them have that virus. Besides, Yolanda ought to be smart enough to ask questions and protect herself," Uncle Doc said.

"I guess you're right. I just wish there were some way I could warn her without breaking my oath."

"Just leave well enough alone. It will work itself out. Scoundrels like this guy can only cover their spots for so long. Sooner or later they show up."

I thanked Uncle Doc and told him he was right. I got up and went to the kitchen to refresh our drinks. This time I poured myself a glass of wine and two capfuls of vodka into Uncle Doc's drink.

"You want to hear some music? Maybe some Billie Holiday?" I asked as I sat back down at the table.

"Naw, I done heard enough singing today. Let's talk. Are you sure that's all that's bothering you," Uncle Doc said.

"The other stuff I can work out," I said. Uncle Doc raised his bushy eyebrows and said, "Are you sure?" I knew I couldn't say yes and make him believe me. So I asked him how long did it take him to get over losing James, his partner for nearly twenty years.

"Well, you never really git over losing someone you love. But you

have to go on. You owe it to yourself and to them. You been thinking 'bout Donald?"

I told my uncle how Donald had been on my mind almost every
other free thought I had when I wasn't worrying about Yolanda. I
shared my plans of going to New York and how I hoped it would
finally let me put my memories to rest. Uncle Doc told me to go if I
really thought it would help, but he also thought I should try and
keep myself busy with work and finding a new love in my life.
"You're still a young man, Boo. You can have love in your life again
if you're willing to try. I don't really think going to New York will
help unless you're going to meet somebody new. I'm going to figure
out a way to git you out more. You ain't gonna meet nobody sittin'
up here in the house all by yourself."

"I know you're right," I said.

"Of course I'm right," Uncle Doc said.

"Tell me the story of you and James again," I pleaded.

"Why you want to hear that story?"

"It makes me smile. I need to smile," I said.

I think Uncle Doc enjoyed telling the story as much as I enjoyed
hearing it. Each time he told me a story he added new details, so it
was almost like hearing it the first time. When he told me his stories
I felt like I was going back in time, like I had lived during the era.
Uncle Doc met James Knight in San Francisco, right after he got
out of the Air Force. Yes, my uncle, who had been gay all his life,
had served in the United States Air Force for ten years. When the
gays-in-the-military issue had come up in 1993, Uncle Doc said it
was much ado about nothing, since sissies had been in the services
since the beginning of time. He didn't understand all the fuss. He
felt the same way about gay marriages. Once Uncle Doc told me he
didn't need a birth certificate to tell him he was born, didn't need a
death certificate to tell him he was gone, and he certainly didn't
need some certificate to prove he had loved.

"Did you know he was gay when you first saw him?"

"Naw, 'cause I wasn't looking at him like that. You know, we didn't call it gay back then. We had our own names, like *dancers*, who were the ones that, you know, like to be penetrated, and *singers*, the ones who liked giving head. We called the butch ones men or husbands," Uncle Doc said. "James was dating one of my female friends, Bertha Lee. She was a fine thing, a red bone with a nice shape, but she was wild. We lived in the same duplex. I had a little apartment downstairs and she lived upstairs. Bertha Lee hung out with me and all my friends in the Fillmore section. They didn't have a lot of clubs for us colored sissies, so we had a lot of house parties. Of course, we could go to the straight clubs if we were so inclined."

"Did he come to one of your parties?" I asked. I really didn't remember what he had told me in the past.

"Naw, he was in the Marines, stationed right outside of San Fran. One night his car broke down and he called Bertha Lee to come and help him. Well, that girl didn't have a car, but I did. But I was a little full, you know, partyin' and all, so Bertha Lee drove and I rode along. When we got there, I told them to let me look at the car and see what was wrong. You know, my daddy had taught me a lot about cars when he was trying to make me a real boy, but instead he got a tomgirl," Uncle Doc said as he let out a sound of absolute delight.

"So you were fixing the car, then what?"

"I had on some short shorts. It was summer and I was built real nice back then. I was bending over lookin' under the hood of his car, when he said, 'You kinda slung low, ain't you, Doug.' "

"Slung low?"

"Yeah, Boo. He was saying I had a nice behind. Which I did." Uncle Doc smiled.

"Then what?"

"So I knew then he wanted some, you know, some of my banana pudding, but I told him I wouldn't as long as he was going out with my girlfriend. To make a low story a high one, he and Bertha Lee had a big fight a couple months later. He was drunk, out in the street callin' her name. It was about four o'clock in the morning and I went out and told him to come into my place before Bertha Lee or one of our neighbors called the police. Told him he didn't want them taking him back to the base in his condition. Well, let's just say that when I gave him a bath and cleaned him up, he pulled me into the tub with him."

Uncle Doc told me how crushed he was that James married a lady back home in Mississippi when he got out of the service a year later. But how they kept in contact through phone calls and Uncle Doc's letters. When Uncle Doc moved to Chicago and started his restaurant, James came to visit him at least three times a year. A couple of years later he moved to Chicago to be with Uncle Doc, leaving behind a wife and two children.

"But he always took care of those children, and I helped out too. To this day I still hear from them. Matter of fact, when James died, I was the one who called his wife. She asked me if there was anything she could do for me with his arrangements. When his daughter got married, she asked me to walk her down the aisle. The only one who gave me shade was that nappy-headed son of his. But his ass is in jail for beating up his wife," Uncle Doc said.

"So his wife didn't have a problem with you?"

"If she did, she never said anything. You know we never talked about stuff back then. Everything was understood. I think that's the problem with the children today. They want to talk about everything. Talk too much if you ask me. Put they business up in folks' faces. We didn't do that and we didn't have the problems like today," Uncle Doc said. "We kept our legs open and our mouths shut. I mean, unless there was something good comin' toward us," he said as he slapped his knee and let out a chorus of mischievous laughter.

"So no one ever teased you?" I asked.

"No more than any other kids were teased. You know, for being too Black or too ugly or too poor. The only thing I remember was once my older brother, Leroy, told my daddy, 'I think Douglas is a little pink.' "

"What did you say?"

"I put my hands on my little hips and I said, 'I ain't a little pink. I'm a whole lotta pink.' That shut his mouth up for good."

"Did you love James?"

Uncle Doc's face broke into a wide smile.

"Yes, Boo, I loved him a lot. And I knew he loved me. He never said it, but I knew," Uncle Doc said as he took a long drag off his cigarette. He had a far-off look in his eyes, and I knew exactly how he felt.

Chapter 18

It was Monday morning. Dwight arrived at his office a little before eight to look over his account profiles for his monthly review with management. On his way to the coffee station he bumped into Barry and Kent, in jovial conversation and carrying steaming cups of coffee. When they saw Dwight they exchanged nervous glances.

"You ready for the meeting?" Barry asked.

"As always," Dwight replied.

"Have you thought any more about the situation at MedMac?" Kent inquired.

"What situation?"

"With the proposal," Barry said.

"I think I've made my feelings about MedMac perfectly clear," Dwight said.

"Why don't we take this into my office," Kent said as he noticed other office personnel strolling into the office. Dwight followed the two of them into Kent's office and he shut the door and offered Dwight a seat. "I'll stand," Dwight said. If this was going to be another meeting trying to convince him to sign the proposal, then Dwight figured it wouldn't last a minute. He was right.

"So, Dwight, are you going to sign the MedMac proposal?" Kent asked with a skeptical, steel-eyed stare.

"No, I'm not," Dwight said firmly.

"Then I think you should offer your resignation," Kent said, not looking at Dwight but at Barry, who was sitting in a chair like a delinquent schoolboy.

"I'll have my resignation on your desk by noon," Dwight said.

Barry jumped up and said, "Why, Dwight? Are you sure you want to do this? All we're asking you is to sign the goddamn proposal. What's so hard about that?"

Dwight looked at Kent and asked, "Is there anything else?"

"I don't think so," he said as he shook his head in dismay.

Dwight walked out of Kent's office, went to his cubicle, and gathered the few personal effects he kept at the office: A plaque the office had given him at the beginning of the year as the top sales engineer, a picture of his mother and him a few Christmases back, a 1996 Hampton University football schedule, and a Bulls cap with Michael Jordan's stenciled signature. He threw the items in his briefcase, removed the office key from his chain, and laid it on the desk. Dwight pulled a sheet of paper from his tablet and wrote: *Effective immediately, I resign from my position of sales engineer, Dwight Leon Scott.* He resisted scribbling some obscenity or something smart like *See ya, wouldn't wanna be ya.* Dwight figured they wouldn't understand.

●　　　●　　　●

Riley was second-guessing herself again. As she finished up the last five minutes on the treadmill, she wondered if she had made the right decision in not going to Hampton with Selwyn. He had convinced her early Monday morning that it made more sense for him to go alone. If Selwyn showed up unexpectedly, the kids might not become suspicious, since they knew he had clients in the area. The two of them showing up at Ryan's doorstep might signal a lack of trust. Selwyn and Riley trusted their kids, but they were concerned. It hadn't been that long ago when the two of them were experiencing their first taste of freedom, without parental restraints.

Selwyn promised he would call Riley immediately after he had seen Ryan and met this Perry guy, and if there was any cause for concern, he would withdraw Ryan from Hampton on the spot.

When the two of them sat in the breakfast nook, drinking coffee together, Riley saw glimpses of the man she fell in love with. Selwyn acted like he cared about how she felt, often rubbing her hands gently as he explained why he felt he needed to go alone. His touch was warm and reassuring, and Riley felt needed. He even told Riley that if she felt strongly about going, he would understand, but thought his plan might be better. He knew how Riley loved her children, and neither of them wanted to see them repeat the past.

Selwyn pointed out that Riley had a lot going on in Chicago, with her workouts, charities, and preparing for her Chicago debut. When she pointed out that everything wasn't final, that Yolanda hadn't said yes, Selwyn surprised her by saying confidently, "It will come through. This is a break you've been waiting for." A couple of times Riley actually blinked her eyes to make sure she wasn't dreaming and was actually having a conversation with Selwyn and not some stranger. When he gently kissed her on the forehead before leaving, Riley still wasn't quite sure it was Selwyn. It had been so long since she'd felt his lips on any part of her body.

After showering, Riley changed in her dressing area, putting on a blue warmup suit she had purchased at Hampton. It wasn't something Riley would normally wear, not even around the house, but she didn't feel like getting all dressed up today. Riley's mother had looked at her like she was a crazy woman when she asked the clerk for the sweatsuit in her size. Riley told her mother it was for her maid, and Clarice looked relieved.

Riley decided to spend the afternoon reviewing mail, finishing up the poem she was writing for her secret admirer, and calling Yolanda for dinner. She needed to know the date of her debut. Maybe she could jump-start Yolanda into making a decision.

Riley was putting back a suitcase she had pulled down in anticipation of her trip, when she noticed a red folder in the inside pocket. She opened the folder and realized it was some of the poetry she had written over the years. Riley could tell from the handwriting that some of the poetry had been written while she was still at Hampton. One poem had *Selwyn and Riley forever* written along the margin. She smiled as she thought back on those times, when life really seemed happy. In the stack of handwritten poems, Riley noticed one that was typed on some heavy bond paper. The paper was a dingy yellow now, but the grade of paper hadn't changed. She looked at the date typed at the top, 10/20/77, and realized it was a poem she had written on a magical evening. An evening when she and Selwyn had gone for a ride in his first new car. Riley sat on her bed and read her words as her eyes blurred with tears:

We rode through the indigo of a cool fall evening
Speaking about destinations reached and sought
As slowly steady soul grooves
Played on your stereo
You taught me why JT has seen fire and rain
(I was impressed)
I told you the best lyrics come from the hearts of true poets
Then you crooned for me
Luther's "Going in Circles"
Not knowing I'm a sucker for a brother who can sing
And you said you were like that wheel
Later, on my couch
When I looked into your big browns and kissed you
With silent deliberation
Out time zones became not so distant

(And my sensibilities waned)
Next we moved to our own beat
(A rhythm too exotic to compose)
And I clung to the promise held by things new and uncharted
I looked to you for salvation
You offered comfortable intensity
So I apologized at my deliverance
With you I see cadences and crescendos
Of delicious melodies
In perfect harmony
You are music gentle warrior
You are peace

Riley felt she would give anything in the world to feel like she felt when she wrote the poem. But now her words felt like little bombs of regret and nostalgia, exploding like Fourth of July fireworks. When Riley began crying, loud sobs jerked her entire body, as if something inside her were lost in a grief deeper than sadness.

Chapter 19

My plan worked like a charm, and Yolanda didn't disappoint me. The girl is all that and then some. We made love so many times, we discovered new paths to pleasure that surprised us both. Each time better than before. I think I might be in love. But I didn't tell Yolanda that. It's not time. It's too soon. But when I'm with her, and even when I'm not, I think I could love this woman so hard—at times I just want to jump out of my body. I want to run—not walk—out of the tunnel of melancholy I've been stuck in and run straight into her arms. It's that serious. Yolanda has made an indelible impression on me.

Her body is as beautiful as her smile, and her brown eyes are so deep, you could drown yourself in them. Yolanda's legs are trim and graceful like a dancer—her breasts are nicely shaped like large plums. When she walked across the hotel suite in the nude, it was like paradise in motion. Makes my stuff hard just thinking about it.

I've had great sex before. But most times, after I get my nut, I don't want the person or persons anywhere near me. I don't want them touching me, kissing me, or holding idle conversation. But I wanted to hold Yolanda forever. I wanted to talk to her and tell her things I've never told anyone, because I know she would be listening. I would tell her how she's the first woman I've been with where I feel complete. How I don't see *him* when I look into her eyes. I know she would understand and care.

Yolanda shows me one of the things I love about women. Like my aunt Lois, they see more in men than we see in ourselves. They overlook who we really are because women see what we can become.

When she talks—it's like going to the movies. She told me about holidays when she was growing up. I could see Iowa—even though I've never been to the state. I could smell the food. I could see her playing chess with her father, letting him win. I could imagine her helping her mother hang up sheets on the clothesline she told me about, and playing jacks with her sister, Sybil. Yolanda made Iowa sound like a magical place.

She's confident, but not in a bitchy sorta way. Sometimes I think if I pulled some of my old stunts, like not calling after I've gotten the draws, Yolanda wouldn't care. I mean, she probably would care, but she'd never let me know. She's not like some of the crazy women I've gone out with in the past. Some of them have been so goddamned psycho, I thought I'd have to fake my own death to get rid of them crazy skeezers. I could just hear Yolanda saying, "Later for you, John Henderson."

When I got back from Chicago, I called my dad and told him about Yolanda. He said he can't wait to meet her and suggested we meet him in Detroit, for Thanksgiving. When I asked him why Detroit, he reminded me my Uncle Mac had moved there with his new wife. I told him I'd think about it. Uncle Mac isn't one of my favorite people in the world with his drunk, no-count ass. He's the original mofo. But you can't tell my dad that. He thinks his younger brother's shit don't stink.

Something wonderful happened with my phone call with my dad. It was the first time I can remember when we had a conversation and didn't talk about football. Not once did he ask me if the doctors had changed their opinion about my chances of playing again.

Maybe when he saw I wasn't going to stop sending him a monthly check, my career didn't seem to matter. I called my aunt Lois and told her about Yolanda. She said she couldn't wait to meet her and then told me she was going to Detroit also for Thanksgiving and how she would love to see me and meet Yolanda. I think she was relieved when I told her Yolanda was Black. Aunt Lois never hid her feelings when I dated women of other races, and told me every chance she got how she couldn't stand my ex-wife, Vickie, partly because she was white. "Don't give that bitch a penny," she advised when I got a divorce. I didn't, but I couldn't tell my aunt how I had managed that trick.

I've talked to Yolanda three times today already. I want to hear her voice again, but I don't want her to think I'm crazy like in love with her. I hope she will call me because she wants to hear my voice. Maybe she will allow me to get her off over the phone with the things I'd do to her if I was in her bed. Just thinking about what I want to say to her, and I feel my stuff growing longer and thicker against the inside of my jock. I take off my sweater and slide my tight-fitting jeans and jock down inch by inch until I'm wearing nothing but gray and white sweat socks.

I go to my refrigerator and grab a beer. I put on the *Waiting to Exhale* CD. I walk through my bedroom and slide open the terrace door. A gust of cool and soothing wind greets me as I walk across the terrace. From there I look across the water and see Brooklyn sparkling in the night. I take a sip of my cold beer and enjoy the glittering lights of the city—and the throb of the music. I decide what the hell, and I rush to my bedroom to call Yolanda. Just as I'm preparing to pick up the phone, it rings, and I'm certain it's her.

"Hello," I said quickly. But it's not Yolanda. It's a man's voice.

"Hey dog, whatsup . . . whatsup . . . whatsup . . . my dog," the man said.

"You got it. Who am I speaking with?" I asked.

"Nigga leave town for a couple months and you forgot 'bout him. Whatsup with that." I recognized the voice. It's music-man Monty.

"Whatsup, Monty? I recognized your voice. Welcome back to the city."

"Did you get my messages?"

"Yeah, but I've been busy. In fact, I just got back in town."

"Where did you go?"

"Chicago."

"Is it cold up there yet?"

"Not really."

"What's this I hear about an injury? You not playing for the Warriors no more?"

"Yeah, that's right. My playing days are over."

"Whatcha up to?"

"When?"

"Right now. I'm kinda near you. I just finished dinner at Mr. Chow's with some of my boys. And I was thinking about dropping by," Monty said.

"Now's not a good time. I'm kinda tied up," I said.

"Who is she? Or is it a he? Either way, if it's a freak, I'm on the way." Monty laughed.

"Naw, it's not like that. Football ain't the only thing I've given up," I said.

"Whatever . . . man. You ain't seen me. I've been pumping iron like crazy. Let me stop by," he pleaded. I wanted to say, dumb mofo—which part of I'm busy don't you understand? But I just said, "I've gotta run."

Monty added, "Holler at a player when you git some time." I hung up the phone, flipped on my answering machine, and turned up my music.

Chapter 20

Black folks ain't shit. It pains me to think and write this, but sometimes the truth is just the truth. I spent the fourth day of my unemployment at the movies. I went to see Spike Lee's **Get on the Bus.** *The reason I'm pissed off is because the theater was nearly empty. I went early thinking I was going to have to wait in line to buy a ticket. This don't make no sense. One of the most important days in the history of Black America is made into a film by an African American man, without the help of white folks, and we won't support it. Pisses me off big-time. What happened to all the promises we made to each other at the March? If half of the brothers who attended the March would have shown up at the movies with their wives, sister, or girlfriend, the movie would have been a tremendous hit. It ain't like they don't know it's out. It's been in magazines, radio, and* **Oprah.** *What else could brother Spike do?*

And to make matters worse, about half the brothers at the film were there with white women on their arms. Disrespecting our sisters who were at the theater alone. I can't figure this shit out. Why we as African Americans can't support one another in something as positive as the March and the film. Now, had this been a movie about Black folks shooting up other Black folks, then the place would have been packed. Don't we as a people realize that all Hollywood is concerned about when it comes to films about us is: How much money was made the first weekend and how many niggers were killed.

But I can't worry 'bout that shit. I got to find me a j-o-b. I love Spike, but he and the other brothers who financed his film are set. Me, well, I think I got about six months before I might have to move back with my moms or to a shelter. Not that I would have a problem living with my mother. I've been thinking a lot about moving back to Oaktown, or to Washington, D.C. Maybe it's time for me to leave Chicago. There is nothing really holding me here but a job I no longer have. I have about $39,000 in the bank and another 20K in a 401(K) I can use. Thank God that after I got rid of Kelli and paying her alimony I went back to living like I did when I was in college. I have always lived below my means. But I was saving this money to surprise my moms with a house for her birthday–Mother's Day–Christmas present this year. But I guess she can't miss something she never had.

I'm trying not to worry about my job situation. I've talked to a couple of headhunters who say with my skills, they shouldn't have a hard time placing me. That's what they say at least. One firm I'm using probably won't send me out for a lot of interviews after I asked the women handling my search why they didn't have any African American headhunters. "We've been trying to find some," she said, sounding like she was looking for some soon-to-be-extinct animal. I started to call my boy at MedMac and tell them what's going on, why I'm no longer on the account, but I don't want to fuck up my severance package. For six months of salary, one of the conditions is that I don't contact my former customers or file any legal actions against the dumb sonofabitches. If they had given me the check in one lump sum, I would have taken the check to their bank, cashed it, and gone directly to MedMac to tell them what time it is.

I should take the money I have, move my ass back home, and start my own business. Something in the community, like teaching brothers and sisters about computers and how to use them. But what if my peoples didn't support my business? Didn't want to learn about something new. I know that would piss me off more than the shit that went down at my gig. There are a lot of African American people in the world like Riley and Selwyn, who feel if it ain't white, it can't be right. Won't give a brother a chance if their life depended on it. When I confronted Selwyn about this a couple years ago, he gave me some lame excuse about choosing the best one for the job, without reference to color. He sounded like a white man, only he was a brother I thought I knew. I guess he learned that at Harvard.

I haven't decided if I'm going to tell the group what happened with my job. I'll probably just tell them I've decided it was time for a change. I've bugged Riley, Leland, and Yolanda long enough. They're not gonna change. But maybe I'll change. A change in employment, locale, and friends. They probably won't even notice I'm gone.

Chapter 21

I wandered uneasily around John's apartment for about a half hour, staring at the phone. I needed to call Riley. She had left four messages at my apartment and two with Monica at my office. From the messages she left on my home answering machine, I knew why she wanted to talk with me. Was she going to open up for Goodfellaz? The answer was still no.

Instead of calling Riley, I sat on the sofa and finished my cold cheeseburger and washed it down with a swallow of diet Pepsi. The autumn afternoon sun painted the living room with soothing shades of ivory and gold. I tried to take my thoughts away from Riley and thought about the meeting I had with a record company executive Lajoyce had arranged for me. The record company wanted me to consult a member of a popular R & B act who was thinking about announcing that he was gay at the same time he was launching a solo career. The executives wouldn't tell me the name of the group or the member in question. I was one of three media specialists they were considering. I did discover he wasn't coming out as some noble gesture, but because members of his own group were threatening to make the information public because of what one record executive described as petty jealousies. A major music industry magazine was preparing a front-cover exposé on the group and its gay member. I started to call Leland and tell him about the meeting, but I knew he'd ask what I had done about Riley.

For a moment I thought I was ready, but as soon I picked up the phone I felt the need to use the bathroom, where I suddenly had a strong desire to read John's sports magazines sitting in a wicker basket. When I came out, the sun was retreating and I was praying that John would turn the key to his apartment, giving me the excuse I needed. But he said he'd be in late, after meeting with his agent and his two-hour workout. I noticed a scrapbook in one of John's bookcases, so I spent some time looking at pictures of John when he was a young boy. He was, of course, very cute, but he wasn't smiling in any of the pictures. He must have been wearing braces or something. After skimming all the reading materials in the house and looking through the scrapbook twice, I decided it was time. I wanted to see how I looked, but I didn't see any mirrors in John's living area. I guess when you looked like John, you didn't need mirrors. I took a long, careful breath, reached for the phone, and dialed Riley's number. She picked up on the second ring.

"Hello."

"Riley, how are you doing? I got your messages," I said.

"Yolanda girl, I'm so glad to hear from you. I'm so excited about singing. I think I've lost about ten pounds from nervous energy," she said.

"How is everything in Chicago? Are Ryan and Reggie loving Hampton?" I asked, ignoring her enthusiasm.

"Oh, Chicago is fine. How long have you been gone? Ryan and Reggie are fine."

"What are you doing right now?" I asked.

"Just sitting here in my office, writing checks to several charities Selwyn and I support."

"You should make a check out for my charity," I teased.

"What charity is that?" Riley asked.

"The I'm-a-broke-bitch foundation." I laughed. It was nervous laughter, but Riley joined in. "Yolanda, you're so crazy. That's what I love about you, honey."

Why did she have to say she loved me, I thought. I spent another five minutes with friendly conversation, though delicately avoiding any mention of Riley's singing. I mentioned the top secret media planning session I was working on, and we talked a few minutes about where Dwight was going to hold the next group meeting. It was his turn, and we knew he'd never have it at his apartment. Riley said, "I just hope it's in a safe place."

"I know that's right. Remember that time he had it in this hole-in-the-wall barbecue joint on the West Side?"

"Yes, girl, Selwyn was so mad at me for taking his new Lexus up there."

"I think Dwight's growing up. Maybe he will choose a place close to downtown."

I was tempted to end the conversation by talking about Dwight, but Riley wasn't having it. "So, Yolanda, have the people made a decision yet? Did you let them listen to my tape? Am I going to sing?"

I started to say, please, one question at a time, but I blurted out. "Riley, you're not going to sing."

"I'm not?" she asked softly.

"No, I'm afraid you're not up to it."

"Is that what they said, Yolanda? Did they tell you why?"

"No, they didn't."

"Then why can't I sing?" Riley pleaded.

"Because your voice isn't strong enough," I said.

"Who said that?" Riley quizzed.

"I did . . . I mean they said that," I stuttered.

"Who said it, Yolanda? Who said I couldn't sing?" Riley asked. A bitter edge had entered her voice.

"No one said you couldn't sing, Riley. We just decided to go with someone else."

"Did you take up for me, Yolanda? Didn't you tell them how important this was to me?" Riley asked as if she were accusing me of incompetence.

I didn't know what else to say. My face became glazed with sweat and there was a long silence. My heart was beating fast. Finally I heard Riley say, "Yolanda, are you still there?"

"Yes, Riley, I'm still here."

"Did you tell them?" It sounded like she was crying.

"Why is this so important to you, Riley? You have so much else to do. I mean, with your charities and your writing. Your poetry has gotten so much better," I said.

"So you're saying I can't write poetry either. Yolanda, I thought you were my friend. Now I get the impression you think I can't do diddle. No, I bet you think I can't do shit."

I had never heard Riley use a curse word. Even when all of us would use them, Riley never did.

"Riley, calm down and listen to me. I was thinking about you when I made this decision. It's tough performing for the public. I think you should consider getting a vocal coach and working on your singing. That is, if singing is what you want to do with your life."

"What's wrong with my singing? You think you know every damn thing. Your life is so perfect, you're so perfect. I need this opportunity, Yolanda, and I thought as a friend you'd see this. But you're so concerned with your own little perfect life that you can't see how miserable my life is," Riley wailed.

I was in shock and didn't know how to respond. I decided to take another deep breath before I lost my composure. I wanted to choose my next words carefully, but Riley didn't give me the chance.

"Yolanda . . . Yolanda," Riley yelled.

"Yes," I said softly.

"You don't ever have to worry about me asking you for nothing. I'll make it on my own, and I'm sure a perfect person like you has no need for a no-talent friend like me."

"Riley, stop it. You know that's not true. You're overreacting."

"You don't know me. You don't know what my life is like." Riley started sobbing so hard that her words became incoherent.

"Riley . . . Riley," I said. But Riley didn't answer. For a few minutes all I heard was crying and then a dial tone.

What to do? Who to call? I started to call Riley back, but I figured she needed to calm down. I called Leland and got his answering machine. I left a message but didn't leave a number since I hadn't cleared it with John. I called Sybil, but she was combing Devin's hair, and I told her I would call back.

"Are you all right, Yolanda?" Sybil asked.

"I'm okay. It's a friend I'm worried about."

"Is there anything I can do?"

"No, I need to work this out myself. Kiss the kids for me."

"I will. But, you know if you need me, I'm here, big sis."

"I know, Syb. I know." I hung up the phone and, just as I was about to let go of the river of tears I was struggling to keep in place, John walked in the door, looking tired and carrying a gym bag. He greeted me with a kiss and asked me how my meeting went. That's when I lost it. I started crying like a baby, telling him about my conversation with Riley.

"Don't cry, Yolanda. I can't stand to see you cry," he said as we moved to the couch. "Your friend Riley will have to get over it herself. You did what you had to do. Doesn't she realize this is your business? Didn't you tell me she had a rich husband supporting her?"

"But I hurt her badly," I sobbed.

"You didn't do it on purpose," John said. "You did what you thought was best."

"What am I going to do?"

"You're going to go in the bedroom. Get undressed. And then you're going to let me give you a soothing bubble bath. After that I'll give you a massage and I'll rub all that tension from your beautiful body," he said. It sounded wonderful, though I didn't think even John could change the way I felt. I had hurt a friend.

•   •   •

The tears had stopped, but a rush of anger swept over Riley again. She sat silently in the library's gathering darkness, staring at a centerpiece of white tea roses her maid had arranged earlier in the evening. Riley absorbed the silence, reflecting back on her phone call with Yolanda.

How dare Yolanda tell her she couldn't sing, Riley thought. Singing and writing poetry were the two activities that Riley did on her own, without the direction of her domineering mother or her over-anal Selwyn. But now one of her best friends and sorority sister was trying to take even that away from her.

Riley noticed the full brandy decanter and started to pour herself a drink, but quickly decided not to plunge herself into self-pity by mixing alcohol with anger. She wanted to talk with someone and share her anger, but the realization that she didn't have a single person to call brought tears to her eyes once again. She couldn't call her mother, because Clarice would probably tell her Yolanda was right and she needed to get on her knees and beg Wanda Mae to give her her job back. Selwyn was at the office, and although he seemed more attentive in the last couple of days, Riley wasn't certain how long this would last. Calling Dwight was out of the question, because Riley knew he didn't really care for her, and was probably the one who had convinced Yolanda she couldn't sing. Leland, she felt, would listen, but would probably suggest Riley seek professional help. The phone interrupted Riley's thoughts, and as she leaped to answer it, she prayed it was Yolanda calling her back to tell her she made a big mistake.

"Hello," Riley answered breathlessly. "Hello, Riley." It wasn't Yolanda. It was her husband.

"Selwyn." Her voice could not hide any more disappointment.

"Yeah, are you all right?"

"Why do you ask?" she asked, wondering if he really cared.

"You sound like you're out of breath," Selwyn said.

"I was on my treadmill," Riley lied.

"Oh, I see. By the way, in case I haven't told you, I'm really proud of the way you're sticking with your new exercise program. Maybe this spring we can start to work out together," Selwyn said. Riley didn't respond. "Riley, are you still there?"

"Yes, Selwyn. Are you at the office?" Riley was wondering what Selwyn was getting at. Didn't he hear she wasn't interested in what he had to say to her?

"Yeah, but I was calling to see if I could bring you something for dinner. What do you have a taste for?"

"I've already eaten. Sire broiled me some fish," Riley said. Apparently the *good* Selwyn was still in Chicago.

"Well, I'm going to stop somewhere and grab something. I'll see you when I get in?" It wasn't like he was making a statement, but a hopeful question. Riley started to give him one of Ryan's favorite retorts and say *whatever*, but she just mumbled okay and hung up the phone.

Riley decided to retreat to her office and write a poem describing how she felt. That would help, she thought. When she turned on her computer, there were no messages from Lonelyboy, but Riley decided to send him a message anyway. She thought about giving him her phone number and asking him to call, but realized Selwyn might answer the phone. Riley was thinking about what message she should send, when she noticed the poem she had recently discovered. This was it, she thought. Riley hit the keyboard rapidly:

This is a poem I wrote so many years ago for someone special in my life. A time when I thought love would last forever. We both know that's not true. But it's still nice to remember love lost, and think how nice it will feel once it returns. This is special to me and so are you. Enjoy.

Riley sent Lonelyboy the poem, and when she hit the send button, she wanted to feel the surge of love, but instead her tears returned once more.

Chapter 22

Dwight's eyes were closed when he broke out into laughter. He was listening to Miss Dupree, a regular on the Tom Joyner morning show, who was sharing her method of picking the numbers with listeners. When his phone rang he assumed it was his mother. He sat up in his bed and removed his hand from just below the waistband of his boxers when he heard what sounded like a white female on the other end.

"Good morning, this is Becky Lowe. Can I speak with Mr. Dwight Scott?" she asked.

"This is Mr. Dwight Scott."

"How are you doing, Dwight? Can I call you Dwight?"

"I don't know, I'm still waking up. Now, who did you say this is?" he asked as he turned down his radio.

"Becky Lowe, I'm with Phillips and Associates. We're an executive search company, and I received a copy of your résumé," Becky said.

"And," Dwight answered in a slightly annoyed tone. He wanted to know how this woman had gotten his information. Rooks and Associates was the firm he had interviewed with.

"The reason I'm calling is we have a client in the Washington, D.C., area who's seen your résumé and really wants to talk with you about a position," Becky said.

"How did you get my résumé?"

"Oh, from the agency you registered with. Most of the high-tech agencies list their candidates on a database, and that's where I got your information," Becky said.

"Okay. What type of position?"

"It's a senior level programming job that can lead to management." Dwight was still a bit apprehensive; he had heard the leading-to-management line more times than he'd like to remember. But Dwight wanted to go back to work, he didn't like sitting at home all morning, waiting for the phone to ring. And as much as he like playing basketball, he couldn't do that all day either.

"So who do I talk with?" Dwight asked.

"You're interested! That's great. I'll make the arrangements," Becky said.

"What arrangements?" Dwight was hoping this wasn't an agency that charged a fee for locating positions.

"Didn't you hear me? The position is in D.C. You'll be flying there for the interview, and if all goes well, it could be your new home."

"New home? Hold up. I don't know if I'm interested in moving to Washington, D.C. I thought the position was in Chicago. I told those headhunters I was interested only in positions in Chicago and Oakland," Dwight said.

"I think you should at least go up for the interview. After the interview, you can express your interest in staying in Chicago or relocating to Oakland. Even though, looking at this information, it's hard for me to tell if they have an Oakland office. It's an African American company that's growing at a rapid rate. The company was started with the backing of some minority venture capitalist and they're already listed in *Black Enterprise*'s top one hundred. They've also been written up in *The Wall Street Journal*," Becky said. The thought of working for an African American company perked up Dwight's interest.

"An African American company, huh," Dwight replied.

"Yes, I could send you over some information. But we've got to move quickly. I don't know how long this position is going to be open. If you're interested after reading the material, you need to call me right away. I'd like to arrange to have you in Washington tomorrow, or at the very least by Friday. They're willing to fly you up to their headquarters. And they do everything first class."

"All right, send over the information and I'll get right back with you. I guess if you have my phone number then you've got my address," Dwight said. Becky read Dwight's address from his résumé, and he confirmed. She promised to have a courier at his doorstep within the hour.

"I think you're going to be real impressed," Becky said. "I've heard nothing but great things about this company."

"What's the name of the company?"

"I'll tell you that after you've reviewed the information. It won't be on any of the material I'm sending you. If you're interested, then I'll share the information. It's company policy. You understand, we don't want you to give the information to another search firm and allow them to place you. We work on commissions, of course, you know."

"So you're like a salesman, huh?" Dwight knew there had to be a catch somewhere.

"You could say that. Thanks for your time, Dwight. I hope we can work this deal out," Becky said.

"Yeah, right," Dwight said as he hung up the phone. Something about a white lady talking like she was selling him to a company didn't feel quite right. But what could a brother do?

•   •   •

The Woodson house was as quiet as an autumn evening, and Riley sat in the library and absorbed the silence. Riley didn't mind the silence while reflecting on the events of the week. The rejection from Yolanda had left her with a huge emptiness, a feeling that started in the pit of her stomach and then worked its way up. Clarice would say Riley was being dramatic, and she needed to forget about singing and writing poetry and get a real job. But those were her mother's desires, and Riley had decided that when her cloud of depression lifted, she would continue pursuing her dreams even more fiercely. Not her mother's, not Selwyn's, and to hell with anybody who didn't believe her. And that included Yolanda and the group.

Riley had spent three days watching television in a mindless stupor until her body would betray her and sleep would come. Sometimes, when she was staring at the screen, Riley could see glimpses of her own life. Riley trying hard to be the perfect daughter, sister, mother, wife, and friend. But her children, brother, parents, Selwyn, and her friends had made her painfully aware that she wasn't perfect at anything.

She was wearing only rose-colored silk pajamas and matching robe. Riley's face was without makeup and her dimples were lost in her strained face, framed by her hair brushed back and held with two gold clips. She canceled scheduled workouts with her trainer. Riley had finally discovered a way of losing weight without the rigors of diet and exercise. Depression.

Selwyn was on the West Coast on business, and the only contact Riley had with the outside world was her maid, who delivered meals that remain untouched. She didn't answer her phone and had instructed the doorman to tell any visitors that she was out of town on a family emergency.

The only time she left the sofa was to go to her office, turn on her computer, and pray for a message from Lonelyboy. But her secret admirer had disappeared. Riley hadn't heard from him since she sent him the poem she had written for Selwyn. Riley had done something she had promised herself and the group she'd never do. At the last minute she had included her private number. Maybe if she heard his voice it would help her recovery. She had instructed him to ring once and then call back immediately so she would know it was him. But the only rings on her private number came in multiples, so Riley just let the damn thing ring.

Riley was thinking about finding her journal and writing some of her feelings down, when she heard someone knocking at her door. She ignored the intrusion, but moments later she heard the key in the door and then a male voice calling her name. "Mrs. Woodson . . . are you in there? This is Jimmy, the building supervisor. I have someone here to see you." Riley pulled her robe together to make sure it was buttoned and got up from the sofa, when she heard her mother's voice.

"Riley. Riley Denise Woodson. Are you in here?"

Riley walked to the foyer of her house and saw her mother standing behind Jimmy. When she saw Riley, Clarice moved Jimmy aside and gave Riley a half-hug. "Girl, you've had me and your father scared to death. How come you haven't been answering your phone? I've been calling and calling."

"I'm fine, Mother. Jimmy, thank you," Riley said.

"I hope I did the right thing, Mrs. Woodson, your mother was pretty nervous," Jimmy said. After closing the door behind Jimmy, Riley walked back into her library and reclaimed her place on the sofa. Her mother followed her.

"Riley, what is wrong with you?"

"I'm fine, Mother," Riley said.

"Well, you don't look fine. Why don't you have any clothes on? Where is Selwyn? You still haven't told me why you haven't been answering your phone," Clarice said. Riley didn't answer her mother, but instead gazed at the muted television. Clarice was shocked. She had never seen her daughter act in this manner, not even when she was a teenager.

"Riley, don't sit there like a bump on a log. What's the matter with you?"

Riley remained silent, so Clarice walked over to the television and hit the power button off. Still no response from Riley.

"You can sit there like you're crazy if you want to, but I'm not leaving here until you tell me what's wrong with you. I can sit here all night, I don't have any place to go," Clarice said as she sat in a chair directly across the room from Riley. Her voice was cool and bitter. Silence swallowed the room.

Almost an hour later, Clarice got up and started talking again, "Okay, miss. You can sit there if you want to, but I think you've lost your mind. I'm going to call your father, and then Selwyn. If I can't get a hold of them, then I'm calling nine one one. If you're sick or something, then you don't need me sitting here. You need to be in a hospital. In all my years of living, I have never seen anything like this. I have taught you better. And if you're acting like this because you think your father and I will be spending all our time with Clayton Jr. when he gets out of that hellhole—then you'd better snap out of it. You can't be sitting up here in this room and let life pass you by."

When Clarice moved toward the phone, Riley realized she wasn't going to leave without dragging Selwyn into her drama. Riley willed her voice into a firm and steady tone and said, "Mother, I'm going to say this only once. I am fine. I want to be alone. You don't need to call Daddy or Selwyn. I'm asking you to leave me alone. I appreciate your concern, but I have to be alone."

"But why? When did this start? Does this have to do with Ryan? Is she okay? Are you upset about Clayton Jr?"

"Mother, I'm sure you've talked with Ryan. She and Reggie are both fine. And I'm happy Clayton might get paroled." Riley started to tell her mother to stop being so messy, but she didn't think Clarice would hear her.

"What if I stay here and leave you alone? I can stay here and sleep in the guest room, or in Ryan's room. Yes, that's what I'll do. If you don't want to talk, then fine. I'll just stay here and make sure you don't do something crazy." Riley was preparing to take her mother by the hands and lead her out the door, when she heard the keys to the door turn again.

"Who is that?" Clarice shouted.

"It's Selwyn. Clarice, is that you?"

"Yes, we're in the library," Clarice said. Riley rolled her eyes at her mother in anger. Selwyn walked into the library and looked at Riley sitting on the sofa with her arms folded and Clarice standing near the phone.

"What's going on?" Selwyn asked as he set down his hanging bag and laptop case.

"That's what I'm trying to find out. Riley, why didn't you tell me Selwyn was coming home?" Riley didn't answer her mother, and Selwyn looked at Riley with a puzzled glance. "Oh, she didn't know I was coming back. I finished my meeting sooner than expected, and I decided I wanted to be home. Riley, are you okay? I called you several times and I didn't get an answer. I was thinking maybe you went to Hampton."

"I don't think she's okay. Selwyn, I think we need to take this girl to the hospital and get her checked out. I've been calling her for about three days, so I came over here and she hasn't said five words to me. Do you know what's wrong with her?"

Selwyn walked over to the sofa and sat next to Riley. He took her hand and asked, "Riley, are you okay, baby?" When she didn't answer, he put his head on her forehead, checking for a fever. His touch felt soft to Riley, but she turned away from him and said, "I'm fine, Selwyn. I'll be fine. I've asked my mother to leave. She won't. Would you please tell her I want to be alone?"

"See what I'm talking about, this girl is crazy, Selwyn. She's talking about me like I'm not here. Riley knows I don't take that kind of mess. We raised her better. Treating me like I'm some sort of disease," Clarice said. Selwyn looked at her and noticed tears were streaming down her face. This was not the homecoming he had planned. He went over to Clarice and put his hand on her shoulders and said very gently, "Clarice, I have everything under control. Riley will be fine. But I think you should leave. I promise I'll find out what's going on and I will call you. Will you do that for me?"

"I'm not leaving, this is my child," Clarice said as she wiped tears from her face. "This is *my* child."

"Clarice, Riley is my wife. I will take care of her. Now, come on, sweetheart. Let me see you to the door." Clarice looked at Riley and shook her head in disgust and rushed from the library and out the door without a good-bye.

Selwyn sat back on the sofa and took Riley's hand again. Staring at the television screen, Riley felt a numbness running through her like something the dentist had given her to ease the pain of root canal. And even though her pain wasn't physical, she still hurt.

"Tell me what's wrong, Riley. Are the kids okay? I talked with them both earlier and they sounded like everything was okay. Tell me what's wrong."

"Nothing's wrong, Selwyn," Riley said. Her voice was calm, though filled with sadness.

"But you don't sound fine. Is there anything I can do?"

Riley looked down at Selwyn holding her hand. "Tell me what happened to us? What did I do to make you stop loving me?" she asked suddenly as she looked up at her husband as if for the first time, wanting him to love her.

"Riley, what are you talking about? I love you," Selwyn said strongly.

"Are you sure?"

"Is this what's bothering you? You know I've been busy with work, and I know I'm not as affectionate as I used to be, but it's not you, Riley. If anything, you've been too tolerant of my negligence. It's me."

Riley's eyes brightened a little. She had never heard Selwyn admit that something was wrong with him. "What do you mean, it's you?"

"I've been afraid. You know, life for the most part has been good for us. I'm making a lot of money. The kids were great, you were great. I just got scared," Selwyn said softly.

"Scared of what?"

"That something would happen, like you leaving me or the kids. Having a family and being a part of a family is something I have dreamed of all my life. When it came together so perfectly, I just figured something would happen to take it away. Like it happened so many times when I was growing up," he added.

"Where did you think I was going to go? And the children? You know how much they love you."

"I don't know. It wasn't anything you or the kids did or said. About three years ago, I started having these nightmares. I'd come home and the place would be empty. The furniture and all our belongings would still be here, but there were no signs of you, Ryan, or Reggie. It was as though you'd never existed. Never been a part of my life. Sometimes I was surprised when I'd come home from long trips and you'd still be here. I think many times I'd left just to experience that feeling I have when I walk in the house and see your face," Selwyn said as he came closer and placed his face against her cheek.

Riley touched his face and then placed her hand near her heart. Then she said, "Why didn't you tell me about your dreams. We could have gotten help. I could have asked Leland about doctors."

"Because I know I can work this out. I didn't want to talk about it. I guess I just needed to say what was bothering me out loud. I've kept it inside, pretending it's not there."

"But that's why I'm here. We used to be friends. I want to be your friend again. I need a friend," Riley said.

"I need a friend too," Selwyn said as he moved his head to Riley's lap, and she gently brushed his face as tears tumbled from her eyes. Tears of joy, the kind you feel when you see an old friend you'd given up for dead.

Chapter 23

"**Excuse me, are** you Yolanda Williams?" a man with a husky baritone voice asked as he walked up to my table at the Fifty-seven Fifty-seven restaurant and bar in the lobby court of the Four Seasons Hotel.

"Yes, I am. You must be Monty Mason," I said as I stood up and extended my hand. He shook it gently and said, "Please, have a seat."

Lajoyce had told me the record company had been really impressed with me and wanted me to meet Monty Mason to determine if the two of us could work together. I had listened to his group's music most of the morning during my workout.

Monty Mason was a handsome, well-dressed man wearing tailored gray slacks and a light blue form-fitting sweater, a little over six feet with slightly rounded shoulders. Monty's skin was a Sugar Baby–caramel color. The first thing I noticed about him were his wide-set puppy-dog brown eyes, and lashes as thick and dark as his closely cropped hair.

"Do you stay here often?" I asked.

"It depends. This place is usually booked. But it's one of my favorite hotels," Monty said.

"So you live in L.A.?"

"For the time being. What are you drinking?" Monty asked as he looked around the restaurant for the waitress.

"Cranberry and 7-Up."

"Sounds good." His smile relaxed and then disappeared altogether. Despite his success as a recording artist, he seemed a little nervous.

"I've been listening to your group's music. It's all that. How long have you been in the group?" I knew the answer, but I was trying to make him feel comfortable with me.

"About five years, as a group with a record deal. But close to nine years altogether. We met in college, you know, just singing in talent and Greek shows" Monty said. The waitress walked over and Monty ordered a club soda. He picked up a handful of the mixed nuts on the table and plopped them in his mouth. His teeth were as white and perfect as the sugar cubes on our cocktail table.

"Well, I've talked with the people at your record company. They're really high on you. Are you nervous about going solo?"

"Not really. I'm just worried how the public might accept me," he said.

This was my opportunity to bring up the subject at hand. I started to ask him how long he had been gay, but I decided on a different approach. "You know, you're a very brave man to do this. My best friend is gay, and he tells me all the time about how difficult it is being gay in certain industries, like R & B music, for instance. Are you sure you're ready to do this?" I wanted to kick myself for mentioning Leland so soon. I hoped I didn't sound patronizing, but I wanted to ask if he was involved with anyone, or if he was interested in meeting a great guy.

"Yeah, I think I'm ready, but I don't know how brave I am. I'm sorta being forced. I've got to beat those knuckleheads to the punch."

"Do you think they would really leak this information to the press? There are other ways around this."

"Jealousy is a muther. The moment I mentioned my desire to go solo, the threats started. I thought we had an understanding that at some point we would all try to go solo," Monty said. "I'm really trying to beat them to the punch. When they find out I've got a record deal and I've already cut the tracks—I know somebody will start talking."

"Why don't you tell me what happened? How did they find out you were gay?"

"I'm not gay. I'm bisexual. I still love women," Monty said firmly.

"Oh, I'm sorry. How did they find out you're bisexual?" I was thinking same thing, or whatever floats your boat, as my daddy used to say.

"I slipped up and got caught. It was a dumb mistake. I'm usually more careful than that. We were over in Amsterdam, doing appearances. All of us had been running the women all week. The travel agency had screwed up our reservations, so instead of it being two of us in a room, we all had to share a large suite. It was nice, you know, we had a pullout sofa and they brought up a cot. But a couple of us had to sleep in the same bed. Well, anyhow, I met this guy backstage and he gave me this look. I knew what was up and whispered what hotel we were staying at and the room number. I had never fucked around when I was on tour with the group." Monty paused as he took a sip of his drink and picked up a few more mixed nuts. I pulled out a pen and notepad and asked if he would mind if I took a few notes. "No, I don't mind. Like I was saying, I gave the dude my information, and I headed back to the hotel. The other members of the group were going to a local club to hang out with some women they had met. I told them I was beat—I was singing most of the leads and so they understood. Pretty soon old boy showed up—we got busy, and I got busted ass-up," he said.

I didn't ask what ass-up meant, but I had an idea. "How did they treat you after that night?"

"A couple of the guys were cool, saying stuff like 'I'm not gay, but whatever is clever.' There was a lot of laughing and whispers of

'Man can you believe that shit. Aw man, pretty boy Monty likes the beef.' I tried to tell them I wasn't that way, that I was just curious. Even made up some lame excuse that the guy must have slipped something in my drink."

"I guess they didn't believe you."

"At first I thought they did."

"What changed your mind?"

"One time when some ladies came backstage wanting to git with us, one of the group members asked them if they had a brother for me. The rest of them giggled like little boys on a playground."

"When did they threaten to expose you?"

"It was when we got back to the States. They heard from our manager that I was going to be the first one to get a solo record deal. One of the guys who thinks he's the shit was so beside himself. Started calling me all kinds of names, until I decked his ass. When I beat his ass, he swore he'd get me. I think he convinced the other guys to back him."

"Are you ready to deal with all the questions that will come up? Most likely, the media will be more interested in your sex life than in your music."

"But that's where you come in, right?" Monty asked. "You can keep that from happening, after we do the story," Monty asked. His voice expressed curiosity rather than fear.

"Not exactly. My job will be to prepare you to handle the press. Once we put it out there, we'll have to deal with it. Now, we can flat-out deny the accusations. The music industry is filled with individuals who at one time or another had been accused of being gay or bi. Then just ride it out. I can prepare a statement and we can stick to that. We can also come up with a list of responses that aren't lies, but that skirt around the gay issues. Making sure we're both on the same page."

"What I should do is bust some of them," Monty said. A bitter edge had entered his voice.

"Bust who?" I asked.

"I'm not the only one in the group who swings the door both ways. I found out through somebody I was dealing with that another member of the group fucks around. With a pro basketball player."

"A member of your group was dealing with a pro basketball player?"

"Yeah, a basketball player. All kinds of men people would never suspect fuck around. Football players, singers, and what have you. I should bust them all."

"Are you certain about this other group member? Did he tell you?"

"Naw, but I know. I've seen him hanging out with his *boy*, and I know," Monty said confidently. I was thinking, then tell me how to know. I guess Leland was right when he said recognizing someone else who was gay was like a sixth sense.

"Yeah, I should bust them all," Monty repeated.

"I don't think you want to do that. If we're gonna come clean, we should keep this on a higher plane. I want to contact *Vibe*, *The Source*, and *Billboard* and give them a shot at an exclusive. Your story. I think we should follow up with interviews in some of the gay magazines," I said.

"Gay magazines. Why should we go there?"

"If we do this with the truth, you're going to need them, Monty. They can be very influential in your public acceptance. They've been wonderful with people like Me'shell Ndegeocello and k. d. lang," I said.

"But those are women. The public accepts that shit."

"Both of them are wonderful talents. Have you heard Me'shell's album *Peace Beyond Passion?*"

"Yeah. Sister's got skillz," Monty said.

"With you being the first Black man to come out in the R & B arena, it's going to be big news. You're really a trailblazer, but you understand it can be a liability also. I've already talked with several gay-oriented magazines. I didn't give them your name, but they were all interested. I think we should talk with *SBC*, *Venus*, *The*

Advocate, and *Genre.* Those are the ones I've heard really good things about. After the novelty wears off—then I think you'll have a chance to show them what you can do with your voice."

"That's what I'm talking about. If they want to give me fever because of the way I am, then fuck 'em. I can sing my ass off," Monty said in a clear, self-assured voice.

"Are you prepared for the rejection you might face from the record-buying public? Part of your appeal has been that you're a sex symbol," I said.

"I don't think that's going to happen. I'll always have a woman on my arm. I'll even get married if I have to."

I started to ask him if he felt it was necessary to ruin some woman's life by marrying her, but I didn't. If he could find a woman fool enough to marry him, then more power to the both of them.

"I'm hopeful that in the end, your talent will be the only thing that matters," I said.

"You know, deep down I don't want to do this, but I refuse to let those bastards have the last word."

"I won't make a move without talking to your manager, the record company, and, of course, you," I said as I stood and shook Monty's moist hand. "Yeah, I need to sleep on this. Oops, that's what got me into the mess," Monty said with a nervous giggle. His body language was a little bit cocky with equal parts fear. I wanted to tell him everything would be just fine, but I wasn't so sure.

Later that evening over wine and a pizza packed with pepperoni, I told John about my meeting, without revealing Monty's identity.

"Why won't you tell me who he is?"

"Because it's business. You'll know as soon as the rest of the public finds out," I said. I reached over to wipe some mozzarella that was hanging off John's chin. He licked my fingers clean, then asked, "Is ole boy sure he wants to do this? I mean, if you think he's going to be big, then he might want to keep that shit to himself."

"Well, I think that's wrong." I didn't want to get in a big moral discussion, so I turned to every man's favorite subject: himself. "What's going on with you and ESPN?"

"Funny you should mention that. I got an assignment this weekend. I'm doing a University of Michigan game in Ann Arbor. It's really big-time," John said.

"The timing is perfect," I said.

"What do you mean?"

"I'm leaving on Friday."

"Aw, baby, stay here. I'd love to come back knowing you're going to be here," John said.

"As much as I love waking up with you every morning, I've got to get back to Chicago. I've got to follow up with some potential clients, like the new House of Blues, and I've got my group meeting on Sunday."

Before John could respond, his phone rang, something it did often during my stay. Most times he didn't pick it up, allowing the answering machine to handle his calls, but this time he reached over to answer. He was so close, I couldn't help but hear his conversation. "Yeah, Casey, I got your message," he said. A few seconds passed and then I heard him say, "I told you I'm seeing somebody. It's a one-on-one thing, hold on for a second. Hello? Whatsup, dude? Yeah, I got your message—I've been busy." After a few minutes of silence John said, "I told you I'm not down with that. Take it easy. Casey, I've got to go."

When he sat back down I teased him by saying, "Aw, Mr. Popular."

"Folks need to recognize that no means *no*. Now, what were you saying, baby?" I loved it when he called me baby.

"I was telling you I have to get back to Chicago for my journal group meeting."

"That group's real important to you—huh?"

"Yeah, it is. Keeps me sane," I said. Suddenly I thought about Riley. I wondered how she was handling my decision and if she was going to show up at the meeting. Maybe I'd try to call her before Sunday.

"What are you thinking about?" John asked.

"I'm sorry. I was thinking about Riley. We might have to get a new member if she drops out," I said.

"You think she will?"

"It's hard to say. We've been together for a long time. Eventually Riley will understand that I did what I had to do."

"Let me join the group. Since I'm going to write a book, maybe I should keep a journal," John said.

"You live here in New York! And meetings in Chicago would be tough. But you should definitely keep a journal. Right now is an exciting time for you, with the new career and all," I said.

"And a wonderful new lady in my life," John said with a big smile.

I blushed. "Didn't you tell me you've got family in Michigan? An uncle, right?"

"Yeah, in Detroit," John said as he took a bite of pizza. His grin disappeared.

"Are you going to see him?"

"Naw, I'll be too busy. We'll see him together."

"We will? What are you talking about?"

"I want you to come with me at Thanksgiving and meet my father and my aunt. We're all meeting at my uncle's for a big family dinner. I've been talking about you so much, they already know you." John paused to check out my reaction. "So what do you think?"

"Sounds like fun. I have to make sure my sister or Leland doesn't have plans for me," I said. I was thinking family was a serious thing. I had introduced only Chauncey to my parents and I couldn't recall the last time a man *wanted* me to meet his parents.

"It would just be the two of us—you know, after the family stuff. Maybe we can head up to Canada and do some skiing. Just so you're with me when the lights go out," John said as he touched my face softly. I smiled and he kissed me, and we leaned back onto the couch, and moments later I felt a soft pizza on my back, but with John on top of me, it didn't matter.

Later that evening John ran a luxurious bath for me, carried me to his bedroom, then oiled me down and gave me the most sensuous massage I'd ever had—from my neck down to my toes. Before we fell asleep, he whispered he loved me, as if he were afraid to say it out loud. I was too stunned to respond.

Chapter 24

For Dwight, Thursday had started earlier than it should have with a four A.M. call from his mother. Sarah never seemed to get the time right and would often wait up until after midnight, California time, to "catch her baby" before he left for work.

"Mama, it's four A.M., whatsamatter?" Dwight answered the phone on barely awake.

"Ain't nothin' the matter, baby. I just wanted to make sure I caught my baby 'fore he left for work. Can't a mama call her own child just to say she loves him?"

"But it's two A.M. there. What time are you going to work?"

"Oh, I'm going to leave about five-thirty. I don't know, I just couldn't sleep. Just want to hear my baby," Sarah said.

Dwight propped himself on his pillows and tried to come fully awake.

"I love you too, Mama. Are you sure everything is all right? Do you need anything?"

"No, baby. You take care of me just fine as it is. I always told you long as you take care of yourself, that helps me out a lot. How you doin'? Am I going to see you soon? You know I'd feel better if I knew when you might be comin' home to see me."

In the predawn darkness of his bedroom, a light went on in Dwight's mind. She had a feeling. She always had a feeling when something wasn't quite right with him. He didn't know how she did it, but she and her feelings were as predictable as the sun rising. Sarah was a mother.

"Mama, I know you gonna find this out sooner or later," Dwight began. "I've quit my job and I'm thinking about moving back to Oakland. I'm sick of working for white folks. Maybe I'll start up my own firm. You think you could stand to see my ugly mug every day?"

"Just this evening I was thinking how good it would be if I could see my baby every day. Now listen to you. God is good, chile. And He is still in control!" Dwight could hear the sudden joy in his mother's voice.

"Now, hold up. Don't get excited yet. I'm just thinking about it right now. I'm still going over some job offers back here, and I'm going on a few interviews before I make up my mind. In fact, I'm glad you woke me up. I've got an early flight to D.C. this morning to interview with a new Black computer company there. I'm at least going to see what they have to say, then we'll see."

"Suga, I hope it goes well. I really do. But any Black company worth its fatback in a pot of greens got to have some openings in Oakland. Now, you know your mama sure would like to have you back home. Have you asked them about a job in Oakland?"

"Naw, Mama. I got to get the job first."

"You will, 'cause God's goin' to work things out for the best. Whatever that may be. If it's God will that I have my baby back here sittin' at the table eating some of my world-famous hotcakes with warm maple syrup and butter drippin' all down the sides—well, so be it!" They both laughed at that.

"I'll call you when I get back, and let you know how it went. I love you, Mama—more than anything."

"I'll be praying for you, son. Good-bye."

Dwight's mother always gave him such a lift. She made him feel like there was someone on his side, someone who loved him no matter what. When his thoughts slid naturally from his mother, his family, to Scooter (aka Sedrick), Dwight jumped quickly from the bed. He showered, dressed in his best three-button blue suit, packed a overnight bag, and headed for O'Hare. A couple of hours later Dwight arrived in the city that just might be what the doctor ordered. Chocolate City, U.S.A.

Jackson-Hill, Inc., was a new player in the computer industry, but its president and founder, Edwin Jackson, had a long and illustrious reputation in the business for innovative thinking and a successful track record with three of the world's largest computer corporations. Edwin was a Hampton grad who had risen to the top of his field by sheer determination. He was an average-sized man, and nondescript in appearance. A medium-brown color and somewhere between forty and forty-five years of age, he wore gold-rimmed glasses and was beginning to gray and bald simultaneously.

A big-legged, short-skirted receptionist in a royal blue tailored business suit led Dwight down the plushly carpeted corridor to Edwin Jackson's large corner office. It was an ole-boy kind of office with an Afrocentric twist. Rich wood paneling covered two walls, the sofas and chairs were leather, the furnishings antique. Original Black art hung in gilded frames along with Edwin's numerous degrees, citations, and awards. Tall potted palms in brass containers stood on either side of the floor-to-ceiling glass walls that formed the corner of his office.

Edwin sat behind his huge desk looking intensely at columns of numbers moving quickly across the screen of his computer. He had removed his suit coat, and his shirt-sleeves were rolled up to just below his elbows.

"Dwight! How good of you to come," Edwin greeted him. His face lit up with a warm smile as he stepped around his desk and vigorously shook Dwight's hand with both of his. A barrage of questions followed.

"Please, have a seat. How's the hotel? Have you had a chance to check in? Did you have a good flight? We've all been eager to meet you. When Becky told me she had a Hampton grad she wanted me to interview, I was excited. Would you like some coffee? Tea? Have you had breakfast? Most important meal of the day, if you ask me. I can have whatever you'd like brought in. Perhaps some fresh fruit? It's no trouble."

Edwin Jackson spoke in such a rapid-fire manner, Dwight had little chance to answer any of his questions before he'd ask three more. Dwight thought Edwin was more nervous than he should be. Dwight was the one being interviewed.

"I'm fine, really, Mr. Jackson. I came here right from the airport. But I'm certain everything will be fine with the hotel. And I had breakfast on the plane," Dwight said.

"Edwin!"

"Beg pardon?" Dwight answered.

"Edwin! Call me Edwin, everybody does. We try and keep a family environment in the office. No stuffed shirts here. Let's get down to business, shall we? Mikal Lewis and Bill Carter are on their way up to meet you. Like I was saying, I've heard great things about you, Dwight Scott. I read your resumé thoroughly; you've got a lot of experience in the area we're expanding. I talked with some people at Hampton who knew you while you were a student. At the top of your class. I like what I hear about the work you're doing with our kids, we do a considerable amount of community work around here too. I figure we have a responsibility to give back to our community, especially our children. Don't you agree?"

"Yes sir. Never forgetting where I came from has always, always been important to me."

"Yes, sir, Dwight, I like what I see," Edwin said.

Dwight liked Edwin immediately and liked him even more by the end of the interview. Mikal Lewis, vice president of sales, and Bill Carter, technical services manager, were obviously eager to have him join the team. They answered all his questions without hesitation, open and honestly. The company was well situated financially, and their plans for growth and development were exciting to Dwight. The salary they proposed was three times what he was making at his former employer, with stock options and excellent benefits.

After three hours of questions and more questions, Edwin called his executive assistant to summon the limousine to pick Dwight up and take him to the hotel for some rest before dinner. It would take him to the Park Hyatt just outside Georgetown, where Dwight promised to review the portfolio of material they had given him before dinner. As the heavy wood door was closing behind him, Dwight turned and caught a glimpse of the three men smiling and nodding their approval. He was in—if he wanted.

Dwight relaxed in the comfort of the company limo. He stretched his legs and thought how wonderful it was seeing Black men excelling in the tough and competitive computer industry. He pressed his head back into the soft leather, and the smoothness of the ride lulled Dwight into a sweet dream of a day when he'd have an office just like Edwin Jackson's.

When he arrived at the Park Hyatt, a beautiful sister named Carmen welcomed Dwight and told him his executive suite was waiting for him. Finally, she listed the many amenities the swank hotel offered its guests.

The suite was impressive, as was the basket of fruit and bottle of wine Edwin's staff had waiting with a note welcoming him to Washington, D.C. Dwight started to order a late lunch, but remembered his dinner later that evening. He remembered Carmen describing the wonderful health club, so he decided to go for a workout and swim instead.

Forty laps later, Dwight stepped from the warm water of the indoor pool and shivered as the cool air hit his wet body. He hugged himself and looked around for his towel. He could see the oversized hotel towel through the glass partition separating the pool area from the weight room. Except for Dwight, both areas were deserted. He retrieved his towel and plastic water bottle from next to the stationary bike he'd ridden before taking a swim, then retraced his wet footprints back to the pool area.

Dwight dried his upper body, and used the towel to pat water from his swimming trunks. He sat on a reclining deck chair and dried off his legs and feet, then threw the towel over the chair next to him. He lay back and closed his eyes. Though the workout and swim had relaxed his body, his mind moved at the speed of light. It had been a very long day.

"Hi! My name is Scotty. What's yours?" Dwight lifted his head to find a thin little white boy in lime-green swim trunks standing beside him. He tried to focus on the child's face, but his eyes were still blurry with sleep. He stretched his full length, then relaxed back into the chair, yawning loudly.

"What'd you say, kid?" he asked.

"I said"—the little blond boy stomped his sandaled feet on the concrete and yelled at the top of his lungs—"my name is Scotty and I'm four years old!" His high-pitched voice reverberated off the pool room walls. Dwight was now fully awake.

"Scotty! Leave the nice man alone. Come over here with Mommy." A pale white woman with shoulder-length brown hair, wearing a yellow warmup suit with gym shoes, sat up in a deck chair a few yards to Dwight's right. A younger child, a toddler, sat wiggling in her lap. She smiled nervously in Dwight's direction. "I'm sorry, mister, I hope he's not bothering you," she said. Dwight didn't respond. He was thinking, of course he's bothering me. I'm trying to rest before my big interview dinner. Scotty couldn't read Dwight's mind.

"You wanna play, mister? I can swim now. I don't live here. I came here on a really big airplane. I bet I can swim all the way 'cross by myself. Wanna see?" Scotty leaned on the arm of Dwight's chair.

"Scott David Taylor! I said come here instantly!" his mother warned, but Scotty kept his round blue eyes focused on Dwight, not even turning when he heard his mother struggling to get up from her chair.

"I got a fire truck at my house and a puppy. Puppies can't go on the airplane, just people." Scotty ran his fingers along Dwight's arm. "You all brown like my puppy. How come?"

Scotty's mom gave the little boy a quick swat on his bottom and jerked him away. Scotty turned to look back and waved at Dwight as his mother mumbled something about him talking to strange men.

Dwight didn't wave back. The "superior race," he thought. Four years old and already comparing him to the color of his dog. When he's forty, he would be a white man treating people like a dog, Dwight thought.

Though Dwight had a natural affinity for children, his feelings toward white people blinded him to Scotty's innocent overture. He had a little brother once. Sedrick David Scott, but everybody called him Scooter from the day Sarah brought him home. Scooter was about Scotty's age, four, when white people let him die. Sat by and watched him die.

· · ·

Dwight was seven going on eight when he became the first person in his family to learn to swim. He had taken lessons from the local YMCA all summer long, finally passing the test and receiving his certificate. Sarah was so proud, she framed the certificate and hung it on the living room wall for all to see. She'd pull friends and neighbors aside after church and tell them: "You know Dwight, my oldest, got his swimmin' papers. Yessiree, my little man can swim, chile. From one end of the big pool to the other. Praise the Lord. You'll never get me in a pool that big, but my baby can swim."

So when Dwight's aunt Ruthie came all the way from Hughes Springs, Texas, on the Greyhound for a visit, Dwight's mom was pleased when she asked for a real live demonstration of Dwight's aquatic prowess.

Wednesdays were "free days," when the quarter admission fee

was waived at the city-owned pool in their neighborhood. And although the facility had been "officially" desegregated years before, the white and Black children maintained an imaginary line down the center of the water. Though they stood in line together, the Black kids jumped off the diving board to the left, and the white kids jumped to the right. Orange plastic chairs lined the walls on both sides of the pool for nonswimmers to sit and watch.

Dwight was in such a hurry to show his mother and Aunt Ruthie what he could do, he had convinced her to take him and Scooter to the pool at eight A.M. It didn't officially open until around nine-thirty, but Dwight knew the big hole in the fence was a way of sneaking in on the nonfree days.

"Watch me, Mama!" little Dwight had yelled. "Watch this, Aunt Ruthie." And Dwight did a spectacular belly flop off the diving board into the deep end of the pool.

"Watch me, Mama!" Scooter copied his brother, standing close to the edge of the pool's shallow end.

"Scooter," his mother had yelled. "Boy, don't you dare jump in that water. Wait for your brother. I'm not playing with you, boy." She was halfway out of her chair, when Dwight suddenly splashed through the surface of the water at the shallow end.

"I got 'em, Mama. C'mon, Scooter, back down the ladder. I'll catch you. You can hold on to the side." Dwight and Scooter looked to their mother. She smiled her approval and Scooter began backing down the metal ladder into the water. When his left big toe touched the water, Scooter squealed and climbed quickly back up the ladder. Sarah and Ruthie had a good laugh, and Scooter sat stubbornly on the edge of the pool and tried to ignore his big brother's teasing.

"You ain't nothin' but a big ol' baby, Scooter!" Dwight said as he dove under the water and surfaced back on the deep end. When he swam back, Dwight noticed he had company, a little white boy about Dwight's age had jumped in the pool. His mother and father sat on the unofficial white side facing Dwight's mother and aunt.

They wore matching tropical print swimsuits. Dwight and the little white boy were taking turns jumping off the diving board, when they heard the scream.

"Oh, Lord! Oh, my dear Jesus! Somebody save my baby!" Dwight's mother was running up and down the shallow end, pointing into the water.

Scooter had just up and jumped feetfirst into the water and was now frantically waving his arms and trying to call for his mama. The flailing of his arms and legs was carrying him across to the other side of the pool. The white couple sat up straight in their chairs and leaned forward to get a better view. Dwight swam as fast as he could toward the shallow end. When he got to the spot where he'd last seen Scooter, he held his nose and searched under the water for his baby brother. Dwight opened his eyes, and the chlorine burned and blurred his vision—he saw Scooter but couldn't tell how far away he was or if he was still breathing. When his breath was almost gone, he jumped up and gulped for air.

His mother and Aunt Ruthie were now pointing to the other side of the pool, in front of the still-seated couple. Dwight did his very best to swim across faster than he'd ever swum before. He thought he saw Scooter's little hand touch the side of the pool at the five-foot mark, then against the six-foot mark before he disappeared again under the water. Dwight swam faster toward the mark, but Scooter had drifted farther toward the deep end. His mother and aunt were running around the pool toward the white side.

"Help me! Help my baby!" Dwight's mother yelled at the couple. "Can't you please help my poor baby?" she begged. "We cain't swim!"

"We cain't either. Yer boy'll get him. No point in everybody drowning," the man said. He turned to his wife and said, "Honey, go get somebody out here to give 'em a hand." The white woman stood reluctantly and sauntered off. Dwight would always remember the heavy clip-clop of her clogs on the concrete as she moved ever so slowly toward the pool office.

Dwight held on to the white side of the pool, his body exhausted, his breath coming in quick gasps. He swam to the eight-foot mark and dove deep under the water—coming up for air and then diving back down again. He couldn't reach Scooter, and his tiny body was sinking slowly to the bottom of the pool.

By the time help arrived, it was too late.

Sarah stood wringing her hands and praying softly, tears streaming down her face as Scooter's limp body was placed gently on the stretcher. Ruthie sat paralyzed with shock and grief. The couple stood side by side with the little white boy hoisted onto the man's shoulder like they were watching a parade.

Dwight stood stiffly at his mother's side, his rage forcing back his tears. "I'm sorry, Mama," he whispered.

His mother placed her hand on his shoulder, "It's okay, baby. It's not your fault." She paused as if to summon all her strength. "Scooter is with Jesus now."

Dwight wanted to lash out at the white couple, beat their little boy until he lay as lifeless as Scooter. But he was weak and powerless. He couldn't even save his own little brother.

A mother's scream brought Dwight back to the present. The painful, vivid memory had tensed his body, and he felt a tightness in his neck and shoulders. Dwight sat straight up and stretched his arms high over his head.

"Help! Somebody help!" Dwight turned to see Scotty's mother running to the edge of the pool. She had left Scotty explicit instructions not to bother the nice man and not to go near the water while she went into the locker room to change the toddler's diaper. Scotty had jumped into the clear blue water as soon as she had turned her back. The loud splash made her turn in time to see Scotty gasping for air as he went under.

She placed the toddler on a deck chair and ran over to Dwight, the toddler's cries and Scotty's gasps piercing in her ears.

"Please!" She grabbed Dwight's arm. "I can't swim. Please save my child," she cried hysterically.

Dwight hesitated for a blink of an eye. He saw Scooter struggling in the deep water, his own mother frightened and panicked at his side. An overwhelming sense of powerlessness and rage gripped his heart. Scotty's blond head bobbed to the surface, his small arms and legs moving wildly in the water. He gasped for air, screamed for his mother, and gulped water before he sank again.

Scotty's mother shook Dwight hard. "Help me!" she screamed in his ear.

Dwight rushed to the side of the pool and dove in. Seconds later he crashed through the surface of the water with a coughing, crying Scotty under his arm. He swam to the side of the pool and lifted the frightened child into the hands of his mother. Grabbing on to the side of the pool, he lifted himself onto the deck. He was surprised to find his knees wobbly, his body drained as though a weight he didn't even know he carried had been suddenly, mercifully, lifted from his shoulders. He got his towel from the deck chair and wrapped it around Scotty's shivering body. Scotty's mother wept, alternately hugging and scolding Scotty. "Thank you for saving my son." Her eyes were filled with tears and gratitude as she looked up at Dwight.

Dwight put one arm around her shoulders and one arm around Scotty and pulled them close to him. Scotty's mother sobbed with relief; Scotty held on tightly to Dwight's leg and cried a scared-little-boy cry; and, for the second time, Dwight wept for the loss of Scooter.

Chapter 25

It finally happened. Like that song goes, I fooled around and fell in love with Yolanda Diane Williams. I'm tripping 'cause it happened so soon, and because I don't know if she's fallen for me yet. But I'm not real worried, she will. Matter fact, I think I'll surprise her and go to Chicago once I finish my college game gig in Madison.

Having her here every evening, waking up in the morning, just talking and enjoying the comfort of each other's bodies, has changed me. I still find it hard to believe I've found a woman who I feel so safe with, where I don't see nothing but love when I look in her eyes. When she left for the airport a couple of hours ago, I repeated what I had told her this week: I love you. I know her silent smile means she feels the same way. She's just afraid to say it.

I was looking in my closet, trying to decide which sweaters and slacks to take to Madison, when my doorman buzzed me. I wasn't expecting anybody, since every time someone called when I was with Yolanda I gave them the old brushoff.

I'd gotten about five calls from Monty, so I shouldn't have been surprised when I was told he was downstairs. Now, this mofo knows

I don't like folks dropping by my place unannounced. But I decided to use this opportunity to tell Monty that we couldn't kick it anymore. It was later for hardheads. I opened my door, and there Monty stood with the biggest shit-eating grin on his face.

"Whatsup, my dog? I didn't think you was going to let me up," Monty said.

"Come on in, Monty, whatsup," I said as I shook his hand and gave him the standard brotherman hug.

"Did you get my messages? Man, I've been needing to talk to you," Monty said.

"Yeah, I got them, but I've been real busy."

"That's right, you're doing the TV thing. That's smooth, man. I saw you once. You look good on the screen."

"Thanks. Come on and have a seat. What do you need to talk to me about that's so important?" We both walked over to my sofa. I started to put on some music, but I wanted to hear what this mofo had to say and get him out.

"Man, you still look good," Monty said as he touched my face. I quickly grabbed his hand and pushed it back. "Naw man, I ain't with that. What do you need to talk to me about?"

"All right, man, these niggers in my group are tripping. I got caught in some shit, you know with my pants down. Niggers are jealous 'cause I'm getting ready to blow up on the music scene. Getting ready to go solo. And I wanted to tell you I think I'm going to have to go public with the other side of my life," Monty said. For a moment I couldn't believe what I was hearing. Monty was Yolanda's client. My body started to feel warm and I twisted my neck and tried to loosen the top button on the knit pullover I was wearing.

"Man, why you wanna do some shit like that?"

"I don't have a choice," Monty said.

I stood up from the sofa and headed to my kitchen to get some water, but first I looked at Monty and said, "Monty, get real. Them mofos ain't gonna say shit. They will be too worried about what people gonna say about them." Monty got up and followed me to the kitchen.

"You think so, man? I don't know. You know niggas, like crabs in a barrel. Don't want to see anybody get to the top. You got a beer, or some wine?"

I grabbed a beer and gave it to Monty. I wanted him to drink this beer and get to steppin' with his dumb ass. I know those mofos wasn't going to say shit. We walked back into the living room and I asked Monty why he thought I needed to know about his going public.

"Just in case, you know, some people might know we used to hang out. And this lady I'm working with on dealing with the public told me reporters might want me to name names."

Without thinking I said, "Yolanda ain't going to instruct you to do some dumb shit like that."

"You know Yolanda Williams? How do you know her?"

I started to tell Monty none of his damn business, but I was proud of my lady. "Yeah, I know Yolanda. And I know she's been working with you. Yolanda's my lady."

"And she told you about me? That's fucked up. The record company told me everything I told her was confidential until we decided whether or not I'm going public," Monty said.

"Naw, she didn't tell me your name. But once you started talking, it didn't take me too long to figure out it's you. I mean, how many singers you know getting ready to do something like what you're thinking about."

"I can't believe this shit," Monty said as he shook his head.

"Can't believe what?"

"That female would be talking about my business."

"What are you talking about? You're the one that wanted to talk. If you had any sense, you'd keep your goddamn mouth shut and just use it for singing," I said. I started to say, *And for sucking dick, since you do that so well.* This mofo was getting on my nerves with his dumb shit. This was the prime reason I wasn't going to deal with a man ever again.

"Whatcha getting upset with me? I just came over here to warn your ass. You keep talking to me like I'm some child or your punk and I'll make sure I leak your name to the press. Matter fact, I could start with your lady friend, Yolanda. Since she likes to talk so much. Let her tell the public that the man she's fucking is just like me," Monty said.

"Nigger, you tripping! You've lost your mind. I ain't even trying to hear this crap. You ain't telling Yolanda shit. Leave me out of this sordid shit. I'm sorry I ever let you get anywhere near me," I said. My voice was rising with anger, and the sweater was making my body itch. I needed a shower and to get Monty out of my apartment.

"Hold up, Basil, you right I'm tripping. I'm not gonna say anything to Yolanda. Maybe you right. I'm going to rethink this. Maybe I should just keep my ass in the group and forget about going solo," Monty said.

"Now you talking. Man, you can't let the public know men like you swing both ways. You think women gonna wanna hear you sing 'bout making love when they know you could be talking 'bout a man. That shit ain't gonna fly even if you put wings on it."

"I know you're right. I'm letting these white boys at the record company make me think everything's going to be all right. When my records don't sell, they'll drop me quick," Monty said.

I was glad to see this fool hadn't lost all his God-given common sense. "And you know it," I said. I was ready for Monty to get his ass out, but he looked like he was getting comfortable on my sofa.

"So what you got up for tonight?" Monty asked.

"Nothing. I'm getting ready to shower and call it a night. I have an early flight in the morning. Matter fact, I need to say good night," I said as I looked at my watch and rubbed my face as though I was trying to erase the fatigue I felt.

"Okay, I'm going to run, but I want you to hear these new tracks and then I'll let you get some rest," Monty said. I liked Monty's voice, so I didn't see any harm in listening to some of his new music.

"Is it a CD or a tape?" I asked as I walked over to my stereo system and hit the power button.

"It's a tape. But why don't you go on and take a shower and I'll set it up. When you walk out you'll be listening to the new sound of Monty," he said proudly.

"Sounds like a plan," I said as I headed to my bathroom, a windowless cubicle only somewhat larger than my walk-in closet. I removed my clothing and washed my face, and then applied a face scrub I used every other day. I turned on the shower and while waiting for the water to get hot, I brushed my teeth. The peppermint flavor of the toothpaste rushed up my nose as I reached for the mouthwash.

A steaming mist was filling up the space, so I jumped into the shower. I covered my body with an almond body scrub and put my head under the water, and for several minutes I enjoyed its soothing roar. Under the water's force I thought back to a couple of days before, when Yolanda and I had shared the shower for almost an hour, washing each other and kissing until we both were beginning to feel like prunes. I missed her so much. I stopped the shower and drenched my body in baby oil and then sprayed my Dunhill cologne in the air and moved my body into the citrus scent. I grabbed a beach-sized towel and realized I didn't bring a change of clothes into the room, not even underwear.

When I opened the bathroom door, I heard Monty's singing, his smooth voice floating through the apartment. I stopped in the hallway between the bathroom and bedroom and enjoyed the mellow beat and flashy rhythms, thinking this mofo might have a hit on his hands. I pulled out a pair of my red baggy boxers and slipped them under the towel. I searched for the matching T-shirt and remembered putting it in the dryer located in the closet next to the kitchen.

I walked through the living area, where Monty was dancing with himself. When he saw me with just a towel wrapped around my waist, he smiled.

"You're sounding real good, my brother," I said as I walked to the dryer and pulled out the shirt.

"And you're looking quite good, my brother. How often are you working out these days?"

"Two hours, six days a week," I said.

"It's working." Monty smiled as he walked toward me.

"So when are they going to drop your music?"

"We don't have a release date yet. Still got to work out that problem," he said.

"Can you leave the tape? I'd like to listen to it on the flight tomorrow," I said.

"Sure, it's all yours. You want anything else?" he asked with a sly smile. I knew what he meant, but I was willing to play dumb.

"Naw, that's it."

"Can I use the bathroom before I leave?"

"Sure," I said.

While Monty was in the bathroom, I immersed myself in the music. When I realized a third song was starting, I wondered why Monty was taking so long in the bathroom. I quietly moved closer to the door to see if I could hear any sounds coming from the room. Just as I was lowering my head toward the door, it opened suddenly, startling me.

"You want to join me." Monty smiled. He was buck naked. Monty had the smooth and muscular lean body of a track man. I felt the muscles in my face soften, my eyes grow wide as I gazed at his body from neck to toe. But I snapped myself out of Monty's magic and shouted angrily, "Man, whatsup with you? I told you I ain't rolling like that anymore."

"Just one more time," Monty said as he moved his hand toward my groin area.

I quickly grabbed his hands before he reached his desired spot and yelled, "Put your shit back on and get the hell out of my house."

"Come on, Basil, just one more time. I promise I won't bother you anymore," Monty pleaded.

"Man, you better git your ass out of my house before I have to kick your faggot ass," I said.

"I got your faggot hanging low," Monty said as he grabbed his piece. "You didn't think I was no faggot the last time. And you'll see how much a faggot I'll be when I serve your story to Yolanda."

"You ain't gonna do that," I said.

"Watch me," Monty said as he turned toward the bathroom. This mofo was acting like a spoiled-ass bitch. I didn't know what surprised me more, his threats or the way he was acting. Like a punk-ass bitch. A madness was welling up inside me. I started to kick him dead up his ass. Beat him down. But I knew where that could lead. But I had to find a way to reason with this fool.

"Wait!" I said.

Monty turned toward me and said, "Wait for what?" You don't know how bad I wanted to just bust him in the face, but instead I dropped the towel from my waist and pulled my limp manhood from my underwear and said, "So is this what you want?" In the back of my mind a reasonable voice was saying *Don't do this. Don't let this mofo blackmail you into giving up the beef.* Monty's eyes landed on my hands and he lowered his face to my midsection. I looked toward the living room, but I heard his knees hit the floor. Before his lips reached my muscle of manhood, he whispered, "Some dicks are made for sucking."

Chapter 26

"Thanks, Ms. Williams, enjoy your flight," the flight attendant said.

"I will," I said sadly.

I didn't want to go back to Chicago and leave behind the warmth of John's bed. But I had to. When I boarded my plane, the airline service agent announced that the flight was overbooked. The airline was offering a free round-trip ticket to anywhere in the continental United States, plus free overnight lodging at the nearby Radisson until the next morning's flight to Chicago for anyone who'd give up their seat. They didn't have to ask me but once. I jumped at it—for more reasons than one. I grabbed my bag from the overhead, deplaned, got my certificate, and caught a cab back into the city. Back into John's strong arms.

During the ride from Newark to John's apartment, I thought about the prior week. I had left John's around six—somewhat reluctantly—after the most enjoyable, passionate, romantic week I'd shared with anyone in ages. I was shocked when he told me he loved me. I believed him, but I didn't feel myself falling in love. At least not yet. I liked John a great deal and I thoroughly enjoyed our long heart-to-heart talks and the time we spent together, but I didn't ache when we were apart. I had Sybil and Leland when John wasn't around, and I'd like to feel that I could include Riley and Dwight also.

The sex was good. *Real* good. But I was old enough to know sex was physical and love was spiritual, and I just wasn't there yet. Maybe, I'd thought, a week of intimacy would push us over the top toward a long-term commitment. But so far it seemed only one of us had felt the push.

The cab pulled up into the circular driveway at John's apartment. I still had the key John had given me when I first arrived, and I slipped the night-shift doorman a ten-dollar bill not to announce my arrival. The doorman said he didn't think Mr. Henderson was home, and I told him of my plans to surprise him when he returned. I wondered where he could be this late, because I knew he had an early morning flight.

It would be perfect, we could take a car to the airport together and say our good-byes at the airport gate.

When I arrived at John's door, I heard voices. Maybe he was home. I was certain I heard male voices as I slipped my key in the lock ever so quietly. I don't ever think I'll forget the image I saw when I opened that door. I was so shocked, I instinctively pulled the door shut again. I didn't—couldn't—believe my eyes. Oh, no, my mind screamed, I know I didn't see what I *think* I saw! My key was still in the lock and I pushed the door open again.

My eyes hadn't lied. There was John, standing buck naked, his underwear down around his ankles. Busted! Busted fucking some man who was bent over the sofa table! The first time, I'm certain they didn't even hear me. Too busy taking care of each other. I could hear lusty moans of pleasure and John's voice barking cuss words I'd heard when we made love. But the second time I opened the door, they both turned their heads toward me, shock and disbelief written all over their faces. My God, the other man was Monty! This so-called want to be the love of my life was fucking my newest client! I didn't know whether to laugh or cry. They looked so ridiculous and so guilty, like little boys caught in the cookie jar. John called my name and pulled away from Monty. As he ran toward me with his underwear shackling his ankles, he fell flat on his face. He quickly got up, tossed his underwear and as he neared the door, I ran. I could hear him calling after me, pleading with me to come back. He could explain, he said. I was outta there! Next thing I knew, I was sitting in a cab feeling like I'd just narrowly escaped a serial killer.

I went directly to the Omni and was able to get a room. As soon as I dropped my bag, I reached for the phone and called Leland.

"We've got to talk, baby-boy," I began. I hoped I didn't sound too crazed. I didn't want to alarm Leland, but I didn't want to tell him long distance what happened. I wanted to see the shock on his face, so I'd have an idea of how I looked moments before. "I'll be back in the morning. Can I come over from the airport?"

"What's wrong, Yolanda? You want me to pick you up? Are you all right? Do I need to come to New York and get you?" I guess Leland had picked up on my somewhat distraught voice, but he was overreacting just a bit, I thought. Or maybe it was just me.

"I'm fine, Leland. Chill. Everything's under control. I just need to talk, that's all. Now, don't worry all night. Promise?"

"I do worry about you, Yolanda. You've been gone a whole week and I haven't spoken to you once. That's not like you. Now I get this call and your voice sounds frantic, telling me you've got to talk as soon as you get off the plane. Whatsup? Are you sure you're all right?"

"I'm fine. Trust me. Didn't you get my messages? I was really busy with this new client," I said.

"Yeah, but somehow we always manage to talk person to person. I was thinking you were upset with me," Leland said.

"Upset for what? You're my best bud. I could never be upset with you. I love you, that's all."

"And I love you, that's all," Leland said. He was reluctant to let me off the phone, but he finally did after promising not to worry too much and to have breakfast ready when I got there.

My mind was a blur of confusing, contradictory images: me and John making love, my meeting with Monty, strawberries and whipped cream, that Raymond guy, Leland giving me the green light but telling me to be careful, John and Monty together, and the kiss at the Motown Cafe that started this shit. I couldn't think straight. How in the hell, I thought, did I wind up sitting here alone on a queen-sized bed in a hotel room in the middle of the night? Tears began to well up in my eyes, but then I had a sudden vision of John with his underwear around his ankles, trying to run after me. Suddenly overcome with a fit of side-splitting, tension-relieving laughter, I fell backward onto the bed. With tears streaming down my face, I laughed until my sides ached. Life is a bitch, I thought. But thank goodness the bitch had a sense of humor.

·   ·   ·

When I saw Yolanda standing in my doorway, it was like watching my life explode like skyrockets. Her lovely face was filled with disgust that in seconds melted into disappointment. For a few moments I was in shock, and then I rushed toward her and fell on my ass. I started to follow her downstairs, but here I was, standing in my living room, naked, with Monty. When he told me not to worry about Yolanda, I snapped.

"Monty, shut the fuck up!" I shouted.

"Don't get mad at me, how did that bitch get in?"

I moved over and grabbed Monty and said, "Look, asshole, I've told you, don't call my woman a bitch."

"I don't think she's going to be your woman after what she just saw," Monty said with a smirk.

"How could I be so stupid, fucking yo' ass," I said.

"Basil, stop kidding yourself! You'd fuck a snake if you could find a way to get up under it," Monty said. I wanted to punch him dead in the mouth, permanently removing that smirk.

"Look, get your shit on and get out of my house. I don't want to see your ass ever again in life. Do you understand?" Monty walked toward the bathroom, then looked at me and said, "Fuck off."

I went to my bedroom and put on a pair of jeans and a sweater. Maybe Yolanda was still downstairs in the lobby. I suddenly wondered how she had gotten upstairs without the doorman calling. This kinda shit pisses me off. I reached for the house phone and a man with a slight accent answered. "How can I help you, Mr. Henderson?"

"Who is this?"

"This is Pedro, sir."

"Who let Ms. Williams upstairs without calling up?"

"It was me, sir. The lady said she wanted to surprise you. I was told you had left permission for her to come up without calling. She said she had a key, sir."

"I didn't mean to let her up when I'm here. I'm going to have your job, Pedro," I said as I hung up the phone. I looked around and saw Monty walking out of the bathroom. He looked at me and I raised my palm in the air in an I-don't-want-to-hear-it stance. Monty got the message and left my apartment in silence.

I was so mad, I didn't know what to do with myself. I just didn't know who I was angry with, Yolanda for coming back without calling—she was supposed to be back in Chicago—or Monty for trying to blackmail me. I should still be kicking his ass. Or should I be mad at my own dumb ass? I could have told Monty no and meant it. Why didn't I just stop with the oral sex? That would have satisfied him. But no, I got greedy. I figured if this was going to be my last time, I should just go for the whole buffet.

I didn't even hear the key turn. My thoughts were lost in the physical pleasure, excited by the power I felt rocking back and forth. I invaded Monty like the Marines arriving on enemy territory. I wanted to make sure I punished him for forcing me to do something I didn't want to do. I was trying to break his back.

In all my years, I've had some close calls. But I have never gotten caught in the act with either a woman or a man. Why, when I finally stopped seeing the faces and was really in love, would my past finally catch up with me? If I was a punk I think I would have cried, but tears of any kind are the ultimate sign of weakness. Instead, I just let off a stream of mumbled obscenities.

•   •   •

Leland was standing in front of his apartment building when my cab arrived. He looked like he hadn't gotten much rest. Although he looked nervous around the eyes, his face lit when I got out of the cab.

"So what's for breakfast?" I asked. "Did you miss me a little?" I teased. "I sure missed my baby-boy!" I meant it too. I was never so glad to see someone in all my life. Leland was my rock, confidant, and soul support. I could honestly say that Leland had always been there for me—through thick and thin. He was the standard for sensitivity, tenderness, intelligence, friendship, and honesty by which I measured his heterosexual counterparts. I felt a little guilty for putting him in this anxious state, but I was so very glad to be with him now. My best friend hugged me so hard, I could hardly breathe. I guess he was glad to see me too.

I was starved, but Leland refused to feed me until I at least began to tell him what had happened. I told him the story—the whole story—over a plate of bacon and eggs. When I got to the last part, I started laughing again, uncontrollably. Leland didn't laugh at all, but sat there across the kitchen table looking at me like I'd lost my mind.

"Leland, lighten up!" I tried to stop laughing. "I'm okay, really." But Leland's somber face didn't change one iota. "Look at me. I'm not hurt. I'm not crushed. In fact, I'm feeling damned lucky. I wasn't in love. But I tell you, he had me fooled right up to that very moment. If I hadn't walked in when I did, who knows what would have happened to me down the line? I guess he had you fooled too. I guess your gaydar isn't working like it used to. I can't believe you didn't know."

"But I did know," Leland said softly. "I knew."

It took a few seconds for that to register in my mind. Did he just say he knew? No, he couldn't have said he knew.

"You knew what? You mean you suspected John might be bisexual? Is that what you mean?"

"No. I knew." All of a sudden this wasn't funny.

"What do you mean, you knew? And if so, why didn't you tell me? How long have you known?" I was so mad, I didn't know what to do. A part of me just wanted to reach across the table and slap his guilt-ridden face as hard as I could. "How long have you known that the man I was sleeping with—about to fall in love with—was bisexual. A week? A month? Leland, I thought you were my friend. Tell me when in the hell were you planning to tell me? I don't believe this shit!"

"Yolanda. Please. Listen to me. I couldn't tell you. I wanted to tell you, but I just couldn't."

"Why, Leland? I can't wait to hear why you couldn't tell your so-called best friend that her very life could be in danger. We've talked about this. Why couldn't you bring yourself to tell me such an important thing? Please! Tell me!"

"Yolanda! Calm down! I didn't know at first. I promise. I just found out, but I found out from a patient who'd had relations with John, or Basil as he called him. He told me during one of his sessions. You know I can't divulge what a patient tells me. It was a matter of ethics, Yolanda. You understand that, don't you?"

"I understand all right. I understand that your fucked-up sense of ethics is more important to you than my safety. Your damn ethics weren't so important when you were discussing Mr. Light-skinned with the group. Have you told the group about dumb-ass Yolanda with the swinging-dick boyfriend? And I guess it's more important to you than our friendship! I don't believe this. I trusted you. I thought you had my back all this time, but I guess you were too busy covering your own ass to think about me. No wonder you were so worried. And here I am thinking you were worried about me. Was it my well-being or your guilt that kept you up all night? Well, fuck you, Dr. Leland Thompson—now and forever." I was so mad, I said a few things I knew I'd regret later, but I was literally seeing red. I steamed down the hallway and out the door before Leland could respond.

For the second time in less than twenty-four hours, in two different cities, I was slamming the door on some man who had fucked me over.

Chapter 27

It was early Sunday morning, and I was lonely. Uncle Doc had been gone for almost an hour, and my body was dry from the relaxing bath I had taken. I put on my terry-cloth robe, and from my bedroom window I gazed up at the layers of puffy white clouds, so peaceful and beautiful. I went into the kitchen and poured a glass of brandy and moved to my den. I started to put on some Billie Holiday, but instead I slipped in Chantay Savage's version of "I Will Survive," my anthem for a couple of decades. After the brandy numbed my tongue, and the music had begun to soothe my soul, I decided to write in my journal.

 Right now I don't know if things can get any worse. First Yolanda hit the roof because I didn't tell her about her dream boy. My dread was justified. I'm shocked at her response. I could see her being a little upset at first, but I thought she would understand. I'm hoping she'll get over this real soon. I already miss her, but I've got to stand my ground. I did what I had to do. I spent days rationalizing what was right. Was I a friend first, or should my loyalty be directed at my profession?

I spent Saturday night with Uncle Doc at a party he was giving with some of his friends. After Yolanda left, I called him and told him what happened. He told me I didn't need to be sitting at home feeling sorry for myself. Usually when he invites me to parties with his buddies, I find a way out. But I needed to talk and just be with my uncle, and hope that his humor and warmth would help ease some of my loneliness. He assured me this was going to be a hot party, with people my age. He was right, his friend's lover was just turning thirty and he had invited a lot of his friends.

The party was packed, I mean it was wall-to-wall men. It had been so long since I been out that I'd forgotten how many good-looking Black gay men called Chicago home. After helping Uncle Doc bring in some of the food he had cooked, I found a spot against a wall unit and allowed my eyes to tour the room. The music was good, and the drinks were flowing. Almost every five minutes, Uncle Doc was coming over and introducing me to one of his friends. All his age. I spotted an empty chair and I rushed to grab it, when I noticed this really fine-looking man, in a dark suit, white shirt, and red tie, walk into the room. It felt like everyone in the room stopped to notice the new guest, including Uncle Doc. He wasn't drop-dead Hollywood handsome, but he had strong Black features, an assertive chin, and a broad nose.

The stranger looked around the room and then I saw him hug one of the guests. Damn, I thought, he's taken. When was this party going to end? I decided sitting in the chair might appear antisocial, so I got up and re-claimed my spot against the wall as if that said more about my social skills. When I looked across the room, I saw him again. I couldn't help but notice the careful trim of his beard and hair. When our eyes met, his thick lips stretched into a sexy smile. I turned around to make sure he was smiling at me, and when I realized that he was, I felt my face getting warm and I lowered my head in embarrassment. A few seconds later I looked up again, and he was still smiling. He took a sip from his drink and licked his lips so sensually that I wanted to run across the room and kiss him.

I kept looking, and smiling, praying that he would make a move to my side of the room. But he didn't, so I decided if I was going to meet this man, then it was going to be up to me. In my head I started to think of what I *would say. I was thinking of saying, I couldn't help but notice you looking at me, I'm Dr. Leland Thompson. Naw, Doctor sounded too damn preten-tious. I could ask him if he lived in Chicago and if so how long. I would simply go over and say, hello, I'm Leland, and you are? I set my drink on a speaker, and just as I was making my move toward his corner of the room, I saw him talking to a guy and decided this love connection wasn't going to happen. I picked my drink back up and noticed that even though he was still otherwise engaged, he smiled at me again and this time he winked at me. Well, that was it—I was going to meet this man. I would simply ignore his admirer. That's when the screaming started.*

"All you mutherfuckers have got to go. Git your asses out. I mean, git out now before I get my mutherfuckin' gun and start shooting up some asses."

All of a sudden people were grabbing coats and dashing like a pack of bulls had entered the room. People were pushing each other trying to get to the door like the place was on fire. I was looking to see what direction the stranger was going, when I saw Uncle Doc. He grabbed me and said, "Git your jacket. This crazy bitch ain't playing. Matter fact—leave your coat, I'll git it for you later. Let's git the hell out of this camp!"

When I asked Uncle Doc what was happening, he told me to wait until we got outside. On the way home Uncle Doc told me his friend had found his younger lover receiving a birthday present, buck naked, from a former lover. I guess John wasn't the only one caught with his pants down! I asked Uncle Doc if he knew the handsome stranger, but he didn't recall seeing him, commenting that with all the men at the party, it was hard trying to decide which way to look. He did promise he'd ask his crazy friend once he cooled down. Adding he was really a nice person until he got some liquor in him. During the ride home all I could think about was the handsome stranger and how every time I think about giving love another try, the unexpected happens. Again I was facing another winter alone.

●   ●   ●

My mind raced from John to Leland to Riley. My head was spinning as I jumped from my bed. I pulled my Celine Dion CD out of the player and turned my radio to V-103, where Luther Vandross and Cheryl Lynn were singing "If This World Were Mine." I located my journal and crawled back into my bed. I suddenly hated songs that triggered memories. Celine reminded me of Riley, who had turned me on to the French Canadian singer, and Luther and Cheryl brought up thoughts of Leland and the group. Right now I don't know if I will ever add anything to that journal, so I thanked God I still had my own.

Men are dogs. Let me clarify that: All men are dogs. I don't care whether they're straight, gay, young, old, friends, or lovers. They're all a bunch of insensitive, self-ish, heartless, unevolved idiots.

When will I learn to stop trusting them with my feelings? What's wrong with me? I'm getting much too old for this.

I mean, John, that's one thing. I can deal with his ass. I still think it was funny catching where he couldn't lie. How else do you explain a naked man bent over on your sofa table, and him being so close, I couldn't tell where their bodies separated.

But Leland? No way. I didn't think I had to pay attention. I just can't believe he'd do me like this. Not my best-buddy-in-the-whole-world Leland. Not I-love-me-some-Yolanda Leland. Not Dr. I've-always-got-your-back Leland. I mean, I've told him everything. Everything about me. No one knows me like he does with the exception of Sybil. But Sybil's family. I thought Leland was too. I've never had a closer, dearer male friend—or so I thought.

How could he possibly know and not tell me about John? How could he hurt me like this? I just couldn't have been that wrong about him. It just doesn't make sense. He says it was a question of ethics. Screw ethics! What about friendship? What about love and trust? Like one of my favorite lines from **Dreamgirls,** *what about what's best for me?*

How could he put his damn job ahead of my well-being? What if I hadn't found out the truth about John until it was too late? Would Leland have said something if I'd married John? What if I'd gotten some disease—AIDS even? Sisters are still among the fastest-growing groups of HIV infection. Then what happens to his precious ethics. He'd be crying over my grave, convinced that he'd done the right and ethical thing. I'd be dead and he'd be right.

Well, he can just go find someone else's shoulder to cry on from now on. Someone else to be his family and social life rolled into one. What's he gonna say to Uncle Doc about betraying his best friend? I'd like to be a fly on the wall for that conversation. Maybe he can call Riley at three o'clock in the morning when he's missing Donald. Maybe he and Dwight can go to the theater and hang out at Miss Thing's together. In fact, maybe old Dwight can teach him a thing or two about loyalty. Someone should.

The group! I forgot about the group. How could I possibly face them after this? Dwight's probably loving this. I think they might offer support on the surface about John, but I don't think I could stand to even be in the same room with Leland again. No, I'm not giving up the group. Let Leland give it up. It would serve him right. He doesn't need the group anyway, he has his ethics to keep him warm.

He doesn't deserve me. I hope he's feeling bad, just like he's made me feel. I'm not sorry for things I said to him. I hope my words hurt him to his heart. I hope he realizes he's lost the best friend he'll ever have in this world.

My God, listen to me! Okay, girlfriend, breathe, baby, breathe. Have I lost my ever-loving mind? I'm sitting here wishing someone I love is in horrible pain. Get a grip, girl. Leland didn't tell me go and have constant mattress gymnastics with John. I chose to sleep with him. I really can't even blame him for nothing but being a liar. What did Dwight once say, "Why do women fall so easy for liars?"

I guess I need to admit to myself and Leland that maybe I was wrong. I guess Leland will have a whole lot to talk about when we're speaking again. But right now I need some quiet time. I don't really feel like making up with Leland, or Riley for that matter. I had to tell the child she couldn't sing, at least not for me. I love them both, but maybe we all need some space. We've got the rest of our lives to continue our friendship.

Chapter 28

Sunday morning came in cool, foggy, and cloudy. It looked like it was going to rain. I was still madder at Leland than I was at John. I hoped Leland would come to the group meeting so I could give it to him one more time. If he even looked like he was going to twist his mouth around an apology, I would let him have it. Then we could move on. As mad as I was at Leland, as hurt and betrayed as I felt, I still loved him.

Before I left my bed, I decided to call Sybil, but I got her answering machine. Knowing my sister, she was in the front row at church with her children. Maybe that's where I needed to be, at God's house, praying for some direction. But I didn't want Trinity United Methodist to crumble when I walked in. It had been that long.

I had to admit that I was a little ashamed at my own behavior. Not for the things I'd said to Leland, but for some of the things I was thinking about saying, like: You and John are just alike and he's a pretty good lay, so maybe you want his number so you two can hook up and lay in bed laughing about how you both duped Yolanda. But I was wrong to even think those things. Leland was and always would be my friend. We loved each other and I knew he was probably beating himself up enough for the both of us. I guess we could both use a little forgiveness. I needed to seek some forgiveness from Riley also. Who was I to throw water on her dreams? This meeting was going to be like an old school pledge meeting. A colored version of *Who's Afraid of Virginia Woolf?* Let the cussing and ass-kicking begin!

By the time I was ready to leave for the group meeting, my answering machine was full. John, John, and more John. Pitiful! Brother, please, I thought. Call Monty. Let it go—I have.

It was Dwight's month to host the meeting, and since his place was so small, he had made reservations for a private room at The Retreat, a quaint Black-owned restaurant on East 111th. It was popular with the after-church brunch crowd. The restaurant was located in a renovated Victorian house with a beautiful cherry-wood staircase, carved fireplace, private dining rooms, and cozy booths. The food was great, with everything from catfish teasers to crawfish étouffé.

I guess I shouldn't have been too surprised when no one but Dwight and I showed up. Considering what had transpired between me and Leland the day before, as well as Riley, well, it would have to be strained at the very least. I had a lot on my mind and Dwight was a blessing in disguise: a neutral corner, a much-needed retreat from issues and people I didn't want to confront just then.

"I didn't think anybody was going to show up," Dwight said as he greeted me with a slight hug and a kiss on the cheek.

"Did you speak with Leland or Riley?" I asked. I wondered what side Dwight would be lining up on.

"I called them to give them the address, but I didn't speak with either of them. I talked to Leland's machine and Riley's maid."

"I started not to come myself," I said. Dwight sat across from me in the cozy booth. Something was different today. He had dressed up for a change and looked really handsome. Maybe that was it. He wore a black shirt buttoned to the collar, a plaid brown and black sport coat, and black slacks. He sure looked good in black. But that wasn't it. Has he always had those long, thick lashes? I thought. I couldn't remember noticing them before. No, it wasn't his lashes and it wasn't the way the black shirt hugged his muscular frame when he removed his jacket. In fact, it wasn't physical at all. What I sensed was more emotional, and there was a warm flicker of light that seemed to dance in his eyes now. He just seemed more relaxed, more at peace. Maybe it was just me. This was exactly the kind of person I needed to be with right now. But maybe I was projecting my need onto the same old Dwight.

But he was giving me eye contact today. Dwight never looked me directly in the eye. He always lowered his lids just a bit—not shyly, just uncomfortably. Not today though.

"Why weren't you going to come?" he asked. "Does it have something to do with Leland and Riley not being here?"

"May I make a long story short and cut to the chase?" I asked directly.

"Okay by me." Dwight put down his menu and leaned back in the booth.

"Well, I told Riley she couldn't sing at my function and then added she couldn't sing anywhere if they wanted a real singer, and I accused Leland of not really being my friend." I paused as his eyes widened. "You think that could have something to do with them not showing?"

"Oh, I doubt it," Dwight said. "Now, if you told Riley her poetry was just as bad as her singing, and accused Leland of being secretly straight, pretending to be gay to learn what women really want, then maybe I could see the connection." Then he let out an avalanche of laughter. I don't think I'd ever heard Dwight laugh out loud myself. His shiny black mustache followed the curve of his full lips and joined a perfectly trimmed, neat beard that highlighted his strong jawline.

"Thank you, Dwight. I need someone to laugh with. Do you mind if I ask you a personal question?"

"Oh, no, don't tell me you brought Riley's cards?" He laughed.

"No, I'm serious," I said.

"Okay, I'm sorry. What's your question?"

"You seem kind of different. I can't put my finger on what it is, but you seem less angry today. You've got a whole 'nother vibe, my brother. Whatsup? You're not in love, are you? You and Kelli aren't back together, are you?"

"Kelli and me? No way, no how. But who would care if I was? I'm sorry, that's not what I meant to say." For the first time this afternoon, he averted his eyes. "No, I'm not in love, but I am going to start loving myself more."

"Well, whatever it is, it looks real good on you," I said, letting the *would you care?* statement fade away between us. For a moment we just gazed at each other, until the waitress came over and asked did we want to wait for the rest of our party.

"No, let's order. It looks like it's just going to be the two of us," Dwight said.

"What will you have?" the waitress asked. Dwight nodded at me to go first.

"I'll have the mustard-fried catfish," I said.

"And you, sir?"

"Let me have the Seafood Trio," Dwight said.

After we ordered, Dwight told me about his interview in Washington, D.C. I didn't even know he was looking for a job. He told me it had gone very well and they had made him a very generous offer just before he left on Friday. He said he was thinking seriously of taking the job and moving to Washington.

Then Dwight surprised me with a story of a little white boy at the hotel pool, how he'd saved him and how grateful the mother was. He told me how they had all hugged and cried together. It was a side of Dwight I had never seen. Then he continued and told me about his brother Scooter all those years ago. I knew he had lost a younger brother, but I think we all assumed it was to some type of gun violence. It was so very sad to me that I could only imagine how painful the memory was to Dwight. I felt tears form in my eyes, and

I touched him. He said the incident at the hotel had been the catalyst he so desperately needed to finally grieve for his little brother, to start his own healing. Dwight said he had spent so many years in denial, substituting his unresolved grief and guilt over the death of his brother for an inordinate hatred of white folks. He had decided to stop blaming the entire race for his loss.

"They aren't worth the years of anger I've wasted," he said. "It really wasn't their fault that he died, and now I know it wasn't mine either. I loved my little brother, still do. And that's what I want his legacy to be—love, not hate." Dwight leaned toward me and the light in his eyes shone even brighter.

"My," I said. "I don't know what to say. I'm happy for you. And so very proud of you, Dwight. He looked at me full face for a moment, then down at his hands resting on the table. "It's hard, I know, to turn around and face yourself honestly. I know it took a lot of courage to just get to this point."

"I appreciate your support. I want to live again. I want to love again. You know I think my anger and grief had a lot to do with my marriage ending," Dwight said.

"You think so?"

"It was a part of it. I mean, I know Kelli and I were never really meant to be together. We're two very different people who wanted different things in life. But that doesn't mean she was wrong or that I was."

"I know the feeling. That's the same thing that happened with Chauncey and me," I said.

"How is old Chauncey?"

"We have to find out what country he's in to figure that out," I laughed.

"Does he know what a great lady he gave up?"

"Oh, yeah. I let him know." I smiled, then added, "You know, I'm really enjoying this. If you ever want to talk about your little brother, or life, you know you can call me. I'm a good listener."

"I'd like that," he said sincerely. "Okay, it's your turn. Now I'll be the listener." Dwight relaxed against the back of the booth as a server brought out our food. "I'm all ears," he said as he released his silverware from the napkin.

I tried to repeat my conversation with Riley word for word, but gave him the *TV Guide* version of the John fiasco, leaving out the intimate details and how I was just a few steps away from falling in love with the jerk. Dwight listened to my tale quietly, never even flinching at John's betrayal, or my unkind words to Leland. In fact, he made no noticeable judgment at all. He interrupted me only once when he asked me to pass the hot sauce. His eyes stayed locked on mine as he listened intently to my every word.

When I finished, he took both my hands in his and held them gently.

"You've had a rough time, haven't you, girl? I'm so sorry. I think you did the right thing with Riley. One day she'll realize that." He squeezed my hands a little. "And you don't deserve to be treated like this John guy treated you. I'm glad you've decided not to hang around and take that kinda mess. A lot of women would stay just because he's a jock. I'm proud of you too. Now, with Leland, I'm going to leave that one alone. You guys are too tight to let something like this break up the friendship," Dwight said as he placed my hands back on the table with a final squeeze.

"I know. I just want him to think about it for a while," I said.

"That works two ways." Dwight smiled.

"I know."

"I want you to know that if you need anything or just want to talk, I'm here for you. Who knows? I might even invite you over to my crib."

"Now, this is too much!" I teased. "But you know I'd be honored."

"You haven't seen my place." Dwight laughed.

"You have made me feel better, Dwight. And I thank you for that. But there is something else you can do for me," I said as I leaned closer to him.

"What?" he asked.

"Don't move to Washington," I said. "Don't move." Dwight didn't respond, and for a brief moment he looked away. Then he turned to me and said, "Let's share some caramel pecan cheesecake. I hear it's da bomb."

Chapter 29

I met Lonelyboy. It was Selwyn. At first I was upset, but only for a few seconds, until the shock wore off. Friday night he walked into our bedroom and said, "I loved the poem when you first wrote it, and I love it even more now." When I asked what he was talking about, he started reciting the old poem I had sent to my secret admirer. Turns out I was not the only lonely person sleeping in my bed.

He told me he didn't realize it was me until I sent the poem, and he finally understood my pain and loneliness over him being so remote. He said some of the things he learned through our cyber-affair would help him to be a better husband. Selwyn added that every one of my notes to Lonelyboy spoke of my desire to have a friend I could trust with anything. He wants to be that friend. We both admitted we had become lovers so quickly that friendship was never really a part of our relationship. We pretended to be friends.

The last couple of days I've felt like I'm in a movie. Selwyn and I are talking like we've never talked before, or at least for a good number of years. We talk like when we first met. When every bit of information was a new discovery. Selwyn told me how he had been trying to find his birth parents for the last two years. When the private investigator discovered his mother was alive and living in Tallahassee, Florida, Selwyn felt he could finally move on from his past. He was devastated when his mother told the investigator she had no desire to meet him. Selwyn went to Florida anyway and had a brief encounter with his mother when she cleaned up his room in a local hotel. She was unaware that it was her son who had left the $100 tip and sat at the suite's desk watching her clean. Selwyn had hoped they would make some type of eye contact and his mother would realize Selwyn was her son. She didn't. She cleaned the suite slowly and deliberately, humming to herself. When I asked him why he didn't tell her who he was, he said she seemed happy and content. He was still hopeful one day she would change her mind. He told me how they shared the same crooked smile and wide eyes. After that encounter and our passionate notes, he wanted to renew our love and use all his energies working on the family he had, to make it better than ever. But I could tell from his eyes that his mother's rejection had hurt him deeply. In so many ways it explains his distance, and I told him I wished he would have told me and allowed me to help.

On Friday night we made love for the first time in years. It was right after Selwyn told me about the poetry. I felt his eyes gaze into the space between my breasts like he was seeing them for the first time. I felt beautiful, and Selwyn told me I was. Our lovemaking took on an intensity I've never known. It makes me melt just thinking about Selwyn. The passion, complete.

I'm writing all this down for me. I think it's time I move on from the group and pay more attention to myself and my husband. Now, I'm not going to completely immerse myself in making Selwyn feel secure, but I'm going to keep our love growing, all we share close to my heart. I realize how very much I love him and how much he loves me.

When I missed the group's meeting today, it was the first time I had ever missed sharing my thoughts with my friends, I mean the group. I am beginning to wonder if I can call them friends. But I didn't miss it, because Selwyn and I spent the entire afternoon at a restaurant located on the north side, Pops for Champagne. We had a wonderful brunch of eggs and baked breads and drank Bellinis as we listened to smooth jazz. Selwyn and I held hands over the table, and almost every five minutes he would kiss each one of my fingers. The waitress asked if we were newlyweds, and we both grinned and said "sorta." We made plans for a winter ski trip with the kids, and promised to sit down and talk with each other heart to heart at least once a week. Even if that means me getting on a plane to meet my husband if he's not in Chicago.

The only thing pressing in my life is telling the group my plans to leave and dealing with my mother. I still have some issues with the group. Perhaps its purpose has been served. I wonder if Leland and Dwight feel the same way Yolanda does about me. When I mentioned this to Selwyn, he pointed out that Yolanda didn't say anything about the friendship, just my singing. He said he understood how her words could hurt me, but pointed out it was only one person's opinion.

My mother, well, that's a whole 'nother story. I have talked with her, but only briefly. Each time she says "Riley, we have to talk," I tell her "I know, Mother, but not now." I'll decide when. I don't know what I'll say or if she'll like the new me. I know I will finally tell her why my poetry and music are so important to me. They saved me when she was busy with her work and the two men in her life. I must give her credit for teaching me that when trouble comes, you have to face it head-on. She was the tower of strength when Clayton Jr. was sentenced to prison. It was Daddy who went into seclusion. It was Clarice who went right out into the community, to church, and almost dared someone to say something negative about her firstborn. It was Clarice who was busying herself, by planning a welcome home party for my brother. Like Clayton was a returning war hero. A mother's love is a powerful thing. I have learned a lot from my mother. But she needs to see me as the strong Black woman she and Daddy raised to be their pride and joy. Not her little girl. Not anybody's little girl.

Chapter 30

I've been sitting here at my desk, staring at my yellow legal pad since the office closed. I hope my last patient didn't realize how distracted I was. Whether he knew it or not, he sure didn't get his money's worth out of me today. I'll make a mental note to make it up to him next week with a little extra time.

Okay, let me get to this note I've been putting off all day. All I have is what I wrote early this morning before my first patient: "Dear Yolanda, Please forgive me for . . ." For what? For being me? For being the man she *knows* I am? She's the one who always praises me for my integrity. She knows I would never compromise my patient's confidentiality. In fact, she's always teasing that she wouldn't go crazy unless she knew she could get an appointment with me.

We've never had to say out loud: "Now, don't tell anyone, but . . ." We both know how to keep each other's secrets. I guess that's what's so hard. I've always told Yolanda everything. But I couldn't tell her this. As bad as I wanted to, I couldn't tell her this. But I'm not the one who lied to her. I'm not the one who dogged her. I know she's hurting, but it's not fair to blame me. I've never treated Yolanda with anything but love, respect, trust, and more love. That's all. But she's still mad as hell at me.

I guess I can't really blame her. How would I like it if the tables were turned? What if she had the dirty lowdown on someone I cared about and she didn't or couldn't tell me? Guess I'd be plenty pissed off too. But what if I *had* told her a patient's business? Would she still trust me with her secrets? The whole thing is out of hand. Not just because of me, but because she was so hooked on that jerk Basil. I guess it looks like we *both* betrayed her. I hope that men like Basil Henderson can't hide in heaven. That there is some special room where you learn you can't hide from your truth forever. But the doctor in me understands maybe why Basil felt he had to lie. The world isn't ready for macho football players revealing their sexual secrets.

Maybe I'm wrong. Maybe she's wrong. Maybe we're both wrong. I'm sick of vacillating. It really doesn't matter anyway. We need to get past this so I can give her the love and support she needs right now. Yolanda is family.

I decided the yellow legal paper wasn't right for the note; instead, I wrote it out on the blue linen stationery she'd given me for my last birthday. After hours of agonizing, and it all came down to nineteen words:

Dear Yolanda,

  Please forgive me for hurting you. I did what I felt I must do. I love you, that's all.

  L.

I decided to mail the letter on my way home. I found a stamp in the receptionist's desk and tucked the envelope in the breast pocket of my coat. I turned out the lights, locked the outer door, and decided to walk home. There was a cool wind blowing, and the sky had softened to an amber color that brightened the city. There was a convenience store near my building with a late-night pickup mailbox out front. Hopefully, Yolanda would receive the letter before the weekend. I could buy a microwavable dinner or deli sandwich and unload my heavy heart in one quick stop.

The emotional drain and tension had taken its toll. After walking twenty blocks, I was physically exhausted too. But I managed to enjoy the beauty of Chicago. A beauty that seems most vivid in the cold months. The lights seemed more brilliant and sounds more dazzling and alive. Despite the colder temperatures, the city exudes a real warmth, like a home with a roaring fire. The glare of neon up ahead told me I was almost home. I couldn't ever recall being this tired after walking from my office.

The fluorescent lighting inside the store cast a garish glow over the rows of snack foods, candy, and personal hygiene items. I headed for the side wall, where a line of glass-doored refrigerator compartments held cold beverages, ice cream, and frozen meals.

I reached for a turkey dinner, and as the door closed, I caught the reflection of a young white man in a black knit cap standing directly behind me. I turned to face him as he stood there blocking my path. He was no taller than I was, but maybe twenty years younger. His heavy navy pea coat was turned up at the collar and missing several buttons. His jeans were dirty and ragged, but his thick-soled brown shoes looked brand new, like he had just walked out of a shoe store.

"Watcha looking at, man! You looking at me?" His speech was slightly slurred and his eyes looked wild with a twinge of meanness around the edges. Drug-induced paranoia, I thought. I've seen it too many times in my business. But I wasn't at work, and all I wanted to do was pay for my food, mail my letter, and get on home. His hands were in the side pockets of his coat, and he stood firmly between me and the aisle leading to the cash register.

"Excuse me," I said, and brushed past him to the counter.

"I said, whatcha looking at!" He followed me to the counter and stood inches behind me. I could feel his sour breath on the back of my neck.

"I'll just take this," I said, and pushed my frozen dinner across to the young woman in an orange and brown smock behind the counter. She took my purchase and looked nervously over my shoulder at the belligerent man behind me. I could see the fear in her eyes and looked in the mirrors mounted on the wall behind her for a security guard. The store was deserted. It was just the three of us, and it was beginning to feel a little scary.

"Do you hear me talking to you, punk! Are you deaf or what?"

"How much do I owe you?" I asked the clerk. I could feel the adrenalin pumping through my veins. I needed to get some space between me and this freaked-out fool so I'd have room to land a punch if need be.

That's when he grabbed me by the shoulder and spun me around. "I'm talking to you, motherfucker."

"Take your hands off me, man," I said very slowly. I was trying to calm him down like with my patients. "I don't know you and you don't know me, and I sure would hate to have to call the police on you. Chill, man." I turned my head toward the clerk, hoping she'd heard me. She did, and reached under the counter to push what I prayed was a silent alarm. "Now, why don't you just step back, give me my space, and we won't have any trouble."

"Call the police? Whatsa matter, blood, can't handle it on your own? You think I'm scared of the fuckin' police?"

"Listen, man. I just came in here to buy my dinner. I know you're a little out of it right now, but don't start something you'll be sorry for later."

"Oh, so I'm fucked up?" He poked his fingers in my chest, giving me a little shove for good measure. I could have just pushed him out of the way and walked out of the store, but I didn't want to leave the young woman alone with this maniac. Where were the police? I would try and calm him down just enough for me and the clerk to get outside.

"Hey, man. Why don't you try and relax. Nobody's trying to mess with you here. Nobody wants to hurt you. Chill."

"Chill, my ass. Fuck you, man! I'm tired of everyone fucking with me. Stop looking at me. I can't think straight. I'm tired of this shit. Why can't you just leave me alone? Why can't everyone just leave me the fuck alone!" His eyes were darting back and forth, and he had a nervous tic—his fingers were shaking.

"Okay, man. Okay. Me and the young lady here are going to leave you alone. Okay?" The frightened clerk came slowly from behind the counter, never once taking her eyes off the man. She stood close behind me and I could feel her body trembling. "It will be all right, just stay calm," I whispered to her.

"See, we're leaving you alone. We're just going to go outside and you can have the whole store to yourself. No one will bother you anymore. We'll tell them all to leave you alone when we get outside. Okay?"

We started backing slowly toward the door, resisting the urge to bolt and run. At first he just stood there, looking confused and panicked. I kept my eyes locked on his, knowing he could explode at any moment. Please, God, I thought, just let us get out safely.

We inched closer and closer to the door. The clerk reached behind her and opened one side of the double glass doors just as two patrol cars pulled up and shone their spotlights into the store. I was hoping they would realize I wasn't the bad guy and not start shooting the moment they saw my Black face with a frightened white girl behind me. Suddenly shouting interrupted my thoughts.

"Sonofabitch!" the man yelled. "You lying sonofabitch! I'm gonna kill you, punk, I'm gonna kill you all!" He pulled a gun out of his coat and aimed it directly at us. The woman froze. I pushed her out the door, blocking her body with mine. I heard a shot. Then another. I felt a stinging sensation, but all I could think was that I should have mailed Yolanda's letter before I came into the store.

Chapter 31

Something told me not to answer my phone, but I didn't listen. "Yolanda, I've been trying to reach you for days. Did you get the flowers I sent?" John asked.

"Yeah, I got them," I said in my dry *I-ain't-even-trying-to-hear-you* tone.

"Yolanda, I'm sorry. We need to talk. It's not what you think," John said.

"We don't need to talk, John, and it really doesn't matter what I think. You and Monty showed me. I don't have any questions. You just go and be happy with yo' boy Monty."

"It's not like that. I'm not gay or bisexual. Let me explain," John pleaded. I was getting ready to tell him to save his words for some woman fool enough to believe him, when I heard my call-waiting tone. "Hold up," I said as I clicked over to the second line.

"Yolanda?"

"Yes?" I didn't recognize the voice right away, but I knew it sounded familiar.

"Baby, this is Uncle Doc. Leland's uncle," he said.

"Uncle Doc, how are you doing? I was thinking about you today.

You know me and my boy are on the outs. But don't worry, it's just a temporary thing, we'll be back hanging before you know it."

"Yolanda baby, I got some bad news," Uncle Doc said slowly.

"What's the matter, Uncle Doc?"

"Baby, Leland be shot! He's in the emergency room at Northwestern Hospital," Uncle Doc said.

"No! Not my Leland," I screamed. What was Uncle Doc telling me?

"Yolanda, calm down. You need to get over here," Uncle Doc said.

"I'm on my way." I hung up my phone and it rang immediately. I had forgotten John was on the other line.

"Hello," I said.

"I'm still here. Yolanda baby, please let me come to Chicago and—"

"John, I ain't got time for you and your lying, need-to-admit-you-gay ass. My best friend is in trouble. Later." Dial tone.

●   ●   ●

It's funny how you behave in an emergency. Your brain seems to kick into automatic, overriding your emotions and getting your body to do what needs doing. I don't remember hanging up the phone, or leaving the house, let alone getting in my car. But here I am, sitting behind the wheel, driving down Lake Shore Drive to Northwestern Medical Center, while my mind is racing through a stream of unanswered questions.

Did Uncle Doc say Leland had been shot? How could someone just walk up and shoot somebody like Leland? How could that be? Leland of all people. Leland the always terminally nonviolent. This man wouldn't hurt a fly. Terminal. Dead. Oh, no, not Leland. Dear God, not Leland. How could I have been so stupid? I didn't even ask if Leland was dead or alive. Please God, let my baby-boy be alive.

Shot. That's what Uncle Doc had said. Leland's been shot. He didn't say killed, he would have said killed, wouldn't he?

Hold on. You're tripping. If Leland were dead, I'd know it. I would have felt something. I know I would. He's not dead. It's probably something like a flesh wound in the arm or leg or something. That's it. He's probably sitting in some emergency room pissed off because he's got a tiny bloodstain on his shirt or his pants leg. He's probably feeling like a jerk for putting himself in jeopardy. He's probably embarrassed as hell. I'll try not to rub it in.

How many times have I told him about walking alone late at night? I don't care how safe he thinks his neighborhood is. He thinks because he's a good person, a decent man, nothing bad will happen to him. I mean, really! He works with crazy people every day. He should know better. I hate to say "I told you so," but as soon as we get him all bandaged up and back home, I'm going to give his ass a good talking-to. Upsetting me and Uncle Doc like this. This will not do. If he doesn't care about himself, then he's got to think about my and Uncle Doc's feelings for him. Got us running to the hospital in the middle of the night, all upset and worried—and for nothing.

What we will do is get him in Uncle Doc's lemon-yellow Caddy. Uncle Doc will take him home and get him settled, and I'll go down to the Walgreens on Michigan and get any medication he's prescribed. I'll stop and get him some Cap'n Crunch and Ben & Jerry's Chunky Monkey. I'll also get him some bubble gum and those apple sticks he loves. Magazines. I have to get some magazines for him to read. No medical journals or business magazines. Just the pop stuff. I don't want my baby-boy thinking about nothing. I'll take good care of him. He's okay. Just a little flesh wound, that's all.

When I got to the hospital, I parked in a restricted zone and plopped my press sticker on the dashboard. As I followed the broad red line painted on the hospital floor to the emergency waiting room, a sense of panic and doom overwhelmed me, shattering my

neat little flesh-wound scenario. I had never seen anyone shot before. Not really. I fought to suppress the terrible images that
flooded my mind. Images from television and movies of bright red
blood against brown skin.

The waiting room was soothingly decorated in muted pastels.
Sofas and chairs were arranged to provide semiprivate areas for
waiting friends and relatives in the warm, open room. A young couple sat huddled together in a far corner, holding on to each other for
dear life. A white-haired, distinguished-looking older man sat in the
chair closest to the door, and beside him was a younger woman—
maybe his daughter? Every few minutes she would reach across the
arms of their chairs and gently pat his knee. They both stared
straight ahead, lost in their own thoughts. I was trying not to stare,
so I sat down in a chair against the wall.

My eyes moved to the door of the waiting room and I saw Uncle
Doc. I leaped from my seat and started toward him. Uncle Doc
paced slowly into the room. He suddenly looked very old and very
tired. When he saw me, I could see he'd been crying. He gestured
for me to follow him outside into the corridor.

"Uncle Doc," I said, surprised at the sound of my voice cracking.
"Is he . . . is Leland . . . is he . . ." I couldn't get the words out.
Uncle Doc held me and said, "He's still with us, baby doll. I don't
have any more information."

"What happened? Did they catch whoever did this?"

"They caught him. But I don't know the details. They may have
to operate," Uncle Doc said. Tears began to roll from my eyes. "Let
it all out now, 'cause I'm going to need you to be strong." I cried
softly into Uncle Doc's frail shoulder and felt some of the tension
ease from my pounding head and strained neck and shoulder muscles. Uncle Doc held me gently, like I was a rag doll, until my sobs
finally subsided.

"What happened, Uncle Doc? Where is he? Can I see him? I
can't believe this is happening. Why would anyone shoot Leland?" I
didn't want to ask where he was shot, or how many times. I didn't

want those images in my mind. I just wanted Uncle Doc or some hospital person to tell me that Leland was all right.

"Yolanda, I've got to go to the airport and pick up Leland's mother. So you've got to pull yourself together. I need you to call any of Leland's friends who might be able to donate blood. I can't lie to you. It's not looking too good. The doctors haven't said that, but I've got this feeling."

"Don't say that, Uncle Doc. Leland will be just fine. Where did this happen?"

"At that little store near his building. I think it was a robbery, I don't know, but it seems like Leland was just in the wrong place at the wrong time. Leland ain't never hurt another soul his entire life, now this. It just ain't right, baby. It just ain't right."

Uncle Doc pulled me close again and we held each other and silently wished Leland all of our strength and love.

"Now, listen," Uncle Doc said. He sat us down on the padded bench outside the waiting room. "You make some calls. I want to be there when Mattie gets off the airplane. Okay, baby? Now, I'm going to find the doctor on my way out, but in case I don't see him, I want you to be here and find out what he has to say. I'm going to pick her up, and then we'll be right back. I hate to leave you like this, but I'll be back directly. Now, do you think you'll be okay?"

"I'll be fine, Uncle Doc. You go on. I'm not going anywhere until I know Leland's all right. Go on, really, I'm fine." But I didn't feel fine. I was scared and really didn't want Uncle Doc to leave me not knowing if Leland was going to live or die. I watched him walk away down the corridor until he turned out of my sight.

I sat in the corner of a sofa and started at the blank screen of the television set mounted on the opposite wall. The white-faced clock on the wall near me ticked off the seconds and minutes in slow motion. Each second felt like a torment, the waiting endless. Afraid to seek out bad news, I sat very still, as if moving would make the news worse. It would have to come to me. I would have to tell Leland's mother and Uncle Doc about our baby-boy. I suddenly remembered Uncle Doc saying something about Leland needing blood. I needed to call Dwight and Riley. I could also call Monica and Sybil. I knew they both would want to help. Just as I stood up, an Asian woman in green surgical gear approached the waiting room.

"Douglas Thompson? Is there a Douglas Thompson here?" She spoke to the waiting room in general.

"Here," I said. "Mr. Thompson had to pick up his sister-in-law, Leland's mother, at the airport. I'm Leland Thompson's best friend, Yolanda Williams."

"I'm Dr. Cheng, Ms. Williams," she said, and reached to shake my hand. "I'll be performing the surgery on Dr. Thompson."

"How is he? Is he going to be okay?" I asked anxiously, a slight tremor in my voice.

"I'm sorry, Ms. Williams. I really need to speak with his next of kin or any relative. I can discuss his condition only with family members." Dr. Cheng spoke quietly, almost patronizingly, to me.

"But Leland's—Dr. Thompson's uncle asked me to stand in for him. Can't you tell me what's going on? This is my best friend in the world we're talking about here!" My voice was getting louder the more frustrated I became, but I didn't care. "Just tell me if he's going to be okay, dammit!"

"I understand how you feel," Dr. Cheng said sympathetically. "But I really must speak directly with his uncle or mother. You should just try and relax, so you can be there for your friend." She turned to leave, then doubled back and took my hands and said, "You do understand, don't you?"

I gave her a weak smile and whispered, "Yes, I understand."

The doctor headed toward the nurses' station, and I headed for the bank of public telephones in the opposite direction.

"Dwight," I said, biting my lips to keep myself from crying.

"Yolanda? Hey, I was hoping you'd call. I've been thinking about our meeting a lot. I want—" Dwight sounded so happy, but I had to interrupt him.

"Leland's been shot!" I blurted out. "He's going to need blood."
I hadn't thought about how to tell Dwight or Riley the bad news,
and the words just came out in a rush, like I had no control over
what I was saying.

"What happened? Where are you? How much blood does he
need? Of course I'll donate," Dwight said.

"I'm at the emergency room at Northwestern. They're going to
operate real soon," I said.

I asked Dwight to call Riley and give her the news and to ask her
to meet us at the hospital. I told Dwight all I knew: that Leland
had been shot, that the surgery was needed to remove a bullet, and
that he was still alive. No, I didn't know how many times or where
he'd been shot. He was alive. That's all I know, I told him. He's
alive.

About an hour later I was relieved to see Riley's and Selwyn's
worried faces coming toward me down the corridor. I was surprised
to see that they were actually holding hands, like very young lovers.
Dwight was right behind them. I felt like the posse had arrived.

"Thanks for getting here so fast," I said, and gave each of them a
hug. "Uncle Doc left for the airport to pick up Leland's mother, and
the doctor won't tell me anything." We turned into the waiting
room and sat down together in silence. Dwight sat close to me on a
sofa and put his arm around me.

"How're you holding up, girl?" His voice was concerned and
private.

"I don't know, Dwight. This is all so strange, so bizarre. I feel
like running, screaming out of this place. I'm so glad you're all
here." My eyes were filling with tears again, but I fought the urge to
break down and cry.

Still holding each other's hands, Riley and Selwyn sat together
across from Dwight and me.

"Didn't you mention something about Leland needing some
blood?" Dwight asked.

"Yes, I guess we need to talk with the doctor," I said.

"You stay here, Yolanda. Dwight and I will go and see what we need to do," Selwyn said as he stood up.

"Were you with him when it happened, Yolanda?" Riley asked.

"No," I said. "Apparently it happened sometime after he left work. We really don't have any details, just that he was shot at a convenience store near his home."

Riley walked toward me and put her hand on my shoulder and said, "Yolanda, you know Leland will be all right, don't you?" I suddenly remembered how cruel I must have sounded when I told Riley she couldn't sing. I wanted to tell her I was sorry. "Riley, we need to—" Riley placed her slender finger on my lips and whispered, "We've got plenty of time for that."

"Riley's right, Leland will be fine," Selwyn said.

"Selwyn, we should go and find out about donating blood," Dwight said.

I looked around at Dwight, at Riley and Selwyn, and felt a powerful love for each of them, for all of us together.

"Before you guys leave, could we pray?" I asked. "Can we just hold hands and pray for Leland?"

Dwight took his arms and put them around my shoulders and moved closer to me. He took my hand in his and reached across to take Riley's hand. I offered my free hand to Selwyn and he grasped it firmly in his. We bowed our heads and the power of our spirits joined as one in prayer for our brother, our friend. It was so strong, I could feel it pressing against my chest, filling the space between each of us, uniting us in love.

"Thank you, dear God. Amen," I said.

"Amen," Dwight, Riley, and Selwyn echoed in unison.

•   •   •

When my phone rang at around two A.M., I prayed it was Yolanda. Maybe she would at least let me explain myself. Let me tell her why she was different and how she had changed my life. But it wasn't Yolanda, it was that mofo Monty.

"Man, I'm just calling to see if you've cooled down," Monty said.

"Cooled down from what?" I started to tell Monty he wasn't calling to see if I had cooled down from shit. This mofo wanted some more beef.

"You know, us getting busted. Man, I'm not going to use Yolanda for business. Matter fact, those fools in my group have come to their senses. They won't be talking since they got their own deals. I won't be going public."

"Good for you, Monty. But it still doesn't change a thing with us. I'm through with fucking around with hardheads like yourself. I've got to go," I said.

"Man, I don't know how you think you're going to do that. You know how women are. Yolanda probably already got that shit on the grapevine. You'll be going through the same shit I just went through," Monty said.

"I'm going to win Yolanda back," I said firmly.

"You think so?"

"Look, I don't even know why I'm discussing my business with you. I wish you whatever, man. But don't call me no mo', got it?" I said as I hung up the phone. The first thing I was going to do the following morning was get another unpublished number.

. . .

"I feel like I already know you, Yolanda," Mattie Thompson said as she gave me a big hug.

"And I feel like I know you. I'm so sorry we're meeting under these circumstances," I said.

"Oh, my baby will be just fine. He's in God's hands and he'll be just fine."

"I know that's right," Uncle Doc said. "Where are the rest of your friends?"

"They're down in the coffee shop, getting some coffee. Have you talked to the doctors?"

"Yes, we just spoke with them. They're preparing Leland for surgery. Where are the young men who donated blood? I have to thank them," Mattie said.

"That's Dwight and Selwyn. You'll meet them in a few minutes," I said.

"I look forward to that," Mattie said as she took a seat on the sofa. She looked tired.

"How was your flight? Do you have a place to stay?"

"Darling, the flight was just fine. And I'm going to split my time between Leland's place and Doc's. Thanks for asking."

The group returned and introduced themselves to Leland's mother. It felt like a family reunion, all of Leland's family and friends waiting for word of how his operation had gone. Uncle Doc had found out from the police that they had apprehended the guy who shot Leland and proudly told us how his nephew was a hero for putting his own body in front of the young lady working at the store.

"My baby always was concerned with others," Mattie said softly. Mattie Thompson, wearing a floral scoop-necked dress, was a short, square-bodied woman with strong shoulders and generous hips. She had calm brown eyes with flawlessly mascaraed lashes. Mattie's long and thick salt and pepper hair was curled on the ends.

"Mattie, ain't you tired yet? Girl, look at them heels you got on. I know at least your foots are tired. Let me take you home," Uncle Doc said.

"I want to wait and talk with my baby," Mattie said.

"That might be a while. Yolanda and them will be here, and they can let us know," Uncle Doc said. "We ain't gonna be no good for Boo if we too tired. We're old folks. We need our rest."

"Speak for yourself, Douglas Thompson. Speak for yourself."

Mattie opened her brown leather purse and it looked like she was organizing its contents. A few minutes later she pulled out a couple of peppermint candies and popped one in her mouth. "You want one of these?" she asked Uncle Doc. Uncle Doc rolled his eyes and said, "What you trying to say, Mattie. Is my breath kickin'?" Mattie smiled and pushed him with her whole body and said, "Take this, you old man." They both laughed and gave each other a supportive hug. I noticed Leland's and Mattie's lower lips tucked under their teeth the same way when they smiled and both had an easy, elegant laughter.

"Mrs. Thompson. Maybe you do need to get some rest. We'll stay here and I'll call as soon as we hear something." I turned to Uncle Doc, who was now sucking on the peppermint with a smacking sound, and said, "Uncle Doc, somebody from Leland's biological family might need to be here or inform the doctor that it's okay to give me information. Dr. Cheng was really strict about following the rules. She ain't giving up *any* information."

"Don't worry, darling. I'll take care of Dr. Cheng and be right back. Mattie knows she needs to get some rest," Uncle Doc said.

When Uncle Doc and Mattie left, the solemn mood of a couple of hours before seemed to lift somewhat as the four of us enjoyed coffee and each other's company, like we were back at Hampton hanging out in front of the Grill. Dwight was almost staring at Riley and Selwyn sitting together, looking like a couple again.

"Riley, if you're tired, you and Selwyn can go home. Dwight and I can stay," I said.

"That's all right, we'll be just fine. I want to make sure Leland's all right," Riley said. Selwyn looked lovingly at her in agreement. Dwight took my hand and said he was going to look for Dr. Cheng and see if he could find out any more information on Leland's status. I nodded my head and glanced back at Riley and Selwyn and saw Riley lay her head on Selwyn's chest while he gently patted her back. They looked like they had years ago, when we were all so very young. How I missed that time.

About fifteen minutes later Dwight returned and said Leland was in recovery. We found the recovery room and were told Leland was being prepared to be moved to the intensive care unit on the next floor. I could feel a subtle creep around my heart, and Dwight held my hands and led me toward the elevator. We rode silently up one floor, and I jumped slightly when the elevator beeped at the fourth floor. I hesitated a bit when the elevator door opened, and Dwight waited patiently for me to take a deep breath and move forward out of the elevator. We walked together down the quiet corridor, and I wanted nothing more at that minute than to turn and run back in the other direction—away from this place, away from this terrible feeling of impending doom.

"I need to go and call Uncle Doc," I said suddenly. "I need to let him know Leland's out of surgery."

"I'll have Selwyn and Riley do that," Dwight said. I guess he could tell I was stalling. I hated hospitals.

The ICU was a glass-enclosed room, cold and sterile. There were three occupied beds inside. Each patient was hooked up to a beeping monitor and yards of plastic tubing. One bed held the frail body of an elderly woman, and another held a middle-aged man. Leland was in the third bed.

My spine tingled and Dwight had to pull me closer to the glass. Leland's eyes were closed. He had a slightly troubled expression and his face and his arms were motionless at his sides. He lay on a white sheet, a white pillow beneath his head. Another white sheet covered him from his feet to just above his waist. His chest was a mess of white bandages. Tubes and wires seemed to extend from everywhere—his chest, his arms, his nose and mouth. I was totally unprepared to see my baby-boy like this, so still, so quiet. I wanted him to open his eyes, look up at me and tell me he "loved him some Yolanda." I wanted him to wake up so I could tell him I loved him too. And that I was sorry for the hurtful things I had said to him. I wanted my old friend back, laughing with me while we shared a plate of Uncle Doc's wings.

"Oh, Dwight. He looks so still," I said. "You don't think we're going to lose him, do you?"

"I don't know, Yolanda. Leland's tough. We don't always see eye to eye, but I've always respected his strength. I look forward to getting the chance to tell him just that." Dwight shrugged his broad shoulders and his chest expanded with a deep, low sigh. We both felt a twinge of helplessness as we stood side by side behind the glass barrier separating us from our dear friend.

"It's all my fault," I sobbed. "If I hadn't gotten so mad at him, maybe we would have been together having dinner somewhere instead of him being in that store. Uncle Doc said the police said Leland was holding a TV dinner. He didn't have anybody to have dinner with. It's all my fault." My admission of being so childish and guilty made me cry that much harder.

"This is not your fault, Yolanda. You didn't have anything to do with this. You didn't make him go in that store and you didn't shoot him. So don't go tripping and beating yourself up. It's like Selwyn said when we were in the coffee shop, things just happen. It's how we deal with what life throws at us that shapes our character, makes us who we are." Dwight pulled a neatly folded white handkerchief from his back pocket and dabbed away my tears. "You've got to be strong, Yolanda. You've got to have faith that Leland will be all right. Despite your little disagreement, Leland knows you love him."

"You're sure he knows it?" I asked. "The last thing I said to him was also the worst thing I've ever said to him. I'll regret those words forever if I can't ask for Leland's forgiveness." I started to cry all over again.

"I thought you promised me you'd be strong?" It was Uncle Doc. He was standing behind me. When I turned around and looked at him, he opened his arms wide to embrace me.

"Come here, baby doll," he said. He let me have a good cry while he talked to Dwight over my head.

"Me and Mattie have been through here already. It was kind of a shock to see him like this." He nodded toward the glass. "Mattie is pretty shook up, but we talked to the doctor and I guess we'll just have to wait and see how the good Lord plays it." Uncle Doc patted me on the back and rocked me ever so gently until I was able to catch my breath and stop crying.

"I left my sister back there with Riley and Selwyn. Sure was good to see them together, all cuddled up and comforting each other. I think it's a sign that everything is going to be okay. Leland knows we're all waiting on him. Anyhow, a little old gunshot wound is a piece of cake for the good Lord."

Dwight and I smiled in spite of ourselves and thought maybe Uncle Doc was right. At any rate, it was out of our hands and all we could do now was pray and wait.

"They gave me Leland's stuff," Uncle Doc said, holding up the plastic bag. "His clothes, shoes, his wallet, and such." He reached into the bag and retrieved a blue envelope. "This here's for you, Yolanda. It was in his coat pocket, they said."

The envelope looked vaguely familiar. I recognized my name and address scrawled across the front in Leland's distinctive handwriting. He had written his return address in the upper-left-hand corner. I took the envelope from Uncle Doc's hand and held it gingerly in mine. Leland had written me a letter. He'd been shot before he had a chance to mail it. I looked down at the envelope in my hand, at Leland's writing, at the blood spattered over the stamp. A gift as precious to me as a good friend.

Chapter 32

On an early Monday morning, the week of Thanksgiving, a dusting of snow left a glittery, fresh surface on Chicago. Across this city, on the North Side, Mag Mile, and in Hyde Park, three friends drank cranberry juice, coffee, and orange juice while writing in journals that kept them sane in the midst of a storm. Not the winter weather outside, but one of the heart.

 I read my mother up and down this morning and felt nothing. No guilt. No call back a few hours later with an "I'm sorry." She made me mad. Again. When she asked why she couldn't reach me one evening, I told her I was at the hospital, visiting a friend. When she asked who and I told her Leland, she said, "Isn't he gay? Didn't his friend die of AIDS? Does he have AIDS?" After I answered yes, yes and no, I told her Leland had been shot, and the questions started again, "Did some man shoot him for making a pass at him? Is he on drugs? Was he trying to buy drugs and some dealer shot him?" These questions I didn't even answer. I told her from now on

out, I wasn't discussing my friends with her and would ask that she do the same and that included Miss Wanda Mae Washington, whom I was not going to work for again under any circumstance. While I was talking to her I was smiling at myself in the mirror and doing circle pops all around myself, thinking to myself, take that, Miss Clarice. But in many ways I'm not really mad at my mother. I'm starting to feel sorry for her. Sorry that she will probably never live her dreams, whatever they are. Me, I think I might have a chance at my dreams.

When I told Selwyn about my conversation with my mother, he told me he was so proud of me. We had just left the hospital and were sitting in the library, having a brandy, just gazing into each other's eyes. I'm loving him more and more each day. This is really love like the first time. When I mentioned the part about Wanda Mae, he asked me what did I want to do? I told him I wanted to continue with the poetry and music. He was supportive and said I could do anything. I'm not so certain I'm ever going to be some diva singer or poet; to be honest, I've finally faced that I probably will not. But I can help others. What I want to do is help young kids, maybe from the lower-class areas, who have an interest in the arts. Maybe they have parents who aren't listening to them, not because they don't care, but because they're too busy worrying about two jobs or how they're going to put food on the table. That's when Selwyn came up with this brilliant idea. Well, it wasn't totally his, because I had thought about it several times but never mentioned it to anyone. "Why don't you open some type of after-school program? Hire some instructors and make it free to the kids you were talking about. We have more than enough money to fund it and it could be a way for you to give back and share your dreams. And you'd get a chance to use that wonderful business sense you have," Selwyn said. All I could do was kiss him all over his face, lips, and hands. He has such complete faith in me and my dreams.

So I'm looking forward to the future, and more important . . . the near future. I think once Leland has recovered, the group will reconvene. I'm praying that it's before Christmas. I need my friends. I need the love of my children, who have been calling almost every other day asking about Leland's status and our ski trip to Vail. I want so very much to share a *wonderful holiday with my family, meaning Selwyn, Reggie, and Ryan and the best gifts of the season—family and friendship.*

God is testing me. My new wave of tolerance, that is. First thing, I find myself sleeping in Leland's hospital room, just so Yolanda, his mother, and Uncle Doc can get some sleep in a real bed. I don't like hospitals, but we, I mean, I want to be there for Leland. Despite our differences, I think he'd be there for me if our roles were changed. I'm falling in love with Leland's mother, Mattie, who reminds me of my mother. Mattie and Sarah would get along just fine. I was telling my mother about spending so much time at the hospital with Leland and she told me how proud she was of me. When I asked her why, she said, "Oh, baby, after Scooter died, I didn't think you'd ever go in a hospital again." I told her I didn't ever remember being in the hospital with Scooter, and she said, " 'Cause you wasn't. You refused to go in. You just stood outside the emergency room door." I didn't tell her I didn't even remember that. I realized there are certain things about that day and the days following I have blocked out. I used to think people were bullshitting when they talked about this repressed memory shit, but I guess it's as real as rain, as Sarah would say.

Being at the hospital has given me a chance to have really long and honest talks with Yolanda and Riley. I've realized they are both wonderful, yet different types of women. Yolanda told me she didn't believe the doctors when they told her Leland would probably recover, but when I said it, she believed it. That's deep. Riley asked me to talk to Selwyn about never knowing my father, because she knew it would help him accept his own family roots. I didn't even know the old boy didn't know his people. He always carried himself like he had the world by the balls. I feel closer to Selwyn knowing where he came from and what he's achieved in his life. It's funny how this new combination of testosterone and sensitivity is working in my body. I guess it was always there, but I never let it show.

One night after leaving the hospital I got home and called Kelli's mom, who I always liked. We talked a few minutes and I asked her for Kelli's number. After a little bit of hesitation, she gave it to me but warned me to hang up if her new husband answered. I called, and when Kelli answered, I said quickly but calmly, "Kelli, this is Dwight. I hate to bother you this late, but there was something I have to say. I'm sorry and I was wrong. I should have given you an explanation, but I was young and dumb. It wasn't you. And I wish you and your new husband well." There was a few seconds of silence and then Kelli said, "Thank you, Dwight. I've been waiting for years to hear you say that. Good night." I made the phone call, not because I felt I had to, but because it was right.

But back to God and his test. I had decided to take the job in Washington, D.C., you know, go and work for the brothers. Becky screamed, "Yes!" when I told her I would accept the offer. I'm sure it was the commission that had her excited. I told them I'd report the second week of January.

But a couple of days ago, when I got back from the hospital there was a message on my machine from Dan Stickens over at MedMac. He wanted me to call him right away, said it was very important. Since it was around two A.M., I waited until the following morning.

When I called Dan he told me he had somebody he wanted me to meet, and he hoped I was available for lunch. I asked who it was and he just said somebody who could change my life. We met for lunch at Glady's and I was a little surprised when Dan walked in with this white man with reddish-brown hair and a full beard. He introduced his associate as Myron Weinstock. I shook Myron's hand and told him it was nice meeting him, but I still didn't know why Dan wanted the two of us to meet. Myron looked vaguely familiar. I think I had seen him around MedMac in the computer room. I assumed he was one of the program contractors MedMac hired on occasion to assist in bringing up new applications while permanent personnel maintained existing systems. Maybe Dan was introducing me to Myron because he could help me in getting a job doing contract programming. But Dan was wasting his time, I wasn't interested.

After we all ordered smothered chicken, Dan told me he was moving to Detroit to help open up a new office for MedMac, so his job as MIS director was open, and he wondered if I was interested in his job. He said they were willing to meet my salary requirements (Like I had some. I was thinking how about a paycheck). Of course I was interested. I knew Dan's role at MedMac and it was definitely a management position. That's when I found out who Myron was and why Dan said he would change my life. As it so happens, Myron was CFO at MedMac and one of the founders. He had been one of the primary investors when the company was founded and had developed several of the software packages the company used. Currently these products were being used by MedMac and their customers, but they were preparing to sell them through a regional sales distributor. And MedMac was preparing to become a public company and if I signed on before the end of the year, I would receive some unbelievable stock options. Dan said if things go as planned, we'd all be millionaires this time next year. I was sitting there in Glady's, letting my food get cold and not believing my luck. I wanted to stay in Chicago. I think I could get used to being a millionaire. I wouldn't change, you know, like drinking champagne and eating caviar and shit, but I could do some things for my mother, and maybe a future wife. I've decided I want love in my life.

So, I'm just sitting there like a stone, listening to Dan and Myron trying to convince me to take this job, when Myron looked at me and said, "Dwight, I've heard a lot of great things about you. And the job is yours if you want it. But I think there is something you should know about me, since it looks like we'll be working very closely. We have big plans for expansion in the data processing arena." I was thinking, what is he getting ready to tell me, that he's white? I could see that. That he was Jewish? The name gave that away and I didn't have a problem with that either. So I looked at Myron and said, "I'm listening." And Myron said, "We have a family environment at MedMac . . . and, well . . . I'm gay. Will that be a problem for you?" I looked at Myron and then at Dan, cupped my hand over my mouth to hide my grin, and said, "No, I don't have a problem with that." And the funny and strange thing for me was, I really didn't care. There was no twitching, my heart didn't quicken, and sweat didn't soak my neck. All I could think was these two men had enough faith *in me to offer me a chance of a lifetime. Man oh man, wouldn't Yolanda and Leland be proud of me. And of course, Sarah and Scooter would be proud too!*

 I'm finally starting to believe Leland will be just fine. I hope our friendship will be the same, if not stronger. The doctors say Leland is still not out of the woods yet, but I believe in something higher than the doctors. My faith. Something I hadn't given the attention I should and need to. It's not like I stopped believing in God or anything like that, I didn't. It's just with my business and all, I got sidetracked with my time commitments. I was working six days a week, so on Sunday instead of going to church I stayed in bed. I know I need church to reinforce my faith. I had always gone to church, but with each new client I signed, church became a lower priority. My mother and father wouldn't be happy about that either. Sybil reminded me of how whenever we ran into a problem, Mama always used to say, "Give it to God. He can handle it." When both my parents died, the grief was unbearable. Even with Sybil for support I didn't know how I would survive without my parents. But I did. I gave it to God. And even though I don't remember the day when the pain left, it did. I was able to accept my parents were in a better place, together forever.

So that's what I've done with Leland's health and our friendship. I've given it to God, and it seems he's sent me an angel to make sure I know he will take care of Leland. The funny thing is, I never thought Dwight would be that angel. He has been so supportive and understanding. Allowing me to talk when I need to talk, and cry when the tears just come. When the doctors were holding information on Leland's condition, I imagined the worst. But when Dwight told me Leland would be fine, I believed him. I don't know why, maybe it was the way he said it. He seemed so sure of what he was saying to me. I'm praying he doesn't take the job in D.C., but if he does, I will definitely go and visit. If he invites me. The job

opportunity in D.C. really sounds like a good one. And Dwight deserves a break.

The other night Dwight and I were sitting in the hospital waiting room, just talking about life. How Leland's tragedy had made all of us take a look at life. How short and precious it could be. How when we were at Hampton we were convinced life would always be as fun as a greek show, a slamming party, or a walk alongside Hampton Creek with that someone special. I don't know, but since Dwight came back from D.C., his face looks younger, like he has not only changed internally, but physically as well. Maybe the tension he used to always carry with him has vanished and took some years with it. He laughs a lot now (mostly at the ebonics jokes he tells me when I look depressed), and when he does, his eyes appear to sparkle like stars against a dark sky. When we talk, I don't want the conversations to ever end. But when Leland leaves the hospital, I'm afraid the late night talks just might.

I also know when Leland gets better, I'll have to deal with John. I need him to understand that friendship is the only thing I can offer. I can't believe he's still calling, sending flowers and expensive gifts. Just a few days ago I noticed a large box inside my apartment. The office management people told me it had been delivered by FedEx, and that some gentleman had called and asked them to put it in my apartment. When I opened it, I realized it was a beautiful Verna Hart painting I had admired when John and I had visited a New Orleans art gallery. The certification papers informed me I was now the owner of a limited edition serigraph entitled "Bass Walkin," a colorful painting of three African American jazz players. It would fit perfectly in my living room, with its blue and red coloring, that is, if I decide to keep it. I think I'm going to call the gallery and find out the price and then send John a check for the amount. He has to know he can't buy my love and affection. But right now John and the painting will have to wait.

Chapter 33

Days passed. Then weeks, and I still hadn't talked with Yolanda. I was exhausted waiting for a call that would not come. There were many days when I felt myself drifting back into my tunnel of gloom. I needed to talk with Yolanda. I knew if I could talk to her in person, or even at length on the phone, I could convince her to give me another chance. Yolanda was the type of woman capable of love and forgiveness. All she needed was a little time. Part of me is trippin' out, wondering why I don't just move on. If Yolanda doesn't want to give me another chance, then I should say to hell with you. Get to skippin', Miss Lady. But I can't.

It was a couple of days before Thanksgiving, and I was still counting on her to go to Detroit and meet my father and aunt. With the exception of Chase, I never wanted my father and aunt to meet a lady I was serious about. Mainly because my father and aunt didn't think there was a woman good enough for me, which was probably true. They didn't meet Vickie until after we were married.

I figured something had happened to Yolanda's friend Leland from the updates she left on her answering machine and with her assistant Monica. "This is Yolanda, and I have had a family emergency and won't be available to return your messages promptly. If this call is regarding my services, please contact my assistant, Monica, at Media Magic. Have a blessed day and pray for Leland." At least, it seemed he was out of danger, and I was hopeful Yolanda would soon be answering her phone. While I was waiting for a food delivery, I decided to give her one more try. My fifth call today alone. I was startled when she answered the phone on the first ring.

"Hello?" Her voice sounded tired, but sweet.

"Yolanda baby, this is John. How are you doing?"

"I'm doin'. I got your messages, but I guess you've heard about Leland," Yolanda said.

"Yes, I heard your messages, and Monica mentioned it when I called your office. How is he doing?"

"Better. He came home two days ago. Thank God, it looks like he's out of danger."

"I'm glad to hear that. Girl, you don't know how hard I've been trying to get with you. We need to talk," I said.

"John, I don't know what we have to talk about. I think I've told you where I stand. Besides the obvious, I have to make sure I'm here if Leland needs me, and I've got to get my business back on track," Yolanda said.

"I understand. But I think there are some things we need to talk about. I don't think you know the whole story," I said.

"John, look, I'm not trying to be a you-know-what. But I don't think we have anything to discuss in terms of a relationship. Maybe after some time has passed, we can try and start a friendship. I don't think I have a problem offering my friendship. But now I don't even have time for that. I don't begrudge you for being gay."

"Yolanda, dammit! I told you I'm not gay. I'm not even bisexual. That's why we got to talk. Please let me come to Chicago. Let me pick you up and drive you to Detroit for the holidays. It sounds like you need to get away for a while," I pleaded. I didn't mean to raise my voice, but I had to make her understand. Things were not what they seemed.

"Thanks, but no thanks. I've already made plans. Look, my other line is ringing. Maybe we can talk at the beginning of the year."

"Yolanda, please, baby. I need to share some things with you."

"I'm not the one, John." I didn't think Yolanda was being cold, she was just direct, but I didn't want to hear this.

"Yolanda, I love you. I mean that. I really love you. Please give me another chance," I said.

"Good-bye, John. Give your family my best." And then a dial tone.

I was so mad, I slammed the wall phone down so hard, it crashed to the kitchen floor. "Goddammit, dammit," I yelled. My body was tight and tense and I felt a rush of anger pass over me. The kitchen felt dim, dismal, and gray, like a storm cloud was hovering right about the stove.

When I heard someone knocking at my door, I was thinking who in the fuck could this be, knocking on my door unannounced. If it's the mofo Monty, I'm kicking his ass from here to Hollywood, I thought.

When I opened the door, this short Chinese guy was standing there with my food delivery.

"Who let you up here without calling?" I demanded. He looked at me like I was crazy.

"Sir, sir. We called. The phone just ring. Doorman said it was okay."

"How much is it?" I asked. Instead of kicking Monty's ass, I needed to kick some doorman's ass. If it hadn't been for the damn doorman, I wouldn't be begging Yolanda to give me a second chance. The delivery guy didn't tell me what I owed. He handed me a greasy yellow slip with $27.96 written in blue. I reached in my jean pockets and quickly realized that I had only ten dollars in cash.

"Do you take credit cards?" I asked, looking at him like *I dare you to say no.*

"Yes, sir," he mumbled while looking down at his well-worn gym shoes.

"What kind? Do you take American Express?"

"Yes."

I pulled my American Express card from my wallet and placed it in his open hand. He looked frightened as he pulled a small credit card machine from the red box that transported the food.

I signed the receipt and slammed the door. Now I wasn't hungry. While I was putting the card back in my wallet, I noticed a business card. When I pulled the card out, there it was: *Raymond Winston Tyler, Jr., Attorney-at-Law.* Below the numbers designated as office and fax was a handwritten number with an *H* at the end. That's who I needed to talk with: Raymond would understand my rage.

But I couldn't call Raymond right away, not when I was this angry. I put on my Brownstone CD, started humming the song "If You Love Me." I ate some wonton soup, shrimp fried rice, dipped an egg roll in some sweet and sour sauce, and drank a beer. My order included some sweet and sour pork, but after pouring it on a plate I decided I was full. Again, I had an urge to call Raymond. Maybe he would understand what I was going through. What I was feeling.

I went to my bedroom and picked up the phone and began to dial Raymond's number. Just before I hit the last number I heard my call-waiting beep. Maybe it was Yolanda. "Hello."

"Basil?" It was my dad.

"Hey Dad, whatsup?"

"I'm doing okay, son. Did I catch you at a bad time?"

"Not really. I was making a call. It can wait." I sat down on the bed and tried to breathe slowly, I didn't want Dad knowing I was upset.

"What day are you and your lady getting to Detroit?"

"I don't know. Right now that's up in the air."

"Why? You are coming, aren't you?"

"I think so. But Yolanda might not be with me. We've got some problems to work out. I might just skip Detroit and bring her down to Jacksonville for Christmas," I said.

"I need you to come on up to Detroit, son. I need a favor." I knew this meant he needed to borrow some money, which was cool. My dad usually didn't ask to borrow anything unless he really needed it. He owned his truck and rig, but sometimes business was slow around winter.

"What's wrong? Is business slow? Sure, I can spot you a loan."

"Business is doing all right. Matter fact, so good I'm taking off a couple weeks in December and January," my dad said.

"So, did you meet some nice new lady and you gonna take her on a cruise?"

"Naw, son. It's my brother who needs the help. Your uncle Mac. He's got cancer, son, and he doesn't have insurance."

Uncle Mac was the *last* person I wanted to loan money or help. I had to stall while I thought of an excuse to say no. "Why doesn't he have insurance?"

"I don't know that. But I told him not to worry. We would work this out. He didn't want me to ask you for the money. But Lois doesn't have it, and I told him you'd be happy to help out." I bet he didn't want my dad to ask me for shit. It was amazing my dad didn't know how much I despised his younger brother.

"I don't know if I can do that. What kind of cancer does he have?"

"I think it's prostate. The doctors say if they operate they'll be able to get it before it's too late."

"I have to think about it, Dad. Most of my money is tied up with investments. I'm trying to buy a new apartment. I'm sort of on a fixed income." I had the money and would give it to my dad in a heartbeat, but not Uncle Mac.

"Can you talk to your people? I really need you to do this. Your uncle really needs your help."

"I'll get back to you, Dad. I've got a call to make." This would have to wait until I changed Yolanda's mind. She was my priority, not my good-for-nothing uncle.

"When?"

"When what?"

"When can you let me know something? They want to schedule the surgery right after Thanksgiving."

"A couple of days."

"That might be too late," he said.

I started to say *that's too goddamn bad*, but I was firm and said, "It's the best I can do."

"Are you all right, Basil?" he asked with a puzzled voice.

"I'm cool. I've got to go," I replied as I hung up quickly. I didn't mean to be rude, but what did he know about me, about any of this? Since when did he care about what I'm feeling and not about what I'm earning. I picked the phone back up and dialed Raymond's number again. I was burning with anger. How dare my dad ask me to help this dumb mofo! Dumb-ass didn't have any insurance. It would serve him right if his ass died for being so dumb.

After a couple of rings, a man answered the phone. It wasn't Raymond. I started to hang up, but the man said, "Hello . . . hello . . . is anyone there?"

"Yeah, I'm sorry. Is Raymond Tyler there?"

"Sure, can I tell him who's calling?" What kinda shit was this, I was thinking. Ole boy sounded like a bitch making sure ain't some other woman calling her man.

"Tell him it's Mr. Henderson from New York City," I said firmly.

"Hold on." Yeah, I thought, *you* hold on, mofo.

"Hello." This was Raymond.

"Mr. Tyler. How ya doing? Guess who?"

"Whatsup, Basil," Raymond said.

"So you remember my voice? See, I knew you wouldn't forget me," I teased.

"What was it, a couple of months ago when I saw you? I did give you my number. I expected at some point you might use it," Raymond said.

I didn't recall Raymond being so cocky, but I liked it. "So is that yo boy who answered the phone? I don't want to get you in trouble."

"That was Trent. And I'm not worried about any trouble."

"All right, then," I said as I stood up and turned open the miniblinds. A milky light filled the room.

"So what did I do to deserve this call?" Raymond asked.

"I guess you just a lucky so-'n'-so," I said.

"It was good seeing you. How's your lady friend?"

"That's up in the air right now," I said.

"I see. So you coming back to the other side?" Raymond asked.

"No way, nohow. That's not why I'm calling. I thought I was going to need your legal help. But right now things are changing," I said, replaying the conversation with my father.

"Are you in some sort of trouble?" Raymond asked.

"Not right now. But I could be," I said. I knew I was being mysterious, but I was still trying to decide if I could talk with Raymond.

"What are you talking about, Basil?"

"I thought I might have to kill somebody," I said.

"You're joking, right?"

"Naw, I'm serious as a heart attack."

"Man, whatsup with that? Are you still tripping on the violence tip?" Raymond asked.

"What are you talkin' about?" I asked.

"Man, how soon we forget. Remember the last time I had to help you out legally? I've forgotten his name, but you know what I'm talking about. The young gay man you beat up for telling the truth," Raymond said.

I started to hang up on his ass, but instead I said, "Man, that's cold. I don't remember that mofo's name." I added, "And if I kill this mofo, it would be for a good reason."

"There is no good reason for killing anyone. You know that. I can't believe you're serious." I heard somebody in the background, and Raymond continued. "And I've got to get out of here. Trent and I are getting ready to go to the movies." I started to say *how sweet*, but instead I asked, "So you wouldn't help an old friend out?"

"Have you killed anyone?"

"Naw, but I still might," I said. I knew I sounded like a little kid craving for attention, but I was feeling something this evening that was more than attention-seeking.

"Then call me then. I don't do criminal cases, but I can make some recommendations," Raymond said.

"So it's like that, huh? You thinking I'm playing, don't you?"

"I hope you're playing. Man, how do you sound calling me before the fact talking about killing somebody. Basil, it's like you haven't change a bit. Man, that's lame. I've got to run."

"Raymond . . ."

"Yeah."

"Wait, I need to talk. Don't you want to know who I might have to kill?"

"Like I said, I pray you're joking. And two, I've got to run. Nice talking with you Basil. Keep in touch."

"Raymond . . ." I didn't hear a response and the line went dead. This mofo hung up on me. I couldn't believe this shit. I got so mad, I destroyed the second phone of the night.

•   •   •

At the mystic moment when darkness and dawn meet, my demons awakened me. My body was moist with sweat. I sat up, in shock, staring at my reflection, backed by a fluorescent brightness in the terrace's sliding glass door. Without the blinds the door is like a full-length mirror cluttered with memories.

A nightmare I hadn't dreamed in some fifteen years returned with vivid details and new characters. Raymond and Yolanda were looking at me lying in my twin bed with the plaid bedspreads and matching curtains. Watching me as my uncle Mac slipped into my room, and then into my bed, at the same time every morning, darkness at dawn. The uncle I would run to greet at the gate whenever he came to stay with me, when my dad's job took him out of town. My uncle Mac, who would let me stay out way past my bedtime playing catch with neighborhood boys and my cousins. Uncle Mac, who would pop corn in a black skillet and then cover it with Karo syrup. My uncle, my daddy's brother, adored by all. And standing there, watching us, were Yolanda and Raymond, shaking their heads in a way I couldn't tell if it was sympathy or shame.

The memories of my childhood are coming to the surface like boiling water. But why now? I ask myself. Memories that are like Holyfield body blows. Any one of them could knock me reeling.

I jump from my bed and race to my bathroom and look at myself in the mirror. A rage warms my entire body. I was gripped with an all-consuming anger, tempted to pick up the phone and call him and say die, you worthless mutherfucker. But I don't have a working phone. I feel at this moment I could kill him. I want to cry, but I can't. I don't cry. Tears are the ultimate sign of weakness. Tears are for sissies. My uncle Mac taught me that.

Chapter 34

"**Leland! What are** you doing answering the door? Why aren't you lying down? Where is your mother and Uncle Doc?" Leland stood in his foyer with a cane, smiling at me like I was his first date.

"Yolanda, which question do you want me to answer first? I'm fine, thank you," Leland said as I passed him and went into his living room. I put my shopping bag of presents on the floor and took off my coat, then stood with my hands on my hips, waiting for baby-boy to make his way down the hall, through the dining room and into the living room. As soon as he made the corner, I let him have it again.

"Didn't *you* just get out of the hospital? Isn't that the reason we're having the meeting here—so you can keep your butt in bed!" I wasn't angry, but I wasn't completely kidding either. It had been only a little more than a month since doctors had removed a bullet lodged so close to Leland's heart, it was God's grace he was still among the living.

"Yogi, I told you, I'm fine. Come on here and give me some love," Leland said as he opened his arms.

The shooting had taken its toll on Leland. But he was on his way back. He had lost weight and his face looked drawn and tired. He was wearing the navy blue pajamas that Riley and Selwyn had given him when he was in the hospital and the paisley silk robe I gave him last Christmas. He was still moving around slowly, as though the slightest twist or turn would cause him great pain.

"You sure I won't hurt you?" I asked before I gave him a hug.

"Like I said, give me some love," Leland said.

"You sure you can take all this?" I asked as I attempted a body-builder, muscle-flexing pose and opened my arms wide to embrace him. I held him as gingerly and as lovingly as I could, planting a dozen kisses on his cheeks, his forehead, and the tip of his nose.

"I love you too," he said, and sat carefully down on the middle sofa, facing the fireplace.

"Leland! This Christmas tree is over!" The huge fir stood glorious in the corner near the windows. It was decorated the old-fashioned way—just like when I was a kid. Strings of colored bulbs criss-crossed all around the tree, ready to shine. Red, green, blue, and gold ornaments hung on every branch, while angels, candy canes, and lots of silver tinsel and a Black Santa with a kente-cloth hat adorned the top. The only thing missing was construction-paper chains we used to make in kindergarten.

"Would you believe Uncle Doc and my mom are in the kitchen stringing popcorn? Maybe if you're a good girl, they'll let you help decorate the tree," Leland teased.

"Despite what you may have heard—I am a good girl. Definitely good."

"You do look good," Leland said.

"You know, Leland, after all that's gone on during the last few months, I'm happy that I'm healthy, that I still got *all* my friends—and I'm wiser than I was before. Life is good, baby-boy."

"Yeah," Leland said wistfully. "Life and God are very good." He seemed to look in my direction, but his eyes told me his thoughts had drifted away from this moment.

"You know something, Yolanda," he said, still staring off into the distance. "I almost died." Leland spoke slowly like he was having trouble believing it himself.

I sat beside him and held his hand in my lap. "I know, baby-boy," I said.

"No, I don't think you can know. It's not like 'Whew! Lucky me, I almost died.' It's like, I should be dead now . . . but I'm not. I feel like I'm not all the way here, at times." He paused, then looked at me directly as he tried to make himself clearer. "I mean, we all know God answers prayers. So many times I've wished, prayed to be with Donald. When I'd get down and miss him so much, I'd pray that the Lord take me too. But he didn't."

"That's because other people were praying also. Maybe he was too busy hearing our prayers that he didn't hear yours. I'm thankful for that," I said.

"Was it the power of other people's love that kept me here? Was it my own will to live? Is there some purpose to my being here? I don't know what it is I'm feeling, what I'm supposed to do now. I just know that I'm desperately grateful to be alive." Leland's eyes welled up with tears, and so did mine.

"I don't know what I would have done if you'd left me, Leland. You know I love you." I took Leland's face in my hands and looked at him hard as though the answer to life were hidden there in his deep brown eyes.

"You *do* know that, don't you?" I repeated.

"Yes, I know it," he whispered. "Give me some love, Miss Thing Alinga. Just hold me."

"Miss Thing Alinga? Where'd you get that name from?" I laughed.

"From Uncle Doc and Mama. That's what he's been calling her all week." Leland smiled. I hugged Leland once again, and then proceeded to cry softly in his arms. And then he started crying, but it felt so good to be with my best friend.

"What the heck is going on here! Mattie! Come on in here and just look at this pitiful sight. God almighty, y'all. It's a week before Christmas and you two are sitting here bawling your eyes out. I thought this was 'sposed to be a party!" Uncle Doc stood before us, smiling from all directions and holding a string of popcorn as long as he was tall. A chef's apron with splatters of different sauces covered his neatly pressed oyster-colored rayon shirt and gray slacks. He sported a big red bow tie with tiny green reindeers all over it. Uncle Doc was the picture of Christmas and good cheer.

"Now, Mattie and me, we know how to party. Ain't that right, Miss Thing Alinga?" Leland's mother, in a red sweater with a decorated fir tree on the front, came and stood beside Uncle Doc. She shook her head and sucked her teeth.

"You're absolutely right, Mr. Thing. This is the saddest thing I've ever seen. Maybe we should just break down and have us a good cry too." She looked at Uncle Doc and gave him a wink.

"I don't think so," Uncle Doc said as he pulled a gingham handkerchief from his back pocket and told us to wipe out faces and cheer up.

"Mattie, these young'uns need a little Christmas cheer," Uncle Doc said.

"I'll get us all some eggnog." Mattie turned toward the kitchen just as the doorbell buzzed. She changed her course mid-stride and added, "I'll get it. Uncle Doc, you bring in the punch bowl and the cups. And, mister? Do not make that eggnog any more 'special' than it already is! Put on some of that Vanessa Williams Christmas music. That ought to get things rolling 'round here!"

"No cryin' on the popcorn, you here me, Boo?" Uncle Doc chuckled and walked off down the hall whistling "Jingle Bell Rock."

"I bet it's Dwight," I said, standing to smooth the wrinkles from my kelly green sweater dress. I found my purse on the floor behind the sofa and freshened my lipstick. I walked into the dining room to look at my reflection in the glass case that housed Leland's African instrument collection.

"So, Yogi, what's up with you and Dwight?" Leland yelled back at me. "Don't you think I didn't notice you two at the hospital. You guys were never there without the other. I saw them looks."

"What are you talking about?" I asked as I checked my curls in the reflection.

"You know what I mean," Leland said. "I don't think I can make it any clearer: What's up with you and my boy Dwight?"

"Let me take your coats," we heard Uncle Doc say as he headed back down the hall. Saved, I thought, though I didn't really know why I was trying to hide my feelings from Leland. I guess I just wasn't too sure how I really felt about Dwight, and after John, I knew I was being overly cautious. I didn't want Leland or anybody to think I was foolish for jumping back into the fire, but I liked the way Dwight and I talked and enjoyed each other's company. Even if it was just friendship. I knew I'd never have too many special friends. Romance could wait.

"Merry Christmas, everybody!" It was Riley, and girlfriend looked fantastic. She wore a bloodred velvet sheath that hugged her body. It had a semi-plunging neckline, and her hair cascaded over her shoulders seductively, covering her cleavage.

"Girl, you look great! I don't know who's in charge. You or that dress. Honey, I'm going to get the name of that trainer of yours," I said.

"Thanks, Yolanda," Riley said. "I feel fabulous."

"You are radiant, Riley. Your hair is flowing, your skin is glowing. Now, your trainer can't be the real secret. Tell me where I can get some of whatever it is you've been using. Has Wanda Mae come up with some new makeup?"

Riley leaned close to me and whispered, "You're right, girl, it's not Wanda Mae, it's not my trainer, it's Selwyn. He's been keeping me *real* happy, girl. Know what I mean?" We giggled like schoolgirls and gave each other hugs and kisses.

"Where have you guys hidden my wife?" I heard Selwyn ask as he walked into the living area. Selwyn's face was almost completely hidden behind a big stack of exquisitely wrapped packages. He had on a red Santa Claus hat with little bells at the pointed end.

"We almost didn't make it after I saw Riley in that dress," Selwyn said as he peeked around the packages and gave Riley a smile full of love and a little mischief. "Tell them, baby," he said.

"You need to stop, Selwyn." Riley blushed too, just a few shades lighter than her dress.

"You both need to stop," I teased, "I know green is a Christmas color, but it doesn't look good when it's envy." I took the top three boxes, while Riley placed her purse and bags on one of the couches.

"Uncle Doc and Mattie have been cooking all morning. I hope you two can keep your hands off each other so you can get the forks to your mouths." The three of us laughed and took the presents and placed them under the tree.

"Oh, don't mind me," Leland said, "I just live here. Can I get some Christmas cheer or what? Come give me a kiss, Miss Riley, with your fine self. I mean, you're *wearing* that red, girl. Hey, how you doing, Selwyn? Good to see you, man. How are the kids?"

"They're doing great! They will be home tomorrow," Selwyn said as he moved toward Leland on the couch.

"Yeah, all three of them," Riley said.

"Three?" Leland asked as he looked at me.

"Yes, three. Ryan is bringing her boyfriend, Perry, home for the holidays," Riley said.

"Say what?" Leland hollered. "How are the two of you handling that?"

"We'll see," Selwyn said as he turned toward Leland and asked with genuine concern, "How're you feeling, man? Shouldn't you be in bed?"

"I'm okay, really. Why don't you guys go in the kitchen and let Uncle Doc pour you some eggnog."

I went and turned the volume down on the music, and then took the popcorn strings from Leland's lap and hung them on the tree. The late afternoon winter light filtered dimly through the blinds and gave the room a cozy, peaceful feeling. I watched as Selwyn placed a pillow behind Leland's head and Riley pulled a quilt over his lap. A room full of love, I thought. That's what we have here tonight.

"I'll get it!" Mattie's voice called out from the kitchen. I heard her heels clicking on the kitchen floor, then the muted sound of her footsteps down the hall. My heart beat just a little faster when I heard her say, "Who is this handsome man? C'mon in, baby, everybody's here. Let me take your coat. Is this snow? Has it started snowing?"

"Just a few flakes," I heard Dwight say as I walked to the door. He was wearing a red sweater with a gray band and black corduroy slacks, and greeted me with a warm smile.

"Dwight," I said, "we were wondering when you'd get here."

"*We?* Did you say *we?*" Mattie teased, sounding more like her son.

"Now, Mattie," I said, feeling my cheeks begin to glow. "It's good seeing you, Dwight. Let's go get some eggnog." Dwight leaned over and gave me a kiss on the cheek. I grabbed his hand and smiled as I led him into the living area. Just before we reached the room, he whispered, "I like that dress."

"Thank you, Mr. Scott, you don't look so bad yourself." I felt warm all over now, and I hoped I wasn't blushing noticeably. When we walked in, Leland looked at me with a huge grin and a *don't-even-try-it* expression on his face. Clearly he was pleased with what he read into our brief exchange.

"So," Dwight said, turning to look at Leland, "how's my blood doing?"

"I'm doing okay, Dwight. Thanks for asking," Leland replied.

"Naw, man. I'm not talking about you. I'm talking about my *blood*! You know you got some of my blood running through you now?"

"Is that why Riley and Yolanda suddenly look so good to me?" Leland teased.

"Could be. Maybe you're ready to change your religion," Dwight joked.

"As long as it doesn't mean I'm gonna be straight!" Leland laughed.

"It could be a movie, like *Black Like Me*," Riley said.

"More like *Blood Like Me*," Selwyn joked, and gave Dwight a low-five. We all shared a good laugh, and Leland tried to contain himself to a smile, but finally burst into laughter too.

"Oh, oh, ow, Donald, I'm coming to join you, baby," Leland joked, placing his hand to his chest, like he was in pain like Redd Foxx on *Sanford and Son*.

"I'm sorry, man," Dwight said, frowning, not realizing Leland was playing. "I really didn't mean to cause you any pain. I wasn't thinking. Are you okay?"

"He's fine, Dwight. Leland, stop kidding him," I said in a protective tone.

"Look at her, taking up for her man," Leland said.

"You don't want me, Dr. Thompson," I said as I pinched his cheeks.

"Stop, that hurts," Leland said.

"When are we going to get started? Selwyn and I need to go home and get the house ready for our children," Riley said.

"I bet," I said. "Don't ya'll mess around and have another mouth to feed next Christmas. And don't you have a maid to do that stuff?"

"We gave her a couple of weeks off. It's just been the two of us, cooking and cleaning," Selwyn said proudly.

"Now, that I'd like to see," Dwight said.

"We do all right," Riley said.

"Riley, did you bring the cards?" Leland asked.

"Yes, and I'll get them!" Riley said as she rushed to get the silver-colored bag she'd left in the dining room. I replenished everyone's eggnog and we all sat back down. Mattie and Uncle Doc came in from the kitchen with a platter of hot wingettes and placed them on the table next to the punch bowl.

"Well!" said Uncle Doc, looking at the half-empty punch bowl. "Looks like my secret-formula eggnog went over pretty big. Say, Dwight! How you doin'?"

Dwight stood up to shake Uncle Doc's hand. "Uncle Doc, that eggnog needs to carry a warning."

Mattie laughed. "You feeling okay, son?" She came and sat down on the edge of the sofa beside Leland. She felt his forehead and patted him gently on the hand. "You want anything?"

"I'm fine, Mama. Just sit here," Leland said as he smiled proudly at his mother.

"Did I hear somebody say something about a game?" Uncle Doc asked. "I like games. You got room for two more players?"

"It's not really a game," Riley explained. "We just pull cards out of the bag and answer the question on the back. See?" She held up one of the cards. "I don't think the group would mind if you and Mrs. Thompson join in."

"That would be nice," I said.

"Yeah, Uncle Doc, you and Mama should play. There is only one rule you guys have to follow," Leland said.

"What's that?" Uncle Doc asked.

"You have to tell the truth, no matter what," Leland said.

"That won't be a problem for me. I always tell the truth," Mattie said.

"Are you implying I don't?" Uncle Doc asked as he put his hands on his hips.

"I didn't say a word," Mattie laughed.

"Since you guys are new, we'll let you go first. And Selwyn's also new. He can go after you guys," Riley said.

"I'll go first," said Mattie. "You all have some snacks and I'll go while you eat."

"How come you always have to go first, Mattie? You don't even know how to play," Uncle Doc said.

" 'Cause I'm a lady," Mattie said.

"Who said I ain't one?" Uncle Doc smiled. "Here, give me a card, Riley. I'll show this old woman how it's done."

"Go on, then, with your bad self," I teased as I did a little bit of a mashed potato step.

"Show me, you old fool," Mattie said. Uncle Doc walked over and put his hand in the bag and pulled out a card.

"Hey! This is a picture of Leland when he graduated from Hampton. I was there. Sat right behind the first row, where all the Hampton dignitaries were," Uncle Doc said.

"That's right! Wasn't that something else," Mattie said.

"Okay, Uncle Doc. Now give the card to me," Riley said. Then she looked at Leland and asked, "Is it okay if I read the cards?"

"Sure, Riley. Knock yourself out." Leland smiled.

"Okay, Uncle Doc. Your card says: 'Thank somebody.' "

"That's it?" Uncle Doc said, puzzled. "'Thank somebody'? That's no question, that's more like a direction."

"See, Douglas?" Mattie gloated. "I told you I should go first."

"Wait just a minute, now," Uncle Doc said. "Just hold on. 'Thank somebody'? I can handle that just fine—and without any help from Miss Thing Alinga." Uncle Doc mulled over his answer for a moment, then said, "I got it! I want to thank a bunch of somebodies. I want to thank y'all for what you've done for Boo here. I don't mean just lately, I mean for the last few years. You've been good friends to my boy and I sure do appreciate it. And—you've been good to me too. Always coming to my eatin' establishment and bringing your friends. I couldn't do it without you. I feel like we're all family here. We can never have enough family or friends. There! How's that?"

"You did fine, Douglas. That was lovely," Mattie said. "Now let me have a card."

Mattie rose from her seat and reached into the bag. She pulled out a card and handed it to Riley, then sat back down. "What does it say? What's my question?" she asked.

"Mrs. Thompson, your card says, 'What are you grateful for?'"

"Her question sounds like mine," Uncle Doc said.

"All the cards are somewhat different from what we usually have, Uncle Doc," Riley said. "Mrs. Thompson, do you want to choose another card?"

"Naw, she don't want another card," Leland said. "We don't get to change cards, so my mother can't either." He laughed. Mattie rolled her eyes at Leland and said, "Hush up, Mr. I'm-So-Sick-I-Could-Just-Cry. And, Riley baby, you can call me Mattie."

"Okay, Mattie, are you ready to answer your question?"

"I have so much to be grateful for. I'm grateful for Jesus Christ," Mattie said as she looked toward the ceiling with a peaceful look on her face. "I'm grateful that my son is on his way back to a total recovery from that crazy man's bullets and that he has such wonderful friends, looking out for him—when his family was far away, both in miles and in the heart," Mattie said as she patted her heart and then blew a kiss toward Leland, who smiled broadly. "And for a reason I don't know why, I'm thankful for my brother-in-law, who's been like a brother and a *sister*, but more than anything, for being my friend."

"Stop it, Mattie, stop it right now, before I start boo-hooing," Uncle Doc said.

"And so much other stuff, but I don't want to take up all you children's time. Thanks for letting me do this. It feels good to say how you feel out loud."

"It sure does," Uncle Doc chimed in.

"Okay, Selwyn, it's your time," Riley said.

"Not yet, ladies first," Selwyn protested.

"But you're not a regular member of the group, so it's your time," Riley said.

"That's right, my man. See what we have to go through? Go on, dig in and pick a card, my brother," Dwight said. Selwyn shrugged his shoulders and reached in and grabbed a card. I saw him wink at Riley as he handed her the card.

"Selwyn, your question is: 'What's the best gift you've ever received for Christmas?' "

Selwyn paused for a moment and looked at Riley as though they were the only two in the room. I was afraid they were gonna just attack each other and start doing the nasty right there under the tree. I guess everyone else was feeling it also, because nobody said a word until Selwyn spoke. "That's easy, I got the same gift twice." He paused and reached across to hold Riley's hand. "The day God blessed me with Riley was the best gift I could ever receive. And this year I got her back." Riley eyes filled with tears, as did Mattie's, Uncle Doc's, and mine.

"Man, you gonna make this tough for us to follow," Dwight said.

"I mean," Leland said.

"Let's take a break," I suggested. "Let's eat some food and then come back and finish." I was hungry and wanted to make sure my makeup wasn't all over my face. I could see Riley's eyeliner sliding down her cheeks, but she still looked beautiful.

Riley and I went into the bathroom and freshened up our makeup. I told Riley how happy I was for her and Selwyn.

"Thanks, Yolanda. I'm so happy, I don't know what to do. Who said you can't have love in your life always and forever. I wish the same thing for you too," Riley said. I gave her a hug and whispered, "Thank you, Riley. You deserve happiness. I'm not so certain about me."

"What are you talking about? Of course you deserve happiness. With love, friends, and your career. Why are you being so hard on yourself?"

"Well, I know you said everything was fine, but I need to tell you again, how sorry I am about what I said about your singing," I said.

"You don't have to do that, Yolanda. One of the things I have always loved and respected about you was that you always deal with honesty. That's how you felt. I don't have to agree, but I want friends who are honest with me. That's why I'm so lucky to have a friend like you," Riley said.

"Thank you, Riley," I said as I grabbed her and hugged her once more.

"No, thank *you*, friend. Thank you," Riley said.

When Riley and I left the bathroom, we heard Uncle Doc yelling, "Ya'll come on and eat 'fore this food gets cold, and don't nobody eat Miss Thing Alinga's gumbo cold." Uncle Doc and Mattie brought out a large smoked turkey with dressings, fruit salad, and steaming bowls of gumbo and rice. When everyone was seated and served, Leland asked Dwight—who he now called "Blood"—to turn on the Christmas-tree lights. The lights sparkled and the tree looked magnificent. At that moment it was the most beautiful tree I'd ever seen, and we all ooohed and aaahed and applauded Uncle Doc and Mattie for a great job of decorating. The gaze exchanged between Uncle Doc and Mattie spoke volumes about love, friendship, and family.

"Leland," Mattie said, "would you please say grace?"

"I'll say it," Uncle Doc interrupted. "Good food, good meat, good God, let's eat!"

"Amen, amen," Leland said.

"Now, Doc, you know better than that. I want a real prayer from my baby. Leland, you remember how your daddy taught you how to say grace? You and your brother."

Leland looked at his mother very lovingly and said, "Yeah, Mama, I remember." Leland bit his lower lip (I'm certain to fight back tears) and began to pray. "Our Father, who art in heaven, we thank you for this chance to thank you once again for your blessings and your grace. We thank you for this food our bodies are about to receive, and Lord God, we thank you for the hands that prepared this food. We thank you for all the families gathered here today, and for the gift of friendship you've allowed us to enjoy and rediscover. But most important, dear God, we thank you for the reason for the season, the birth of our savior, Jesus Christ. We ask that you watch over us and all your children, those who know you and those who don't, not only tonight, but now and forever, amen."

"Amen, amen," Mattie said in a voice so loud, it shocked a few of us. "I told you my baby could pray." Then she added, "Let's eat!" And Mattie was right, after Leland's prayer, there was nothing else to do but eat.

•   •   •

When it was all said and done, we had each eaten more than we should have—and enjoyed each and every bite. To my surprise and Riley's too, Selwyn and Dwight did the dishes, then joined us in the living room for coffee and some of Uncle Doc's *make-you-wanna-slap-your-mama* pound cake with lemon icing, while Stephanie Mills's Christmas album played in the background.

After we finished, Selwyn suggested he take Mattie and Uncle Doc to see *The Preacher's Wife*, allowing the four of us time to talk privately.

"That's a good plan," Leland said. "Mattie needs to get out of the house."

"I don't wanna go too far, my baby might need me," Mattie said.

"We'll take good care of baby-boy," I said.

"I think it's playing at 900 North Michigan," Riley said.

"The theater near Bloomingdale's? You would know that, wouldn't you, sweetheart," Selwyn teased. Riley smiled and winked at Selwyn.

"I don't know when was the last time a man invited me to see a movie. It might be the last time. So git your coat, Mattie, before this fine young man changes his mind," Uncle Doc said.

"Leland, you sure you gonna be all right?" Mattie asked.

"Mattie honey, I ain't gonna tell you again. Git your coat. This big ole rusty-tail boy will be just fine," Uncle Doc said.

"I love you too, Uncle Doc. Ma, I'll be fine. Go on, enjoy the movie. I heard it's great. As much as I've been playing the sound track, you two will know the entire movie," Leland said. The sound track, along with Jody Watley's *Greatest Hits*, were in a gift package I had brought Leland at the hospital. He told me those were his two new favorite CDs, but mentioned he hoped Santa Claus would also bring him the *Evita* sound track. I told him I'd talk to Ms. Santa and see what she could do.

While Mattie and Uncle Doc grabbed their coats, I heard Mattie saying how much she loved "that little Whitney Houston" and Uncle Doc saying Denzel was his man.

After Selwyn, Mattie, and Uncle Doc left, the four of us gathered in the living room. Riley and Dwight were sitting on the floor, and I sat on the sofa with Leland's legs in my lap. This chile loved being spoiled. Typical man, I thought.

"So what are we going to do? I don't have a lot in my journal," Riley said.

"Me either," Leland added.

"Why don't we just talk," Dwight suggested.

"Talk?" I asked.

"Yeah, why don't we just tell each other what's on our mind. The truth and nothing but the truth," Dwight said.

"Sounds like a plan to me," Leland said.

"I'm game. What do you think, Riley?" I asked. I didn't want her to think we didn't appreciate her doing special cards for Christmas.

"That's fine with me. Who wants to go first?" Riley asked.

"I will," Dwight said. Dwight cleared his throat, and then coughed as he looked around the room. "I just wanna say thanks to you guys . . . you know . . ." Dwight's voice seem tangled in his throat, but then words of friendship and love surged through. "I hope one day to be as good a friend as you've all been to me. So . . . well . . . I guess that's all I have to say, except that I'm making some changes in my life. I've released some anger, and I want you to know I love you all and—" Dwight stopped abruptly and looking somewhat embarrassed, stared at his hands in his lap.

"We love your old ass too, man. My blood brother. You know I feel like I should break into a verse of 'I Am Changing' from *Dreamgirls*. Riley, you know that song, don't ya, sister?"

"I don't think so, let's leave the singing to Vanessa and Stephanie." Riley smiled. Leland's comment and Riley's cute response quickly dissipated the awkwardness that had descended upon us. With his head hanging low, Dwight whispered, "Thanks, my brother."

"I'll go now," Leland said. Leland looked at me and said, "I'm truly blessed to have Yolanda, Dwight, and Riley for friends. True friends. I can't thank you all enough for your love and care this last month. It's meant the world to me. I wish Uncle Doc were here so I could tell him how wonderful it is to have an uncle who's a friend, and my mother, how happy I am to have her back in my life. But I'll tell them later. You know, I'm blessed, I guess, I know, just to be alive; to be here with you all like this. I realize that I've spent a lot of time in last years thinking about death, but now I want to concentrate on living. Riley, it was a brilliant idea you had to bring us all together like this so many years ago. I don't think I knew then how much it would mean in my life, thank you," Leland said.

Fighting back tears, Riley said, "Thank you, Leland."

"And I'm especially grateful to have a new brother—a blood brother. Thank you, Dwight. And, Yolanda sweetheart, I love you, that's all."

We sat silently and let Leland's words sink in. I think we all got a little misty around the eyes. It was a good feeling that wrapped around us, bonding us together in mutual love. After a few minutes, Riley started talking. "Well, I would like to say first that I feel like Leland said—blessed to have you all as friends. I really feel lucky because I've learned what being a friend really means. I don't know if I knew that when we started this. Friendship doesn't always look like I thought it did. Sometimes being a friend means you have to be true to yourself. You have to be honest, even when it hurts. And you have to trust that your friends will be honest with you, even when it hurts. Yolanda, I want to thank you for the gift of honesty and for the book you gave me."

"What book?" I asked.

Chapter 35

It's Christmas Eve and my nightmares won't leave me. I didn't go to Detroit for Thanksgiving and I didn't call my dad to explain why. He and my aunt Lois called almost every other day, but I didn't answer the phone or return their messages.

I almost made it to Detroit, but instead I went to Chicago. I was going to convince Yolanda to come to Detroit with me. I knew if I saw her face-to-face, she'd change her mind. I checked into a hotel near the airport and called Yolanda every hour on the hour. When I couldn't reach her, I went back to some of my old habits. I went to this club, the Excalibur, near downtown Chicago, and met this big-hipped, small-breasted lady. I don't even remember her name. Yeah, I do, it was Kathy—Kathy with a K, she had said proudly. I bought her a couple of drinks and brought her back to my hotel.

After a few more drinks, I was going for the draws. We had oral sex, but when I wanted to take it further, she insisted on a glove. I didn't have one. Kathy got up and dressed quickly, saying something corny like, "If the glove don't fit, then keep the dick." All I could

"*Lessons in Living.* The Susan Taylor book. When I was having a tough time, I read that book over and over. There was a line that stuck with me. I think in chapter eight she said something about the paths to realizing our dreams is never smooth. But we have to say I will—claiming my power to choose. I choose you all as friends for life and wish you safe and peaceful paths to your dreams," Riley said.

"Thanks, Riley," Dwight said. "I think we should put that in the *If This World Were Mine* journal."

"I do too," Leland said. "That's beautiful. I want a copy of that book."

"I think Ms. Santa already took care of that," Riley said as she looked toward the presents under the tree. Suddenly everyone looked toward me. It was my time.

"First, I'm just thankful to be here and have friends like all of you. I know everybody has said that, but today I feel it in my heart. I feel it all over this room. I've learned some lessons in the last couple of months. Friends are forgiving. I'm thankful for that. Like life, friends are precious gifts. They should both be honored and treasured. That's what I've been blessed to learn."

"I think this is going to be the best Christmas I've had in a very long time," Riley said as she stood up and moved near the tree, and the Christmas lights cast a warm glow over the room.

"It's the best for me too," Dwight said, "in a lot of ways." He looked over at me and smiled that smile again.

"Me too," I said. "How about you, baby-boy?"

"I think it's already the best," Leland said. "You've all filled my home with so much love, so much friendship and warmth, I don't think there's any room left for old memories and broken dreams. I'm ready to move on. With friends, of course," he said as he grabbed my hand and squeezed it tightly.

I knew at that moment that no matter what happened to each of us in the future, this would be a day we would always remember, a day and night we would cherish for the rest of our lives.

think was *dumb bitch*. I took Kathy with a K back to the city and then I stopped at a seedy male bookstore near downtown Chicago and got an anonymous blow job through a tiny hole in a booth.

It didn't make me feel any better.

When I got back to New York, I felt guilty for losing my courage and not going to Detroit and doing what I had to do. I had rehearsed the scene in my mind, almost every day since I had my first nightmare. I would go to my uncle Mac's house and say nothing. I was going to stare him into a confession in front of the entire family. Then I'd make him get on his knees while I held a gun in his mouth, so he could plead for his low life. Instead, I just came back to New York. I punked out.

One day I got a note from the New Orleans art gallery stating a credit had been issued against my credit card, because Yolanda had sent a check to pay for the painting I sent her. That hurt me deeply. The days since Thanksgiving passed slowly and painfully. I spent a great deal of time staring at my phone and listening to Luther Vandross crooning "Goin' out of my Head." I was. I knew I needed to call my dad, but what would I say.

Instead of calling my dad, I picked up my phone and dialed Raymond Tyler's number like I dialed it every day. He picked up after the first ring.

"Merry Christmas," he said in a cheerful voice.

"Whatsup, guy," I said.

"Basil, I was hoping you'd call back," Raymond said. If he was, maybe Christmas wouldn't be so bad after all.

"So you've been thinking about me," I said.

"Yeah, I have. I was pretty tough on you the last time. I'm sorry. How are you doing?"

"I'm doing," I muttered.

"Did you get that problem solved?"

"What problem?"

"The person you were talking about killing. Were you able to work that out?" he asked.

"Not really, but I have to forget about it. What are you doing for Christmas?"

"I'm going home tomorrow and then it's off to Orlando," Raymond said.

"What's going on in Orlando?"

"My family's going to the Citrus Bowl. Northwestern playing Tennessee. I'm hoping I'll get to see my little brother score a touchdown on New Year's Day," Raymond said.

"You're really proud of him, aren't you?"

"Yeah, I am. We all are," Raymond said. While Raymond was telling me about his holiday plans, I was thinking how lucky he was to come from such a close-knit family, where there was love and no secrets.

"Raymond, can I ask you something?" I asked after he finished detailing his plans.

"Sure, Basil. Whatsup?"

"How did you do it?"

"Do what?"

"Get your family, especially your father and brother, to accept your lifestyle?"

"My life, Basil. It's not a lifestyle, it's my life. And to answer your question, it wasn't easy. I still haven't had *the* conversation with my little brother. But I will, and soon," Raymond said.

"Do you know what you're going to say?"

"No, but I'll know when it's time. Maybe I'll write him a letter. It's not like it will be a total surprise. I've been living with Trent for almost five years, and he's usually with me. I think it's clear we love each other very much."

"So, you're just going to write him a letter? Is that what you did with your father?"

"Yes and no. My father and I talked, but I still wrote him a letter to explain my life more clearly. It's never easy for fathers. Especially Black fathers. They always think it's their fault. Don't tell me you're getting ready to come out," Raymond said.

"Naw, it ain't nothing like that. I'm not going out like that. There are just some things I need to tell my father. Things that happened to me," I said.

"Then tell him," Raymond urged.

"I don't know if I can," I said.

"Then write him a letter," Raymond suggested.

"I've never done that."

"Basil, I know whatever it is can't be easy. I can hear it in your voice. I've never heard you sound so unsure of yourself. You're one of the most confident men I've ever met. That's why I was sorry for being so short when you called the last time. To me, it just sounded like you hadn't changed a bit. You know, when you start to tell the truth about who you are, life becomes much simpler, much sweeter," Raymond said. I was thinking that was easy for him to say. Raymond always had the world by a string.

"You think I'm confident?"

"Some might call it arrogant, but yes, I think you carry yourself with a certain power that's attractive in a way."

"There are some things I need to say that I've never said to anyone. But I don't know if my dad can handle it. He might really be pissed off."

"Is this causing you pain?" Raymond asked.

"Yes," I said softly.

"Then you've got to talk with someone. If you don't, Basil, whatever it is will destroy you," Raymond said.

"Can I talk to you?"

"Do you consider me a close enough friend? It sounds like you have something really heavy. I care for you as a human being, and as a brother struggling with issues I've had to deal with. But I know you must have some friends who would understand," Raymond said.

I wanted to tell him how when I made love with him I didn't see my uncle's face in his eyes. That he and Yolanda were the only two people I had been intimate with where the invisible presence of my uncle didn't interfere with our lovemaking. In my eyes, that made Raymond and Yolanda special.

"I think I could talk with you. But not on the phone. I need to see you in person," I said, almost pleading.

"When?"

"I'll fly to Seattle, Alabama, Orlando. You just tell me the time and place."

"It will have to be at the beginning of the year. Are you still in New York?"

"Yes, that's where I am now. I don't know if I can wait that long."

"Then write the letter. You'll be amazed at how much stress it will relieve. You don't have to mail it. But you have to write it. Give me your number and I'll call you in a couple of weeks. If you still want to talk, we can get together. I may be in New York on business anyway," Raymond said.

I gave Raymond my number and then asked, "What kind of business?"

"My best friend and his wife adopted a new baby and they've asked me to be godfather," Raymond said proudly.

"Do you know how lucky you are?" I asked.

"I know I'm living under a state of grace. I know I'm blessed, and I try to remember that every day," Raymond said confidently.

"So that's all I have to do is write a letter?"

"Write the letter, Basil. It will at least be a start."

"I'll think about it," I said.

"Merry Christmas, Basil. We'll talk next year," Raymond said.

"Good-bye and Merry Christmas. I hope I can wait that long," I said.

"You can. You will. I've got to run," Raymond said.

"Yeah, me too," I said as I hung up the phone. This time I let the phone remain intact. I had a phone call to look forward to.

I spent Christmas Day alone. For dinner I had a smoked turkey and cheese sandwich I ordered from a local deli that never closed. I watched a basketball game and a college football game. I suddenly missed sports. When I was playing, the holidays didn't seem any different from other days because I was usually involved with practice. I couldn't remember the last time I had spent Christmas with my family.

But I always talked to my dad on the holidays, and at around ten o'clock I decided this year wouldn't be any different. I wondered if he had spent the day with my aunt Lois and her family or if he had some new lady friend he was sharing his holiday with.

When his answering machine picked up, I was relieved. I could leave a message. "Dad, Merry Christmas . . . sorry I haven't talk to you . . . I've . . ." Suddenly I heard a clicking sound and then my dad's voice. "Son, hold on, I'm here. Let me turn this thing off."

"Merry Christmas, Dad," I said.

"Same to you. Where have you been? You had me and your auntie worried. We were looking for you in Detroit. You missed a meal and all your cousins were asking 'bout you."

"Something came up. I'm surprised you're at home. What did you do today?"

"Aw, I spent the day over at Lois's house. We had a nice dinner," he said.

"Sorry I missed it. Well, I was just checking on you and letting you know I'm doing all right," I said.

"Are you sure, Basil? Are you really all right? Now, if you're worried about that money I asked you for, don't worry. Lois and I are going to get a second mortgage on our houses. Mac is our brother. He's not your responsibility." Now he was really making me feel like crap.

"I'm okay. Are you sure you want to do that, Dad? Isn't your house almost paid for?"

"Yeah, so I should be able to get enough money to pay for Mac's operation."

"You really love him, don't you, Dad?"

"He's my baby brother. He's family. Of course I love him."

"Dad, I want to explain why I won't lend Uncle Mac the money," I said softly.

"It's your money, son. You don't have to explain," he said. If I didn't know better, I could swear I heard my dad sniffling. He couldn't be crying. I had never seen my dad shed a single tear.

"Are you all right?" I asked.

"Yeah, son, I'm gonna make it. I just wonder how a son of mine could turn his back on his family. I mean, damn, Basil, I thought I raised you better than that!" My dad's voice moved up in volume and then I thought I could hear those sniffles again.

"Let me explain," I said.

"No need. Merry Christmas, son. I hope you and your money will have a nice holiday season," my dad said as he hung up the phone.

I started to call him right back, and then I started to call my aunt Lois. Maybe I could talk with her and explain why I couldn't help Mac. That's when I noticed the yellow legal pad with a black ballpoint pen lying on the coffee table. I had pulled it out after I talked with Raymond, but I hadn't written a word. I could hear Raymond's voice ringing in my ear. *"If you don't, Basil, whatever it is will destroy you."* I wanted to shout from my terrace, "It already has!"

I picked up the pen, but I didn't know where to start. I put the pen to my lips and then on the paper.

Dear Dad,

This is the hardest thing I've ever had to do. But this is something I must do. First, I love you. I know I don't tell you that often, but I do. Dad, there are some things about me you don't know. I pray you don't know.

When I was around nine years old, something terrible happened to me. You had left on one of your trips and Uncle Mac had come over to stay with me. Up until that night I loved it when Uncle Mac came to stay with me. He was your brother, my uncle, and I loved him.

    I don't need to go into details, but Uncle Mac's usually soft touch became unkind. On that night I became a little boy who wanted so badly to trust the world, but after Uncle Mac left my bed, I knew I couldn't. I could no longer pretend the world was unknown to me or I would enjoy what I would see. That touch would also make me unkind to the world, and the people who crossed my path.

    I have carried that night and the guilt I felt all these years and never told anyone. But I know if I continue to pretend it didn't happen, it will become worse than the molestation. Yes, that's what it's called, child molestation.

    I know you love your brother, and right now I'm trying to discover some of that love, but I'm afraid my love for Uncle Mac ended with the memory of a clean and innocent nine-year-old boy.

The memories of that night were suddenly so vivid in my mind, I had to stop writing. I felt my eyes watering, but I still had the power to stop them. I read what I had written and I knew how much my letter would hurt my dad. I didn't want to do that. So I ripped the page from the tablet and balled it up with a maddening force.

I went and picked up the phone and hit redial. A few rings later, my dad answered the phone. He sounded defeated. "Dad," I said.

"Yes, son."

"You don't have to apply for a second mortgage. I'll take care of Uncle Mac, but I want you to know I'm doing this for you."

"Thank you, son, but why do you suddenly have this hatred for my brother?"

"It's not sudden, and I can't talk about it now. I don't know if I will ever talk about it. Just take the money and do what you have to do," I said sternly.

"Thank you, son, I will."

"Good-bye, Dad. Merry Christmas. My accountant will call you tomorrow."

"Thanks again, Basil. You're a good son."

I hung up the phone, hit my CD player with Luther's "Goin' out of My Head," and I picked up my pen and started to write again.

Dear Raymond,

Horrible things often begin softly, like a kind touch. There is a story I must tell you.

And Then . . .

The balance of the Chicago winter wasn't cold and was short on snow. Right now, the city is in a final slide toward summer. I'm feeling almost brand-new. As if the bullets never came close to my heart, ending my dreamless life.

But as my mother said, "Leland, when God is in control, things happen for a reason." I now treasure life . . . this life and I'm dreaming again. I went home with my mother and Uncle Doc after the first of the year. I had a great time visiting all my family and friends and met my mother's man. He's really a nice man and I think Mattie hears wedding bells.

A lot has happened for me and the group since winter. I think maybe my friends and family have learned from my brush with death. Yolanda and Dwight are expanding their friendship, with a slow-moving kind of passion. It's really wonderful watching them fall in love. I talk to Yolanda almost every day, and with Dwight at least twice a week.

Riley is busy with her new project! A new baby. On Valentine's Day she and Selwyn adopted a beautiful little boy, named Yourdan. I think the only singing she's doing is in the nursery, and the way

Yourdan smiles, Riley's singing voice might be improving. Selwyn recently got a big promotion that allows him to spend more time in Chicago with his wife and new son.

The changes in my life have been good. I've reduced my client load and joined the staff at Michael Reese Hospital treating adolescents who have been sexually abused. I made this decision after reading about the plight of a nine-year-old Chicago girl who was raped and left for dead in the Cabrini Green projects. Her story touched me deeply and reminded me why I wanted to be a psychiatrist. I may never be able to help Girl X personally, but being on the hospital staff I will be able to help other little girls and boys like her.

On the personal tip, I'm dating again. After I got back from New Orleans, Uncle Doc called one evening and told me to rush over to Miss Thing's Wings. He said he had a present for me.

When I walked into the restaurant, there sitting at my favorite corner table was the stranger from the party. His name is Dorian, and as the kids say, he's *all that*. Dorian is a teacher at Westside Preparatory, and we have so much in common it's scary at times. But not so frightening that I want to run away.

Who said you couldn't have happy endings? Who said you can't have new dreams? Not me.

About the Author

E. Lynn Harris is a former computer sales executive with IBM and a graduate of the University of Arkansas—Fayetteville. He is the author of four previous bestselling novels, *Invisible Life*, *Just As I Am*, and the *New York Times* bestsellers *And This Too Shall Pass* and *If This World Were Mine*. In 1996 *Just as I Am* was awarded the Novel of the Year prize by Blackboard African-American Bestsellers, Inc. *If This World Were Mine* was a finalist for the 1997 NAACP Image Award and winner of the James Baldwin Award for Literary Excellence. Harris currently divides his time between Chicago and New York, where he is working on his fifth novel.